Southern Fried
SUSHI

Southern Fried
SUSHI

Jennifer Rogers Spinola

ISBN 978-1-61626-364-5

This book is a work of fiction. Names, characters, places, and incidents are either products of the author's imagination or used fictitiously. Any similarity to actual people, organizations, and/or events is purely coincidental.

For more information about Jennifer Rogers Spinola, please access the author's website at the following Internet address: www.jenniferrogersspinola.com

Cover design: Faceout Studio, www.faceoutstudio.com

Published by Barbour Publishing, Inc., P.O. Box 719, Uhrichsville, OH 44683, www.barbourbooks.com

Our mission is to publish and distribute inspirational products offering exceptional value and biblical encouragement to the masses.

Printed in the United States of America.

Dedication

To my mother, Doris Lambert Rogers,
whose only resemblance to Ellen Jacobs was steadfast faith
until her last petal fell. Thank you for singing so beautifully. 1952-1996

Acknowledgments

People often ask me how a writer gets published, and I have to be frank: I have no idea. Why me? Why now? Why this book?I can't answer the whys, but I know one thing: apart from God's extravagance and helping hands along the way, I'd never be seeing my work in print. Although my name appears on the cover, it's not just me who's written a book.

It's Roger Bruner and his wife, Kathleen, whose first exuberance over my manuscript put hope in my heart, and whose encouragement and editing ideas kept me going along the way. It's my deputy cousin Lessa Goens, whose quick-fire texts when I desperately needed a plot twist or rescue or piece of legal info kept me from chucking everything out the window.

I thank teachers all the way back to my third-grade teacher, Sandra Thompson, who took me seriously enough to read over my handwritten manuscript (and not laugh!), to college professors Dr. Gayle Price, Dr. June Hobbs, Bob Carey, and Jennifer Carlile who pushed me forward and encouraged my writing for life. At my first job it was Anita Bowden and Mary Jane Welch who refined my verbs and helped me find my voice; Mark Kelly and Erich Bridges showed me how to change the world through words, one article at a time. You are all my heroes.

I'd be lost without my crit partners Jennifer Fromke, Shelly Dippel, Christy Truitt, and Karen Schravemade, and even more lost without the love and hands-on help of my handsome Brazilian husband, Athos Spinola, and the cooperation of my two-year-old son Ethan. I love you both more than anything.

Mom, Dad, and Winter, I remember your encouragement through those long years of handwritten stories and hold them close to my heart. Thanks also to Aunt Lois, Aunt Ruth, and Grandma for reading so many of those little stapled-together books and always making me think they were wonderful.

To my editor, Rebecca Germany, thanks for taking a chance on an unfamiliar face. April Frazier and Linda Hang and Laura Young at Barbour, thanks so much for your hard work.

To Jesus Christ, my Savior forever, I owe you everything. You are my life. Why me? I will never understand.

To those who have stood by my side: there are no solitary journeys. This is all your work. Thank you from the bottom of my heart.

Chapter 1

"Uh-oh." Kyoko peeked over the cubicle at me with suspicious black-lined eyes. "They got your work address."

I stared at the envelope Yoshie-san dropped on my desk. Citibank Corp, it read. Not good.

"*Mou ichimai*," said Yoshie-san slowly, sifting through the mail stack. "One more. For Shiloh Jacobs." At least he meant to say "Shiloh." His thick Japanese accent rendered it so incomprehensible, it might have been "Spaghetti."

"Busted," whispered Kyoko insolently.

I waved her away with a scowl. "Mind your own business."

"*Sumimasen. Mou nimai.* Sorry. Two more." Yoshie-san's ink-stained fingers stopped on two more envelopes. "American Express. Daimaru."

I snatched them out of his hand and shoved them under my notebook. "You don't have to read my mail out loud!"

"You have a Daimaru card?" Kyoko stared. "From that big department store?"

I ignored her. "I'm busy. My big story on the Diet's due."

"I want a Daimaru card. How'd you get it?"

"Go to Daimaru and find out yourself."

"You know, it's pretty much impossible for foreigners to get credit cards here. What'd you do?"

I launched a paper ball over the cubicle wall and socked her squarely on her sleek bob, tinted with that mod dark purple-red tone we saw everywhere. In fact, I don't remember seeing anyone in Japan with black hair except Yoshie-san, the office helper. I saw chestnut and auburn and bleached blond in abundance, but no black. I should make a list.

Black hair? Yoshie-san. Mod purple-red? Kyoko. My next-door neighbor, Fujino-san. I added some more ticks. I should do a study on this for my master's. "Modern Japanese and Hair Color: A Study in Transitions."

"Ouch. What's your problem?" Kyoko rubbed her head. She spoke with perfect coastal English that betrayed her California roots. If I didn't look up, I'd think I sat across from a surfer.

The cursor blinked on my screen, and I typed a few more lines about the Japanese legislature, otherwise known as the Diet. When previous Prime Minister Koizumi's son starred in an ad for diet soda, I'd begged to write the article. The puns were too tempting. But thankfully somebody axed the idea before it ever made it to editor Dave Driscoll.

Somehow I'd become the reporter Associated Press tapped for political stories. Kyoko dabbled in legal articles.

"Wanna go to lunch?" Kyoko could change subjects in the blink of an eye.

"Meeting Carlos. In Shibuya." The corners of my mouth turned up.

Tap, tap, tap from Kyoko's side. "Wanna join us? He's bringing along his new roommate. Wants me to check her out and make sure she's. . .you know. Normal. Not psycho or anything."

"Her?" The tapping stopped. "You're kidding, right?"

"I said the same thing. But he told me not to worry. Just business, and he's not attracted to her and whatnot."

"They all say that."

"He's engaged. To *me*." I waved my ring at her.

"Doesn't mean a thing."

I glared at her again. "I trust Carlos. He's never lied to me."

No response. Just those black, overplucked eyebrows. She thinks I'm a moron.

"Do you want to come or not?"

"I'd better. Moral support. 'Cause believe me, you're gonna need it."

"Whatever."

"Five more minutes. Gotta get this to editing ASAP."

I added a few more lines, saved, and turned off the screen. The end of this month made two years working for the Associated Press bureau in Tokyo as a news reporter—a heady jump from college papers and my aspirations of the *New York Times* for as long as I could remember.

Not that I hadn't worked for it though. I'd grown up in Brooklyn, read every page of the paper since age eight, and studied my tail off at Cornell—double majoring in Japanese and journalism. Studied a year abroad at Kyoto University, number two in the country, and homestayed in Nara. Interned at the *Rochester Democrat* and *New York Post* and worked six months at my beloved *Times*. And suddenly I found myself in Shiodome, Tokyo, in a brand-new office, halfway through my online master's program in journalism and ethics. With awards lining up behind my name.

Kyoko slung her black skull-printed purse over her shoulder and played with the mouse while I gathered my purse and keys.

The corners of the envelopes stared at me accusingly, and I quietly slid my notebook back.

Shiloh P. Jacobs, they read in stern, accusing fonts. No mistake. Not only was there no possibility of another Shiloh Jacobs in the entire country, but the amazing Japanese postal system once delivered my friend's letter from New York when the address smudged. They read the names in the letter, guessed the recipient from the context, and forwarded the letter—to my correct apartment no less. Back in Brooklyn I still got mail for Mr. Pham, who'd moved back to Vietnam in 1987.

I was still staring at the envelopes when Kyoko scared me by appearing over my shoulder.

"Uh-huh. As I suspected."

I slapped my notebook down over the envelopes and pushed her with both arms. "Out! Now!"

"How much did your last trip cost?" We walked through rows of cubicles with reporters typing furiously and piles of paper, sprawling books, and boxes stacked everywhere. Reporters never close books or throw paper away; they just stow them somewhere for future use.

"Which trip?"

Kyoko stared at me. "What do you mean, 'which trip?' To Brazil of course." She pretended to smack me in the forehead. "That must've cost a fortune!"

We closed the glass office door and pushed the elevator button. "I couldn't miss Carnaval, Kyoko. The biggest Mardi Gras in the world. It was the trip of a lifetime."

I closed my eyes and remembered the wild samba, the crowds, the late-night euphoria and thick salt air of the beach. Lights reflected over the dark water, mirroring the two famous bulges of Pão de Açúcar mountains. I'd flown back to Japan with confetti in my hair.

"Well, you'll pay on it for a lifetime." Kyoko folded her arms grumpily.

A Japanese woman with fake blue contacts got on, and I quietly made a tick mark in my reporter's pad under Sandy Blond.

"What's that?" Kyoko demanded.

I put a finger to my lips and put the pad back in my jacket pocket. The elevator dinged, and the woman got out.

"Research. I'm doing a study on hair color in Japan for my master's."

"Aren't you studying ethics?"

"Sure. The impact of Western imperialism and globalization on traditional cultural attitudes. What do you think?"

Kyoko raised her eyebrows. "You're just weird. Period."

I smirked. The elevator was empty, so I turned to the mirror and brushed lint off my new navy-blue jacket. A lightweight silky weave from Comme des Garçons—a super-spendy splurge after a particularly heated argument with Carlos. But I have to admit, it did suit my straight, dark brown hair and hazelish-greenish eyes with their distinctive flecks. All the summer pastels seemed to wash me out, but this did the trick. And my Louis Vuitton silk scarf pulled everything together. Just one Louis Vuitton. I promised myself.

In my teenage years I'd dressed like a bum: torn-up jeans, T-shirts. But this was AP and Tokyo, and the combination reshaped me in ways I'd never imagined. It also reshaped my wallet.

The doors opened with an automated announcement from a high-pitched woman's voice, and we stepped out into the brilliant late-June sun. And heat.

I took off my scarf immediately and folded it in my purse. And my jacket. Draped it over my arm.

Kyoko wiped her brow. "This is awful! I feel like I'm in New Mexico. Ro-chan. . ." She moaned. "Are you really going all the way to Shibuya? Again? It's like the third time this week!"

I grinned at the nickname she'd given me: "Ro-chan." Chan is an honorific, so she called me, in effect, "Little Honorable Ro." Kyoko would never admit in English that I had any honor, but in Japanese it just sort of happened.

Ro? That's another story. Not only did I have to repeat my unusual name—Shiloh—over and over to Tokyo-ites in various red shades of embarrassment, but it's utterly impossible to pronounce in Japanese. And not just for Yoshie-san.

Just trying to sound out the warped vowels and syllables to

fit in the Japanese phonetic alphabet was sheer torture. It ended up something like "Sha-ee-row," since there exists no *"shy"* sound or *L* in any form in the Japanese alphabet, and gave us all a headache.

My mom had single-handedly given me a name where each and every syllable got butchered in Japanese. She'd accomplished a pretty good feat; I'd never seen another name like it. I hoped she enjoyed her little prank.

"Carlos wants me to," I pleaded. The oppressive heat rushed at us in all directions, making it hard to breathe. "He's really busy."

"And you're not?"

"Not as busy as he is, I guess." My red face dripped sweat, and my clothes stuck to me.

"Thank goodness!" Kyoko grabbed a mini pack of tissues from a noisy gaggle of spiked- and dyed-haired young people on the sidewalk. Companies and stores gave tissues away by the pack as advertising, boasting bright pictures on the clear plastic. She tossed me one, and I mopped my forehead.

"Good thing, too. My collection at home is getting sparse. With freebies like these, I never have to buy tissues anymore." I turned over the package and read the kanji characters. "Kinoko Records. Checked it out yet?"

"Yeah. It's all right. I found some good Ramones stuff there once. And a bunch of Japanese punk albums. More punk than post-punk, but darker than New Wave."

I never knew what Kyoko was talking about when she started in on her music, which included a heavy dose of retro '80s stuff, so I pulled out my reporter's pad. "Did you catch the hair colors back there? At least one neon blue."

"You're wasting your time."

Maybe. But I knew Kyoko's secret from the distant gleam in her eyes. She adored "Akiba"—Akihabara, Tokyo's geeky electronics district. That's where all of her extra cash disappeared.

Video games, cool stuff for her computer, anime comic books. Record shops reminded her of electronics shops. She was probably plotting her next trip now.

"Akiba this weekend?" she suddenly asked, and I laughed out loud.

We ducked into the subway station already jammed with people jostling in line for tickets that popped out of a machine. The turnstiles opened, and we joined the waiting throngs.

The next two cars were so full we couldn't even get on, with people squishing out of them and white-gloved "pushers" shoving arms, legs, expensive purses, shopping bags, and occasionally heads through the slowly closing doors.

On the third try the crowd finally spit us into the subway car and smooshed us up against the glass with contorted faces. Kyoko, dressed all in Gothic black, looked scary as she grimaced and sponged her forehead with another tissue.

"Is that a real Louis Vuitton?" she demanded, snatching the corner of my scarf out of my purse when I dug for my tissue pack.

I snatched it back and zipped my purse shut. "Why do you care?"

Her reflection stared back at me in the glass. "Girl. You are a spender."

"Just like you in Akiba."

"I bet all my comic books cost less than a corner of that little silk thing in your purse."

"I bet they don't."

"So Carlos has a girl living with him now?" She wrinkled her nose, and her piercing glittered. She'd just done the one-second subject change again.

"For now. Says it's temporary. The last guy had gang tattoos and never paid rent." I put my nose in the air. "I don't see any problem with it, provided she respects our relationship. I'm a modern woman."

Kyoko shot me a look. "She better be ugly as sin. That's all I'm saying."

"Then don't." I turned my thoughts to Carlos. Carlos Torres Castro hailed from Argentina (or, as he pronounced it, *Arhentina*) and in the words of more than one female friend was a knockout. Dark lashes and even darker brows framed gorgeous almond-shaped black eyes, and his skin glowed with a perpetual tan. He was a stockbroker, twenty-seven, just three years older than me—and he let his wavy hair grow just a little over the collar of his fashionable dark suits. Total Arhentinian style.

I fingered the big diamond on my left hand, wondering if I'd lost my sanity to get engaged four months ago—in only my second year at AP. But we're talking about Mr. Right here. Mr. More-Than-Right, with a Spanish accent.

He'd offered me the ring over wine and steak. "Sí?" he'd said, turning those pleading eyes to me, almost too beautiful to look at.

"Sí," I replied and slipped it on my finger. It dazzled in the candlelight like fire trapped in glass. And so we were affianced. No wedding date in sight, perhaps not for the next two or three years. But it would happen. We just needed time.

Time. I checked my watch for the tenth time, still too many stops away from Shibuya. The train lurched to a halt, opened its doors, and out rolled a moving sea of people. Kyoko and I hung on to the rings dangling from the ceiling for our lives. The tide poured back in, blasting us like seaweed in a typhoon.

Red kanji characters burned overhead as the doors closed, announcing the next stop, and my eyes bounced over silent, charcoal-gray-clad businessmen avoiding eye contact, a subway map, and too-colorful advertisements for green tea and soap. No one spoke. Kyoko stuck her iPod buds in her ears, harsh guitar chords audible even over the chunk-chunk of the tracks.

When the subway car finally eased to a stop at Shibuya station, I'd melted into a rumpled, wrinkled mass of sweat. We stumbled out into the station and across the platform, following humanity up, up, and up the stairs toward daylight.

We didn't have to think. The crowds moved us along without effort, like a piece of flotsam in a flood. I just had to remember to keep right so running businessmen could speed past on my left.

The right-left thing changed, though, from city to city. So I had to stay on my toes.

"What's the *P* in your middle name stand for?"

Obviously I had to stay on my toes at all times with Kyoko, too. I narrowed my eyes at her. "Nice try." This time she'd done the split-second subject change on purpose. Trying to catch me off guard. "I'll never tell. So you can stop asking."

"Must be pretty wild if you don't use it instead of your first name."

"Wouldn't you like to know." I stuck my tongue out at her.

"Where are you meeting?"

"At Hachiko. We always meet there."

People crisscrossed our paths yakking into tiny flip cell phones, sucking Starbucks straws, and tuned out with iPods. No two faces looked alike: topped with a delivery cap, wrapped in an Indian turban, or hair cut in the fashionable, shaggy Japanese teen look. But all were on a mission: lunch. And air-conditioning.

I took my scarf out of my purse and tied it on then put on my navy-blue jacket. Even in the heat. And my new pricey sunglasses. Rolled on a bit of perfume from the glass tube in my purse.

"Done yet?"

I sniffed at Kyoko. "Can't help it I want to look nice. Look! There's Hachiko."

As we grew closer to the unassuming bronze statue of a dog, I felt a lump strain my throat. According to the story, Hachiko waited at Shibuya Station every evening for his master to arrive—until the day the man suffered a stroke and never returned. Still Hachiko waited. Even after they gave him away, he escaped and waited at the station at the time of the train. For ten whole years until he finally died in 1935.

No story had ever gripped me as much as Hachiko's, and nothing in my adult life—ever—had made me want to cry.

Hachiko chose to love. And stay. Unlike everybody else in my so-called life.

I blinked under my sunglasses at Hachiko's characteristic bent ear in bronze.

"You okay? You haven't even met her yet."

I whacked Kyoko with my purse. "I don't care about her! Will you forget it? Honestly!" I crossed my arms and scowled at a group of boisterous European tourists, laughing and taking pictures of three delicate Japanese girls, all decked in colorful cotton yukata kimonos and shyly waving fans.

I started to say more, but a pair of black eyes lazily strode into view. "Little late, aren't you?" he said in his spicy accent, kissing me lightly on both cheeks. Not a bead of sweat—even in a full suit. Tropical blood, I guess. And he smelled wonderful. I leaned closer and tried to memorize the scent.

"It's rush hour, babe." I took his arm.

He tugged on my scarf. "Is that real? What am I gonna do with you, spending all your money?"

"It cost about as much as your Italian shoes," I shot back, reddening not just from the heat.

Carlos spoke as if he hadn't heard me. "We're going to Friday's, but first. . .oh, I see her. Wait a minute."

"Hello?" Kyoko waved her hand in irritation, but he didn't notice. Not unusual. Carlos didn't care much for Kyoko, and she mirrored his feelings. Plus some.

We strained our eyes through Japanese *gakusei* (high schoolers) in their blue Prussian-style uniforms, spike-haired store clerks with chopsticks wolfing down rice from to-go boxes, and a TV crew setting up to film a sweat-drenched guy dressed like a piece of sushi. A man yelled angrily into his phone in

Arabic. Cicadas sawed with a ringing sound, and it all swirled together in a hot, sweaty mass.

"Uh-oh." Kyoko's voice fell flat.

"What?" I asked sharply, shielding my eyes. "I don't see anyone remotely. . ." My breath deflated. "Oh no."

Chapter 2

Kyoko wisely kept her mouth shut as we wended our way across the crowded plaza. There on an iron bench sat a vision of a girl with thick, white-blond ringlets stylishly done up in a messy bun. Her cheeks bloomed pink, yet she remained cool and refreshing in a white skirt and sandals.

She looked up from typing text messages, blinking the palest green eyes I'd ever seen—like translucent sea glass. "Cahlos?" She stood, giving an enchanting, warm little smile that seemed to know no strangers.

He gave her the same two kisses he'd given me, Argentinian style, and I bristled. Did he do that with everybody?

Carlos cleared his throat and looked disinterested. "Mia, meet. . .um. . .Sh–Shiloh. My girlfriend."

I stared into his perfectly sun-browned face. He stuttered. Carlos never stuttered, not even the night he proposed. I'd only heard him stutter once: before a big company presentation with the president. From nerves, he'd explained.

"Fiancée," I corrected and gave her a stiff smile. Not only did she dazzle with all her perfect hairs in place, but that accent only made her cuter.

"Shoy-loh," she said delicately, betraying her Aussie roots.

She smiled and fanned herself with a pretty paper fan. "Ploised to meet you. Mia Robinson. I'm from Sydney."

She dug in her purse for a business card—the quintessential Japanese "who's-higher-on-the-totem-pole" accessory—and I reached for it with one hand. Not two, per Japanese customs of respect.

"I've been to Sydney." I didn't even glance at her card, which—if either of us were Japanese—would have insulted her immediately.

Instead I squared my jacketed shoulders, deciding to pull rank as well as height, since petite Mia barely reached my nose. Not that my height was anything to brag about. "Kyoko and I work for the Associated Press bureau in Shiodome. I'm a reporter." I offered her a business card from a professional card holder inside my purse. With two hands.

"Associated Press." Mia blinked adorable lashes, those frosty green eyes shining like sea foam. "How exciting! I know someone there—Nora Choi. We studied Japanese together in Kobe University."

"Nora. Yes. She's our coworker." I straightened my slipping purse strap, miffed that Mia had somehow entered the AP circle, if only by acquaintance. The mystery I'd hoped to convey faltered.

Carlos stood there like an idiot, hands in his pockets, and then finally cleared his throat. "Well, let's go then." And he turned and headed off through the giggling high school girls. (One of whom tried to take his picture, blowing kisses after him.)

I came to my senses and trotted after Carlos, leaving Kyoko and Mia chatting behind us. I took his arm and tried to talk, but he seemed a million miles away. "The heat, *amor*," he said shortly.

"But you're not even sweating!"

"Well, it's still hot." He walked with a sort of swagger. "I'm getting promoted, you know. I'm top seller of the month. Again."

"You told me. Congratulations."

"It's really hard to beat my record. But it's easy for me. I was born for sales. In fact, they might transfer me to Beijing with a promotion."

"What? But I thought. . ." I looked up at him in horror.

"I know. You like Japan."

We turned a corner, and I coughed back my astonishment. Beijing?

"Hey, *porteño*," Kyoko called to Carlos over the street noise, using the nickname for Buenos Aires natives. Her world knowledge never failed to impress me. "Did you hear Shiloh's story on Kobe won—"

"I know. Some little. . .award," Carlos interrupted, checking his cell phone.

"It's not little," I retorted. "It's a big deal." All the press crowds, snapping photos while shaking hands, and international telegrams and wires made sure it was a big deal.

"Sure." Carlos glanced back at Mia and smiled. Looked at me, struggling for conversation.

We walked in silence a few blocks, interrupted only by the ringing of cicadas and endless chatter on cell phones. A *bento* (lunch box) delivery motorcycle buzzed past.

Behind us I could hear Mia's musical little laugh as she and Kyoko talked. About what, I have no idea because Kyoko sometimes made a piece of shrimp look sociable.

"So you're going to room with her?" I peered up at Carlos suspiciously through my sunglasses.

We passed an udon noodle shop where businessmen stood slurping bowls of steaming soup through their chopsticks. The delicious smell made me pause for a minute before he pulled me along.

"I guess."

I wrinkled my nose. "You really think it's a good idea?"

"Why? You're not jealous, are you?" He locked black eyes on me. "Stop being childish, Shiloh! This is business. I could use the money. I mean, I've got an extra room I don't use."

"Well, why don't we. . .?" I fingered the ring again. I didn't want to push things too fast, but if we got married now, then. . .

He touched his forehead, which started to glisten slightly with sweat. "I don't think now's a good time. I can't take vacation yet, and a wedding is a big deal. I want to get married back home. It's better to wait."

"Bring your parents here. I can help out with the cost."

"I've got a big family, amor. You have no idea how big."

"I've got money," I pouted again, feeling stung. "I mean, I do work for—"

He tugged on the corner of my scarf, and I snatched it off in exasperation and stuffed it in my purse. He didn't even notice. "And that trip you took in February? To Brazil?"

"So what?"

"You should have gone to Arhentina. We've got a better Carnival. The Brazilians think theirs is so wonderful because they've got samba. But we've got something better."

"What?"

"Arhentinians."

I rolled my eyes. Carlos could be such a nationalistic snob sometimes.

I glanced back at Mia, fluttering her fan while a breeze tossed those white-blond corkscrews. Her celadon eyes glimmered in her happy face as if playing a practical joke on my heart.

"How old is she?"

"Twenty-three."

I narrowed my eyes. "I'm not sure I like it."

Carlos rubbed his face with a free hand in annoyance. "I'm helping her out, that's all. It's more for her sake. I feel sorry for her."

"Well, she can come live with me then if she needs help."

Pure bluff. Housing at the AP apartments would never allow it, and besides, they were already too small. I felt as if I lived in a closet. A nice closet, but still.

"Don't be silly. You know she can't live there." He stopped abruptly on the sidewalk and faced me. "Do you think I would bring her here to meet you if I had other intentions?" He stared me down.

I turned away, blushing. "I guess not." What a lame answer.

"Then forget it. She'll only stay a few months. I promise."

"Months?"

"Weeks. Whatever."

I laced my fingers through his as if to make sure he stayed with me, no matter what, and tried to push Mia Robinson out of my mind.

Kyoko didn't say much on the way back. She pretended to be absorbed in her cell phone, typing out text messages nonstop until I finally grabbed her phone and snapped it shut.

"Hey! What'd you do that for?" She scowled. "Now I have to type it all over again."

I tried to erase the troubled line from my brow, but I couldn't. "You think it's a bad idea? Mia and. . .?"

Kyoko shrank her eyes into dark lines. "You really want to know?"

I swallowed hard. "Yes."

"Yes."

"Yes what?"

"Yes, it's a bad idea. A very bad idea," she hissed.

I lifted my chin. "Well, you don't know Carlos."

Kyoko grabbed her cell phone back. "Do you?"

"What's that supposed to mean?"

"I just mean you haven't known the man for what. . .eight months? It raises a lot of red flags."

"Ten. And what do you know about red flags?" I played with the zipper on my purse and fumed. It was also a Louis Vuitton. Okay, so I'd broken my promise. But just that once.

"You asked. I answered."

"Well, you'll see. It'll turn out fine."

"Besides, Ro, is that even legal?" She squinted at me. "I mean, the company obviously pays for his housing. I doubt they'd be too keen on subletting, no matter how many rooms he has. Did you ever think about that?"

She had a point. Leave it to legal Kyoko. I caught a flash of my face in the glass, lips curved into an unhappy frown. I forced a smile and lifted my head.

"Carlos is my fiancé. I can trust him." I changed the subject. "Did you go to law school or something?"

She ignored me. "Just the same, better keep him away from Miss Australia for the time being."

I plodded back to the office in silence, straightening my hair and tying on my scarf in the bathroom mirror. Kyoko reapplied her already dark eyeliner and some purple-brown lipstick. She pressed her lips together, looking like one of those sad, black-clad rockers strumming guitars in subway corners.

We had just come through the glass double doors of the office when Bob the copyeditor jumped out at me. "Good thing you're back. Dave's waiting for you."

"Dave? Why?"

"Says you're late on a story. He's not happy."

I recoiled as if bitten by one of the Japanese monkeys that hung out near the hot springs. They routinely stole lunches and grabbed soft-drink cans. One even tried to carry off Kyoko's gigantic purse, which is nearly as big as me.

"What? I turned everything in! The Fujimori speech with the faux-pas reference to the shrine. The new recycling bill. The one about—"

"The prime minister's wife," Bob finished in irritation.

Sudden horror rose in my stomach, and I felt the floor suddenly buckle, earthquake-like. But I steadied myself and feigned relief. "Oh, of course!" I waved it aside like a pesky bug.

"I'll send it to you."

"He's scheduled a meeting with you at two fifteen."

I glanced at the clock. Forty-five minutes.

"No problem. I'll talk to Dave."

I hurried back to my desk, pins and needles tingling at the ends of my fingers. My breathing turned shallow, and I sat down quickly at my desk, rubbing my face with trembling hands.

Calm, calm, I willed myself, trying to get a grip. The prime minister's wife story. I remember it now. I'd been so consumed with the Diet story and understanding the complex Japanese government issues (and equally complex Carlos, I had to admit) that somehow I'd forgotten the PM's wife.

I opened my calendar and flipped back through my list of assignments, and to my horror red ink glared at me—deadlined for Wednesday. Today was Friday. Afternoon.

I grabbed my Rolodex and riffled through it with shaking fingers, nearly tearing the pages until I came to the official governmental numbers. Normally I'd have gotten a secretary to make the appointment for me days ago, but in the haste somehow I'd forgotten.

How? How? I pounded my fingers into the soft fabric of my chair, wondering how on earth something so important could have slipped my mind. I'd never, ever turned in a story late—especially one so stunningly important. Shiloh the award-winning rookie—barely out of college and halfway through her master's—did not turn in stories late.

If I failed now, I'd fail at everything. Dave would bawl me out. He'd never said a cross word to me, although once I saw Nora Choi fleeing to the bathroom in tears after a heated discussion in his office. The same day he broke the copy machine in half.

What would I say? "Sorry, Dave. I haven't even started"?

I grabbed the phone and punched in some numbers then hung up. What am I doing? I don't want Kyoko and the whole world to hear me calling the Japanese government at one thirty in the afternoon on a Friday! I snatched up my Rolodex and fled to a conference room then shut the door and dialed again. I could hear my panicked breathing as I waited for the sound of ringing.

Please, please pick up!

No answer. I dialed again desperately, keeping an eye on the slowly moving second hand on the clock. Tried another number then another. Finally the beautiful sound of a human voice.

I blurted out my request in my best Japanese, begging for just five minutes to speak to the prime minister's wife or one of her representatives. I'd just started my lengthy Japanese apology when the receptionist abruptly put me on hold.

I tapped my foot impatiently, maneuvering myself over to the sleek computer on the desk, phone under my chin. Opened a fresh page and set up all the correct headings and formats to save time. I could type the interview, if a miracle occurred, straight into the story.

"*Moshi moshi*?" asked a professionally crisp voice. "Hello?"

I introduced myself and begged his mercy then pleaded to speak to the prime minister's wife. I knew I'd breached all possible protocol, and even Japanese etiquette, by demanding something on the spot—but it was my last recourse. They should know me by now. I've interviewed the Japanese prime minister, for crying out loud! I'm dependable! I'm good! I'm. . .

He was saying something about France. "I'm sorry?"

"France," he repeated. "The prime minister's wife is in France."

I lowered my head to the wall and banged it silently. I knew that, I knew that! They'd given me her schedule already. "I'm sorry. Could I please speak to someone else? It's urgent, and I really need to—"

"*Sumimasen*. I'm sorry." And he hung up. Didn't even bother to give me the typical Japanese runaround where they put you on hold for two hours and rummage for something in a nonexistent file, too polite to actually say no.

I put the phone back in its cradle and slumped there in front of the computer, looking at the empty story with no lines of text. Just a headline and subhead and my poor little by-line looking lost and lonely: Shiloh P. Jacobs.

The cursor blinked.

A scant thirty minutes stood between me and SHILOH GETS BAWLED OUT BY DAVE DRISCOLL—with a possible sidebar on bodily injury and severance pay.

AP reporters never missed deadline.

And especially not for Dave.

I took a deep breath and glanced shakily up at the clock. That useless phone call just cost me ten precious minutes. I shuffled through my notes to find anything I could write about, racking my brain to think where I could get some information fast. I almost ran to Kyoko for help, but she'd yell at me, too. Besides, she didn't usually do Japanese government stories.

Tokyo (AP)—, I typed.

At that exact moment, as the cursor winked, something caught my eye: a little blue icon opening the Internet.

I licked my lips and stared at it, trying to think through my racing pulse.

I moved my hand to the mouse. And then, all of a sudden, I clicked on it.

"What took you so long, Jacobs?" snarled Dave as I handed him the hard copy. "You've worked here almost two years. You should know better!" His craggy face looked perpetually angry, as if he couldn't wait to take out his frustrations on the desk or coffeepot.

I knew how to handle Dave. Cringe. Wait. Look properly ashamed, but don't grovel.

"LATE!" he shouted in sixty-point font, waving me to shut up with his arm. "What kind of flunkies am I hiring to turn in stories late?"

"I'm sorry." I ducked as his words rattled the glass office window. "I won't let it happen again."

"You're right you won't! The next time you're sloppy I'll throw you into one of those daft hot-noodle shops to wait tables!" He banged his fist on the table, overturning a coffee cup, and roared some swear words about rookies.

"I understand." Shiloh P. Jacobs, wiping soy sauce bottles. I forced back a smile.

"No, you don't understand! You don't understand that every single hour, every single minute we're late on news, we're losing dollars! Maybe our shirts!"

He ranted awhile, face the color of a dark red *umeboshi* (pickled plum), and I tried to identify his hair color. Gray-brown? Slight comb-over? I need to add that to my notebook.

But I tuned in when I saw him winding down. "Am I clear, Jacobs? If not, go sell records or something. I hire reporters!"

He was testing me. "Yes, sir. No thanks. I'm aware of that." Three statements, three answers.

He slapped the paper down on his desk. "Did you get Schwartz to edit this? Because I'm not wasting any more time doing it myself!"

"Yes, sir. It's ready to go." I hadn't, but it was perfect.

Dave narrowed his eyes at me and banged his index finger into my story. "And if you referred to her as the First Lady I'll fire you on the spot because that's for presidents' wives, not wives of prime ministers! The classic rookie blunder."

"No, sir. I knew that."

He waved me out of the room with a furious hand, and I closed the door cautiously behind me. And walked straight back to my desk with my head up. No way I'd go out crying like Nora.

I straightened my desk and pretended to work on the Diet story, but I could hardly stop my fingers from shaking. So, after a carefully timed ten minutes, I gathered up my purse and headed to the restroom.

Kyoko swung through the door on her way out, wiping her hands on a paper towel. "You okay?" Her eyes popped. "I saw you got called into Dave's. Did you have the story?"

"Of course," I fudged. "He just told me to make my deadlines."

"That's all? I thought I heard him yelling."

"Not at me. That vending company he hates called."

"Oh, that one. Whew! Good for you." She blew out her breath. "I've heard he can be pretty tough."

"Yeah. I was lucky."

I pretended to casually check my makeup in the mirror until Kyoko left and then fled for one of the stalls.

Do not cry! Do not cry! I told myself severely, holding a wad of tissues to my eyes. It would smear my makeup, and I'd have red eyes for an hour. Besides, I don't cry. I just don't. Shiloh P. Jacobs does not cry.

I leaned my head against the cold metal door and breathed deeply, feeling light-headed. I'd done the deed. And if I could slip through, just this once, I'd never do it again. I'd never steal somebody else's words. And I'd never include quotes that I myself didn't elicit.

At least I hadn't invented the quotes. The prime minister's wife did say them—she just didn't say them to me. So what's the big deal? It's not like I lied. Exactly. I merely lifted information someone else had posted. On the Internet, of course, where millions of people browse every second, and who put what first just sort of blurs. Public domain and all, right?

First and last time. I promise. I'll never do something so stupid again as long as I live.

I pressed my fingers to my forehead, feeling a headache coming on. If I stayed too long, Kyoko would think I was crying, so I flushed the toilet and took another breath.

Japanese toilets are amazing. First of all, they have padded, heated seats to warm legs and posteriors. Plus a bidet function that sprays water, at the touch of a button, and a whole panel of other buttons to adjust temperature, flush, and—my personal favorite—make a flushing sound. That way if people are shy about the sound of nature's call, they can cover it with a flushing sound and not waste water. Some toilets even play music.

I had just come out of the bathroom and into the office when Dave powered past me on his way to something important. I felt ice in my stomach.

"Good story," he growled. And stomped off.

I went back to my seat on rubber legs. He didn't notice. He had read my story, and he hadn't noticed. Maybe I was in the clear after all.

I picked up my notes on the Diet and hastily got to work.

Chapter 3

I stayed late at the office until Kyoko finally got tired of waiting around. "So, Ro-chan, Akiba this weekend?" She shouldered her huge purse, which could probably carry a folding chair.

"Sure."

"It's almost seven thirty. On a Friday. What's so all-fired important?"

I sighed and shuffled my papers. To tell the truth, I had nothing all-fired important. Guilt just weighed heavily, as if I ought to make up for what I'd done.

I looked up sheepishly. "Going out tonight?"

"Nah. I'm a little bushed from researching Japanese legal stuff all day. Dave's been breathing down all our necks lately."

I pretended not to hear. "Takeshi out of town?"

"Takeshi's over. Too *otaku* for me. Just weird." She tapped a message into her cell phone without looking up. A little plastic dog thing dangled from her cell phone, bouncing back and forth.

"I thought you like geeky otaku guys. With their big glasses and plaid shirts and reading comics all day."

"Otaku is one thing. A guy who takes you to a *pachinko* parlor on your first date epitomizes weird."

"He took you to one of those annoying gambling places?"

I'd seen them before, with their flashing lights, weird sounds, and rows of people seated in front of what looked like pinball machines. I never understood the attraction.

"He won a green pepper."

I smiled. Pachinko prizes sometimes ranked lower than white-elephant gifts.

"Besides, he's thirty-four and still lives with his mom. Gives me the creeps." She shuddered. "Dinner. . .I don't know. Maybe an *onigiri* at 7-Eleven or something." Kyoko snapped her cell phone closed and waited. She knew food held a persuasive power over me that little else could rival. Except maybe Carlos.

Onigiri. I could almost taste the crisp green nori seaweed wrapper, slightly salty, wrapped around a triangle of fresh white rice. I loved the dab of tuna or shrimp and mayo in the middle, or sometimes salmon. I even liked the salty pickled plum, too, but Kyoko called me crazy.

And never before had modern Japanese technology and creativity shined as much as they did with onigiri wrappers.

"You know, I'd lived here six months before I realized the numbered tabs on onigiri wrappers were for you to open them in order?" I saved my half-finished story and started to shut down my computer.

"So what did you do, just rip them open?"

"Yeah. Didn't you?"

She gave me a look. "No. That's why there's a number one. You open that tab first. And then the second and the third. Did you think they printed the numbers there for looks?"

I shrugged. "I don't know. I figured it was something like stroke order—you know, the Japanese way of writing kanji characters up to down, left to right. Any other variation and you've done it wrong."

"Well, there's a purpose in the wrapper, genius. It's to keep the seaweed crisp and separated so it doesn't get soggy against the rice. When you pull the tabs, it slips right into place. Brilliant.

Unlike us Yanks, who just slap plastic wrap and Styrofoam on everything."

"Now I know. But I still haven't figured out the purpose in stroke order. I mean, who cares how I do it if it looks the same?"

"It doesn't look the same. We foreigners just can't see it."

"Most things in Japan are like that, aren't they?" I turned off my screen and stood up.

"So, changing your mind about pulling an all-nighter?"

"Yeah."

"Onigiri?"

"Nah. Something more substantial. As long as you don't say a word about Carlos." I hadn't eaten much with Mia's frosty eyes twinkling across the red-and-white-checked table.

"*Tonkatsu*?"

Fried pork? I brightened. "Now that's more like it. There's that Momiji place on the way home."

"Momiji it is."

We walked out into the deepening blue twilight, and a strange sense of peace fell over me as we crossed the street without speaking. Evening in Japan descended warm and quiet, and the streets lost their boisterous clamor. As far as I could see glimmered lights, lights, and more lights: full-screen TVs flashing advertisements, neon signs, and futuristic glass buildings like they'd popped out of a Jetsons cartoon.

I loved the city, and I loved Tokyo. Surrounded by waves upon waves of buildings like galaxies of stars made me feel at home, at rest, and comforted, like long-lost friends. Inside those offices and rooms and subway cars were people just like me, all searching for their tomorrow, their greatness, and their way home.

And I had found it.

I turned in a full circle, taking in the dizzying immenseness of it all. Skyscrapers lifted their arms up into the perfect indigo dome as if reaching for heaven.

We all did, in a way. Trying to improve, perfect, and attain the next great thing. . .and for what?

Yet for the moment, I was content just to be a little dot on Shiodome's sidewalk, dwarfed by a colossus of concrete and stone, by the sprawling harbor and mazes of endless streets and neighborhoods. We moved through Tokyo's sidewalks like blood in its giant arteries, pumping, pumping through its great heart.

"Do you miss California?" I asked abruptly. A guy sped by on a bike, smooth spokes purring into the distance.

Kyoko stuffed her hands in her pockets. "Yeah."

"Really? Why?"

She pushed the button at the crossing. "Well, California's my home. I miss my mom and dad, my brothers, and. . .well, you know, the idea of home."

I tried to understand, but a Japanese paper lantern caught the corner of my eye, pricking me with an almost painful longing. "How so?"

The crosswalk opened with a birdlike chirp, and we walked across the black-and-white-striped crossing with the crowd. Not a single straw paper littered the astonishingly clean streets, unlike New York, and we felt perfectly safe to walk alone at night. Darkness and streetlights made everyone look ghostlike.

"Well, I grew up there. My roots are there. Japan's great, but it's very homogenous outside Tokyo and the big cities. If you're different, it's not such a good thing."

"But you're Japanese!"

"No. I'm American." Kyoko spoke in a tone I'd only heard when she was mad, and I kept my mouth shut. "But people expect me to act Japanese because I look Japanese. They expect me to read and write perfectly, speak with all the honorifics, and dress myself in a kimono."

"Are you kidding? I needed two people to help me get into mine!"

"Ro." Kyoko rolled her eyes. "Try getting stuck in the

bathroom—on the toilet! With that stupid obi thing wrapped around my. . ."

"I get it! You can stop now."

She glanced at me bitterly. "But people don't expect you to be Japanese—not with your pretty foreign face. You so much as spit out a sentence, and people fall all over you like you've won the Nobel Prize."

Um. . .that was actually true. Never once, in all my time in Tokyo, had anyone said a negative word about me. (Except Dave, but I heard he criticized a squid at Tsukiji Fish Market until the white-booted fisherman threw something at him.)

Kyoko didn't look at me. "My grandmother lives in Aomori, up in the north. I visited her one time."

"I remember that."

"And probably the last time, too."

"Why?"

"She hated my makeup, my piercings, my hair, my clothes, everything. She called my parents and scolded them for raising an American vagabond who can't even speak Japanese. Said I was too big for a proper Japanese girl."

I sucked in my breath. "I'm sorry, Kyoko. I had no idea."

She shrugged in annoyance. "Ah. Who cares? She grew up in a different era, a different world, and she can't expect me to fit in it. I couldn't do the Buddhist chants right, the claps and candle-lighting and stuff, I spilled tea, and my knees hurt to sit on the hard floor. It's just not me. I'm San Fran. Trolley cars. Freedom. No stroke order. Know what I mean?"

Funny, but I did. At the same time, Tokyo flowed in my blood, and I had somehow become its child. As much as I loved dirty, messy, brawling New York, smelling of garlic and garbage and the harbor, I couldn't forsake Japan. It had adopted me.

Down that street stretched a quiet little park just after Mitsukoshi, the ritzy and crowded department store where I bought *senbei* rice crackers and imported spices.

On the next street I could find Kitamura with fantastic *gyoza* dumplings and curry, the post office with its friendly, uniformed staff, my favorite karaoke place, and Inoue's grocery/convenience store where I bought those onigiri rice triangles, cold jasmine tea, and bunches of fresh green onions. Ancient Mrs. Inoue always smiled her wrinkled grin and gave me handfuls of ginger candy.

And down that street, my all-time favorite: Beard Papa's, the cream-puff shop with yummy custard filling. They'd even expanded to New York, making my two favorite cities now sisters. All thanks to Beard Papa's cream puffs.

"I could stay here forever."

A shiny bus swooshed by in a rush, blowing our hair slightly in the evening breeze. The exhilaration of speed and distance made me tingle all over, like a whiff of Carlos's sultry cologne. The bus was headed somewhere, on a mission, and I wanted to go with it.

"I love Japan. I never want to leave."

"Not me. Don't tell Dave, of course. But one day soon my time here will end, and I'll move on to the next thing."

"Where?"

"I don't know. Maybe Europe. Maybe home."

We stopped in front of the hanging cloth curtain, split in the middle, that indicated Momiji. I lifted it aside and stepped into the brightly lit room filled with rustic wooden tables. The cozy yellow glow reached out to welcome us like a friendly relative.

"*Irashaimase*!" chirped the crisply uniformed girl, bowing in greeting. "Welcome!"

I stared at her hair: a dark caramel color, cut in long curls with fashionable shaggy bangs swooping to one side. I pulled out my reporter's pad and made a tick.

"Argh." Kyoko turned her eyes heavenward. "The hair-color thing again. Give it up, Ro-chan!"

"Wait and see. I'll include it in my master's thesis somehow."

She flickered the first hint of a smile I'd seen in a while. "The scary thing is that I'm sure you will."

We sat against a wall with a window behind us. The girl brought us each smooth, glazed earthenware bowls with ribbed insides, perfect for grating fresh sesame seeds, and thick, blunt, knobby sticks for stirring. We set to work grinding the piles of black and white seeds into a tantalizingly fragrant powder.

"Tonkatsu is my favorite food in Japan," I announced, inhaling from my bowl. "Who would've thought to grind sesame seeds?"

"You say that about every food." Kyoko looked grumpy and pounded her seeds.

"True. But tonkatsu really is."

We ordered—tonkatsu (breaded, fried pork) for me and chicken katsu (the same thing with chicken) for Kyoko since she always watched her weight. I could hardly wait until the two trays came, steaming, loaded with little bowls and plates. There sat our hot katsu, golden brown and perfect, surrounded by a mound of pale green shredded cabbage, a dish of hot white rice, and a bowl of tasty, salty brown *miso* soup. A glorious Japanese feast.

We broke open our chopsticks, said the traditional, "*Itadakimasu*!" with palms pressed together to give thanks, and dug in.

Heaven, covered with a crispy coating and out-of-this-world sauce. A smudge of hot mustard made me murmur my delight out loud.

I'd eaten half my plate when Kyoko squinted at me, nose ring shining. "Don't you miss your family?" she blurted.

I poured more thick, sweet brown sauce into my ground sesame seeds and mixed it with my chopsticks then drizzled it over my pork. "Me?"

"No, the waitress. Yes, you."

I looked up in surprise, stirring absently with my chopsticks. "Well, to be honest, I don't have much of a family. My parents are divorced, and I never, ever hear from my dad. He used to send checks at Christmas, but a few years ago he just sort of stopped. And so did I."

"Bummer."

I shrugged. "It's not like I miss him anyway. He worked ninety percent of the time, was angry the other ten, and left for good when I turned seven."

"Remarried?"

"Yeah. To some woman named Tanzania who's young enough to be my older sister. She's a belly dancer or something. I think she has a kid. No, two."

Kyoko's dark eyes beamed back unexpected sympathy and ever-present cynicism, as if that's how everything turned out. "I'm sorry. Where does he live?"

"Tanzania," I snipped, and Kyoko choked on her wisp of cabbage between two chopsticks. Glared at me.

"He lived in Canada for a while, but Tanzania wanted a warmer climate, so they moved to Mexico City. His retirement money goes pretty far there."

"What a globe-trotting family. And your mom?"

I grimaced. "I don't even know, to tell the truth. She's just so weird. After Dad left she just sort of lost it. Nervous breakdown or something. She would mutter to herself and send me to school with an onion in my lunch box."

"An onion?" Kyoko put down her chopsticks and sipped her hot green tea.

"Yeah. Unpeeled. Just sitting there." I chuckled. "It's kind of funny now, but at the time I was hungry. And mad. I learned how to eat out of school vending machines, but then they took away the vending machines because of nutritional debates, and I couldn't find anything else to eat. Until they caved in to big money and started putting franchises like Burger King and Pizza Hut in the bigger schools, and I could eat to my heart's content."

"Obviously." She scowled at my nearly empty plate. She still had half her food left. I cautiously hovered my chopsticks near a crisp, succulent piece of chicken.

"May I?"

"Go ahead." She shoved her plate in my direction and looked sullen. "I don't know how you stay thin when you eat like you do."

"I run?" I offered hesitantly, taking a bite.

"Please." Kyoko snarled. "You run, what, around the block?"

"Um. . .yeah. But that counts, right?"

"I could do marathons all night long, and I'd still look like this."

"Like what? You look great. Stop it."

She really did. I don't know why Kyoko thought she should look skeletal—like so many hollow-cheeked Japanese fashion models.

"Who asked you?" She sounded mad again, but I knew her weight bothered her like always.

Genetics played favorites like a spiteful grandmother—blatantly and unjustly arbitrary. All running aside, I could eat and never gain a thing, whereas Kyoko could have a little dish of rice and put on pounds. Or kilos, since we lived in Japan.

Since she was twenty-six, she loved to remind me how the weight would pile on once I hit thirty—and I could kiss my french-fry addiction good-bye. Well, at least I had six more years to go.

"I dispense my opinions for free. You're one of the lucky few, Kyoko. You really should be more grateful." I took a long sip of green tea and another piece of her chicken.

She drummed her nails in irritation. "So, do you ever see your mom?"

I made a face. "No. Why should I? She's just. . .in her own world. She joined cults all the time. Especially the one about aliens." I thought hard. "Something about beaming us all up to our celestial home. Or is that *Star Trek*?"

"Raelians. I've heard of them. There's a bunch of them in San Fran."

"There's a bunch of everything in San Fran. But my mom just. . .doesn't fit in my life anymore. She swears she's quit cults and all that, but who knows what she's into now?"

I rubbed my forehead in annoyance. "The past year or so she's been bugging to talk to me again, sending me letters and stuff, inviting me to visit, and. . .I don't want to. What's done is done. I've moved on."

"Where does she live?"

Color crept into my face. "I'm not exactly sure." I picked up some rice with my chopsticks. "She moved a couple of times, and I sort of lost track. Atlanta or something."

"Ah, the South!"

"Yeah. Of all places."

"Don't they still believe the Civil War is going on?" Kyoko smirked.

"Apparently." I leaned closer. "I knew this guy from Alabama once. They said he married his cousin. Don't they have laws against that?"

"Not in some states." Kyoko, the legal expert on inbreeding.

"Let me guess. . . . West Virginia?"

"Wrong."

"Really?" I looked up in midbite. "Where?"

She winked. "California."

I laughed, hands circling my green-tea mug. Kyoko wasn't kidding about her San Fran freedom. Truth be told, we actually weren't that chummy at work, where Kyoko could be ice cold and somewhat competitive. But in the soft drone of voices and laughter around us, the amber glow, everything seemed to soften.

"You'd like the food in the South though. I hear everything's deep fried." Kyoko's eyes peered at me over the rim of her shiny lacquer teacup.

"Really?" My ears perked up.

"Yeah. Like pork rinds and deep-fried moon pies."

"My mom sent me some stuff once here in Tokyo. A bright pink coconut thing, which probably soaked up more red dye than those Chinese 'congrats-on-your-new-baby' eggs."

"Wow."

"Yeah. But the weirdest thing she sent was a mini pecan pie, enshrined in plastic. I still have it at home."

"Did you eat them?" Her eyebrows contorted in horror.

"No way. I kept the pecan pie as a memento."

"What do you mean you 'kept it'?"

"Well, the pink thing started to. . .well, not look so good anymore, so I threw it away. But the pecan pie never changed. It just sits there staring at me. I think it's made with formaldehyde or something." I shuddered.

She stared at me, mystified. "Funny. So that's your mom's legacy."

"Yeah. My half sister told me Mom got a good job doing something. . .forgot what. . .and makes a good living, so I didn't worry about her anymore."

Kyoko surprisingly said nothing. She twirled her teacup. "So you have a half sister?"

"From my dad's previous marriage. No relation to my mom, but Ashley lived with us until Dad left."

"Do you keep in touch with her?"

"Sort of. We e-mail once in a while. She's pregnant and lives in Chicago." Obviously Dad, not Mom, named Ashley. "And she's a pain. Now she just sends a Christmas card every few years."

"Oh. Well, I guess that sort of makes you free to live where you want, doesn't it?"

"Exactly." I smiled. A twinge of sadness flickered across my thoughts, but I grabbed my reporter's pad instead and made several ticks. "Hair dye companies must do a roaring trade in Japan. Great investment potential, don't you think?"

"As if you have money to invest." Kyoko sniffed. "Gucci girl."

"What? I only have one thing from Gucci."

"Really." She didn't believe me.

"No." I smiled and asked for the check.

Quiet settled over the streets when we stopped under the streetlight next to my apartment complex. Which wasn't as nice as Kyoko's a few blocks away, since she'd been at AP longer.

"So you really want to stay here forever?" asked Kyoko, digging in her purse for a lighter.

"Yes."

"Does Carlos?"

I played with my silver watch strap. "Not exactly. But maybe I could convince him."

She harrumphed. "You'll have enough trouble convincing him to leave the Girl Down Under alone."

I sniffed and said nothing. Kyoko lit up a cigarette, which I hated. Hands down her worst habit. "Why'd you have to do that?" I whined. "It's bad for you. And for me." I faked a cough.

"No worse than your fried whatever. Besides, it helps me keep the weight off."

"That's no excuse."

"Hey, you gotta do what you gotta do. That's life." She made an exaggerated point of blowing smoke on me. "Gotta step on some toes sometimes."

In an instant I thought of the PM's wife article and knew exactly what she meant. "Well, you're right about one thing, Kyoko. Whatever it takes." I gave her a mock salute. "Well spoken. You up for a run?"

"Tonight? Are you nuts?"

"Sure. Just over to the—"

"No." Kyoko tapped the ashes off her cigarette and scowled. "Any other silly questions?"

I hid a smile. "Okay then. I'll go alone. I'm definitely up for

Akiba tomorrow though. I'll call ya."

She saluted me back and disappeared down the street until I could only catch a little orange glimmer of her cigarette. Then my cell phone buzzed. DOES THE P STAND FOR PERSEPHONE? she texted.

The split-second subject change again. NICE TRY, I texted back.

MARRY A JAPANESE GUY. THEN YOU CAN STAY HERE.

NOT POSSIBLE. I'M IN LOVE WITH CARLOS. ADIOS.

DOES HE LOVE YOU?

I stared at her brazen letters in disbelief. The cursor winked. OF COURSE HE DOES!

I snapped my phone closed in annoyance and headed up to my apartment on the eleventh floor. Technically it was the tenth floor, since Japanese are superstitious about the number four, which sounded ominously like the word for death—*shi*. So occasionally Japanese airlines have no row number four, and some high-rise complexes omit the fourth floor, too, like mine.

Funny, the first three letters of my name started with the letters "shi." Why had I never thought of that until now?

I hoped it wasn't an omen.

The door to my little flat opened quietly, and I dropped my keys and purse on the long wooden table. Inside, rows of tiny "cubicles" held my shoes so I didn't dirty the inside of my apartment, per Japanese custom. It reminded me of the "capsule hotels" where Japanese businessmen sleep in a rented tube to save money. I hoped my shoes slept comfortably.

I slipped them off in the *genkan*, a sort of uncarpeted entranceway, and stepped into padded Japanese slippers, feeling the weight of my too-chic heels melt.

"*Tadaima*!" I said to no one in particular. "I'm home!"

I shrugged off my expensive jacket and hung it in the small wooden wardrobe near my bed. My apartment looked more like a mini hotel room: sterile modern furnishings, tiny spotless rooms, solid white paint and carpeting. The "living room" (more like a "six-by-six-foot living space") barely contained a sofa and tiny table, a narrow hallway with a mini fridge and stovetop, and just enough room to swing my legs over the (single) bed without hitting the wall.

I was lucky; most of my expat friends lived in one-room efficiencies or cheaper underground pads. Bill Gates made chump change compared to staggering Tokyo rent.

My favorite feature: the mini balcony, where I could look out over the city and watch it twinkle and sparkle into the night. Even my new flat-screen TV, which I'd wedged next to the table, took a backseat. I couldn't fit a chair on the balcony, but I could sit on the arm of the sofa and look out, out, as far as I could imagine. In fact, in a few minutes I'd take my favorite seat and dream, and maybe call Carlos.

My second favorite feature: the toilet-sink. Yes, my toilet did play music, but the top of the toilet tank also sported a faucet, scooped porcelain, and drain—making its own little sink. As Ben Franklin said, "Waste not, want not."

I doubt he referred to space, but in Tokyo, every millimeter counts. The Japanese did it again—and not just with onigiri wrappers.

The apartment still smelled of newness and carpet. A minimalist design, certainly, but I'd brightened it up with memories of my two years in Japan: brilliant red-and-white carp streamers, colorful kites, paper lanterns, a blue-and-gold silk wall hanging decorated with kimono patterns.

On the corkboard in my bedroom I kept a stash of mementos: special news stories I'd written, ticket stubs, pictures of *Kinkakuji* (Golden Temple), an iconic "I LOVE NY!" postcard, letters from friends, pressed gingko leaves, a flowered kimono hairpiece, and my mom's mini pecan pie.

I'd skewered the pie there by the corner of the plastic with a thumbtack. It looked sticky but otherwise the same as it did six months ago.

The collection of absurdities displayed my life, in a strange little nutshell.

I pulled my hair back into an elastic band and took off my bracelets, setting them in the artsy dish on my dwarfed bedside table. I was just reaching for my running shorts when I noticed the blinking light on the answering machine. Fourteen messages.

No. Please no. Dread crept up my spine. What if Dave. . . ?

Impossible. He would have called my cell phone. He knows I'm almost never home.

Right?

Nobody calls my home phone except occasional salespeople, who are too cheap to pay the more expensive cell-phone rate. The number 14 flashed red again like a warning, and a tremor of fear passed through me.

Four. Shi. Death. Mine, at the hands of Dave Driscoll.

As if on cue, the phone jangled loudly, startling me in my silence.

Chapter 4

"Hello?" I nervously picked up the receiver.

The line crackled. "Shiloh?" asked a choked-up voice. "Are you there?"

I stared at the wall, the tremor of fear increasing with every second. "Who is this?"

"Shiloh? This is Ashley."

My half sister? I could barely hear over incoherent sobbing.

I stood up and grabbed the phone as if to cling to something, anything. I sensed bad news and approaching fast. Ashley never called me. The pit of my stomach shook like when I felt an earthquake coming on.

"Ashley!" My voice rose. "Speak to me! What's going on?"

No answer, just sniffling.

"Did you lose the baby?" I couldn't think of another possibility. . .unless her husband, Wade. . .

"Shiloh, I didn't want to be the one to tell you, but. . ." More sobbing.

"Ashley!" Panic prickled.

Muffled noise sifted to my ear, some staticky clicks, and an embarrassed male voice sounded on the line. "Shiloh? Hi. This is Wade. Sorry about that."

"Wade. So you're okay." I sat down warily on the side of my bed, coiling the phone cord tighter around my white fingers. "She lost the baby, didn't she?"

"No, Shiloh. The baby's fine. Ashley's fine. We're all. . .fine. It's your mom."

Instinctively my eyes turned to the pecan pie on the corkboard. "What's wrong with Mom? Is she. . .sick or something?"

"No. Yes. Uh. . .no."

"Huh?"

Wade sighed. "Shiloh, I don't know how to tell you this. I'm really sorry. It's just. . .she. . .well, she's gone."

"Gone? She's. . .missing?" My mom's photo on a milk carton flashed through my mind.

"No. She passed away."

The line buzzed faintly like static. I rubbed my ear to see if I'd heard right.

"Excuse me?"

"She passed away, Shiloh. I'm sorry."

I felt my throat tighten, but no tears came. I couldn't speak. The wind had been knocked out of me. Literally. I slumped from the bed to the floor, landing in a pile.

"She. . .what?"

"She passed away early this morning. At the hospital. The doctors say she had a brain aneurysm. They tried to help her, but. . .they couldn't. It happened so suddenly. Nobody ever expected it in a million years. She was fine and healthy. . .from what I. . .you know, hear. . ."

I felt numb and strange, as if hearing two perfect strangers having our conversation. I had the urge to hang up and pretend everything had never happened, that I'd dreamed it all up. The room shimmered transparent, unreal.

"Shiloh, are you there?" Wade's voice again.

"Hmm?" I had lost the feeling in my fingers. I unwound the cord slightly, letting blood flow back into the tips.

"Are you okay?"

"I'm fine," I stammered. "Fine." What else could I say? "Does Dad know?"

"Yeah, he does. Ashley just talked to him. He and Tanzania are. . .well, really sorry. She meant a lot to all of us."

I thought of Dad, off with his belly-dancing wife in Mexico City, and felt a wave of fury heat my blood to boiling. Not only did Dad know before me, but he could care less about Mom. Sorry? He doesn't know the meaning of the word sorry!

Wade cleared his throat. "I know she was. . .well, her own person, in her own special way."

Hot anger toward Wade stabbed me so fiercely I could hardly think. How dare he say anything about Mom? He never knew her, probably never even spoke to her. Ashley didn't even invite Mom to her wedding.

"How did it happen?" I barked, trying to keep my voice from shaking.

"Well, Ashley said Ellen—your mom—was out working in her garden when she just fell over. A neighbor saw her and called the ambulance, and. . .they pronounced her dead at the hospital. That's really all we know."

"How did Ashley find out?" I could feel my voice rising. "How does she know everything?"

"It's okay, Shiloh. I know you're upset."

"I'm not upset!" I hollered.

"Okay." Wade sighed, sounding tired. "Do you want to talk to Ashley?"

"No. She's probably still. . .no. Forget it." I don't do crying. Ever. My stomach tightened at the thought. "Sorry, Wade. I'm just surprised. That's all."

Wade took a deep breath. "Some of your mom's friends called Ashley. She had listed Ashley and me as emergency family contacts since you live overseas, so. . ."

His voice just hung there in the air. "Are you still there?"

"I'm here." Some of my anger had subsided.

"There's something else, too, when you're ready for it."

I gripped the phone cord. "What else? Go ahead. My day's already ruined."

"Wait. It's not bad. Not really. I mean, I don't think so."

I raised an eyebrow. "What?"

Wade cleared his throat. "Well, you know the house she lived in. . ."

"No, I don't."

"Well, a house. Her house. She left it to you in her will."

"Her house?" My throat closed again, and I sagged back against the bed. "What do you mean?" I was really making this hard for Wade.

"She had a house, Shiloh. It's not much, apparently, but she paid for it, and she wants you to have it. She knew Ashley and I already have our own house, and besides, you're her daughter. . . . So it's there, waiting for you. You can sell it, which is what I figure you'll want to do, and put the money in your bank account. It can't hurt with the economy the way it is."

I grunted my understanding as the words wrapped themselves around my fogged brain. "She left me her house." I said my question as a statement.

"Yeah. Something like that. I. . .uh, suppose you'd like to know about the funeral, too, which will be there where she lives. It's Monday if you can. . .you know, make it. I guess it might be difficult for you to come, but. . ."

I didn't speak, so he cleared his throat again. "It would be good, though, if you could, so we could get the house business squared away."

"The house," I repeated stonily.

"I didn't mean the house is more important than. . ." He sounded frustrated. "You know what I mean, Shiloh. If you can come, it would be great. If not, Ashley and I will try our best to fax you the stuff. . .get your signature and. . .whatever. I know you're busy there. It's up to you."

"Yeah." I rubbed my head in a daze.

"I also thought you might want to. . .maybe. . .go through your mom's things and see if there's anything you'd like to keep. Something with special memories or something."

I almost laughed out loud. Special memories? Mom? Dad? My family? What a joke! My special memories had been success. Work. A few friends who helped me make it through dark and tangled years. Even Ashley hadn't been around that much, although to her credit she always kept in remote contact, even after my dad left.

"Is Ashley okay?"

"She's fine. She'll be okay. Don't worry about her." He paused. "She just wishes we'd been there more for your mom."

"Ashley never got an onion for lunch," I shot back.

"A. . .what? Sorry?"

"Never mind." Suddenly I couldn't talk a second longer. I could hear Ashley blowing her nose. "I've got to go. I'll call you. Thanks."

And I abruptly hung up.

I sat in a daze for I don't know how long, and the room seemed to fade.

Mom is dead.

The thought stupefied me, as if I were trying to comprehend a difficult Japanese sentence and failing blankly. I tried to think and rethink it until it made sense, but it did not. I began to wonder if Wade was joking or if I was asleep. Certainly Mom did not die; things just don't happen that way.

He'd made a mistake. I'd call and tell him I didn't care for his silly stories and to stop worrying me with ridiculous nonsense.

Wade. What a bonehead my half sister married.

I found myself in front of Inoue's convenience store in my house slippers. Really. I had no idea what I was doing there or why I had on my slippers. I just saw myself looking up into the lighted sign front, with several Japanese people staring at me as they walked past.

"Taking it easy tonight?" laughed an unmistakably British accent as a lanky someone, maybe a foreign-exchange student, pushed open the glass door.

I turned unseeingly to eyes I didn't recognize. Looked back at the INOUE sign and down at my striped slippers.

Call Carlos. I need to call Carlos. I punched in his number, and it rang and rang. No answer.

In an uninhibited stupor that accompanies shock, I dug for Mia's business card and dialed her number. Again, no answer.

Mrs. Inoue appeared in the store window, head covered in a kerchief. Obviously wondering why I was standing on the curb. I dialed again.

"Kyoko?"

"Ro-chan? What's up?"

"Come get me."

A strange silence. "Where are you?"

"I have no idea."

And I shut the phone.

Chapter 5

I was playing a Tetris-like game on my cell phone when a taxi zoomed up the street and stopped in front of Inoue's. Kyoko burst out, flushed and worried, then sprinted over to my side. I didn't look up.

"Ro-chan, what's going on?" She stopped, panting. "What are you doing? You've got your. . . Are you okay?"

I looked up at her and then back at my game. Kyoko snatched the phone away from me and snapped it shut.

"What?" she demanded, shaking my shoulders.

"Green onions." My voice came out small and quivery. "I need to buy some green onions, I think. And some jasmine tea."

Kyoko stared at me in absolute shock. "If you called me over here just to buy groceries, I'll. . ." Her eyes widened. "Something happened, Ro. What? Why won't you tell me?" She flailed her arms in exasperation.

Mrs. Inoue hovered at the window. Then she leaned through the glass door, holding it open for me.

Kyoko nervously followed me inside, as if afraid. She greeted Mrs. Inoue briefly, and they exchanged remarks, and I bowed politely. Tried to smile. It seemed a toothy grin to me, like a wolf might make, but I couldn't remember how to do it right.

I wandered over to the tea section, unable to force out the words. Maybe if I didn't say them they would somehow not be true.

Kyoko trailed me, hands on her hips. "Okay, so you want some tea?" she asked in a surprisingly gentle voice. "Will that make you feel better?"

She pulled open the thick glass door with a suction sound. "Which one? This one? I think that's your favorite, right?"

It wasn't even jasmine tea. It was a weird brand of green. But I nodded anyway.

Kyoko pulled out the bottle and just stood there. Finally she closed the door. "Okay. Anything else?"

I tried to think.

"Is it. . .Carlos? Did you guys have, like. . .a fight or something?"

"Carlos?" I glanced at her foggily. "No. But he didn't answer the phone."

"But you did call him?"

"Yes. Mia didn't answer either."

She wisely restrained her eyebrows. "Something at work?" she ventured.

"No."

Kyoko shook her head as if lost, drumming her dark nails on the tea bottle. "Okay. . .something at. . .home?"

As I raised my eyes to her, looking lost and shell-shocked and even guilty, something inside her seemed to understand.

"Your parents?"

"My mom." I couldn't say any more.

Kyoko opened and closed her mouth then guided me to the register. She paid for the tea and spoke to Mrs. Inoue, who worried over me with crossed arms. Mrs. Inoue gave me a bag of ginger candy, wrapping her hands around mine. She dropped in some senbei rice crackers for good measure then accompanied us to the door.

I suddenly reached out and hugged her, something I had never done. Japanese generally don't hug.

She patted my hair in a motherly way, muttering something soothing in Japanese with her wrinkled lips.

Maybe I'd come for that reason. Maybe, for just one moment in my addled brain, I wanted to reach out for two things I suddenly could not obtain: a mother who acted like one—and a mother who was still alive.

"Do you want to go home or come to my place?" Kyoko held open the door for me.

"Your place." I couldn't stand the idea of going back into my bedroom and seeing that phone again.

Our taxi stopped at Kyoko's apartment. She flipped on the light and seated me on the sofa with a blanket and a bowl of *mikan*—small, deliciously sweet tangerines packed with flavor. They reminded me of those ancient Bonkers candy commercials where huge fruits suddenly crash through the ceiling when you ate one.

I gently tore off the soft mikan skin, pressing the pieces against my nose to inhale them. It made Kyoko's living room smell less like carpet and incense and more like summertime. If they made a perfume scented like mikan, I'd wear it. In fact, maybe I could just wear the peels like a necklace or something. I rehearsed the Japanese phrase I'd use at the perfume counter to ask, "Do you have bottled mikan?"

I was making no sense. I popped a section of mikan in my mouth, and the intense burst of sweet, tart citrus flavor seemed to bring me out of my fog.

"She was only forty-nine," I said in a small voice, dropping my head into my hands.

Kyoko came from the kitchen with two glasses and stopped short. "What do you mean 'was'?"

"I mean, how could she do that? I should have been there, and she should have waited for me. I mean, how do I know those doctors actually tried to help her? I should see the records! If I sue, I'll sue big-time. You can help me with all your legal know-how. It's their fault. Completely."

I didn't touch my tea. Condensation frosted on the side.

"Come on—forty-nine? People don't die of brain aneurysms at forty-nine. People live to eighty. Or nowadays, ninety, with all our medical care. What about longevity? Vitamins? She was healthy. This shouldn't have happened."

Palpable sorrow glowed in Kyoko's dark eyes. "I'm so sorry," she whispered.

I barely heard her. The dam had broken, and the tidal wave curled up, ready to slap. Just like Hokusai's famous painting.

"Maybe those freak friends of hers took too long to call the medics. Or the ambulance. Maybe it didn't get there fast enough. They took the wrong road, or got stopped by traffic, or. . .would that be the city's fault? Maybe somebody poisoned her! Help me, Kyoko! You're the legal one. Who can I sue?"

I blabbed on for about five more minutes, and Kyoko graciously didn't try to stop me. When I finally sagged against the sofa and sipped my tea, she clumsily patted my shoulder.

"I'm so sorry, Ro-chan. I know you weren't. . .you know, close. . .but I know she mattered to you."

For some reason I sensed none of the anger I'd felt toward Wade when he said basically the same thing.

"I should have tried harder. I should have been there."

Grief obviously didn't put Kyoko in her element, and I knew she felt uncomfortable. But she just stayed there in her armchair, legs curled up under her, looking glum. She picked at her dark green toenail polish.

"Wanna try Carlos again?"

I shook my head. "Let's just go there. He doesn't answer his phone."

"Okay. Do you want to call Dave? Or I'll call him if you want."

Kyoko? Call Dave? Kyoko Morikoshi had suddenly moved beyond crabby office lunch-mate to friend. "Would you?"

"Sure. I guess you're going for the funeral, right?"

"Yes." My determination surprised even myself.

"Really? You sure? I thought. . ."

"I'm going."

Her smile beamed slight tenderness. "Good for you, Ro," she said, voice softer than usual. "The rest of us can cover for you. It's not a busy month."

She scrolled through a computer calendar and squinted at me. "Aren't you supposed to renew your visa next week?"

"My what?"

"Never mind. You can do it in the States. Just don't forget."

I played with my glass and ate another mikan while Kyoko discreetly made phone calls from the other room. A purple lava lamp bubbled. My eyes passed over her walls scattered with old Goth and dark post-punk rock posters: Bauhaus. The Cure. Joy Division. And some scary-looking blond Japanese guy in all black called Gackt. Where did Kyoko come up with this stuff?

She came back in and fiddled with her laptop on her desk. "Your story on the PM's wife posted."

I looked up. "Oh." Some other time I'd celebrate.

"Do you want to make some airline reservations? I can help if you want. Then we can go to Carlos's place."

I dragged myself over to the couch and plopped down in front of the computer. Clicked a few pages. Rubbed my face. Typed *Tokyo (Narita)* under FROM.

The cursor blinked at me under To.

"Where does she live?" Kyoko started to correct herself and say "did" but stopped.

I banged my head against the keyboard, typing rows and rows of b's.

"Ro? Are you okay? Calm down! I'll do it." She leaned over me and took control of the keyboard. "What's her city and state?"

I rolled my head back and forth in misery. "You know what? I don't even know."

Tokyo at night had a soothing feeling even my mood couldn't shatter. A taxi over to Shibuya would cost a fortune, so we took the subway. I already had too much on my credit card to buy first-class tickets, so I got coach and hoped Kyoko hadn't noticed. She paid for our subway tickets.

A group of platinum-blond Japanese girls with eerie white-and-blue makeup and silver-white lipstick strummed guitars and sang on the side of the street. A perky summer love song, ironic for how I felt at the moment.

The subway crowds had thinned, so Kyoko and I sat side by side on the seat, purses on our lap and staring straight ahead per Japanese custom. A drunk businessman tried vainly to hold on to one of the rings, advertisement cards overhead swatting his balding head, and he finally stumbled into a seat across from us. He slumped against the glass, tie askew and mouth hanging slack. I felt like doing the same thing.

"Thanks for letting me call Wade and Ashley."

"No problem, Ro. Just don't forget to go to the consulate and renew your visa while you're in the US, or I'll be visiting you in the deportation wing of the airport."

"Yeah, yeah. I hear you." I tried to smile but couldn't. "Do you really think it's okay to take off a whole week?"

"The office will find some way to go on." Kyoko stopped abruptly, remembering to turn off her sarcasm button. She tried again. "Dave was really sympathetic, wasn't he? Probably a first for him."

"I know. Will you talk to Mrs. Inoue? I like her a lot."

"Certainly."

"And you're sure? You really don't mind putting me up for the night and taking me to the airport tomorrow?"

She flicked my head. It stung, and I scowled and rubbed the spot. "Stop worrying about everything! Take a nap like that guy is doing."

I followed her curt nod to a thin businessman in an open-mouthed sleep, head bobbing forward as the subway car jolted. There's a disease in Japan called *karoshi*—death from overwork. One could only take so many eighteen-hour days, eating vending-machine noodles and sleeping in tubes.

"I'm worried about Carlos," I finally whispered. "And Mia. I don't like it."

"Now you're coming to your senses."

"He called me childish."

"He's the one who's childish. If he thinks for a second he's immune to Little Miss Green Eyes, or any other attractive woman under the age of fifty staying in his apartment, he's deluded. *Ploise.*" She fluttered her eyelashes.

"I thought you're from San Fran!" I protested. "Freedom and no stroke order!" Honestly, Kyoko struck me as the last person on earth to object to Carlos's female roommate.

She stared at me. "I'm not stupid, Ro! Freedom doesn't mean ignorance. Wake up and welcome to the real world!" She tapped me on her head with her cell phone.

"Besides, he always makes you go meet him," she grumbled. "He doesn't even care that you love Japan and want to stay here."

"He works hard. And he loves Argentina."

"Then get used to playing second fiddle, babe."

"I can't just expect him to drop everything for me!"

Kyoko turned to face me. "Everything? Know what I see, Ro-chan? A man who hasn't given up *anything* for you! At all! He does his thing, and you come at his beck and call. You don't even talk to each other like you're in love! He. . . Forget it."

Kyoko looked furious. She mashed the keys on her cell phone violently, and her cheeks reddened. Finally she broke the icy silence. "I think you should dump him."

The ring on my finger sparkled, and I curled my hand into a fist in defiance.

"I can't."

"You can."

"I can't."

"Shut up." She turned away.

We didn't speak until the subway slid to a stop at the station. I knew in her own way Kyoko bared protective claws, and it made my heart swell a little. Someone cared; someone thought my happiness mattered.

We walked through the turnstile and started up the hill to Carlos's apartment, breathing in the cool, damp night air.

"Look, I'm sorry," she muttered. "I shouldn't keep bringing it up, especially with all you're going through now. He's as good-looking as sin, Ro, but he still bugs me. Something just isn't right. I don't want to see you get hurt."

"It's okay." Our footsteps echoed on the pavement. "I understand." I took her arm. "You're a good friend, Kyoko. Thanks."

"Nah. It's nothing. You'll probably get married as soon as you get back, and I'll have to eat crow." She disentangled her arm and patted me—or rather, smacked me—on the back of the head. I'm assuming she meant it affectionately, since that's pretty much as close as she came.

We entered the super-chic, chandeliered lobby of Carlos's building, and the receptionist nodded at me. He loved practicing his English, and I loved gawking at the fine furnishings and imagining I lived here. Stockbrokers obviously made more than reporters.

"Is Carlos home?" I asked in English.

"Yes, I believe he is. Shall I ring him for you?"

"No thanks. We'll go up." I nodded my thanks.

We stepped into the shiny gold elevator, but when it stopped at Carlos's floor, my hands twisted nervously. Why hadn't he called me? Certainly he'd seen his messages by now if he was home. Maybe the receptionist made a mistake.

I buzzed the button outside Carlos's door. Kyoko twisted a dark silver spider ring, looking moody.

A flurry of footsteps pattered, and my heart picked up. A fumbling with the lock.

The door opened slowly, and there he stood. A little rumpled in shorts and a T-shirt, but still gorgeous. "What's wrong, *chica*?" His eyes widened as he spotted my sad face. "Chicas?" he amended upon seeing Kyoko.

"Can we come in?" I reached out to hold his hand.

"Of cou. . .uh. . .sure. Sure." He held the door open wider and cleared his throat. He stuttered again.

We filed in, and there in the darkened living room sat Mia, looking pretty in a pair of fuzzy cotton pajamas, curled up in an armchair. A bowl of popcorn at her feet. She looked up in surprise.

"Um. . .hi." Her nervous gaze bounced from me to Carlos, those glass-green eyes looking blue in the glow of the paused TV. For good measure, she quickly sat up straight and wrapped a blanket around her shoulders. I shot her a look, but she seemed quite absorbed in scrubbing something off the arm of the chair.

"We were jus. . .watching a movie." Carlos assumed his place in the armchair opposite Mia and leaned back in overdone relaxation, hands behind his head. They sat pretty far apart, but he ran his hand through his black hair a tad nervously.

Carlos gestured to the sofa and turned on the lamp, bathing us all in light.

"What's wrong, babe? You okay? You look upset." He reached out muscular arms, and I just stood there.

"She tried to call you all evening," said Kyoko, sharper and louder than necessary. "Is there some reason you didn't answer?"

Carlos's jaw dropped. "You called me?"

"Your house phone, too. Care to explain?" She glared at Carlos and then at Mia, whose cheeks turned pale.

Um, maybe we should try a different tactic. I sat nervously on the edge of his armchair.

Mia blushed and excused herself with an embarrassed "I'll be right back," but I knew she wouldn't.

"Whoa, whoa, whoa," snapped Carlos, flaring up. "What is this, the Inquisition?"

"It's okay." My fingers fluttered to my forehead. "I just needed to talk to you. About something important."

"What's so important?" Carlos smoothed my hair. "You know I want to talk to you, amor. I'm just tired. Long day. Didn't feel like answering my phone. Headache. You know how it is when you've been talking to people all day?"

Actually, I did. His accent soothed my raw nerves, and I leaned back against him.

"I'm sorry, *princesa*. I didn't mean to hurt you. Forgive me?"

"Sure." My resistance melted like a cone of shaved ice at a Japanese summer festival.

"So what's the big deal?"

On the way home I forced myself to talk about something—anything—but Carlos. I'd accepted his apology, but something unsettling still lurked. Kyoko didn't need to mention she'd made her point.

Carlos held me and whispered his sorrow. Wished he could take me to the airport, but he couldn't miss his big presentation. Held my face in his brown hands and promised he'd be waiting for me when I got home. Those deep eyes, rimmed with tears, so beautiful I couldn't turn away. I pressed my head to his shoulder and wished I could stay.

Kyoko went out on the balcony and smoked. Mia never reappeared.

I turned my attention to the trip home. My foggy brain still churned.

"I need to call that person Wade and Ashley told me about," I said as we turned on the lights in Kyoko's apartment. It felt dark compared to mine, decorated in Gothic art, mirrored Indian pillows, and a whole bookshelf of creepy-looking anime comic books. A record by somebody called The Psychedelic Furs mounted on the wall. The Psychedelic what?

I suddenly felt exhausted and rubbed my eyes. "Maybe I'll just call tomorrow."

"It'll be in the middle of the night there," Kyoko warned. "Better do it now."

"Then I'll sleep until noon tomorrow. I'm worn out."

"You miss your flight and I'll beat you silly." She scowled at me. "The phone's there. I'm getting ready for bed. Help yourself to anything in the fridge."

She closed the bathroom door, and I slipped over to the fridge. In the bright light I found nothing but healthy food: tofu, some languishing green onions, a bit of Brie cheese, and a white Styrofoam container of some kind of leftovers. I grabbed the Brie and rummaged through her cabinets until I hit pay dirt: chocolate. I just hoped I wasn't ripping into a precious care package stash.

Kyoko's mom sent her Reese's Peanut Butter Cups. Mine sent me artificially colored curiosities. Huh.

Only now she'll never send me anything again. Ever.

I dropped the Reese's Cups back in the cabinet, feeling queasy.

"Call yet?" Kyoko poked her head out the bathroom door, toothbrush in her mouth and barely intelligible.

"No." I picked at a piece of lint in the rug.

"Do it." She dropped the phone in my lap and went to spit.

"You have a real sink. Not a toilet sink."

"Do it. Or I will, and I'm too tired to be polite."

I picked up the paper where I'd scratched the number. Some older woman who knew Mom and had keys to Mom's house.

"Faye Clatterbaugh," Ashley had said.

"Clatter-what?"

"Clatterbaugh. It's her name."

I sighed and dialed the number. It toned several times—that weird, overseas ring—and then someone picked up.

"Hello?" said the voice in a Southern accent.

"Hi. I'm Shiloh Jacobs, Ellen's daughter. Calling from Japan. My sister Ashley said you wanted to give me your number."

"Oh hi, sweetie. I've been waitin' for yer call. I'm so sorry about yer mom, sugar. So sorry."

She sounded sadder than I did, and I felt ashamed. "Um. . . thanks. I appreciate it."

"Just call me as soon as ya get here, and I'll make shore ya get everywhere you need to be. You're welcome to stay with me, too. I've got an extra room." I suddenly thought of Carlos and his "extra room," and fresh anger swept through me.

"No, that's all right. I've already made hotel reservations. But thank you."

"Are you shore, honey? You do what you want, but ya don't need to spend your money. You'd be welcome at my place."

Southerners sure were friendly. But I needed space, not friendliness, now.

"Thanks, but I'm fine. I just need to get to the funeral on Monday. What time will it start?"

"It's at four p.m. If you tell me your hotel address, I can leave directions there or even come an' pick ya up. Ain't no trouble."

"Okay."

"An' when you're ready, anytime, I'll show you your mom's house or anything ya need at all."

"Thanks. That would be great."

"I imagine you've got a tight schedule, so I'll let you go, doll. Sleep well, and I'll see ya on Monday. I'm lookin' forward so much to meetin' ya."

"All right." I shrugged. "Well, good night then."

"Good night, doll baby. Have a safe trip."

I crawled into the bed Kyoko had made for me on the floor, feeling like the 116-year-old Japanese woman I'd seen on TV.

Chapter 6

At an ungodly hour, sky still brooding, I found myself on a plane headed across the Pacific in a number 47 seat. Three rows behind the number 44. Japan Airlines apparently didn't honor superstitions.

I rubbed my forehead, remembering the blur of events: Awakening on Kyoko's hard floor with an angry Indian elephant tapestry brooding down at me. Back to my apartment, where Kyoko helped me shove things in suitcases and then haul them up onto the conveyor belt at the airport. Luggage checks, security checks, passport checks, jarring announcements on the loudspeaker, my tickets, fumbling for my foreigners' ID card, a boarding gate, crisply dressed Japanese stewardesses.

And here I slumped, eyes glazed over with sleepiness and shock.

The big news: Mom lived in Virginia of all places—not Atlanta. She'd never lived in Atlanta. Wade said she almost took a job there once though, so I wasn't completely out in left field. But she'd settled in Virginia about six years ago.

The city itself where Mom lived mystified me and, in some ways, made me nervous. For starters, maps showed no airports close by. Actually, they pretty much showed nothing close by.

Worse, Mom actually didn't live in town at all. She lived in "Churchville," which coughed up little on the Internet except—I kid you not—photos of livestock auctions. Not a good sign.

Churchville? Ironic for me, a nonchurchgoer. Chalk up another one for ol' Mom.

How much would a house sell for in a place like Churchville? Enough to cover my debts? I hoped?

I'd spent my preboarding time researching Staunton, the closest city to Churchville. If I could call a place with barely twenty thousand people on a good day a city.

Kyoko had printed off reams of info on Staunton, Churchville, and Virginia in general and shoved them in my hands before I left. Consummate on-the-spot reporter that she was. Since I couldn't sleep, I flipped through them.

Virginia: "Old Dominion," Jamestown and Pocahontas, tobacco, James Madison, Thomas Jefferson, Colonial Williamsburg, Patrick Henry's "Give me liberty or give me death!" speech, capital Richmond also former capital of the Confederacy, the Pentagon, Blue Ridge Mountains, top ten in education, dogwood, bluebells, Chesapeake Bay, peanuts, Edgar Allen Poe, Langley Air Force Base, Katie Couric, Sandra Bullock, blah, blah, blah. Motto: *Sic semper tyrannus*, or "Thus always to tyrants."

Sandra Bullock? I looked at the list again. Where did Kyoko come up with that?

Staunton: Home of old Western State Lunatic Asylum.

I shouted out loud, clapping my hand over my mouth, and several annoyed Japanese faces frowned in my direction. I managed to bob my head in an embarrassed "sorry, excuse me" and flung the papers in the empty seat next to me with a shudder.

Mom was just weird. End of story. If I ever needed proof, it grinned right back at me in black and white.

Honestly! My hands curled into fists. Couldn't Mom do anything normal? Even her last domicile proved her freakishness to a *T*.

I glared at the paper again, hoping her house wasn't on Western State Lunatic Asylum property. Or that she wasn't a resident.

The thought flashed through me so quickly that the paper wavered, and I slowly lowered it to the folder. Mom did have psychological problems at times. . . . Do you think. . .?

The plane droned. The window turned navy and then black. I opened my laptop and tried to work on some news stories. Halfheartedly ate a soba noodle dinner on a flimsy tray—likely the last Japanese food I'd have for a while. But for the first time I could remember, I didn't feel like eating.

When people started turning out their lights and putting on slippers, I reluctantly flipped on my reading light and tried again.

Staunton: Home of old Western State Lunatic Asylum, home of Virginia School for the Deaf and Blind (okay, so maybe Staunton-ites had big hearts toward those with physical challenges. . .good, I suppose), home of the Statler Brothers (some kitschy old country-western band), Woodrow Wilson birthplace, Confederate supply base, farming, poultry, apples, livestock feed, Amtrak, Mary Baldwin College.

Churchville: NOTHING.

Half the stuff Kyoko printed out referred to Churchville, New York.

I put the stack down and thought about Mom, and a light glinted in my head. Physical challenges. Teaching. Hadn't Mom talked about doing special-ed teacher training all those years ago? I mean, when she wasn't unemployed or working at diners or laundry services because her tax center boss fired her again?

She talked sometimes about her younger brother, Billy, who'd been born with severe learning disabilities, including deafness and bad eyesight. She'd cared for him and tried to teach him, and apparently she'd had some measure of success before Billy died at age six. He affected her deeply. Could Mom have worked at the Virginia School for the Deaf and Blind?

Mystified, I recalled snatches of conversations I'd pushed aside so many years ago: "Billy learned his alphabet. . . . They said he couldn't, but he did. . . . Wish I could have gotten a degree. . . . Kids with difficulties shouldn't get sent off to institutions and forgotten. . . . If I had more money. . .if I could do it over again. . .if I had a chance to do what I did with Billy. . ."

At the time I could only hear complaints and injustices, pressed down so tightly they overflowed like a plugged sewage pipe. More lectures about Mom's problems, way too big for my own shoulders, and more things to blame on Dad.

I tried to imagine Mom working with blind students, pressing their hands to pages of braille, and felt a sudden warmth flood through me. . .a strange aching that also condemned me. I should have spent more time with her. I should have known who she was. I should have cared about what she wanted.

"Tea?" The starched-uniformed flight attendant scared me by stopping the cart by my seat, and I jumped.

I accepted the steaming cup. The fragrant, slightly grassy scent reminded me of Shiodome, morning sun through the buildings, and the call of crows.

As I stared into the chartreuse depths of my teacup, I wondered how much more of Mom's life I had missed.

Chapter 7

Traffic cleared out once I circled Richmond in my rented Honda, leaving me with wide open lanes and endless thickets of pines. Not a car in sight. The college rock station crackled and finally disappeared. I was really in the middle of nowhere. Which was probably good, considering I'd tried to drive in the left-hand lane at least three times, like back in Japan. Cars honking angrily as I swerved out of the way.

I stretched my legs, clad in preppy dark blue jeans and high-heeled boots, tugging on the scarf tied around my neck in the heat. Turned up the air conditioner.

Sunday already, and Mom's funeral tomorrow. I'd fallen asleep still in my traveling clothes in the hotel bed, completely "flown out." My flight from Chicago was delayed, and I'd been lucky to make it to Virginia, even half asleep.

My eyes sagged. I yawned. Tried to remember what my businessman seatmate told me about Staunton—a "stopover," he'd called it—where tradition still lives and will probably rise again. "The Civil War and all that."

He corrected my pronunciation, too. "It's STAN-ton. You'll sound like a Yankee if you call it STAWN-ton."

"I am a Yankee."

"Well, then, good luck. But remember how to say it."

I yawned again, turning the radio dial as my mind blurred with sleep. Static. Nothing but static. And then a shaky organ.

"Welcome to Bible Today," said the announcer. "We're glad you're listening."

Great. Sunday in the Bible Belt. And apparently Bible Today had forgotten to pay whoever was supposed to come up with catchy titles.

A bunch of sermons hardly piqued my interest, but my eyes were glazing. I rubbed them with the back of my hand, yawning again. I needed something, anything, to keep me awake.

"When you rely on yourself and your own abilities to accomplish everything in your life, some might call that self-confidence," the kind-voiced man was saying. "But in 2 Corinthians, Paul writes that our sufficiency is not from us, but from God.

"Why did God create us then? To know Him and be known by Him. To give Him glory. We deserve death—the wage we earned for our sins, says the Bible—so He sent His Son Jesus to die in our place and give us eternal life.

"God urges us to call on His name and be saved. 'Choose life!' He says. 'I have set before you life and death, blessings and curses. Now choose life, so that you and your children may live and that you may love the Lord your God.'

"And because of Jesus, we can now cry out like the Psalmist, 'I will not die but live, and will proclaim what the Lord has done!' "

The message poured out before I could stop it. My hands tightened angrily on the steering wheel, and I swerved, whacking at the radio button.

"But have you chosen life through Jesus Christ, the sinless Son of God? Or are you following your own way and believing that you, and you alone—"

I finally jammed the button off. Jerked the steering wheel back and calmed my breath, staring angrily at the desolate yellow lines stretched out on endless asphalt. Maybe it was better to fall asleep and plow into the guardrail than spend my first few hours in Virginia getting a lecture.

Nobody could tell me I hadn't earned my job or my good standing. I'd received my academic scholarship at Cornell fair and square, night after night of endless studying. After all, what else could I do? Stay at home with Mom and listen to her rant about aliens?

I'd worked hard to pay my bills, unlike my richie-rich friends who bought Mont Blanc watches for Christmas presents and traveled to Europe for spring break.

I, Shiloh P. Jacobs, had done it. Without help from any supernatural source. Don't tell me I need God or any other crutch to give the credit to! I fumed, knuckles still rigid on the wheel. I deserve my success, and yes, Carlos, my Louis Vuitton scarves!

My cell phone rang, and I hastily stuffed my Bluetooth in my ear. "Carlos?"

"Ro-chan!" Relief poured through me at the sound of Kyoko's voice, even far away and crackly. "Where are you?"

"On the way from Richmond to Staunton."

"Lots of traffic?"

"Not a soul. Sunday noon, so everybody's at church I guess." I made a face.

"Are you all right? Do you need anything?"

"I'm fine, Kyoko. Really. I just need to get to the hotel and eat something and sleep. I'll feel more. . .normal." I tried to rub sleep from my eyes.

"You? Normal?" Kyoko snickered. Then her voice abruptly sobered. "The. . .uh. . .service is tomorrow?"

My grin faded. "Yeah. I'll find out more when I get there."

"So what's Virginia like?"

"I have no idea. So far. . .flat. Lots of trees." I peered out my windows. "And deer-crossing signs."

"Good weather?"

"Yep."

"Hmm. Good." Kyoko wouldn't say it, but I could hear the worry in her voice. "You really doing all right, Ro?"

"I am. Really. And thanks for everything, Kyoko. You've been great. You've helped me so much." Nothing would make Kyoko flee faster than heartfelt praise, but I said it anyway. Thought briefly of Hachiko the dog, perched on the edge of Shibuya station.

"Yeah, well. . . I'd better let you drive. Call me when you get checked in, okay?"

"Sure. Thanks again."

"Stop thanking me. You're getting on my nerves."

"Sorry." I bit back a smile. "By the way, has Carlos maybe. . . called you? To check on me?"

"Carlos?" she snorted. "Don't be ridiculous, Ro. Why, you mean he hasn't. . .?"

I bit my lip. "He's probably just busy."

"Ahem. Well. Don't get run over by any turkey trucks." She'd actually been reading up on western Virginia.

"Funny."

"I try. Well, bye."

"*Matta.*" The Japanese short form for "see you," which is different from "good-bye" (*sayonara*).

By the time I reached the Best Western hotel in Staunton, I could hardly move my legs. The water and ham biscuit I'd bought at the run-down, Podunk gas station just past Afton Mountain had dissipated hours ago. The one with the ticking NASCAR clock, cowboy-hatted patrons, and unintelligible saleswoman. Sheesh.

"Hi there!" said the desk clerk a little too brightly. I must have looked tired because she gave me a sympathetic look. "Long trip?"

"From Japan." The lobby, decorated in a country-ish pattern of florals and cranberry colors, smelled distinctly of swimming pool and coffee.

"All the way from Japan!" Her eyes popped as she took my credit card. "Patty," read her name tag. She really did look like a friendly Peppermint Patty from the Peanuts comic strip with her honey-brown bangs and freckles. Before long she'd start calling me "Chuck."

"Well, what brings you here?" She pushed buttons and printed out stuff as we talked.

I winced. Why did everyone have to ask me that? "Funeral."

"Oh dear. I'm sorry. I hope not anyone in your immediate family."

"Well, yes, I'm afraid so."

"I'm so sorry." Patty finished putting together my information, using a gentler tone of voice. "Well, I hope you enjoy your stay. There's a coffeemaker in your room, and. . ."

I nodded, not hearing anything. Patty handed me the key. "Is there any place to run around here?" I yawned, hoping I'd remembered to pack my tennis shoes.

"Not really." Patty hesitated. "I guess you could follow the parking lot up to Cracker Barrel or the other way past Mrs. Rowe's."

"Where?"

"That red restaurant." She pointed out the window.

"Oh." I turned to look. "What's their food like?"

"Lands! People come from all over just to eat there. It's been in business since 1947. She died a few years back though. It's a bit different, they say, but still really good."

"She?"

"Mrs. Rowe."

"Oh. Any recommendations?"

"Breakfast. Everybody loves the pecan rolls. And then there's her daily specials, like fried ham and fried chicken with mashed potatoes and gravy."

"Do they have anything not fried?" I tried to keep back a smile. I'd heard lots about the South. Some places even fried weird stuff, like candy bars and dill pickles, which were never meant for the deep fryer.

"'Course they do. They've got the best barbecued pork sandwiches. And spoon bread and collards. And lands, the pies! My favorite's coconut cream."

"Spoon bread? Collards?" I didn't understand half of what Patty just said.

Patty smiled. "You're not from here, are you?"

"If you mean Staunton, no." Thank goodness for that!

"Well. You've got to try them. And then there's the steakhouse and a Cracker Barrel up on the hill with the best dumplings and corn muffins you've ever tasted."

"Probably the only ones I've ever tasted." Redneck food heaven! Here I come.

"Knock yourself out." Patty grinned.

I wheeled my stuff up to my room, neat and decorated with similar cranberry colors, and dumped my suitcases.

This room would function as my home for the next week, so I'd better get used to it. I took off my boots at the door and pulled a pair of Japanese slippers from my suitcase. Padded into the room.

First things first. I turned past the hair-dye ticks in my notebook, which I'd intended to use to prove a point about Western influence on Asian culture, and found a fresh page.

Southern Speak, I wrote at the top. And then, "Lands!"—exclamation; "these parts"—around here, when referring to Southern localities. Then I divided a page into columns and wrote, Southern Foods: Fried and Nonfried. Not that I minded partaking of either.

Tapped my pencil against my chin, wondering how long it would take me to fill up the Fried column. Five bucks said after one dinner at Mrs. Rowe's.

I changed into a soft little dress, one of the most comfortable things I owned, and sandals. Pinned my hair up. Lay across the bed to stretch my back and then glanced reluctantly at the clock, figuring I'd better call Faye What's-her-name.

I reached for the phone and punched the buttons without getting up, and she answered. She called me honey, although her accent didn't hurt my ears like the gas station lady's where I'd bought lunch, and asked if she could meet me for dinner.

I started to say no then sighed and heard myself saying yes. Why not?

"Mrs. Whatever is next door. I'm worn out."

"Good thinkin', doll! I was jest gonna suggest it. I'll bring the key to yer mom's house, some paperwork, and other things. Unless you'd like to do all that later."

"Maybe later." I rubbed my eyes. "But dinner sounds good. If I can stay awake."

"Shore, sweetie. Whenever you're ready, jest let me know, and I'll give ya the keys. Then you can see her house and go through her things whenever you like."

I felt like a criminal the way she said it, like I was riffling through someone else's pockets.

"So I'll meet ya in the lobby in half an hour, okay, sugar? Call my cell phone if ya need anything."

I wrote down her number and hung up. Faye seemed so sweet. A shame we had to meet over the ruins of my mom's life, although I had an inkling she'd fill up my "Southern Speak" journal in a minute.

I guessed Faye before she introduced herself. Late fifties, I figured, with a sweet face. Glasses. Soft, sandy-gray hair curled in a shoulder-length style that made her look young. Cute. I smiled in spite of myself.

"You must be Faye. I'm Shiloh Jacobs."

She took my hand, which I'd crisply stuck out in an overly businesslike manner, and then hugged me. I awkwardly put my hand away and hugged her back.

"I'm Faye. So pleased ta meet ya." She looked me over then gave me a sort of shy smile, patting the side of my head. "You do look a little like yer mom. Yer pretty eyes, mainly, with all them gorgeous colors."

"Yeah. My eyes are the only thing though. I don't look much like either Mom or Dad." Thankfully. I didn't mean to think that, but it swelled up against my will. The less I had of them in my life, the better.

"Hungry?"

"Very."

"Let's go then. We can talk on the way."

We fell into step side by side. Faye smelled of something sweet, like violets. A scent older than I would wear, but becoming on her. "So how do you know Mom?"

"From church."

"Church?" I tripped over a patch in the sidewalk. "You're kidding. Mom went to church?" I tried to cover the derision in my voice with surprise.

Faye didn't seem to notice. "Yes, sweetie. She did. She went there for about two and a half years before she passed away."

I cleared my throat to keep from saying something rude. "Well. That's a surprise."

The evening whispered soft and indigo. I didn't need the sweater I'd brought just in case.

"Is it?" I couldn't tell if Faye was genuinely surprised or if she wanted to ply me for more information.

"You know Mom had. . .well, issues, right?" My voice sounded harsh against the soft, humid evening and clumps of fragrant trees.

"I do. She went to counseling for a long, long time, so she told me, to work out some a them issues. And. . .well, doll, I have to ask ya. How much of this do ya really want to know?" Her eyes shone sober and blue.

I swallowed hard, not sure how to respond. I almost preferred to live in my make-believe world, where no information was good information. I could fill in the blanks as I pleased.

But something inside insisted, despite my misgivings.

"None of it. But I need to. I should want to. Tell me everything."

Faye put an arm around my shoulders in a tight hug, and I didn't pull away. "Well then, sugar, let's talk."

Chapter 8

Mrs. Rowe's gleamed with red paint, barn-like and welcoming. From the sound of voices and clinking glasses, the dinner crowd had already beaten us to the tables. But we didn't have to wait long. A young hostess seated us, looking not yet out of high school, and we picked up our menus.

"What do you recommend?" I paged through the list, hoping to find something not covered in cornmeal or lard.

"Well, I like a lot of things, sugar. This is my kinda cookin'. I like the Virginia ham with coleslaw and collards."

"Collards again. What are those?"

"Greens. You know, cooked with ham. Ain't you had 'em before?"

"Nope."

"My husband used to say they taste like grass. 'Course he was from Montana, so what would he know? Some people like 'em with vinegar."

"Well, I had really salty ham for lunch, so maybe something else?"

"Fried chicken's delicious, sweet pea, although maybe a bacon, lettuce, and tomato sandwich would do you better after all that travelin'." She turned over the menu. "Or broiled trout."

Japan. Fish. Trout. "Definitely."

"Oh, it's delicious. If I keep thinking about, I'll get it, too. But I want something differ'nt. Oh, and did ya know you ken get spoon bread here if they have enough?"

Now I had slurped all kinds of strange noodles in Japan and eaten sea creatures scientists probably hadn't identified. But spoon bread? Where would that go in my "Southern Speak" journal?

"Never had it? It's like a sorta. . .I dunno. Soft bread. You eat it with a spoon."

The look on my face gave me away.

"Well, why don't you get rolls, and I'll get spoon bread. You can try a bit if ya like." Faye pursed her lips. "I think I'll go with the fried chicken. Ain't had it in a while. Did ya choose yer vegetables?"

"I think. . .salad and those collard greens." I closed my menu, still trying for a bit of adventure.

"Don't say I didn't warn ya." She winked. "Oh, and dinner's on me."

"Oh no. You don't have to do that!"

"Shucks. Don't be silly. I imagine that plane ticket wasn't no five-dollar special, right?"

I had to smile. "Ten. With tax."

"See? Raisin' the rates like that. The nerve." She gave her menu a decisive look. "What'll you have to drink, Shiloh?"

"What's iced tea taste like? I've only seen it in movies. Is it sweet?"

Faye gave me a funny look. "I thought Japanese people drank tea."

"Well, definitely not sweet. And no ice."

She shook her head pityingly. "Gracious. What y'all been missing!"

"I'll try it then."

"You won't regret it. Oh, and don't forget to save room for

dessert. Her pies are absolutely the best."

It struck me as funny, and even charming, how people continued to refer to "her" as if she were alive and standing in the next room.

A waitress took our orders and brought us two tall glasses of caramel-brown tea, packed to the brim with ice. No wonder tepid-water Europeans made fun of us. In Italy you were lucky if it came room temperature.

I bobbed my head at the waitress in thanks, Japanese-style, and quickly realized no one else did that in Staunton, Virginia. Just me.

"Like yer tea?" Faye smiled across the table, not noticing my gaffe—or pretending not to.

"I do. It's really. . .sweet." But also herbal, slightly. . .bitter? The wedge of lemon cut the sweetness beautifully. I drank without stopping, much thirstier than I realized.

"It's like water here. Good as anything on God's earth." Faye set her glass down. "So, sugar plum, let's talk about yer mom. You seemed surprised she came ta church with me."

"Well, yes. But then again, Mom always did try anything." I waved it away, playing with an empty straw paper. "You just told me she went to counseling. What else do you know about her?"

Faye sighed. "She'd just had a rough time, dearie. That's my impression. 'Course I don't know the whole story. I'm just sayin' what I saw. I knew yer mom—Ellen—for about three years. She moved here some five or six years ago, I think, from North Carolina."

I stirred my tea with my straw, feeling color creep up my face. Mom had lived in Staunton for six years, and I didn't even know what state she lived in.

"She said she'd divorced and yer dad remarried, and ya'd gotten accepted by someplace real important and worked in Japan." Faye unlaced her fingers and laced them again. "She'd sort of lost touch with ya over the years and felt sorry for it."

"I can explain." I tossed the straw paper down harshly. "I know from the outside Mom looks like this poor, mistreated soul whose family just left her. Dad was wrong, for sure. But there's more to it than that."

"Of course, sweetie. I know that. There's always more than one side to ev'ry story. Ellen said it was her fault."

I raised my head. "She did?"

"Yes. She said she only wanted to try an' reclaim what she could. She talked about ya sometimes. . .how wonderful you are and how badly she'd messed up."

"Well, she certainly did." I snorted and looked away. "I don't know about you, Faye, but I never had a mother growing up. And once Dad left with that Tanzania woman, I didn't have a dad either. Not that he behaved like much of one before.

"And Mom? She was unstable—not just sad, but unstable. She cried all day and talked about suicide. Hit me sometimes. She either took depression medicine until she turned into a zombie, leaving me to take care of her, or she didn't take it at all and went ballistic. She joined cults who swindled her out of her money and filled her head with nonsense then disappeared with them for days."

I picked up the straw paper and twisted it so hard it snapped in half, but I didn't stop. "She left me with drunk neighbors who tried to whip me—or worse, their creepy boyfriends who couldn't keep their hands off me." My cheeks flushed with anger, and I avoided Faye's eyes. "That's how I started sleeping at the homeless shelter because nobody would bother me.

"She couldn't keep a job because she didn't show up on time or just disappeared for days without calling. I just. . .grew up alone, raising myself and taking care of her. We got evicted all the time. I always went to bed afraid we couldn't pay the rent and I'd have to go into a foster home or I'd come home and find her. . ." I dropped the straw paper and pushed it away. I'd said too much. And I was furious.

I let out my breath and tried to relax my shaking fingers, ashamed at how much I'd spouted off. What were you thinking, Shiloh P. Jacobs? I needed to be more objective. Reporter-like. The clink of glasses, light conversation, and laughter floated across the restaurant in condemnation.

Faye's lip trembled. "I'm so sorry." Tears glistened in her eyes. "I'm so sorry for ya, havin' to grow up that way. It must have been awful. I can't even imagine."

I sipped my tea awhile before answering and forced myself to calm down. "It's over," I said lightly, giving a brusque shrug. "She means nothing to me."

"So sorry." Faye smoothed a rumpled napkin, as if wishing she could smooth my life out the same way. Well, good luck. It's a bit late for that.

"Does what I told you about Mom surprise you?" I shook off her pity.

"Actually, no. She told me some about it."

"She did?" My eyebrow arched skeptically. Mom always had excuses for herself.

"Not all, sugar, but a lot. Said she didn't expect you or anybody else to come after her, but she wanted ta try an' make something of her life while she still could."

Hence the boxes and occasional letters she'd sent me. The weird pecan pie. As if they were supposed to make everything better. Make me forgive her. Sorry, Mom. I'm no sucker.

"Where did she work?" I changed the subject abruptly.

"At the Virginia—"

"—School for the Deaf and Blind. I knew it."

"She told you?"

"No. I guessed. She always talked about her younger brother, Billy, and I just put two and two together. Why else would anyone come to Staunton?"

I clapped my hand over my mouth. "I'm sorry. I didn't mean. . ." What had I meant? "Really. No offense, please, Faye.

I'm sure it's a great place."

Faye looked down shyly, still smiling. "None taken, sweetie. An' you're right. It ain't like people are knockin' down our doors to get here. Kids don't stay here much after they grow up, and why should they? Except now people are realizin' what a beautiful place we have, without much crime and pollution, and they're buying it up lot after lot.

"Staunton's always been a small town. But some of us sorta like the quiet life, watching the seasons change and living where people know your name. I'm happy here. Doubt I'll ever move. After my husband died I thought I might, but I feel closer to him here. It's my home."

I sighed, feeling depressed. There sure was a lot of dying in this town. The waitress poured more tea with a pretty tinkling sound into our glasses.

"I imagine you've seen whole worlds I cain't even imagine, an' still in yer young years," said Faye a little wistfully. "I guess I'm too old for sushi, ain't I?" She laughed.

My tongue tingled at the memory of salty soy sauce and pungent ginger. "You've never tried it? Where can we find sushi around here? I'll treat you."

Ah. Sushi. Now we were speaking my language.

"Here? Shucks. I don't reckon Staunton's got any."

I blinked as if I hadn't understood. "You're kidding. I mean. . . nowhere? Not even. . .?"

Faye thought hard. "They had a couple a places in the past, I reckon, but they didn't last real long. That last place got shut down."

I stirred my ice, choking back a snarky comment.

"But if you find it, I'll try it! You bet yer boots!"

I managed to smile back. For some reason I liked this woman, even if Staunton left. . .ahem. . .lots to be desired.

"Oh, look. I think that's our dinner."

The steaming tray loomed larger than I'd imagined,

threatening to spill over. The waitress set in front of me a huge trout, golden-brown and crisp, along with my salad and a plate of something dark green and slimy looking.

Aha. The collard greens. I poked at them with my fork, and pink bits of ham smiled back.

"Well, here we are." Faye smiled happily. "Do ya mind if I pray for our meal?"

I quickly put my fork down. To each his own. "Uh. . .sure. Go ahead." And she took my hands.

She prayed for the food, for the hands that prepared it, and for me as I faced all the difficulties of the coming days. Then she said, "Amen." I looked around to see people staring at us, but no. In Japan two foreign women holding hands with closed eyes would definitely attract attention.

I picked up my fork. "What's 'amen'? Everybody says that. What does it mean?"

" 'So let it be done.' Something like that."

We dug into our food. Right. Landlocked Staunton doesn't have sushi. I poked at my golden-brown fish with a fork, hoping some redneck didn't haul it here in his filthy bait bucket.

And the collard greens looked exactly like chopped grass, but tasted salty, hearty, meaty. From there, though, the meal went downhill. Faye's spoon bread had a gross, spongy texture, like soggy breakfast cereal.

To cover my disgust, I excused myself and took a picture of my collard greens for Kyoko.

Faye chuckled. "You got one of them expensive pitcher phones, don't ya?"

"Yeah." I took a picture of Faye and asked her to take one of me with my collards. "But the TV doesn't work. I've got to get it upgraded."

"TV?" she gasped, turning my phone over. "On yer phone?"

"Sure. This model's been out for years in Japan."

"How do I press it ta take a pitcher? Like this? Did I do it?"

I examined her fuzzy picture. "Not bad. See? It's a lot of fun."

"That's the first time I've ever taken pitchers with a cell phone this snazzy. I've seen 'em, but I never used one."

If I'd come here even a month ago, I could have had this conversation with Mom. The thought sobered me. I stabbed at my fish and pulled out a bone.

"Did Mom. . .like it here?"

"She did, sweetie. She said it 'fed her soul.' She loved the autumn leaves an' the fresh air. She helped out at church a lot. We ate here sometimes, she an' I an' a couple a other ladies because we were all single. Or wanted ta be." She giggled girlishly.

I looked around the restaurant with new eyes. Mom had sat at one of these tables. Sipped tea from a glass like mine. I took in the simple country paintings, the crowded tables, and waitresses handing out plates of fried chicken and mashed potatoes.

"Was she. . .normal?" I didn't know how else to put it.

"She was." Faye suddenly took my hand in hers and patted it. "She'd struggled a lot, cried sometimes, but by the time we met I think she'd found some answers for her life.

"She was a good teacher, ya know. Helped a lotta kids. Not very rewardin' work at times, in the way we might think of rewardin'. Sometimes these kids don't outwardly show much progress. She got tired, but she loved it. I wish you coulda met her in her better days." Faye looked sad. "She shoulda invited ya here."

I bristled. "I don't think I'd have come."

"I know, honey. But. . .we just never know what the Lord is up to in all a this. He has His ways, an' He saw fit to allow her to live her life—an' end it—the way she did."

"Do you really believe in God like that?" I asked skeptically, poking at my collards.

"I do, sweetie. With all my heart."

"Did my mom?"

"Toward the end, yes. Absolutely."

So that's what she'd meant in her random letters about finding new meaning for her life. At the time I'd wondered if she'd met a man or gotten a dog. People sometimes go overboard with animals. I heard about a woman who married a dolphin.

"Do you have children?" I pulled a Kyoko.

"No, I don't." Faye folded her napkin. "Mack and I. . .well, we couldn't, an' at that time it was difficult to adopt, so we didn't. I wanted to."

"But I thought you believe in God." The contradiction made me grumpy. I hated contradictions and how people keep on believing them anyway. Like the Japanese housewife offering daily tea and rice to her ancestors but saying she doesn't believe a word of it. Why not forget the whole thing and eat the rice yourself?

"I believe in Him with all my heart, honey. But that doesn't mean we get everything we want in life. God's ways are differ'nt. He never promised heaven on earth."

I felt a whole bitter diatribe coming, but I pressed it down. Our conversation had slipped into directions I didn't like.

"So how about the funeral? Who's even doing it?" I felt confused. The family should, right? But Mom, for all practical purposes, had no family.

"Some friends from church and VSDB. We got together and agreed we'd honor her memory because she'd become so dear to us."

"What about the arrangements? The flowers and. . .and. . . everything?" I couldn't bring myself to say "casket," but I knew the zeros lined up behind those price tags. A proper funeral, plus burial plot and headstone, cost thousands.

"The church and all of us took care of things, and your father sent a check."

My father. Who did nothing but leave occasional messages on my cell phone, which I deleted immediately.

"Really." Everything made me angry. What if I wanted a

different casket? What if I didn't like their choices?

Well, Shiloh, you could pay for a different one, couldn't you? I snapped silently. I was even mad at myself. *But you know in your heart you wouldn't want to spend your money on that.*

Maybe now I would.

Maybe now it's too late.

Horrified, I looked up from my inner conversation. Was I schizophrenic? Had I followed in Mom's footsteps without realizing it? I put my fork down, feeling shaky.

"You okay, honey?" Faye looked up from her chicken. "Too much all at once, I reckon."

"I'm okay." I forced a smile and rubbed my forehead, jet-lagged and exhausted. Half-awake and half-asleep. "Just need to get used to everything."

"I guess you'd better get some shut-eye." Faye got out her wallet to pay. "Take a warm bath when you get back to your hotel room. That'll help ya wind down."

She closed her purse. "Want me to pick you up t'morrow, or are ya gonna drive yourself?"

"I'll drive. Thanks."

Faye left me at the hotel lobby with a warm hug, and I felt a bit like I was leaving Mom behind. Almost changed my mind and went with her. But since I'd paid for my room, I said hi to Patty and took the elevator up. Parked my shoes by the door and turned on the bath water.

Tomorrow would be a big day.

I just had no idea how big.

Chapter 9

I awoke at 9:42 a.m., leaden-eyed. I'd overslept. The hotel radio clock had been playing country music since eight.

After dinner with Faye the night before, I'd taken a warm bath but just couldn't seem to get sleepy. Sent some stories to Dave, texted Kyoko and Carlos. Kyoko and I chatted for a few minutes online, but Carlos's account showed a red bar across it: offline.

As soon as I got comfortable in bed, the room vibrated. I scrambled under a doorway for protection out of habit, mistaking it for one of Japan's famous earthquakes. But no, a midnight train rumbled past. Patty had failed to mention it.

Then another at 1:27, and another. No whistle, just the whir of tracks and wheels.

The last time I looked, the clock read 3:49, and I hadn't slept a wink.

And it was too late now. I grabbed my stuff for the shower and flew through the bathroom, drying my hair and digging frantically through my suitcase.

I didn't know what was appropriate to wear to a funeral for one's mother, so I threw on an ugly black dress I'd bought at a street-side sale in Yokohama. I'd considered it a deal at five dollars, but it was ill-fitting and too dark for my coloring. But it did the black and sorrowful job well.

I pulled on a dark-colored headband and a pair of black ballet flats then added somber makeup. I studied my black ensemble, feeling like Goth Girl from one of Kyoko's bands.

But all the black reminded me I was indeed heading to a funeral. A good-bye. Mom's good-bye. The thought put a damper on my already sour mood.

I grabbed a small black purse from my suitcase and shoved some stuff in it then locked my door and ran down to growl at Patty about the train. Instead of Patty I found Bobbie, an older woman with too-long hair and big bangs.

I crabbed with Bobbie about how I couldn't sleep, how the Best Western ads didn't show any train, and I demanded to change hotels. She promised me a room on the other side of the building, but I'd have to wait until tomorrow to move.

"Fine," I grumbled, even though it wasn't. I grabbed some coffee and a banana on my way out the door.

I sat in my car with the door open and sunglasses covering my puffy eyes, trying to make sense of Faye's hand-drawn map. My mind wasn't cooperating when she drew it, and she might as well have been playing tic-tac-toe. If I'd just written down the address, the GPS could have done the rest. But alas. Jet lag. I kicked myself for not letting her drive me to the service.

But my bad luck was just beginning.

I pulled out my international calling card, but the paper with Faye's number was gone. I riffled through my purse and dumped it on the seat. Sorted through my credit cards and "Southern Speak" notebook, shaking it upside down. In a panic I ran back up to my hotel room, where I emptied the desk drawers and checked every pocket. Tore through my suitcase, throwing clothes on the floor.

I gripped my head in my hands, trying to focus. It must be in the car. It had to be.

I rushed back down to the Honda, door still open, and dug around on my hands and knees under the seat. Bumped my head on the steering wheel. Hit the windshield wipers by accident, and when I swiped to turn it off, turned on the car alarm.

And for all of that, nothing under the seat but a suit-coat button the rental company's vacuum had missed.

I wearily plopped back in the seat and called information. I tried to remember Faye's last name and groaned loudly into my hand. Snapped my phone shut in a huff. There I sat, not knowing a single soul in Staunton who could help me.

I gave a long, angry sigh and slapped the map out straighter. Now I'd have to go to a gas station and get directions, wasting more time, because I sure wasn't talking to Bobbie again in my frame of mind.

Out of the corner of my eye I saw someone brushing mulch around a small tree, baseball cap pulled low. Gardener or something. He looked up at the same time, and I grabbed my map and stalked over.

"Excuse me. Can you help me?" I pulled off my sunglasses.

"Sure. You seemed a little frustrated over there. Lost?"

"Yeah. I need to get to. . .here." I poked my finger at the funeral home.

His stood up and studied the map, and his eyes met mine. They were bluish-colored, or grayish, nondescript—but kind. "I'm sorry."

I guess my black dress did make me look like a mourner, and my mood festered by the moment. "Thanks. Do you know the street address? I could use the GPS system."

"Sorry, I don't. But I can tell you how to get to the funeral home. It's out in Churchville."

"Churchville?" I started. "You've been there?"

"Sure. Lots of times." He squinted at me strangely. "You're not from here, are you?"

"I get that all the time." I made a face. "No. But I needed to go to Churchville anyway, so now I can kill two birds with one stone."

"Well, as long as you're killing birds, make them starlings."

"Sorry?"

"Starlings. They're little black birds."

"Like crows?"

"Smaller."

"Why? Do they dig in the trash here, too?"

"No, they bully the native birds out and take over. Sometimes they sit there and watch them build a whole nest before kicking them out of the tree. Or steeple. Or whatever it is they want. And they flock in the thousands—imagine the mess."

I raised an eyebrow. "You sure study your birds." I made a mental note to write *starlings* in my "Southern Speak" notebook. I'd already started the second page, thanks to Faye and Bobbie.

One corner of his mouth turned up in a smile. "I try. So, Churchville. Let me see the map."

I followed his directions, asking questions, until he drew a big circle around the funeral home. "That's it right there, just off 42. Or Buffalo Gap Highway. But you might not see any road signs. Out there things are a little. . .well, less posted. People just sort of know where they are. So look for these things." He drew in some more notes and—I'm not making this up—something like bugs with stick legs.

"What are those?" I asked, not intending to sound rude. "Roaches?"

"Those are cows. There's a pasture here."

"Oh." I covered my mouth. "Okay. I'll look for them."

"I never promised artwork. Only directions." He gave that slight smile again.

"No, really. I appreciate it. Thanks."

"Sure." He straightened his baseball cap and looked at the map again. "Just in case you get lost, though, here's my cell phone number. I can try to talk you through wherever you are."

He wrote it on the corner of the map.

"Thanks." I took the map back, a spurt of honest-to-goodness gratitude springing up. I had no idea people here were so helpful, and despite my sarcasm and grumpiness, he'd just done me an enormous service. "You've really helped me."

"No problem. Hope things get better for you."

I sighed and put my sunglasses on. Now back to the funeral. Half of me wanted to go, and the other half wanted to skip the whole thing and pretend it never happened.

He called something after me.

"Huh?"

"You okay?"

I paused, fiddling with my purse strap. "I'm fine. Just have a long day ahead of me."

He gave a sympathetic smile and turned back to his mulch. And I got in my car and headed for the last place in the world I wanted to go.

Chapter 10

I half-hoped I'd need to call the gardener just so I could thank him, or even just get my mind off the funeral, but he'd written perfect directions. Even the pasture, just as he'd drawn, scattered with loafing cows. At first I breezed through Staunton without noticing much—just an older small town as expected—but when the buildings began to melt into pastures and farmland, my sad heart lifted just a little.

Sloped, jagged mountains loomed blue and stalwart ahead of me, strangely comforting. They'd come with me along the Interstate like a good friend. Sort of like having Kyoko in the car, minus the cigarette smoke and snide remarks about Carlos.

Pastures gleamed brilliant green, like something out of a fantasy movie, shining in the sun and dotted with trees. Even the roadsides gleamed with color, all splashed with wildflowers and pink sweet pea vines.

The sun hid in and out of clouds, and during one darkish moment I rolled down the window and let in the summer breeze. If they could capture this fresh, clean, earthy scent, it would sell better than bottled Japanese tangerines.

I found myself in the middle of nowhere surrounded by

woods. Just as the gardener had labeled it: "Middle of nowhere." I chuckled as I checked my map.

I turned right at a lonely intersection and passed a long, low brick school, again as indicated, smack in the middle of a giant, rolling cow pasture. Thus the cow drawings. I laughed again.

When pastures gave way to a CHURCHVILLE sign, I slowed the car and stared at large, blocky farmhouses from eras long gone. If I blinked, it could be 1850. Only cars, asphalt, and power lines gave us away. Which one's Mom's? That one with the porch falling in?

And then right in front of me stood the funeral home, already full of cars.

I felt numb, light-headed, and suddenly sick to my stomach. I parked. Sat there, unmoving, until a woman who looked like Faye hurried out to meet me.

She hugged me and sat in the passenger's side, talking to me, and I responded, though I recall not a word of what we spoke. She held my hand. Then she put her arm around me and led me inside. And then, thankfully, the curtain of shock fell, and everything drifted into a haze.

I remember very little about the funeral. People, people, and more people filed past—none of whom struck any chord of memory in my brain. A big-haired woman crying into a handkerchief. An older African-American couple hand in hand. Families with disabled children. . .Mom's students?

Flowers filled the room in fragrant bunches: lilies and yellow spider chrysanthemums. I mouthed unknown names from the cards: Stella Farmer. Covenant Baptist Church. Frank and Beulah Jackson. I wondered if Dad sent any flowers.

They'd saved a special spot for me. A program, with Mom's picture on it. I looked at her face, so much like her in life that

I couldn't believe she was gone. Not Mom. Not smiling like that.

The room reeked of flowers. A pastor with a kind face gave some kind of message, and people sang. I gazed at the carpet, at a spot on the wall. At the chrysanthemum-covered casket with another picture of Mom looking young and happy. I tried to understand why I sat there, all dressed in black. Why people wept into crumpled tissues.

This isn't happening. In a few minutes I'll wake up in Shiodome and realize I'm dreaming. A horrible, too-long dream. I'll call Kyoko, she'll rant about weird music and the '80s, and everything will go back to normal.

People hugged me, people I didn't know. Who are they? Why are they here? I felt sleepy, jet-lagged, and ghost-like, slipping in and out of reality.

Then somehow I saw Faye's car ahead of mine, driving slowly down a long, curvy road in the middle of emerald forest-y trees, behind a long, black car. An iron gate opened for us from an ancient stone wall, and we followed the hearse up a tiny dirt road between rows of old headstones.

Green Hill Cemetery. And appropriately named. It was a cemetery. It was green. It was on a hill.

We stood in the middle of a meadow, surrounded by forest, and my eyes focused, uncomprehending, on Mom's name on a flower wreath: *Ellen Amelia Jacobs*.

The pastor opened his Bible and spoke as we gathered around those awful chrysanthemums in the breeze, trembling in their colorful stands and bunches. The ugly green canopy. Gaping brown earth. The casket. The pastor prayed, and people sang, and then I saw myself unlocking my car, fumbling with the keys.

Faye was speaking to me earnestly, begging me again to go to her house or to go eat at the church. She pleaded and reached for my hand.

I shook my head no. I needed to be alone, to shake the cotton out of my head. To collect my thoughts.

When she stepped away for a second to speak to someone, I left. Just like that. Turned the key in the ignition and drove.

And didn't look back.

Chapter 11

The map fell on the floor of the car, but I didn't stop.

I thought somehow I could end up back at the hotel, but instead the roads turned more and more unfamiliar. Narrower and more remote, lined with ancient barns, grasses, and thin, twisted trees. A red light glimmered from my dashboard, but I kept on driving.

I barely noticed when my speedometer slowed. I pressed the accelerator, but my speed still decreased.

The red warning light. I gazed at it, unblinking.

Just around the grassy bend snaked a deserted road with an even more deserted church, and I pulled the steering wheel hard and let the car coast into the gravel driveway and expire. I just sat there. Took the keys out of the ignition and rolled down the window. Then got out and leaned against the hood of the car.

I didn't cry at the funeral. I wouldn't cry now. But my throat swelled so tight I could hardly breathe.

The swelling whisper of cicadas drifted from fragrant locust and birch trees: soft, comforting, summery. The sun hid behind a silver cloud, and a puff of wind lifted my hair and cooled my sweaty neck and forehead. A horse in a nearby pasture chewed and snorted at me, swishing its tail.

I was really lost. And out of gas. I had no idea how I'd gotten here.

"God?" I whispered. I meant it as an accusation, a request, a question, and a plea for relief from my pain, all rolled into one. I couldn't pray. I didn't even know if I believed in Him. But my lips moved, and His name was all that came out.

In Japan I radiated strength and confidence. I could do anything. My power fizzled here, leaving me helpless. Like a fragile morning glory on the pasture fence, quivering in the breeze.

Leaves shivered across the meadow, soothing and soft. I smelled wild mint, rain, and grass.

I came partially to my senses and pulled the expensive international calling card from my wallet. Tried information again and made up some last names, but no dice. Dug through my purse again.

Kyoko might answer if I called, but that wouldn't do any good. Besides, it was four in the morning there, and she'd yell at me for driving off. Ten minutes passed. Twenty. Forty.

I sorted through the cup holder and ash tray for Faye's number, even though I knew they were empty. Felt a little bit hungry for the first time all day and genuinely worried. I didn't know a soul in Virginia.

I sat helplessly in my car until my eyes lighted on the crumpled map, still on the floor. In desperation I dialed the number for the gardener.

"Hello?"

My heart leaped with relief when he answered. "Hi. This is Shiloh. . .the girl from the hotel. You gave me directions this morning."

"Sure. Did you find everything okay?"

"Yes, but actually, I'm lost now." My voice sounded small

and pathetic. I couldn't bring myself to explain why I was sitting in front of an empty church with no gas.

"You're lost?"

"I took some wrong roads on my way back. And. . .I think my car ran out of gas." I felt incredibly stupid. How could I have taken leave of my senses and gotten myself into this mess?

"Out of gas? Did the gas light come on?"

"Yes," I quavered. "And it just stopped running."

An odd silence. "Well, lack of gas does that. Can you. . .um. . . describe where you're at?" Something roared like a motor behind him, and I pressed my other ear closed to hear.

"Well, there are some trees. And. . .and a horse."

"Okay. . ." He cleared his throat, obviously trying hard.

"I'm in front of some church, too. The sign says Jerusalem Chapel something."

"Oh, Jerusalem Chapel. I know where it is."

"Can you just tell me how to get to the main road?"

"You go left, past. . ." He sighed. "It's kind of complicated." I heard some muffled voices behind him, and he told me to wait a minute. "Hello?"

"I'm here." Where else could I go?

"I'll go out there, but it'll take me about twenty to thirty minutes. Can you wait that long?"

"What? You don't have to come all the way out here!" I sputtered.

"Well." I guess he wondered why I'd called him. "Do you know anyone else who can get there faster?"

I bit my lip, thinking hard for a miracle. "Um. . .no."

"Then I'll bring you some gas."

"No! You've got stuff to do. I don't know why I called. I just. . . don't have anybody else here. In the whole state." That was the honest truth.

"Well then, let me bring you some gas, and I'll get you back to the hotel."

I hung my head in humiliation. What other alternatives did I have? I didn't see a tow truck turning into the church driveway.

"I'll be there in about twenty minutes. Just sit tight."

"I'm so sorry. You have no idea how sorry."

"Forget it."

"No, it's my fault," I repeated miserably. "I shouldn't have driven off like I did."

"What are we going to do, leave you there for the wolves?"

"Starlings," I corrected, my throat tightening. I wasn't meaning to be funny.

"I warned you. Bye."

I gloomily hung up the phone, feeling like the dumbest girl in the world. And more lost and alone than I'd ever felt in my entire life.

Chapter 12

While I waited for the gardener, I fed grass to the horse. Yanked big handfuls and offered it to him. He snorted and wanted more. Showed me his yellow teeth. It was therapeutic somehow, all that ripping and chewing.

Two cars had come by, one blasting country music. Something peacock-like crowed in the distance. The breeze stirred.

Then a little green sedan crunched into the parking lot. Instead of the baseball-capped gardener, a smiling blond girl poked her head out of the window. Not particularly pretty, but she sparkled like her insides glowed.

"Ya outta gas?" she called in a thick country accent.

I dumped the grass over the fence and trotted over. "How did you know?"

"Adam called me! I live jest up the way." She got out of the car. "I don't got no gas, but he'll bring some."

"Oh. Okay."

"He said I should keep ya comp'ny till he gets here!" She smiled that infectious smile again. The poor girl looked like she'd walked out of a 1980s country-western store: jeans, jean jacket, flowered shirt, white tennis shoes, white socks, big bangs. I had the urge to take a picture.

"My name's Becky Donaldson. And you?"

"Shiloh Jacobs." I felt strange talking to some country girl I didn't know in a place I didn't know.

"Wow, what an amazin' name! It's a battlefield, ya know. From the Civil War."

"And a place in Israel."

"I'm just plain ol' Becky." She laughed.

"Yeah, well, Becky is easy to say in Japanese." I stirred the gravel with my foot. "Sorry to trouble you. I didn't pay attention to the gas light, and here I am."

"Shucks! It's nothin'. I done that before. Once it happened in the snow on the way ta school. Had ta push it over to the side a the road an' walk 'bout a mile up to get help. Or was that the oil? I cain't remember."

She said oil like uhl. It rhymed with pull. I thought of whipping out my reporter's notebook, but it would be rude. Kyoko would have done it anyway.

"So how do you know Adam?" I asked, just trying to make conversation. We leaned against the back of my car together.

"Adam? We been friends since I was a kid," she said with a giggle, showing slightly bucky front teeth. "He's kinda like my brother, only I don't got no brother. I'm a only child. I always tell him we was separated at birth. Went to the same high school, same church, ev'rything. Stuffed his locker top to bottom with them packing peanuts one time!" Becky tittered. "He built a snow fort 'round my car so I couldn't git it outta the driveway. That kinda stuff. But we've always stuck together." She smiled a distant smile.

"Just friends?" I smiled, too, but for a different reason.

"For shore! We might be rednecks in Virginia, but thinkin' a your so-called brother that way is just weird. Shucks, I'm married!" She laughed and showed me her wedding ring and tiny diamond engagement band, both old-fashioned yellow gold. "To Tim. We been married four years now. Ain't it sweet?"

"Four years?" I gaped at her. "Aren't you pretty young?"

"Twenty-five," she said proudly. "Tim's twenty-seven."

"Wow. Congratulations!"

"Thanks!" She beamed. "I cain't imagine bein' married to nobody else!"

"How did you meet?" I tried to hide my own diamond, but she was too quick for me.

"Mercy!" She grabbed my hand and turned my ring in the light. "That's some rock! Wow! What's his name?"

The large, ice-clear diamond and exquisite cut still stunned me. I had to admit, Carlos had impeccable taste. "Carlos. From Argentina."

"A Latin lover," sighed Becky dreamily. "Wale, that's jest won'erful! Did ya meet him in Argentina?"

"No, in Japan. Where I live."

"You live there? Where, in To-kee-o?" We Americans tended to add an extra syllable in the middle.

"Yes. I'm a reporter."

"Do you like it?"

"I love it."

"Is it real differ'nt?"

"Well, yes, I guess so. When I first moved to Tokyo I felt some culture shock. But every place is different, if you think about it."

"I reckon. But some's gotta be more'n others." Becky reached down and plucked a yellow dandelion sprouting up through slate-blue pebbles. "I've lived here all my life."

Somehow this revelation didn't surprise me.

"But ya know somethin'? I don't think I could be happier. Tim's just the most fabulous husband ever, and I wanna have kids somethin' awful! We're jest waitin' on the Lord's timing."

"I can't imagine having kids." I didn't mean to say it out loud. "They're cute at first, but then they turn into messy little brats. I'd just rather get a dog."

Becky stared at me and then laughed, something innocent

and sweet in her eyes. I liked her in spite of myself, the way I'd liked Faye. "Aw, shucks, Shah-loh." Even the way her accent rolled my name. "I reckon that'll change when you get married, don't ya reckon?"

"I don't think so."

Carlos echoed my sentiment. "Money grubbers," he called kids. Said they interfered with life and fun.

"I cain't wait to have kids! I'll teach 'em 'bout God, how to read the Bible, and about snowflakes an' fall leaves, an' how ta tie them Boy Scout knots. . .tha way to pet a dawg and hold an old person's hand. . ." She looked like she might cry. "I just wanna see somethin' good in this old world full o' sin. Somethin' honorin' to God that me and Tim can be proud of."

I cleared my throat, strangely moved.

"This hair'll turn white one day." Becky held out a blond strand. "Better do what I ken with the life I got!"

I didn't know what to say. I thought suddenly of Mom, and looked down at my black clothes.

"Oh, I'm so sorry!" Becky gasped, as if remembering herself. She clapped her hand over her mouth.

"For what?"

"You just come from a funeral. Adam said so. And me runnin' off at the mouth like that! I'm so sorry."

I waved it away. "I needed something to get my mind off it anyway. I'm glad you came." Somehow I meant it. Becky lent a sort of clean-scrubbedness to my dark mood—an aura of simplicity and belief that life really could be good after all.

Becky rubbed her feet in the gravel and looked down. "Did ya lose somebody close?"

"Well, yes and no."

She gave me space and didn't comment. Just nodded.

"My mom." I cleared my throat, which for some inexplicable reason felt tight again. Scratchy. Maybe I'd gotten a cold from the plane.

Becky's eyes welled up, and her face turned blotchy red. "I'm so sorry! I don't know what I'd do if my mama. . .mercy, Shah-loh! I had no idea."

It struck me as odd that tears streamed down her cheeks and not mine.

"It's okay. We didn't have. . .uh. . .a close relationship."

Becky wiped her eyes with the back of her hand and sniffled. "No?"

"Not for a long time. She wasn't. . .well, the easiest person to live with. We'd been apart for years."

"That's a shame. Family ken be so wonderful, ya know?"

"I guess." What a lousy answer, and an untrue one at that. Family had drained the life out of me as far back as I could remember.

"But we got our problems, too, Lord knows! Some things're jest real difficult to work through. I guess I'm luckier than most. I love my parents." She looked up. "Was yer mom. . .sick? Or ya don't wanna talk about it? It's fine if you don't. Ain't none a my business."

"No, it's okay. She died suddenly. A brain aneurysm, supposedly. I need to review the medical reports myself, but. . ." My voice trailed off. All my talk of suing doctors had dissipated because not a lawsuit in the world could bring her back.

"I'm awful sorry, Shah-loh. Fer all of it. That's just terrible."

I looked out as a lone car drifted by on the road. "Yeah. Well. I'll be fine." I crossed my arms stiffly.

Finally Becky spoke. "How long ya gonna stay in town for the funeral an' all? Ya got family here?"

"No family. I go back to Japan in a week. I just have to sell the house Mom left me, pay off some loans, renew my visa to Japan, and get back to Tokyo. That's where my life is."

"Wow, a house a yer own! How excitin'!"

"Yeah." My voice conveyed the opposite. "It sounds terrible, but I could really use the money. More than the house."

"Ain't nothin' wrong with that! Well, let us know if you need any he'p with finance stuff. Tim's an accountant."

"Thanks. I'm not so good with numbers."

"Yeah, me neither. But Tim's a whiz! He done he'ped people with all kinds of financial stuff before. So you jest call us if you need anything at all. Here's my number." She reached for my cell phone to type it in. Sans business card, like most people outside of Japan.

"Wow, that's some snazzy cell phone!" She grabbed it out of my hand. "Why, it's one a them models with a cotton-pickin' TV! I seen the ads!"

Did all conversations go like this in Staunton?

"That's wild! I've heard of 'em but never seen one. What else's it got?"

I mumbled some things, suddenly embarrassed at my fancy stuff. I'm sure they sold them here, but they weren't a necessity for most people. Including me.

"Well, I'd love to have one with a real good camera like yours, but they're kinda pricey." She punched in her number. "To take pitchers of my kids." She grinned. "Well, when we have kids, anyway."

Just then a blue pickup truck rumbled slowly, paused by the parking lot, and turned in.

"There's Adam," said Becky, heading across the driveway with a friendly wave.

He turned off the truck and hopped out, taller than I remembered him. He ruffled Becky's hair affectionately and walked over carrying a gas can.

"Hi. Adam Carter."

"Hi." I wiped my hands. He put his out to shake it, and I balked. "I don't think you want to do that. I've been feeding that horse, and he's pretty slobbery."

Not the best way to introduce myself. I tried again. "I'm Shiloh Jacobs. I live in Japan, but I'm here for. . .well, a funeral."

Becky's eyes were still red. "Becky's been keeping me company."

"I'm sorry. I mean, about the funeral."

In other circumstances his comment would have been funny. "It's okay. Thanks."

Adam turned my key in the ignition. The Honda gave a sick little chug and died. "It's dead all right. Just needs a little gas. This your rental?"

"Yeah. From Richmond." I colored, afraid he would ask me when I'd last gotten gas. In fact, I hadn't. "I'm sorry to make you come all the way out here. I can't tell you how embarrassed I am."

"Nah. It's nothing a little gas won't solve." He unscrewed the gas cap. Compared to Becky, he spoke English perfectly. A little touch of Southern drawl, maybe, but impeccable grammar.

I studied him as he poured gas in my car: kind-faced and sober, with a much younger face than I expected. Some sandy hair poked out from under his cap.

I wouldn't describe him as especially handsome, perhaps, but he looked. . .dependable. I don't know why. But he did. Sturdy and dependable.

The kind of guy you could count on to bring gas to a stranger in the middle of Nowhere, Virginia.

"So you're the gardener at the hotel?" I felt stupid just standing there while the gas glugged into my tank.

"No. I'm a landscaper. Run my own business."

"Wow."

"Not a big business. But I make do. Companies, or sometimes people, hire me to landscape their grounds."

The gas can made a tinny pop as it emptied. "Do you like it?"

"I guess so. I like working with my hands and making something natural out of our concrete world." He shook the can and went back to the truck to get another one. Poured it in my thirsty tank. "What about you?"

"She's a reporter," said Becky with bright eyes. "In Tok. . .

how'd ya say it? Ya said it differ'nt."

"Tokyo. Without any syllable in the middle."

"Tokyo," repeated Becky, getting her sparkle back. "Wow, I sound so chic, like I know what I'm talkin' about." She giggled.

"That'll be the day," said Adam playfully.

She whapped him with her dandelion. "As if you would know. Ya off fer today?"

"Yeah. I guess so."

"I'd invite y'all to go out to dinner, since Tim's working late, but I don't know if Shah-loh's up to it."

I desperately needed to be alone, but truthfully, I was starving. I'd skipped the church potluck, and my hollow stomach complained.

"I'm really hungry," I admitted. "I could go."

Adam brushed a chunk of hair back under the bill of his cap with his free hand. "Aw, look at me. I'm a mess."

He was, actually. He had dirt all over his jeans and shirt like he'd been crawling on the ground. Stray pieces of mulch clung to his dusty work-boot laces.

"And that's differ'nt from any other day. . .how?" teased Becky.

"Ha. Okay. If we go, I pick."

"Shoot."

"Tastee Freez. The one in Churchville."

"Okay. If it's good with Shiloh."

"You like burgers and fries?" He straightened his cap. "Not my normal fare, but the best I can do dressed like this."

A hot, identifiable, non-deep-fat-fried, un-Southern hamburger!

"Yes!" I said quickly, before they changed their minds and had me eating that awful spoon bread. "But I've got to stop at a gas station first."

Becky chortled and tried to cover it with a cough. "There's one in the same place as the Tastee Freez. It's kinda expensive, but it'll gitcha back into town."

I turned the key in the ignition, and my Honda roared to life. Purred. I felt sorry for putting her in this predicament.

"Bye, horse!" I called, waving. He swished his tail and snorted, rooting for more grass as I followed Adam's blue pickup into Churchville.

I parked next to Becky at a tiny fast-food place in "downtown" Churchville. The concept of "downtown" was hilarious because (1) there existed no town, unless I counted a few scattered houses, (2) there were no stop lights, and (3) Tastee Freez, along with one run-down gas station and an even more run-down grocery store advertising lima beans and beer, constituted the only franchises in Churchville.

I'd call it "in-between-the-horse-pastures-and-shops-that-have-seen-better-days," not "downtown."

The Tastee Freez was conveniently located right next to the local dump. I swear Kyoko would have a field day here.

For a redneck fast-food chain, though, I had to say this: Tastee Freez served up some pretty good burgers. Beautifully salted, crispy fries. I ordered root beer per Becky's glowing recommendation, a mistake I certainly wouldn't repeat. It tasted horrible, like bad cough syrup.

Halfway through my country-music-glossed dinner (which they both paid for) I opened my wallet to show them some Japanese yen bills, and out floated that little scrap of paper. With Faye Clatterbaugh's phone number in perfect pen.

"I found it!" I excused myself and turned away from Becky and Adam, punching in the numbers on my international phone card. I pressed my ear closed and listened for a ring, nearly knocking over my cup in my haste. Not that spilled root beer would have been a travesty.

"Shiloh? That you?" Faye cried even before I could say her name or identify myself. "I tried and tried ta call you! I'd almost dialed the sheriff's department to come find ya when you called just now! Lands, Shah-loh! You just took off, an' I got so worried!"

I suddenly found my cheeseburger difficult to swallow. "Thanks." That made no sense. But I meant it.

"I drove around awhile and tried to find ya, even went by the hotel an' got real worried when ya didn't show up!"

"I'm so sorry. I misplaced your number." I picked up my cup and straw to drink then sniffed noxious root beer fumes and pushed it away.

"Where'd ya go? China?"

"Sorry." I nibbled a fry. "I shouldn't have. I just needed to drive."

Becky and Adam pretended not to hear, laughing quietly over something printed on the paper-tray liner.

"Are you all right, doll?" Faye asked after a long silence.

"I'm. . .I'm okay. Thanks." My voice softened. "If you wouldn't mind, I'd like to meet you again. Maybe we can go to Mom's house tomorrow."

"You bet, sugar. I'll pick you up."

Adam heard it and raised an eyebrow slightly, and I made a face back. As if Faye wouldn't take the chance of letting me drive on my own.

One more thing. "I left a bite for ya ta eat at the hotel," said Faye. "Hope you don't mind."

Back at the front desk, Patty handed me two overflowing paper plates from the hotel refrigerator, loaded down with the works: barbecued chicken, baked beans, deviled eggs, potatoes with cheese, green beans, some kind of foamy pink Jell-O salad, a dinner roll, and pieces of coconut pound cake wrapped in foil.

She'd left a note: *Eat up. See you tomorrow. Faye.* And some plastic silverware wrapped in a napkin.

If Faye called this "a bite," I couldn't imagine the full spread.

Warmth crept into my shut-up heart as I carried the heavy plates, wedged in a plastic bag, to the elevator. People had brought me gas, paid for my dinner, and left a feast at my hotel room door. Why me?

It almost didn't seem fair, like I should. . .I don't know. Pay them or something. My heart stung with overflowing emotions I couldn't place.

I peeled off my black clothes and sank into the tub, trying to forget the funeral, then hauled myself out and collapsed on the bed. Train or no train, I was going to sleep. My horrible day had finally come to an end.

My bedside telephone jangled.

I woke, disoriented, and fumbled for the clock on the bedside table. Three in the morning.

The ringing stopped, and I rolled over to sleep again. My thoughts had just fizzled into delightful darkness when this time my cell phone vibrated, rattling against the table.

I groped for the lamp in annoyance, blinking in the harsh light, and scrolled through the missed calls. Ten of them. International calls.

Huh? Of all the weird. . .! I rolled back through the list, not recognizing anything but the Japan prefix code. Is Carlos finally trying to call me from a phone booth or something?

I waited, but my phone sat silently. I switched off the lamp. The pillow felt so soft and fluffy compared to the thin airline cushions, cupping my cheek gently as if made out of marshmallows. Yellow ones. Marshmallow Peeps. Peeping incessantly, louder and louder. Shouting, squawking, flapping feathers.

The hotel phone on the bedside table shouted in my ear, and I woke with a start.

What on earth is going on? I flipped on the lamp again and grabbed the phone.

"Carlos?"

"No. This is Kyoko."

"Oh, Kyoko. Hi." I slumped back down and closed my eyes. "What a horrible day."

"I know. I'm sorry."

She didn't sound like her usual self. "Is something wrong?"

"Ro-chan, I don't know. But I need to talk to you. About something important. I'm sorry. I know it's the middle of the night there, and right after the funeral, but. . .this is serious. Really."

I was suddenly awake. "What's going on? Is everyone all right?"

"Well, health-wise, yeah. I don't know about Carlos, but the staff is fine. But you've got to talk to me. Now. Before Dave calls you."

"Dave? Why? What's going on? Is it because my no-vote story is due? Kyoko, I'm really sorry, but I was at a funeral for crying out loud. I turned it in as soon as I could get a connection."

"No. It's not that." Kyoko sounded deathly serious.

"Then what?" I felt annoyed. And sleepy.

"Ro-chan. Tell me something. Did you talk to the PM's wife?"

All at once my heart leaped up and hit the ceiling.

Chapter 13

I couldn't speak.

"Ro-chan. Please. Tell me you talked to her."

I felt sick, and my mouth wouldn't move. "Kyoko, I. . ."

"You didn't. Oh no. Oh nooooo," she moaned.

I tried to think what to say. Should I tell the truth or make up another lie? No, I'd better stop at one.

"What happened?" My hand shook so much I could barely hold the phone.

"The PM's wife is upset. Said she never talked to you or even had an interview scheduled with you about that issue. She told AP she'd only had one interview with Asahi Shimbun, and she felt they misrepresented her position."

My lips went white. "But she did say those things."

"Not to you. And she can disagree all she wants with Asahi, as long as she said it. But if she didn't talk to you, then. . ."

Silence.

"Kyoko, help me!" I pleaded.

"I want to, Ro, but I don't know how I can! You goofed this one big-time! Did you really copy from Asahi?" Her voice rose shrill in my ear.

I swallowed hard and tried to stop shaking. The room

vibrated. That dumb train again. "Kyoko, I'm so sorry. I didn't mean to."

"What do you mean you didn't mean to? Either you copied or you didn't! It's called plagiarism, and you can get in major trouble! You should know that by now!"

"I know. But I missed my deadline!" I gasped, needing oxygen. "I just blanked and forgot a story, and I couldn't face Dave. I've never done either of those before—running late or. . . lifting. From the Internet. I didn't think it would make much difference."

Kyoko's voice crackled with fury. "I can't believe it! Ro, of all the dumb, stupid. . .honestly! What got into that head of yours? Do you have any idea what you've done?" She was practically shouting now. "You're studying ethics, for heaven's sake!"

Ethics. I covered my face with my hands. "Have you ever copied a story before? Or parts of it? Tell me the truth!" Kyoko didn't answer. I thought she would deny it immediately, but she didn't. She didn't?!

"Tell me the truth, Kyoko!"

"I'm at work!" she whispered fiercely.

"I don't care! Tell me."

"Yes," she hissed. "Of course I have! We all have. Probably Dave has. How else do you think we turn hundreds of articles around in minutes?"

"Then why is one little incident such a big deal?" I whined.

"Because you got caught, Ro-chan! The big no-no! If you're going to do it, do it right!"

I blinked. "That's it? That's my advice?"

"Look, all I'm saying is you'd better think of something really good to tell Dave. He's ballistic. He'll probably call you any minute."

I rubbed my face in misery. "Is there any way out, Kyoko?"

Silence. She sounded weary. "I don't know, Ro. This is pretty big. I don't see how even you can dig your way out of this one.

If it goes out that an AP reporter plagiarized. . .oh, Ro," she moaned. "Uh-oh. He's coming this way. I've gotta go. Call me." And she hung up.

Images swirled in my head: The glass-encased news office. Mrs. Inoue reaching handfuls of ginger candy into my cupped hands. My Louis Vuitton scarf. The mountains. The horse chewing grass. Mounds of fresh brown dirt piled around a yawning hole in summer grass.

Sensations of hot and cold swept over me. Light and heavy. My stomach heaved; I needed a doctor.

"God." My lips moved again. Why on earth I was talking to Him, I didn't know. "Get me out of this mess. Oh, God." I buried my face in the blankets.

And the hotel phone rang again.

Nothing, I thought, could ruin my day more than Mom's funeral. But Dave's tongue-lashing sliced me to ribbons. He yelled so loudly I held the phone out from my ear. Used swear word combinations that defied grammar. Broke a mug—no, two—and something else heavy.

Dave blasted my lousy reporting skills until they bled and shouted that I had no business working at a professional establishment like the Associated Press.

"You're fired!" I heard him holler loud enough for Patty to hear down at the front desk. "So don't bother coming back to Shiodome!" He slammed the phone down, leaving a harsh dial tone grating in my already sore ear.

The words floated past my ears as if transparent.

I forgot time as I sat there frozen, immobile, empty phone still in my hand. My world crumbled and quaked, dissolving with a roar like one of those powerful Japanese earthquakes.

What have I done? What have I done? The dial tone whined like an annoying mosquito, yet I made no move to hang up the phone. To close the circuit connecting me to Japan and to the last remnant of my life in Shiodome.

I could live without Mom. I had already done that for years. But I could not live without Japan. Without Tokyo. Without the bright morning skies over Shiodome, the crows swooping, the friendly "*Irashaimase!*" welcome greeting from smiling, bowing Japanese salespeople.

I had literally nothing left.

My head fell into my hands. Japanese samurai ritually took their lives after failure or defeat. I couldn't imagine pulling a knife blade, but I realized as I stared at the clock, which glowed 4:16 a.m., that my life had indeed come to an end. Just like the samurai.

I thought desperate thoughts. I'd run away, or change my identity, or. . .

My eyes fell on the room phone, still hanging limp and pitiful in my quivering fingers.

And in complete and total despair—the wild, desperate kind that only comes from feeling your life bleed out before your eyes—I dialed Faye.

Chapter 14

She met me in the lobby, hair a fright and eyes ringed with dark circles. But she came. She wrapped her arm around me, and I followed her out to the car. She'd left a blanket for me on the passenger's seat and a mug of hot chocolate in the cup holder. The most thoughtful things, maybe, anyone had ever done for me.

I wrapped the blanket around my shoulders, vainly trying to keep out the chill, and watched the dark city glide past me. I didn't care where we went. Staunton, Siberia, Mars. It was all the same. Stars hung cold and condemning outside the car windows.

"Machiavelli said to do everything bad at once, and everything good slowly," I blabbered.

"Who?"

"Machiavelli. An Italian diplomat and philosopher. Well, I followed his advice. I've officially ruined my life."

In Japan Kyoko was taking the subway home from work now. Without me. Forever.

Even the mountains kept their black silence, dark shapes against the indigo sky.

Faye tried to talk, but I didn't respond. She finally turned on a Christian radio station, and I made no move to turn it off or even protest. Just leaned against the window, watching the streetlights and wondering how on earth I'd made such a mess of my life.

Shiloh P. Jacobs didn't need God. Didn't need help. Shiloh P. Jacobs had always worked her way up, not down.

Staunton's shop-lined sidewalks breathed quiet compared to Tokyo streets that never sleep. No neon, no subways. We wended our way through the country, where the air smelled pleasantly of damp leaves and soil and something indescribably sweet, like flowers. Cicadas whispered in shimmering layers, filling the air with their swelling sound.

If I'd been in my right mind, I would've put my window down like Faye and tried to weep, to feel the perfumed night breeze on my face.

But I didn't. Nothing mattered but Japan.

Especially when the air turned sharp and pungent: the classic aroma of cow. I stuffed the blanket over my nostrils and tried not to breathe.

Faye parked the car in front of a nice two-story, cabin-like country house. I got out, still holding the blanket around me, and looked up at the stars. Streaks of pale blue ribboned along the horizon.

I stood there stiffly, watching pink glow over the mountains. Blooming in the hour of my greatest defeat. Robins chirped from the trees.

"I've lost my job. Everything. All I need to do is throw my ring across the yard, and it'll be complete," I whispered.

"Don't do that," said Faye, her light tone sounding a bit forced. "It's pretty expensive."

"My life is over."

"Aw, honey. There's always a silver lining. Wait and see."

I should have hated her for saying something so insipid, but I didn't. I felt nothing. I stared up at the sky until chill and dew got the best of me and stumbled into the house after Faye.

Chapter 15

Bright sunshine streamed through ruffled curtains, and scents of bacon and coffee teased my roiling stomach.

I still had on my jeans and kelly-green-striped J.Crew polo shirt—the first thing my hands found when I'd rooted through my suitcase in the dark back at the hotel. I grabbed my cell phone, scrolling through the sudden mound of text messages. Hundreds of them from Kyoko.

DAVE SAYS YOU'RE FIRED. I'M SO SORRY.

YOSHIE-SAN'S BOXING UP YOUR STUFF. I CAN'T BELIEVE IT! CALL ME.

CALL ME!

WHAT DO YOU WANT ME TO DO WITH YOUR THINGS? CALL ME.

RO-CHAN, YOU CAN'T LEAVE JAPAN! YOU JUST CAN'T! CALL ME.

I KNOW YOU'RE UPSET. DON'T DO ANYTHING STUPID, OKAY?

RO? ARE YOU THERE? CALL ME! KYOKO.

NORA'S TAKING OVER YOUR SPOT. SHE'S A PAIN. WHY, WHY DID YOU COPY?

CALL ME!

I couldn't read them anymore. I liked Kyoko, but suddenly I could no longer relate to her. She still worked for AP; I didn't. She still saw Japanese sky as she stepped out of the subway tunnel I loved; I did not. Kyoko had become a friend far away, over a gap I couldn't cross.

My dad had sent a few messages, too, about Mom, but I deleted them. Thinking of him only made matters worse.

Reality began to dawn when I went to my e-mail inbox and found scores of messages from AP's human resources department. Last paycheck information. Questions and instructions about the apartment.

I rubbed my face to shatter the bad dream, but when I opened my eyes, Faye's flowered guest bedspread still smiled back at me.

And after all this time, Carlos hadn't called me. Not even once.

My thumb scrolled and scrolled, searching for something—anything—from Carlos Torres Castro. But his name refused to show itself, like my hope.

I took off my diamond and shoved it in my pocket. Who wants to marry a guy who could care less if I'm breathing?

I dialed Carlos's number and got voice mail. "If you don't call me back immediately, consider everything off, and I keep the ring." I hung up. The expensive ring, at least, would make him jump.

In two minutes (I timed it) the phone rang. "Look, I'm in a meeting," Carlos retorted, voice coolly restrained. "You know I care, Shiloh. But I'm busy. You can't expect me to drop everything for you."

"No, I don't know you care. How have you shown it to me, Carlos?"

"I'm here for you. I'm waiting for you to come back. I'm just. . .I can't bring your mom back, okay?"

I flinched. "I didn't ask you to bring her back! I don't even want—" My voice stopped, and my fingers holding the phone tightened. "I just want you to call me! Do something!"

I expected him to apologize, but instead he remained quiet.

"Kyoko's called me a million times, and you haven't even so much as sent me a text message."

I shouldn't have mentioned Kyoko. Carlos snorted angrily. "What does Kyoko have to do with anything?"

"She's a friend. And you're. . .silent."

"Oh, so I'm not a friend now? That's what you think?" His tone turned angry. "Well, Mia said you. . .she said. . ."

I sucked in my breath. "What did you say?" The color drained out of my face so fast I held on to the bed to keep from falling.

Carlos knew he'd blundered. "I don't. . .know why I said it. Forget Mia. I don't care about her. I mean, I do of course, as a. . . as a friend, but not. . .I just. . ."

"What did you say?" I gasped, trying to count how many times he'd stuttered.

"You're making a big deal out of nothing!" His Latin temper flared, and he muttered something in Spanish. "And you think I'm. . .with. . .you're accusing me?"

"Should I?" My voice rose to meet his like a twisted tango. Appropriate, considering Carlos's Argentinian roots.

"I don't need the third degree. How about you? How do I know who you've been seeing back home?"

"You wouldn't because you don't call me! And Virginia isn't my home."

"Like that would stop you."

My eyes bugged. "Me? You're the one rooming with another woman. Go ahead—tell me you don't have feelings for Mia!"

"You're crazy! I don't care one bit for her," he barked. "There, are you happy now?"

Happy? Happiness sank to the bottom of my barrel like homemade Japanese pickles, fermenting under layers of sour mash.

It occurred to me as I sat there, staring up at Faye's flowered wallpaper, that Carlos's words were as fragile as folded origami paper.

How could I know if he was telling the truth? After all, I played hide-and-seek with lies all the time. No didn't always mean no. And now, when I really wanted the truth, Carlos handed me paper. Which took the shape of anything he decided.

First a lily. Now a crane with folded wings. Fold and unfold, running a brown finger along the crease.

If I didn't cradle it carefully, it might crumple in my hands.

"I've gotta go." Carlos's voice was cold. "Call me when you're in a better mood."

"Fine. And take your own advice."

"Whatever. Bye."

I took out my ring and watched it sparkle in the morning light, like cold, unfeeling snow—beautiful, but dangerous.

Faye was sitting at the kitchen table reading a Bible devotional, a mug of coffee by her down-turned head. Bacon and eggs waited on the kitchen stove, covered by a napkin.

"You awake, lamb?" She looked up. "Sleep okay?" If she'd heard me arguing with Carlos, she didn't mention it.

"Fine. Thanks." I awkwardly sat down at the table.

"How about some breakfast?" She didn't wait for me to answer, just got up and served me a plate. Put some fresh bread in the toaster.

"You look good in green, honey. Brings out the green in those pretty eyes. How 'bout some coffee?"

I nodded. I couldn't talk; I could only eat and feel pain rising steadily in my chest in waves. I gazed out the window at the sunny morning, which looked too happy for me.

Something mushy and ivory-colored stared up from my plate—like soft rice, but granulated, almost like sugar. "Uh. . . what's this?" I poked at it with my fork.

"Grits, honey. Ain't ya ever had 'em?"

"No. Are they. . .potatoes?"

She chuckled. "Corn, sweetie. White corn. With butter."

I reluctantly tasted. Soft and salty. Strange. Almost tasteless. I took another smaller forkful and swallowed then downed it with toast.

Japan had ushered in a whole new world of food: sweet azuki bean paste, squid liver sushi, sea urchin. Fermented squid intestines, a sticky pink paste on rice. I thought I'd seen it all. The South, though, offered an equally formidable culinary adventure.

"Takes some gettin' used to, people say. I've ate grits all my life."

I ate in silence. "What do you do when everything's falling apart?" I finally asked, stabbing a piece of bacon.

"Pray," she replied with a little smile.

I glared at my plate. "I mean practically. What helps you? Any. . .secret?"

"None that I know of, sugar. I prayed through all my hard times. They didn't always get better right away, but I always had the Savior holdin' my hand."

The. . .who? Oh. I get it. I kept forgetting the Bible Belt thing.

"My relationship with Carlos stinks," I retorted as if I hadn't heard. "Nothing's going right, Faye. It's hopeless."

"Nothing's hopeless, doll." She hesitantly patted my hand. "You've jest been through a lot a changes. A lot a loss. Give yerself some time."

"You can say that again." I stared into space, swirling my coffee in my mug and trying to jog my exhausted, jet-lagged brain into action. "I just want to go back to Japan. I've got to renew my visa, and. . ."

I set my mug down hard. Renew my visa. My journalism visa, tied with AP.

"I know, sweetie. I'm sorry. You do have a return ticket, ya know. You gonna go back?"

"Of course I'll go back!" I shot back as if she'd asked me to stop breathing air. "I can't leave Japan."

And then as I picked at my grits, I realized the absurdity of what I'd just said. Go back to Japan for what? To hang around Shiodome? I don't even have an apartment anymore! And without a visa?

I felt that same panicked haze closing over my mind like when I fled to Jerusalem Chapel, not caring where I went.

"Maybe I can find a job somewhere and. . .teach English. . . or. . ." I pushed my plate away, sick to my stomach.

I'd need a different visa for teaching and probably a degree in education, too, which I didn't have. Japan was a stickler for proving job skills for foreigners—especially teachers.

I wasn't a teacher. I was a reporter. For AP.

Only suddenly I wasn't.

My breath came in shallow waves, and I felt the room spin. My stomach churned.

"You okay, doll?" Faye put a hand on my arm. "Ya look awful pale." She quickly opened a window and fanned me then pressed a glass of water into my limp hand.

"Shiloh?" She knelt next to my chair.

I looked up, unseeing. Tried to make the two images focus into one.

I had become, in one night, a girl without a home.

Chapter 16

I drank and rubbed my temples, letting the feeling ooze back into my head. I needed something familiar, something that reminded me of my roots. Despite my best intentions, I needed a mom.

I set my glass down and pushed back my chair. "Let's go see Mom's house."

"Now? Are ya sure?"

"It'll do me good." I balled up my napkin and reached for a fresh one. Wished I could do the same with my life.

"You wanna take a shower first?"

"Yeah." I started to head back to the room then leaned over and gave Faye an awkward half hug. "Thanks. You've really helped me out a lot. I mean it."

"Aw, shucks, sweetie. Don't ya worry about it. You just git on your feet again, and ev'rything will fall inta place." Her eyes reflected so much sympathy I turned away. "You know yer welcome ta stay here as long as ya like. Don't forget that."

Faye gave me soap and towels, and I found myself in an unfamiliar pink-and-white bathroom decorated with candles and smelling of rose-scented soap. Yet somehow I felt more comfortable here than I did at the hotel—as a friend on some (strange) level and not a patron.

I couldn't fathom not going back to Japan. I'd find a way. I'd sell Mom's house and use the money to. . . I don't know. Pay my debts and beg Dave to change his mind.

I picked up the pink bar of soap and determined to push all my bad luck behind me—the way I'd done with tragedy all my life.

I rolled down the car window and let the sun stream in, watching the two-lane country road meander into a green forever. Fields of emerald and apple-green glided by, crooked creeks reflecting the blue sky.

"It's beautiful," I managed, watching the mountains over a splash of white wildflowers.

"I think so. I like it here. It's always beautiful no matter what time a year."

"I've heard." I tried not to think of Japan's red maples or the snowfalls of pale pink cherry blossoms. "Aren't I keeping you from. . .work? Something?"

Faye laughed. "I'm not as busy as you are, hot stuff. I take care a my house, cook good meals, help with a ladies' Bible study, go to church. . .those sorts of things. I work at a greenhouse, too, doin' bookkeepin' just to keep the bills paid and give me somethin' to do."

"A greenhouse?"

"Sure. Not far from my house. It's so fresh and beautiful, just like Eden."

"Sounds like something Adam would like." I almost made a pun about Eve, too, and thought better of it.

"Who?"

"Oh, just the gardener I met at the hotel."

"Adam Carter?"

I turned in surprise. "You know him?"

"'Course I do. He goes to my church. Runs a landscaping business."

I rolled my eyes. "Everybody knows everybody around here, don't they?"

"Well, not always, I reckon, but. . .sorta. A good guy, that Adam."

"I thought so. He brought gas out to my car. Seems young to have his own business."

"I reckon he's about twenty-two. He's been through a lot, he and his family. With his brother and all."

"His brother?"

"Ah." Faye waved a hand. "I shouldn't chatter on so much about somebody else's business."

I laughed. "Twenty-two? He's practically a baby." I graduated from Cornell at twenty-two, giddy and full of plans. Before AP. It seemed like an eternity ago, although really not that long. The thought stabbed fresh pain through me.

"Not Adam," said Faye gravely. "He's one grown-up young man."

We passed a field full of something yellow, and I forgot our conversation. "What's all that?"

"Reckon it's dandelions. Pretty, ain't it?"

I stared out the window, wondering if Mom's lawn in Churchville was splashed with yellow, too. In the past, the only houseplants that survived her mayhem were of the hallucinogenic variety.

"So Mom lived near the funeral home? In one of those big farmhouses?"

"No. It's farther out, in a little neighborhood called Crawford Manor."

The name conjured up images of a stately English cottage, all covered with roses with horse stables behind. "What's it look like?"

Faye cocked her head. "Well, it's perty nice, you could say. A little neighborhood with family homes. Small, mind you."

"How small?"

"Smaller than my place. Two bedrooms or so. Maybe three. One bath. Little starter homes just right for families with kids."

Something in my look must have given away my thoughts. "Ellen wasn't a rich woman, honey," said Faye gently. "She did a great job with what she had. Got financial help. Started savin' and puttin' her paychecks in the bank. Bought and paid for one of them little houses and was so proud. I think you'd a been proud a her, too."

I gulped. If I'd put my AP checks in the bank and started a savings program, I could probably own two or three of those "little" homes myself.

"So what do people do in Staunton?"

"Lots a farmers. Don't sniff at 'em. Their farms are worth millions, and the prettiest land you've ever seen." I believed her. "Teachers. Real estate. Small businesses. That sorta thing."

We followed the road through a lightly wooded valley and came up over a hill. The mountains and a stretched-out patchwork of blue, green, and gold suddenly appeared, like a mirage. I felt on top of the world.

"What's yer daddy do?"

Besides pamper spoiled, belly-dancing Tanzania and her two kids? "Sales. He retired early after making it good some years ago. And finding a freak wife who's closer to my age than to Mom's." My jaw tightened.

"That's a shame, honey. Have ya talked to your daddy any?"

I stiffened. "No. Why should I?"

"Well, he's yer daddy. He might not be the best of men, but. . ."

"I don't want to," I said sharply. "End of discussion."

Faye made no response but kept driving.

I hung my head. She'd picked me up in the middle of the night, made me breakfast, and was driving out to do my business just out of the goodness of her heart.

"I'm sorry, Faye. I didn't mean to speak that way. I just. . . don't want to talk about it. Dad's not a nice person. He was never there for me growing up, and I don't want anything to do with his life. He can call me a thousand times and apologize, but he can never fix the mess he made."

"I understand, sugar. But I still think ya might try. People change."

"Dad doesn't. Or rather, he has. For the worse." I crossed my arms. "I'll never forgive him. Or Mom either."

"You're just awfully alone in the world is all, honey." She gave me a sympathetic look that struck me to my core.

"Alone is fine. I'm better off without him."

We buried the topic. Faye turned down an even more remote country road, and I didn't know so many tones of blue and green existed, separated by wheat-colored grasses and orange daylilies flanking country mailboxes. Then she turned onto Crawford Drive. Little nondescript ranch-style houses with shutters and gravel driveways lined the street. Flowered mailboxes. A giant indigo mountain loomed behind them, its angular shape cutting into the hazy western sky.

"Here we are, doll." Faye turned in, gravel crunching under her tires. And shifted into PARK.

I blinked at Mom's house. My house. Cream-colored, with a brown shingled roof and chocolate-brown shutters. Neatly trimmed trees and shrubs. Probably a late '70s model prefab, shaped just like all the others. On the side a wooden deck peeked out, flanked by a riot of pink, white, and red roses in the flower bed.

I started to ask whose white Honda Civic sat in the driveway then stopped myself.

"What happens to the car?" I asked, finding my voice. At least Mom and I had the same taste in cars. Japanese.

"It's yers, too, sweetie. Everything is."

Faye took a jingly packet from her purse and pressed it into my hands, and I pulled out a key chain. A VIRGINIA SCHOOL FOR THE DEAF AND BLIND logo dangled. I squeezed them, wishing I could make them warm from Mom's hand.

"Ya all right, baby doll?" Faye put a gentle hand on my arm. I realized I'd been standing there a long time.

I didn't answer. Crunched across the driveway and up the wooden deck steps, glancing out at the large backyard—green and grassy with lanky, leafy locust trees, shimmering shade in cool patches. I shielded my eyes. A rope swing dangled, gently rocking in the breeze.

Faye took off her glasses and wiped her eyes. I pretended not to notice. Abruptly unlocked the screen door then the wooden door, my movements harsh. It creaked open.

We stepped inside, hushed, as if we might encounter some remnant of my mother's life: her scent, her voice, the sound of her laugh.

"Laundry room," I heard myself say to cut the emotion. The room was plain, with a washer and dryer and closet. I tried not to look at the basket of laundry, imagining her hands—just days ago—folding the towels.

The large kitchen and dining area made me raise my eyebrows: wallpapered in a hideous brown-and-white floral pattern obviously left over from the '70s. Windows trimmed with frilly country-style curtains, and a large wooden country table. Framed pictures covered one wall.

I pulled out a chair and sat down, taking in the room where Mom ate, watched the snow fall, washed dishes.

"She was some woman, that Ellen." Faye's voice faltered as she ran a hand around one of the frames. I heard her sniffle then dig in her purse for a tissue. I should have gotten up. Gone to her. Put my arm around her shoulders.

But I just sat there, hard and bitter, like a frozen scoop of Japanese green tea ice cream.

"Do azaleas grow here?" I turned my head away. "She loved azaleas."

"No, sweetie. Gets too cold in the winter." Faye finished wiping her eyes and spritzed water on some limp houseplants. "But she's got those roses growin' real well outside."

I forced myself to look up at the pictures and saw myself as a baby, chubby face upturned. My high school graduation picture. An artsy black-and-white photo of my five-year-old hand holding hers.

I recognized Billy in faded colors, with his heavy glasses and round face. Mom's funky retro bob and smiling face next to his.

And then Mom, like she must have looked last year or so, next to a skinny, smiling boy in a wheelchair. She looked mature, rested, happy. Her hair flyaway as always, but nicely styled. I squinted closer in surprise. Highlights? On Mom?

All around gleamed little framed photos—on top of the microwave, on the refrigerator, in the living room—of Mom with her little students. Pictures of Mom smiling. I'd never seen her smile so wide, so real. The corners of her eyes crinkled pleasantly.

The house felt suddenly empty, and a cool breeze from the door ruffled the curtains.

"Let's see the rest of the place." I pushed my chair back. My voice came out harsh and abrupt, almost flippant. But I needed Faye. Her voice, her support. I just couldn't let her see it.

"Of course, doll baby." She appeared like an angel. "Don't you worry. Ya don't have ta do everything all at once, ya know, like that. . .Italian whatever fella you were talkin' about earlier."

"Oh, I'm just fine. Don't worry about me." I stuffed my hands in my pockets roughly, and she patted my shoulder. Faye would have made a good mom. I almost said so, but the words stuck in my throat.

We walked through the living room, with its large picture window and view of the mountains. Swallows or something nested up in the corners of the porch eaves, with Mama Bird perched on a nest. Mom's bedroom, bed neatly made and slippers still on the floor. A library with an armchair. A guest bedroom. A tiny bathroom.

At last I leaned against the horrible kitchen wallpaper, exhausted. Someone drove by blaring country music.

"I'm ready to go." I took out my cell phone and tapped some silly text message to Kyoko, not letting my eyes soften for one second. "Thanks for bringing me."

"I don't blame ya," said Faye, putting her arm around my shoulders. "Keep that chin up. Things'll get better."

But Faye couldn't have made a worse prediction.

Chapter 17

I spotted Adam in the hotel parking lot, planting shrubs and hauling bags of mulch. He waved as Faye dropped me off at the lobby, and the two of them lingered there talking. Voices lowered. Faye shielding her eyes in the sun.

Before I could slip up to my room I saw him coming, shaking the dust off his baseball cap.

"I'm sorry about your mom, Shiloh. I knew her from church. Not well, but I knew her."

"You probably knew her better than I did." I tried to keep my voice light. "We weren't that close."

"I'm really sorry." He just stood there, looking down at me with a deep, sober expression.

"Thanks." I never knew what to say in these conversations.

"Becky's been asking about you. She wanted me to invite you over for dinner before you leave."

"Over? As in. . .?"

"To her house. You up for it tomorrow night? Maybe around five?"

I bit my lip, ready to say no.

"If it's too much—the house and funeral and all, I understand. We can—"

"No, I'm completely fine. Tomorrow sounds great."

Adam hesitated. "Are you sure? I mean, losing your mom must—"

"We've been apart for years. I'm fine." I checked my watch in irritation.

Adam took a step back at my tone. "Okay. Anything you don't like?"

"Like? As in, spiders or earthquakes or. . .?"

He laughed, the first time I'd seen him do it. "To eat."

"Oh. No. Except maybe spoon bread." I almost said root beer, but Becky had bought it for me, so I stayed quiet.

"What? No. Becky and Tim are grilling out. So watch out." A glimmer of a smile lit up his face.

"That bad?"

"I'm kidding. Their food is great. Faye's coming, too."

"She's wonderful."

"She sure is. Would have made a great mom to somebody." Adam took off his cap and wiped his forehead then plopped it back in place. "Faye said you haven't had lunch yet. I can recommend some places."

"Nah. I'm not hungry." Shuffled my feet. "I've got some airline crackers or something up there."

"Well, take care then, if you're sure. I've got to get back to work, but Faye can drive you to Tim and Becky's. After all, we can't have you running out of gas again." He sized me up. "Maybe I should give you a spare gas can."

I wrinkled my nose. "Oh, so you don't trust me anymore."

"Not much."

"Well then. See you tomorrow."

I plodded up to my room and sprawled on my bed, thoroughly worn out. I didn't move until someone knocked on the door, and I padded wearily over to the peephole in my house slippers. Front-desk Patty stood there holding a bag.

"Adam sent this up for you from Mrs. Rowe's. Enjoy!"

Without looking I knew the cup brimmed with sweet tea and ice. I opened the to-go box and found a steaming pork barbecue sandwich, all moist and hot. Coleslaw on the side.

I lied. I was hungry. Very hungry.

I closed the door and took a bite, surprised at the burst of tomato and vinegar in the spicy sauce. The bread tasted homemade—soft and buttery. And not a pork rind or deep-fried Twinkie in sight for Kyoko to scold me about.

I ate it all, licked my fingers, washed it down with cold sweet tea, and made a mental note to thank Adam.

My mind cleared a bit, and I hooked up my laptop and got online. I sent Kyoko a quick message and scrolled through e-mails from AP. Deleted my half-finished story on the Japanese no-vote issue.

Something niggled inside me, and I thought of Carlos. It was odd that he hadn't written or called since I left Japan, except when I'd threatened him.

I tap-tap-tapped to his profile on Azuki, a Facebook-like social networking site we used in Japan, and found his photo smiling up at me. I leaned closer. He'd changed his profile picture. And who was standing next to him? The photo cropped out the face, but someone's white shoulder and filmy silver dress strap pressed a little too close to Carlos's side.

I zoomed in on the photo, heart speeding with each second. That's not my shoulder! And his arm's. . .around her? I bristled.

To my utter shock, Carlos had changed his relationship status. Instead of *Engaged to Shiloh Jacobs,* it now read—in hateful black letters—*Don't ask.*

"Don't ask?" I snatched the ring out of my pocket and hurled it on the floor. "Don't ask?"

Thanks for the fun evening! beamed Mia's curly script, capped by three smiley faces. *I loved meeting your colleagues!* And then, *Don't forget to send me the pics!*

WHAT?! Carlos was too busy to call me, even once, but had

plenty of time for parties and sending pictures?

I'm wrong! Carlos loves me! He wouldn't. . .

My hand hovered over the photo icon, and I hesitantly clicked. And there, in all their unabashed glory, glimmered photos of Mia and Carlos. Hand in hand at a black-tie dinner. Giggling like kids. They looked like Hollywood premiere shots: Carlos in an expensive Italian suit, gorgeous dark eyes, and Mia with her curly blond updo and innocent, red-lipped smile. Silver dress. Filmy little straps.

My mouth went dry. I clicked through the photos: Carlos and Mia at a table with his workmates, his arm around her. Toasting with sparkling glasses. And then Carlos, kissing her naughtily behind a paper fan.

My Carlos. My fiancé.

I snatched up the phone and dialed Carlos.

Chapter 18

"You're calling me a liar?"

"A rotten, double-crossing, Argentinian liar!" I knew how to push Carlos's buttons.

"Oh no, you don't!" he hollered, letting out a tirade in Spanish.

"Say whatever you want, but you've been schmoozing on a girl while your fiancée stands by her mother's grave. I didn't know even you could stoop so low!"

"You're not coming back anyway. I know you got canned," said Carlos coldly. "Someone told me."

Hot color rushed to my face. "Who?"

He didn't answer.

"Mia?"

He didn't answer again, meaning yes. Of course. Nora. Friends with Mia. Of all the low, dirty, rotten. . .

"Well, you can tell Mia you just got canned!" I snapped. "We're done, Carlos. Over! *Adios!*"

"At least send me my ring."

Stupid diamond. It glittered there in the carpet like broken glass.

In the back of my mind I saw Hachiko the dog, his bronze

statue and bent ear gleaming in the Shibuya sun. Waiting, waiting, ever so faithfully for the master he loved—not leaving his side even for death. My throat contracted painfully.

"You said you didn't have feelings for her."

"Maybe I lied."

Carlos's paper promises crumpled in my fingers. "Thanks for the origami stinkbug, you creep." I banged down the phone.

First thing Wednesday morning I moved to a train-free room and, after a sweltering run along the highway inhaling truck exhaust, tried to put the shambles of my life in order. I'd spent half the night talking to Kyoko, who was still mad at me.

Not only did she remind me that she'd predicted Carlos's unfaithfulness, with staggering accuracy, but informed me—courtesy of Nora—Carlos had been "entwined" with Mia for. . . well, a while. She repeated so many I-told-you-so's I threatened to hang up.

In reply, Kyoko offered to send the Japanese *yakuza* (mafia) after Carlos. Whether she was joking or not, I couldn't tell. But then again, Kyoko astounded me—and sometimes scared me—in ways few other people did. I'd hate to be on her bad side.

"Good riddance!" she snarled. "What a jerk!"

"I know." I blinked dry eyes, wishing I could cry.

"So Nora ratted on you."

"Seems like it."

"I'll hack her computer and take down her files. Little brat! Man, Shiloh, what great friends you have!"

My eyes popped open. "You know how to hack, too?"

"Hmm." Kyoko's way of saying yes. What could she not do?

"Then hack into Carlos's page and take down his pictures of Mia."

"It'll just make him more protective of her, Ro. Men are like that. It'll be counterproductive."

"How do you know so much about men?" I snapped.

"Life, Ro-chan. Makes a believer out of you."

"A believer in what?"

"Reality. Just live it up while you can and play some really good music. I don't need a man to be complete."

"But you date way more than me!"

"I date. Never said I intended to keep them around very long. Live and learn, babe!" Her voice was hard. "And I'm certainly not wasting my time on clowns that aren't worth the time of day. Like your egocentric, 'world-revolves-around-me' Carlos. What a snob."

"But he's gorgeous!"

"Incredibly. His pretty face, however, didn't stop him from being a jerk."

I played with the satin hem of my pajamas, raw heart aching. "I guess not."

"Guess not? You're a sucker, Ro. I could see him lying through his pearly white Argentinian teeth a mile away! Why can't you stop seeing things like you want them to be and just face reality?"

"Maybe reality stinks." My voice shrank to a whisper.

"Well, welcome to life!" Kyoko's harsh tone made me pull the phone away from my ear.

No one spoke for a while. Maybe she was right. In her own dark, depressing way, Kyoko often was.

"I know one thing that would really make him mad," I said finally.

"Spill it."

"Can you hack into Azuki and change his nationality from Argentinian to Brazilian? Those two countries have a huge rivalry. Soccer and so forth." I'd learned that much in my four days in Rio de Janeiro.

I could almost see her smiling. "Now that I like," she replied evilly. "Now you're finally using your head."

As soon as I hung up with Kyoko, the hotel phone jangled. I snatched it up, half-wishing for Carlos's voice on the other end. Begging my forgiveness.

"Hi, sugar. It's Faye. Just called to see how you're doin'. Feelin' all right?"

My heart slumped. "Me?" I tried to laugh. "Okay."

"Just okay?"

"Sure." I scrunched my eyes closed. But for some reason I couldn't lie to Faye. "Well. . .uh. . .not exactly. Carlos has been sort of. . .you know. Seeing another girl." My throat swelled until it felt like choking.

"Sugar. I'm so sorry."

"Yeah." What else could I say? I'd successfully lost everything that had ever mattered to me. Not a bad feat even for me.

"Oh, sweetie. . . I wish I could take ya to lunch, but I work until three."

Funny how everything revolved around food in the South. Which made it, in that aspect, my kind of place.

"Don't worry about me. I'll get a salad at Cracker Barrel. I'm not hungry."

"You're still comin' to Becky's tonight, aren't ya, sugar plum? I think it'll do ya good."

I looked around at the charming but impersonal wall decor, feeling startlingly lonely. Everything was plastic, strange, cold. "Sure. I'll come."

"I'll come pick ya up then. An' if you want, I'll take ya to Mrs. Rowe's fer coffee beforehand so we can chat. How about it?"

"Why?" I blurted. "Why do you take time for me?"

"Why not, sugar? You're Ellen's sweet girl, and you're both so special to me. Besides, I'm always up for some gab." She chuckled, trying to lighten things. "Aren't you?"

You're both so special to me. You are. She had used the verb in the present tense. Faye, in her own gentle way, hadn't forgotten Mom. She hadn't swept her up like a day's work and tossed her in the trash. My heart flickered.

"I'll wait for you in the lobby."

"Wouldn't miss it for the world, doll."

I grabbed the stiff hotel towel and headed for the bathroom. A shower made everything feel better, as if all my problems were swirling down the drain. Kyoko would probably tell me it was psychological, like Lady Macbeth.

I dried my hair, donned my darkest blue jeans, a frilly red shirt that made me feel like a femme fatale, and sassy heels. Tied an imaginary *hachimaki*, or Japanese warrior-student-whoever-needed-extra-oomph headband, around my forehead.

Time to do battle with the bureaucracy dragons.

After an hour on the phone with the Japanese consulate and Japan Airlines, alternately on hold and arguing my throat hoarse, my Karate-Kid pose began to waver.

Japan Airlines was unapologetic. The emergency flight had been to the funeral, not back from it, so I couldn't change the date without a hefty fee—nearly the price of a new ticket. And the last thing I needed to do was spend more money.

"I'm sorry, Mizz Jacobs," chirped the attendant's voice. "Is there anything else, Mizz Jacobs?"

"Yes. I still want to change the flight, and you haven't helped me."

"I'm sorry, Mizz Jacobs. We cannot rebook once the flight is reserved. Is there anything else, Mizz Jacobs?"

"Stop calling me Mizz Jacobs. You don't know me."

"I'm sorry, Mizz Jacobs. Is there anything else I can help you with today?"

And so it went until I banged the phone down in frustration.

I talked to the rude woman at the Japanese consulate until I turned blue in the face, but my efforts got me a headache—and nothing else.

I had a journalism visa, tied directly to AP, and without them backing me I no longer qualified. In fact, not only was I unqualified for any other work visa whatsoever, but I couldn't even get a tourist visa.

A tourist visa, for crying out loud! And why not? No medical insurance, which was also tied directly to AP, and no financial means to (1) support myself in Japan or even (2) buy a return ticket to the US. Even if I wanted to go back as an English teacher, which I wasn't sure I did, I had all the wrong qualifications. How many years would it take to go back to school and get a teaching license?

I tried buttering up the consulate woman by speaking flawless Japanese, but I might as well have read the ingredients off a corn-chip bag.

I groaned and dropped my head in my hands. I needed air. Now. And a temporary place to stay in the US until I worked things out. I slammed the door on the stifling air-conditioned room and stalked down the stairs to a bench in the shade. Then flipped desperately through my cell-phone list.

"You're welcome to stay with me, Shi. Any time."

"Uh. . .no thanks. I'm not Mia Robinson."

"Huh?" My old Brooklyn friend Vito strained to hear over the background noise. "Mia who?"

"Never mind. I appreciate the offer though. I'll keep looking."

"You're always welcome at my sister's place, too. Keep in touch, okay? We've missed you."

I hung up and crossed his name off the long list, a knot forming in the pit of my stomach. People my age weren't settling down. They were moving. Changing. Marrying. Studying. Going places.

Unless I wanted to live with Vito's sister's crazy Italian family (three kids and one on the way) in Indianapolis, my luck had run out.

I hadn't helped myself by going off to a foreign country and letting contacts fall by the wayside. I hadn't meant to. But my life was there, not here. Japan had been everything to me. And Carlos.

Suddenly I had neither.

I slumped in front of a country hotel in the middle of Nowhere, Virginia, sun sweltering over a land as far from my own as Shiodome.

I found one small moment of evil pleasure between crossing out names. Just before closing time, I drove to the nearest post office and requested a padded envelope. Chucked the ring inside and wrote Carlos's address. Started filling out the customs form.

DETAILED DESCRIPTION OF CONTENTS: I tapped my chin purposefully with my pen. Just how spiteful was I?

Very.

Waste of eight months, I wrote neatly in the blank.

APPROXIMATE VALUE IN US DOLLARS: *$9,000.*

And I signed the form. Sealed the envelope. Handed it to the postal worker.

His face whitened. "Is this a. . ."

"Ring. Yes."

"You don't want to send a ring that way." He shook the flimsy envelope and pushed it back across the counter.

"I absolutely do." I pushed it back.

"You know envelopes are the worst way ever to send something valuable, that anybody could slit open the side and take it out?"

"Of course."

His eyes bugged. "You know somebody's gonna have to pay one whopper of a tax, right?"

"I know. It's not a problem."

He shook his head, muttering something about crazy females. "So I guess you're gonna want a ton of insurance?" He clicked the computer keyboard, hand on his forehead. "We start at—"

"No. None."

He dropped the mouse with a clatter. "Aw, no. No way. You can't send it like this."

"Why not? I'm paying the postage. You've offered me insurance and I've refused. So. . .if you'll just tell me the amount?"

"Lady, do you have any idea what's gonna happen to this?" He jabbed his finger at the envelope, everyone in the post office turning to gawk. Including the advertising cardboard cut-out dangling overhead.

"If it even makes it out of this post office intact, and I'm not guaranteeing that, somebody's gonna slit this thing open and take it home to his girlfriend within five minutes. Do you know what you're doing?"

"Are you going to tell me the postage, or do I need to go somewhere else?"

He shook his head in disgust and slapped on a label. "Five dollars and ten cents." He glared.

I counted out the bills and change. "Thank you."

And I took my receipt, smiled, and left. It was my finest moment.

"Ready for that coffee?" Faye pulled up at four o'clock in a snappy emerald-green jacket and that violet perfume.

"You have no idea."

A waitress seated us near a window, and I looked out over the railroad tracks in the back, all flanked with trees. Listlessly stirred sugar and cream into my coffee cup.

In Japan, coffee came in vending machines in skinny metal cans, black and bitter and cold and slightly sweet. Or piping hot, depending on the preference. We could buy pretty much anything from vending machines: cigarettes, beer, tea, juice, bags of rice, meal tickets, live beetles. Kyoko told me it was so people didn't have to talk to each other to make a transaction.

When my heart sagged with sorrow, I understood them.

"So, hot stuff, tell me about that young man." Faye's spoon clinked against her coffee cup.

"That young man's a two-timing snake," I retorted, louder than I should have. Faye raised her eyebrows but did not flinch.

"Got a girl while you were gone?" she asked quietly.

"Yes. Apparently he had his eye on her before."

"Were you engaged then?"

"Yes," I mumbled, humiliated, and the story of Mia slipped out. Her sea-green eyes. Her innocent smile. Her "date" with Carlos while I wore black to Mom's funeral.

"Well, doll baby, good thing ya got rid of him now, before you got married." Faye didn't seem shocked over Carlos's living arrangements or scold me for allowing it. "Rovin' eyes are jest the kinda thing that brings people to divorce."

"Divorce." I stared moodily into my cup. "Then I'd be exactly like Mom, wouldn't I? Wrecking my life and getting divorced."

"Well, honey, that's up to you." She gazed at me soberly again, speaking almost sternly. "Her life and mistakes affected you, but in the end these are all your decisions. What ya do with your life is your choice."

"Yeah. Well, I haven't done well so far." I rubbed my forehead, feeling a headache throb again. "I thought I had, but. . ."

"Well, you can follow in your mama's footsteps and wallow in your pain, or you can get up and move on." Faye's eyes bored into mine. "I don't mean to speak outta turn, sugar. But I can see you're at a crossroads. You've gotta choose, baby."

I didn't respond. Just stirred my coffee, even though it didn't need any more stirring. "Choose what?"

"To keep yer chin up. To wait for a good man, a man who'll

stand by ya, even if he ain't such a fancy looker like your boy in Japan. Mack wasn't so much to look at." She sipped her coffee, eyes softening. "But he was good. We loved each other somethin' awful."

She set her cup down. "Believe me, sugar, if a fella'll cheat on you, he'll cheat on that little girl he's got now. I promise ya."

I sighed. Maybe Mia would cheat on Carlos first. Little dagger-to-the-heart that she was. "True. You're probably right, Faye. Sounds like your Mack was a good guy."

Her gaze drifted. "He wasn't perfect, but he loved me."

"See, that's just it. Where do you find a good man, Faye? Like Hachiko?"

"Who?"

"A Japanese dog." I was too depressed to explain. "How do I know he'll stand by me?"

"The dog?" Faye screwed up her forehead.

"No. A man." I covered my eyes. "And please don't say, 'You just know.' It drives me crazy."

"I won't, 'cause you don't just know. You look at his life. You pray a lot. You look how he treats the people around him, and then you can make a better decision." Her cup clinked on her saucer, and she leveled kind eyes at me. "But Shiloh, I don't think a good man is what you need right now."

"Why not?"

"I think ya need to work on you. On gettin' back on your feet and fillin' those holes in your pretty heart. On seein' what God has for you now. Do you believe in God, honey?"

She caught me off guard, and I almost spilled my coffee. "I. . .I don't really know. I think I did once, maybe, but. . .it's been so long, and so much has happened."

"That doesn't mean God's not there," Faye insisted gently. "I can't make you believe, but I can tell ya so many things in your life begin to straighten out when you give it to Him. You'll find peace in your soul, man or not."

I expected to put my guard up when Faye talked religion, and I did. But I also left my heart open just a crack. I overflowed with pain; it was like trying to cork the Pacific.

"What do I do with all the hurt?" I asked in a burst of vulnerability. "I have so much."

Then Faye did the kindest thing. She reached out and touched my cheek softly, like a mother would do. Tears welled up in her eyes. "Give it to Jesus, honey. Give it to Jesus."

I never expected her to say that. I started, surprised, and then stared numbly out at the railroad tracks. Felt her pat my hand. I let my fingers wrap around hers, needing no words. I couldn't remember what it felt like to hold a mother's hand.

If I could cry, I would have, right then, right there in Mrs. Rowe's with a red-haired waitress bringing glasses of iced tea to the table of four right behind me.

But I could not. Instead I thanked God, if He existed, for Faye.

Chapter 19

We wended our way to a little country house, ranch-style, brick, down a lane dotted with pines. I recognized Adam's dark blue pickup truck, parked next to Becky's green sedan and a white truck probably belonging to Tim. I felt suddenly nervous—I hardly know these people!—and honored at the same time. A few days in Virginia and I'm invited home for dinner.

As we crunched over pinecones in the perfect green grass, I smelled smoke. Meat. Barbecue sauce. My mouth watered.

"Hey y'all!" yelled Becky, bursting out the door and down the steps like a happy kid. "I'm so glad ya could make it!" She threw her arms around us. An enormous hound bayed somewhere inside the house then appeared on the front porch, barking and quivering all over from wagging his tail.

"Aw, simmer down, Gordon!" Becky patted him. His tail wagged harder, and he gave us an open-mouthed grin, nudging his big head against my jeans.

"Gordon?" I scratched his ears as he slobbered kisses on my wrist. He smelled rank, bulged like a tick, but his toothy smile won my heart.

"My fav'rite driver. Before I got married, of course!"

The confusion on my face must have shown because she

laughed and slapped her knee. "I forgot ya ain't from here! NASCAR! Ya know, them cars racin' around in circles for hours? Well, this one driver was a real hottie when he started out. And since I'd already named my hound, well, weren't much Tim could do! Right, Gordon?"

He bayed again in excitement, dog tags jingling.

She swept us both by the arms into her simple little house, decorated in country blue and cream, and then out the back sliding door to the patio. Evening summer sun slanted golden-orange onto the pines and wooden deck, making them look all yellowy, and a whiff of smoke puffed across neatly planted marigolds and petunias. Country music crooned from an old radio.

"Shah-loh, meet my mama, Tina," said Becky proudly, introducing a plumpish blond lady.

"An' this is Adam. . . . Oh wait, ya know him already!" He waved, sans cap and dirt and mulch stains, showing his head full of sandy hair. I waved back. He stood next to a lanky guy in a NASCAR T-shirt who alternately flipped burgers and swatted bugs. "And that's the louse of a husband I have."

She convulsed into laughs and squeezed him tight, and he pretended to poke her with the meat fork. Becky was hilarious. She radiated joy, even giddiness, but there was something right about her. Even if her clothes were all wrong. Tonight she had on an oversized black County Bean Festival T-shirt, ill-fitting light blue jeans, and bad loafers. A faded white braided leather belt.

Kyoko, who turned her nose up at traditional fashion sense, would have dropped her iced tea glass. And that said a lot.

Tim waved and grinned at me. He had a mustache plus short hair in the front and some longish stuff hanging down in the back. My eyes widened. A mullet! I'd always heard about this haircut but never seen it on a real, breathing person. I had the sudden urge to take out my phone-camera and snap a picture. I resisted with difficulty, hands twitching.

"Howdy!" Tim speared a hamburger and turned it over. It sizzled, and I took a step closer. "Becky says ya run outta gas the other day at Jerus'lem Chapel. How long did it take ya to figger out the little red light means gas?" He winked.

"Now, Tim"—it sounded like Tee-um—"you stop pickin' on her right now! Ya hear?" She threatened him with a meat cleaver. "And this is my mother-in-law, Jeanette, the mother of that awful goon. She takes the cake." Becky introduced me to a sweet-faced lady, taller than me, with tasteful makeup and neatly styled brown hair.

"Aw, darlin', you were born cake." She kissed Becky on the cheek. Not exactly the evil mother-in-law type you see on the movies.

"Shah-loh lives in Japan, like I told ya. She lives in Tok-ee-yo—no, wait, Tokyo. . .did I say it right?—an' she's got a hot Latin fiancé. Right, Shah-loh? And one humdinger of a rock! Take a look at. . ."

My cheeks suddenly blanched. Becky reached for my ring hand, but I whispered something quickly and grasped for any other conversation. "Faye says all Jeanette's sisters are so nice," I blurted.

Becky reddened but recovered as her mother-in-law nodded placidly. "Well, we're all a mess though, I tell ya. Six of us young'uns." She proceeded to tell me about her uncle Ernie Addler and his farm, and all the girls trying to ride the prize steer, until Becky pulled me aside.

"Mercy, Shah-loh. I'm so sorry! I had no idea!" she whispered. "Ya broke up over the phone?"

"He's a cheater."

She turned red and white at the same time in little blotches. "Yer kiddin'!"

"Nope." I sighed, looking out over the bugs twinkling in the sunlight over the summer grass.

"I'm awful sorry." She rested her arm on my shoulder. "I

jest. . .don't even know what ta say. You've been through jest so much."

I shrugged, keeping my face light. "I'm over him. Really."

Adam appeared with frosty glasses of sweet iced tea, and we accepted them gratefully. He smelled nice, and I turned without thinking.

"Well, look who cleans up so good," Becky purred. "Decided to take a bath this week?"

"That's next week. Don't want to overdo it," he quipped over his shoulder, giving another rare smile, making his bluish eyes shine.

"His brother's doin' better." Becky lowered her tone confidentially.

"His brother?"

"Got blown all to pieces in the military. In Afghanistan. Lost both legs below the knee and almost died."

I choked on my tea. "You're kidding!"

"Wish ta goodness I was. But he's a trouper. This week some a the infection went down. Adam's been he'pin' take care a him and his mama and daddy and little brother."

I felt like I'd been blasted out of my funk. My life wasn't the only sour one out there.

"No wonder he never smiles."

"I reckon. He's a good kid." Becky's lips turned upward faintly. "What am I sayin'? He ain't no kid! He's one a the best people I know. 'Cept Tim, of course, the lout! I love him somethin' awful, when I ain't makin' fun of him!" She laughed and blew him a kiss. "Didja hear me, Tim Donaldson?"

"Woman, I ain't heard nothin' but yer complainin' all day!" he hollered back in a funny falsetto. "Now git over here and make me some biskits!"

"Git yer mama to make ya some biskits!" Becky yelled back.

"Now, don't pull me in! Uh-uh!" came Tim's mother's voice. "I ain't doin' nothin'! You invited me ta eat, and eat I'm gonna do."

I doubled over with laughter. These people made my shoulders shake, made me forget Carlos for a few pain-free moments. They were clean and wholesome, like medicine pumping into my sick body. They might be dumb as rocks—that remained to be seen—but they sure could laugh.

I'd seen drunk Japanese businessmen spend the whole evening senseless over *sake*, only to wake up depressed again the next morning. These people lived on joy. Simplicity. It was almost too easy, like I'd missed something.

"Grub's ready!" Tim shouted. "Let's eat, ya'll!"

We crowded around the grill, and Becky took my hand in one and Tim's in the other. Everybody formed a circle on the deck, around the chairs and tables, and bowed their heads. Becky turned down the radio. I just stood there, not sure what to do, until Tim began to pray.

I quickly scrunched my eyes shut. I'd learned that much in the Jehovah's Witness day care Mom left me at for a year. Before it got closed down by the health department for things I can't repeat.

"Lord, we thank You fer this food, fer this country, an' fer all the good things Ya give us. We don't deserve none of it, Lord. But Ya give us friends an' family and Jesus to die fer our sins. We thank Ya, Lord. In the name a Yer Son, Jesus, amen."

Amens murmured across the deck. At least I knew what they meant now.

A soft evening breeze whispered, and I felt something stirring inside me. When I raised my head, Adam's deep eyes looked right at me like he could see my soul.

He knows my heart is empty.

My cheeks burned, and I looked away. I'd never said I believed the way they did or even implied it. I didn't. I didn't believe anything.

But a tiny part of me wanted to, despite my rationalizations.

I couldn't shake that feeling as I filled my plate with the rowdy others: baked beans, hot dogs, chips. Listened to the joyful dance of fiddles. Dumped ketchup and mustard and pickles on my hamburger and laughed when Tim snatched Becky's burger right out of her hand and took a bite. Roared when Tim and Adam played "Dueling Banjos" on a harmonica and the tines—I'm serious—of a garden rake. Listened to "you might be a redneck" jokes until my eyes watered. Accepted another glass of iced tea. Slipped stinky Gordon handouts while he chewed his rawhide bone by my feet and thumped his tail.

I even dug into some pale green, foamy Jell-O salad stuff quivering in a glass bowl. I don't know who made it or what they put in, but it was fantastic. I tasted marshmallow and pineapple.

I can't believe it! I'm turning trailer park, I thought as I got another spoonful of Jell-O salad and filled up my iced-tea glass. *Next thing you know I'll be ripping into those pork rinds I bought for Kyoko as a joke!*

"How'd ya like it?" asked Becky, draping an arm around Tim. "We country folk know how to have a good time, don't we?"

Words failed me. Normally "having a good time" meant smoky clubs, disco balls, and unreasonably handsome men waiting at the bar. Whirlwind trips. Caviar. The works.

This was a couple of hamburgers and a radio.

But to my astonishment—"Yes," I said out loud. "Absolutely."

"So, when ya goin' back ta Japan?" asked Tina, balling up her napkin and dropping it in her paper plate. "Next week?"

My heart skipped a beat. I opened my mouth to lie again, to make up some crazy story, when I caught Faye's eye. And I just. . . couldn't. I cleared my throat. Looked down at my plate.

"I. . .uh. . .might not be."

Instantly everyone silenced. Adam and Tim stopped their impassioned conversation about politics, football, and who had the biggest ears back in high school. Becky paused in midsip, ice clinking. Even Gordon stopped chewing his bone and pricked his ears.

"What did ya say?" Becky demanded. "Because of. . .ya know. . .what ya told me. . . ?"

I shook my head, my light manner faltering. "Um. . .no. Not exactly."

I couldn't look anyone in the eye. Pretended great interest in my plastic fork. Plastic chopsticks never went over well in Japan. To-go chopsticks are wooden, connected at the end to snap apart, and tucked in a little paper sleeve.

"Is it money er somethin'?" cautiously asked Tim, the financial advisor. "I mean, if ya don't mind me askin'?"

I put my fork down. "Well, money, yeah. And no." I bit my lip, color shooting into my face. "I lost my job."

Tim froze. "Laid off?"

I started to nod. Laid off. Sure. And then glanced guiltily up at Faye. "No. I. . .uh. . .got fired."

Adam stared at me. I fidgeted with the napkin in my plate. Heard the scrape of Faye's chair and felt her arm on my shoulder.

"This young'un's been through a lot," she said softly. "But she'll make it. She'll be okay." She patted my arm firmly. "Don't ya worry, kiddo. Things'll look up."

I reached up and hugged Faye with my free arm, humiliated. Becky and all the others would probably see me as the fraud I really was. Me, with the thousand-dollar cell phone and no place to call home.

Instead, they scooted closer. Becky took my hand. Tina called me "darlin' " and told me it would all work out.

"You can only go up from here," said Adam with a sympathetic smile. "And we've all been through rough times before."

"I did something stupid," I confessed in an almost whisper, too ashamed to raise my voice. "Really stupid. And now I don't even have a place to live."

Without my meaning to, the story slipped out. I told them about Dave making Nora cry and my late story, about Kyoko, and how I marked person after person off my cell phone list to no avail.

When I finally stopped, a pale violet twilight had settled. Moths hovered around the porch light, and cicadas began to whisper from the trees. Gordon snoozed and snored, front leg slung across my foot. Still they sat, chairs pulled close to mine.

"Sorry," I apologized, patting Gordon's fat belly in humiliation. "I've ruined everything."

Becky waved me away. "Aw, quit. We're here to help, ain't we? Ain't none of us here who haven't never made a mistake."

Everyone nodded. Faye squeezed my shoulder again. I felt embraced, warmed, drawn in to the little circle. A pearly crescent moon rose over the trees.

"Whatcha gonna do with yer mama's place?" Tim finally asked over the peaceful hush. "Ya gonna sell it?"

I shrugged. "Of course. Right?"

"Well, it's up to you. Ya gonna go try an' find another job?"

"I want to go back to New York, but. . ." I looked away, embarrassed. "I haven't found a place to live there yet. Besides, I don't have money to pay some inheritance tax on my mom's place. It's better to sell."

"You don't pay inheritance taxes on that," interjected Adam.

"No? Are you sure? I'm positive you have to."

"No sirree. Not unless yer mama's house is worth more than a million bucks, in which case we're havin' burgers at yer place next time, not here," said Tim. The others chuckled.

"So I don't have to pay anything?"

"Shouldn't. It's yers. The will was clear, ain't that right?"

"Guess so. Right, Faye? That's what my copy said and what the lawyer told me. There were no other beneficiaries."

"Wale." Tim shuffled his cowboy boots. "It's all yers then, every dime. I'm sorry ya had to come by it through tragedy, Shah-loh, but you can thank God for your blessin'. We'll be payin' on this place a few more years."

I stared up at the sky, which was turning indigo just through the trees. Fireflies began to sparkle in the grass.

"Where you going to stay until you sell? If you decide to?" Adam asked.

"Of course I'll sell! I just don't have a place lined up in the meantime. Yet." I couldn't keep paying for hotel rooms, but. . .

Tim shuffled his boots again. "This might sound kinda weird, but why don't ya stay here?"

"Why, of course she can stay with us," Becky said indignantly. "Ya reckon I didn't think a that? Don't got much of a guest room, but there's a bed in there."

"Well, yeah, baby, that's fine, too." He kissed her cheek. "But I meant her mama's place."

The thought struck me like a sumo wrestler falling on my head. "Mom's?"

"Well, from a financial point a view, it makes a lot a sense." Tim leaned forward. "It's done bought and paid for. Don't owe no rent. No bank payments. Just yer utilities an' nothin' else. Not a cent. Ya even got a car. All dropped right in yer lap. Might be smart of ya to settle in for a little while till ya get yer bearings. Stop payin' a hundred bucks a night at Best Western and do yer own cookin'. That sorta thing."

I gasped for breath. Stay at Mom's? No way. Too much of her stuff. Her memories. Surrounded by a bunch of redneck wackos.

"It's out in the country!" I cried.

Tim laughed. "Well, so's we!" He rocked back on his heels. "Ain't half bad neither! Ya got a perfickly good house sittin' there empty with your name on it."

"But I'm selling it! I can't stay here!"

"Sellin' don't happen overnight, doll," interjected Jeanette. "It takes time. Sometimes years. You might save yerself some money while ya put it on the market."

An owl hooted from the dark shadows at the edge of the yard. "Is it. . .safe?" I felt light-headed again, like I had when I heard the news about Mom.

"Churchville? One of the safest. Nobody does nothin'

out there 'cept shoot starlings," said Tim, and I instinctively exchanged glances with Adam. "People leave their doors unlocked an' whatnot in some parts, although that's still perty dumb if ya ask me."

"But. . .I don't have a job! Or anything! No income!"

Tim shrugged. "Well, git one, I guess. Whatever you can find ta tide ya over."

"I could drive the car to New York." I thought fast.

"And stay where? Do what?"

Becky tried to help me out. "Reckon ya could git another high-payin' reportin' job anytime soon? Like at the *New York Times*?"

I shivered. Wrapped one arm around myself, trying to stop shaking. Only it wasn't cold out. At all.

Adam tossed a jacket to Faye, and she draped it around my shoulders.

I couldn't look at Becky. Couldn't answer. Just numbly played with my iced-tea glass until I got control of my chattering teeth. "Once you get fired for something like plagiarism, your name's mud. Over. Done with. Nobody ever trusts you again."

"Can you teach. . .ya know, like at a college?"

"I'm not done with my master's. You've got to have a master's. At least. And without a decent income now, I'll have to drop out or. . ." I huddled under the jacket, nauseated. "I just know how to write. And nothing else."

My beloved world slipped further and further out of reach, like the moon disappearing behind a whisper-thin cloud.

"Well, it might hafta be something not so great for a while," said Jeanette gently. "Workin' at a store or somethin' till ya git yer bearings. We've all been there before, sugar. It ain't so bad."

My hand shook, and I spilled my tea. Faye quickly grabbed something and mopped it off the wooden deck slats.

A store? Like, with cash registers? Oh no. Oh no.

The panicked look on my face must have worried Tim.

"Savings account? Stocks?" he asked, trying hard to save me.

I put the glass down and pulled the jacket tighter. "I don't even have a car in Japan to sell."

"Wale." He leaned back and slapped his knees pensively. "I guess ya got yerself a dilemma. If ya cain't find somebody like your dad to take care of ya for a while, I'd recommend you stay put."

" 'Til. . .'til. . .what?" I felt panic—mixed with fury—rising inside.

" 'Til you can git yer debts paid off, find a good-payin' job, and get a new start. Then you can sell yer house an' take off." Tim spoke seriously. "If you got a mountain o' credit cards, you need to get them paid off. Pronto. The interest'll kill ya if you drag it out, 'specially if ya ain't got no job."

It already was.

"You can do whatcha want, of course. It's just what I'd do if I was you." Gordon rolled over and groaned his agreement.

Becky patted my hand and grinned. "Well then, Shah-loh, welcome to Staunton."

Chapter 20

Thursday reality set in as I tossed and turned about what to do with Mom's house. With my life.

Carlos had really left me. I found more photos of Carlos and Mia on his Azuki page and little love messages that made me slam the computer shut in anger. I'd never look again. He had fallen for Mia, really fallen for her, and I—as usual—was left on my own. My left hand achingly empty.

For the first time I wished I hadn't sent his ring back so fast. Having it at least left me with the memory of someone I had once loved. And someone who had once loved me.

Despite all my attempts to keep a brave face, Carlos's mutiny hurt more than losing my job. A lot more. Dave had done what he had to do; no head of a respectable media service would have done less. I could forgive him for that.

But Carlos had known me and still chosen Mia. It stung. Deeply. It was a rejection not of my skills, but of me.

I wanted the ring back. I wanted Carlos back. More than I could admit.

I was seven again, staring out the window at Dad's retreating back in the dusky streetlight, one hand carrying a suitcase. Warm tears on my face, salt on my lips, and a ripping sensation inside my chest. He didn't look back.

If only I'd been better. . .if only I'd tried harder. . .if only I'd helped Mom more. . .

I looked in the mirror, staring at my morose hazel eyes and trying to figure out what I had done wrong. I'd put tears behind me forever. I'd dressed the part. I'd climbed the ladder. And still, after all my efforts, I'd lost. To a twenty-three-year-old blond who batted her eyelashes.

I'd never felt emptier in my whole life. Like my hotel room—full of nice furnishings, but with inhabitants who quickly came and went, never staying long enough to bring warmth or call it home.

And at the end of the day, it never really belongs to anyone.

I started my day with a run in the rain then spent the day making more calls and finding less and less possibility of moving to New York. The Internet went down. I crabbed. Bobbie apologized.

I gave up. Spent the morning with Jeanette in Wal-Mart, restocking my toiletries and gawking over American stuff I'd missed for two years. Shook a jar of pickled pigs' feet, by far one of the grossest things I'd ever seen. Ogled cans of hominy while Jeanette explained it was corn soaked in lye.

"You eat lye?"

"No, it jest sorta makes the corn swell up."

I looked horrified. It sounded pecan pie-esque, like I'd be sprouting a third limb in no time. "Are you sure this stuff's safe?"

"I been eatin' it since I could walk." She chuckled. "Guess it ain't hurt me yet."

I looked over her strong, wiry body, much younger than her sixty-some years indicated, and had to agree. But I still left the cans on the shelf and tried to remember not to bow or pay with my cell phone. Old habits die hard.

Then Faye accompanied me to the courthouse to do a bunch

of boring document stuff on the house. We took my red Honda back to the rental car company, and I paid a hefty fee for only driving it one way.

And then went to pack up my things for tomorrow's move.

After sending my cell phone photos to Kyoko Friday morning, I signed off and hauled all my suitcases downstairs to the front desk. Opened my wallet to square up with Patty.

But at the bottom of the form, where the total should be, it showed zero. Comp, it read next to the room charges.

"Comp?" I repeated, handing the form back to Patty. "I don't understand. My room charges aren't on here. Can you fix it?"

She smiled, and those freckles seemed to smile back at me. "It's fixed. It's correct." Patty lowered her voice. "It's taken care of."

I blanched. "I don't understand."

"You don't have to pay anything," she whispered. "Adam told us about your mom. Bobbie's daughter goes to the Virginia School for the Deaf and Blind. We're real sorry about what happened."

I tried to find my voice. "So Bobbie knew my mom?"

"Not directly. But she knew who she was, and. . .well, it's our way of saying thank you for your mom's service."

Something prickled behind my eyes. But I stood there dry-eyed, fumbling with the pen. Shiloh P. Jacobs does not cry.

I stared at the blank sheet, listing night after night with comp stamped by it. Thought of how I'd given Bobbie a piece of my mind about the train and the Internet. Thought of Faye taking me home, of Becky coming to meet me at Jerusalem Chapel, of Adam buying me a sandwich from Mrs. Rowe's.

Giving seemed to be so natural here, like the summer air outside. I don't think I'd ever been the recipient of so much giving.

"Wow." I closed my mouth. "Thank you, Patty. Really. I

don't know what to say."

"It's no problem. I just hope things go better for you. We all do."

You and me both. I thanked Patty and wheeled my suitcase over to the lobby to wait for Faye.

"Well, farewell for now." I tucked the cell phone stoically under my chin and plopped in an armchair. "I'm going to Mom's."

Kyoko sighed. "I wish I knew what to say, Ro-chan," she replied, sounding depressed. "The office isn't the same without you. I even miss your dumb thousand-dollar scarves."

Coming from Kyoko, I should take it as a compliment. "*Domo*," I said hesitantly. "Thanks. I miss you, too. A lot. I wish I'd never left. Staunton doesn't even have a Japanese restaurant."

"No sushi?"

"None. And if there was, I probably wouldn't want to eat it."

"Of course not! It'd be possum or something."

"And deep fried."

We chuckled. "Subway?"

"Kyoko. There isn't even a bus system."

Silence stretched out.

"I know, I know. It's my fault." I kicked a spot on the rug miserably. "And. . .I guess this means good-bye."

"You've got a journalism visa through AP," Kyoko groaned. "Not good. I could hack something, but it's risky."

"You'd have to hack extra cash in my bank account, too."

"I'll give you a loan! You can stay with me!" she offered compassionately. "Really, Ro-chan, if it'll help."

"Thanks, Kyoko. I really appreciate it. But. . ."

"I know. Impossible." Legal Kyoko knew the system better than I did. "Have you talked to Dave? Kissed his feet? Begged him to come back and be the office staple cleaner?"

"Kyoko. You know Dave."

"Unfortunately, I do know Dave." She sighed again. "And that means Nora will keep bothering me while you send me postcards from Podunk-ville until you move back to New York. Although"—I could hear her smile. It was uncanny—"I did enjoy seeing Nora yesterday, I have to say."

Something about hacking Nora's files. . .? "You didn't!"

"Didn't what?" I couldn't see her, but I knew Kyoko was pulling the innocent act, studying her nails in the light of her Cheshire-Cat grin.

"Talk about a sweeeeeet reward," she purred. "She went ballistic! Had the tech guys on their knees taking apart her computer all day long."

"Kyoko, you're kidding!" I gasped.

"Yeah, and Tsubasa-san, the main techie, is actually quite a hottie. I'm thinking about crashing my own files tomorrow just so he can come fix my computer, too."

"I can't believe you!"

"Ah." She grunted. "Nora's fine. She didn't lose anything major. Her story on public transportation stank anyway—what she'd written of it. I don't know how she even works at AP. Her parents must have paid Dave off."

"Did you. . .um. . .do anything to Carlos's Azuki page?"

Kyoko's response horrified and intrigued me. "See for yourself. Oh, and he'd blocked you, but I took the liberty of adding you back to his friend list." She snickered. "Hope he doesn't mind."

I grabbed my laptop, and thanks to wireless Internet—which was finally working—click-click-clicked to Carlos's page.

Kyoko, in her infinite sneaky wisdom, had changed his nationality from Argentina to Brazil.

My jaw dropped. Not only had she plastered his page with iconic samba and grinning Brazilian soccer star photos, but every post, as far as I could see, was absolutely scandalous—especially for an Argentinian nationalist: "I LOVE BRAZIL!" and, "*Os brasileiros são os melhores!*" ("Brazilians are the best!") and, "I'm thinking of changing my citizenship to a real country."

Kyoko had even managed to Photoshop a little green, yellow, and blue flag into his profile picture.

"How did you write in Portuguese like a Brazilian?" I tried to get air back in my lungs, still scrolling.

He hasn't seen it yet. I stopped short at a huge photo of the triumphant Brazilian soccer team hoisting a World Cup trophy. Blue-and-white-clad Argentinians weeping in the background. *Ooo, Kyoko! You've outdone yourself.*

"Easy. Internet translator. I signed him up for some mailing lists and groups and stuff, too."

I kept my mouth shut. If I got on her bad side, no telling what she'd do to me.

I could hardly speak, still gawking at that trophy shot. Trying to imagine Carlos's furious reaction. "You're really good at this payback stuff."

"Yeah. You should see Mia's page." She preened and then put the compliment aside. "So you decided not to pawn your scarves and stay at Ye Olde Redneck Hotel indefinitely?"

"I guess not." I closed Azuki. "It's temporary of course—just until I find somewhere else to live."

Kyoko was surprisingly understanding. "Why not? Free rent. Just don't put a giant satellite dish out back and start buying TV dinners."

"I'll have you know I have fond memories of TV dinners. Especially the Salisbury steak with mashed potatoes. They were so wonderfully rectangular."

"I heard if you leave them out of the refrigerator for weeks they won't spoil. Too many preservatives. Sounds like embalming, if you ask me."

I turned green. "Thanks, Kyoko. I'll keep that in mind next time I buy pickled pig's feet."

"Pickled what?! Send me a picture."

"I promise, Kyoko, you don't want to see it wobbling around in the jar."

"I've seen worse here at the fish market, and now I'm curious. Send it!"

"Ugh. And you say I'm weird." Kyoko seriously needed help. "Just wait until I upload the photos from my cell phone."

"Like. . .belt buckles? Gun racks?"

"Confederate flags. Jacked-up trucks. Corn soaked in lye. The works."

Kyoko hmm-ed. "Hey, what's that sport where people watch cars drive around a track?"

"NASCAR?"

"Do you know any of the drivers?"

"Well, there's Jeff Gordon, and Tim said something about this guy named Vic—"

"Okay, Ro-chan, that was a TEST!" she roared, startling me. "You were supposed to say, 'No, what's that?' You're scaring me now. GET OUT OF VIRGINIA, Ro! You've been there too long already!"

I glanced up miserably. "There's Faye."

"Any last words?"

"Funny. How about, 'Forgive me, Dave?' "

"Do you want me to repeat his response?"

"Forget it." I closed my laptop. "I'll call you."

"Good. If they know what phones are out in the sticks."

Chapter 21

"How ya doin'? I'm here already! Brought reinforcements."

I heard Becky's cheery voice on my cell phone as we turned into Crawford Manor. "Huh?"

"What, ya thought we was gonna jest dump ya here all by yerself?"

Faye parked in Mom's driveway, and sure enough, Becky's green sedan grinned back at me. I blinked. And Adam's dark blue pickup? The conspirators sat on the deck, boxes on the steps.

I got out to thank them, but the sight of Mom's empty house stopped me. Her white Honda. The brown-shingled roof. Bright and cheery roses blooming in the flower bed, as if Mom stood just in the other room like Mrs. Rowe, watering can in hand.

Fortunately Becky's smile warmed everything as she appeared at my car door. "Ya ready for this?" She grinned, arms full of stuff. "Welcome to yer new pad! We're gonna have a reg'lar housewarmin' party!"

Adam clipped his hedge trimmers in anticipation.

I dug in my purse for the keys, trying to keep my voice light. "Come on in! Make yourselves at home."

Becky turned on the radio and opened the windows, and we set to work putting the house in order. She and Faye cleaned and shined and washed, making the small house smell of crisp pine cleaner and laundry detergent while I tried not to look at Mom's pictures.

Tina showed up with pound cake and some cute new teacups, and she spritzed water on all the houseplants. Stripped Mom's bed and put on clean sheets. The washing machine swished and swirled to life, giving me energy I didn't have.

"Which bedroom do ya want, honey? Yer mom's or the spare one?"

"The spare one," I answered quickly. "I like blue."

"I reckoned so. The bed looks real comfortable." She threw on fresh linens and pillowcases, dusting from top to bottom and vacuuming the pale blue-gray carpet. Got Adam to move in a chest of drawers from Mom's room.

After boxing up Mom's pictures and medicines and things, Faye set to work cleaning out the refrigerator and polishing the furniture with lemon cleaner. Tina drove to IGA and bought me some fresh stuff: a loaf of white bread, grits, and so on. No hominy, thankfully, or pig's feet.

By the time Tim arrived in the evening with Jeanette, they'd all made the whole place shine. Becky found one of Mom's funny old Statler Brothers CDs and put it on so we could all hear and laugh. Or occasionally dance, as Becky tried to do with Jeanette.

I wondered if Mom ever had friends over, ever laughed, ever danced. The smiley pictures now packed in a box suggested she had. I was just too late to see it.

"Yer turn, wild woman!" hollered Tim, slapping down another card as we played UNO and ate surprisingly good delivery pizza. A welcome change from potato and tuna pizza back in Tokyo, or the spicy fermented kimchee cabbage version Kyoko liked. Japanese pizza was certainly nothing to write home about.

"I'm goin'! I'm goin'!" Becky threw down a Skip card, high-fiving Tim as Adam grumpily missed another turn.

I'd always thought games like UNO were stuff for third-grade slumber parties. But the lamplight and music made me feel warm, blooming, innocent in a way I hadn't experienced in years.

"Go, Shah-loh!" Tim grabbed another slice of pizza. Outside, evening fell softly, turning sapphire over a pale sunset, all lit up with stars and the sound of crickets and cicadas. The house glowed with laughter.

Mom's house. My house. Talk about surreal.

"Well, I gotta hit the sack," said Jeanette, putting down her cards and kissing me on the cheek. "I'll bring ya some 'tater bread next week."

"We'll be prayin' for ya, sugar." Faye hugged me tight. "If ya feel like comin' ta church on Sunday, give me a ring. Night or day, if ya need anything."

Tim, Becky, Adam, and I lingered, watching part of a funny movie and sopping up the famous garlic-butter sauce and breadsticks that came with the pizza. I didn't want them to leave.

"I gotta get some shut-eye," said Becky finally, yawning and leaning against Tim. "I'm volunteerin' at the nursery t'morrow for the church's couple's retreat. Too bad yer Carlos is such a knot head. He coulda come with ya."

His name drove a painful dagger through me, but I played it off, flipping through the UNO deck. "Carlos thinks Protestants are on par with McDonald's and Nikes. You know. Invading the beloved country." I made a face. "Although I think he wore diapers last time he went to mass."

"Jesus ain't no McDonald's," retorted Becky, arching an eyebrow. "He ain't no Happy Meal neither."

"Apparently not, with all the bad things that happen in life. But I thought He's supposed to answer prayers." And He sure hasn't answered mine. And I did pray as a child, years and years ago. Before I grew hard. Cynical. Like Kyoko. "Why pray then?" I played with a stray UNO card.

Becky didn't flinch. "If ya reckon yer gonna get a toy in every box, think again. Life ain't all handouts, and my Jesus ain't neither."

Adam cleared his throat. "She means Jesus isn't Santa Claus, Shiloh. Life throws us all kinds of things—good and bad—and just because we believe in Him doesn't mean we get a free ride."

"Yeah. Faye said something like that." I picked at my cat-patterned Japanese house slippers. "It figures. Life's just rotten for everybody."

"The Bible says the rain fawls on the just and the unjust," stated Tim, crossing his cowboy boots and reaching for some more garlic-butter sauce. "But when ya think about it, we's all unjust." He winked at Becky. "'Specially that'n."

She tickled his side, and he squawked.

I must have still looked brooding because Adam eyed me. "You really think there's nothing good in life?"

"No, but. . .why believe in God if it doesn't do you any good?"

"I didn't say it doesn't do any good. But all our problems don't magically disappear. Jesus suffered, and so do we. We go through it with Him. Together. We're not alone anymore. We're invited up into an adventure. . .a mystery. . .a relationship that changes our lives and makes us better people."

I raised my eyebrow at Adam's sudden eloquence over an empty pizza box.

"It's like a romance," said Tim, putting his arm around Becky's shoulders. I couldn't tell if he was joking or serious.

Together. A relationship. A romance. I hugged my knees, wishing it were true, because I longed for it like nothing else in the world. Someone waiting for me like Hachiko, straining to see my face from afar.

But like everyone else, He'd forgotten me, too. My heart felt bitter and empty, the way it had on the long drive from Richmond to Staunton, staring out at the mountains and listening to Bible Today.

Tim drained his Dr. Pepper and ruffled Becky's hair. "Reckon we gotta skedaddle, rug rat."

My eyes bugged out. "Sorry? Can you translate?"

"He means we've got to go," said Adam, cracking his occasional smile. "Skedaddle. Scram. Get out of here."

"How do I use it in a sentence? Is it a verb?" I'm writing that down the minute he leaves!

Adam and Tim exchanged serious glances. "A verb. Definitely."

I smiled, surveying the littered—but cleaned and vacuumed—living room. "And thanks so much for today. You can't ever imagine what your help means to me."

Becky hugged me. "Shucks! Ain't nothin'! Least we could do. I'll call ya t'morrow to check on ya."

Tim looked around blankly. "I don't know 'bout y'all, but I came for the pizza. Was there. . .somethin' else?"

I grinned, thinking of him vacuuming the living room and watering my front lawn, after he'd worked overtime at the accounting office.

"Be safe." Adam double-checked my door locks. "We'll call you."

And one by one red taillights glimmered down the driveway. Into the streetlights lining dark Crawford Drive. And disappeared into the country night.

I stood at the door a long time, porch light shining and door open, watching the swallows dart in and out of the front-porch eaves. Dark streets and dark houses were illuminated by yellow windows into the distance.

The mountain loomed shadowy under the stars, and the yard slept in dewy coolness, moist, heavy with the scent of grass. Breathtakingly quiet. I could hear the gentle thump of the dryer in the laundry room as it finished the last load. Down the street wafted a distant strain of country music.

I slowly eased the screen door closed, clicking the lock. Closed the front door tightly and locked it.

The house felt immense. My whole Tokyo apartment could fit in the kitchen.

Tokyo. Shiodome. My toilet sink and mini balcony. I should be in Chicago now, boarding a flight for Narita Airport.

Pain swelled into choking acid before I could stop it, and for an instant I hated Mom's dumb house. I hated myself.

And the one thing I hated most of all was redneck Staunton, Virginia.

I was still leaning against the closed door, head in my hands, when the house phone startled me with its unfamiliar ring.

"Hey, Shiloh. It's Adam."

"Oh, hi, Adam." I wound the cord around my hand, relieved to cut the silence. "I should give you my cell number because Mom's landline hasn't been paid. It'll probably cut off any time."

He paused. "Um. . .I don't think that'll work, unless we all call internationally. You've got a Japanese number."

I smacked my forehead, still sore at the memory of Japan.

"You might be able to buy a chip or something, but I'm not sure."

"The phone's Japanese, too," I reminded him. "The right chip might be hard to find here." I didn't want to hang up. Even a little conversation made the empty house seem brighter.

"Listen, I'm sorry to bother you, but I forgot some tools out back. I need them for a job in the morning."

"You work on Saturdays?"

"Duty calls. That's running a small business."

"Sorry."

"Nah. I'm used to it. Would you mind if I came back and picked them up? I'm just down the road."

"Of course not."

"Thanks. I'll be there in a second."

I clicked off the phone, grateful at the thought of a visitor in the too-still house.

Within minutes headlights beamed on the living room curtains, and I opened the front door. Moths swirled around the porch light. Mama Bird peeped at me suspiciously, reflections glinting on her tiny eyes.

"Sorry," said Adam, coming into the warm glow. He stood almost a head taller than me. "I forgot my wallet, too."

"That's right. You paid for the pizza, and thanks again. Come on in." I held the door open for him.

To my surprise, he balked. "I'm sorry. I. . .uh. . .can you just get it for me? It's on the table."

I stared at him. "Sure. But. . .why?"

Color rose in Adam's cheeks, and he shifted his weight uncomfortably. "Well, it's just. . .you're single, and I'm. . .you know. It wouldn't be a good idea."

My jaw fell open. "To get your wallet?"

"Uh. . .yeah. Sorry. If it's a problem I can come back another time." He scratched his head nervously.

Jerusalem Chapel. Becky's sedan. I narrowed my eyes at him. "Is that why you sent Becky to meet me when my car ran out of gas?"

"Sort of. But for your sake as well."

"My sake?" Anger burned, although I had no idea why. If Adam wanted to stay on my front porch all night long, I could care less.

"You think a single woman would feel comfortable having some strange guy she just met come find her in the middle of nowhere?" His eyes bored into me. "Ever think of that?"

Actually, I hadn't. I'd become so accustomed to working with men in super-safe Japan, even having my boyfriend live with another woman, that such a thing never occurred to me. Then again, Mia's pajamas definitely had an effect on Carlos. I let the screen door bang shut and went looking for Adam's wallet.

He had paid for dinner. I could at least be civil.

"Here." I stood partially on the porch. "Does it bother you if I stand here?" My nerves were shot, and I couldn't resist sarcasm.

"No. It's fine, Shiloh. Don't get the wrong idea. I just want to be careful how I live. For you as well."

"Really." I said it as a statement. A moth flew in through the crack in the door and began to circle the living-room light. I shut the screen door behind me.

Adam ran his hand through his hair in frustration. "Look, maybe it doesn't mean anything to you, but it does to me. You obviously have no idea what a small town is like. Do you want your neighbors thinking you've just shacked up with some guy the first night you move in? Is that the kind of reception you want?"

"Who cares what they think?" I waved a bug away in annoyance.

"Well, I care. About your reputation and about mine. I intend to practice what I preach, even if it's weird. To you or anyone else. I'm sorry, Shiloh. I certainly don't mean to offend you. But this is who I am."

I sniffed then leaned against the pillar and looked out at the black night. "I'm not offended." Bunch of stiffs! Religious freaks! Bible Belt! Kyoko warned me about this!

A long silence billowed between us, and I sensed Adam shifting uncomfortably again. "Maybe not. But you seem to be."

Finally I plopped down on the porch and put my chin in my hands. Adam hesitated then awkwardly sat down next to me. Keeping (I noticed) a safe distance between us. The fragrance of dew and grass swelled up, fresh and sweet like after a rain.

"Sorry." I sighed. "But I'm not the Big Bad Wolf."

"Well, neither am I," said Adam a little more gently. "But what if I was? You should be more careful, Shiloh. The world can be an ugly place."

I rolled my eyes but said nothing, resting my chin on my

knees. "Yeah. I guess I've gotten used to it."

"I can't say I blame you. But. . .well, I do what I can. Most of the world probably thinks I'm weird, but this is the way I want to live."

Crickets hummed in gentle waves, pulsating through the dark trees and faraway hills. An enchanting sound, almost hypnotic.

"I envy you," I finally said softly. "I don't know how I want to live anymore."

"Of course not. Your life has been turned on its head, and it'll take time to sort things out."

"Time. Yeah, maybe." I played with a blade of grass by my foot, feeling bitter. "But I wonder if time will really fix things. I've made a big mess of my life, and sometimes there's no going back."

"There might not be any going back, but there's always going forward. Don't forget that. We've all made mistakes."

"You've never been fired, have you?" I snapped back, a little more harshly than I intended.

"No."

"Well, have you ever lost a girlfriend then? If that's not too personal?"

"Yes, I have."

I didn't know what to say. I'd expected him to say no, saintly soul he appeared to be.

"I've gone through a lot of things. We all have. Tim, Becky, Faye, everyone. That's life."

I snorted. "Everybody keeps saying how they've suffered, but you all are still smiling! If it was bad enough, you wouldn't."

Adam shook his head. "No, Shiloh. I don't think that's true. We have plenty of reasons to smile every single day. The sun, food, friends, the seasons, the earth. . .and most of all, Jesus. God gives us far more than we deserve."

Missionary! I fumed, running my fingers through the moist grass. "I don't think so."

He pressed his lips together. "I'm sorry to hear it. But that doesn't change the fact that Jesus loves you and died for you."

He said it so simply, so honestly, I didn't even have time to retort. I wished I could believe in something with all my heart, the way I did with Faye over coffee. But I couldn't.

"If He does, He sure has a funny way of showing it."

Adam leaned back on his hands. "It might seem like it sometimes, I guess. But I never thought of it that way. Even in our hardest times, we know He's there, working everything out for our good."

"I know about your brother," I blurted a little too abruptly. "Becky told me. I'm sorry he lost his legs."

Adam blinked, obviously stunned. "Uh. . .thanks. But I wasn't talking about Rick. I was talking about Becky."

I jerked my head up. "Becky? Why? She has a perfect life! A husband and mother-in-law who love her, good friends, living in the same place she grew up. Soon she'll have a houseful of kids and everything she ever wanted," I grumbled, stabbed with unexpected jealousy.

Jealousy toward Becky Donaldson—who still curled her bangs with a curling iron. I was pathetic.

Adam's eyes were luminous. "Becky can't have kids," he said hoarsely.

Chapter 22

I must've heard wrong. "Sorry? What?"

"Becky has some. . .problem. She can't have kids, and nobody really knows why. They've been trying for four years, and she's tried in vitro for free, mainly because a rich doctor felt sorry for her. She told Becky if it didn't 'take' the third time, she'd have to give up. But Becky keeps believing for a miracle."

My mouth fell open. "Has she done it the third time?"

"Yes." He swallowed hard. "All her tests and readings are showing up the same, regardless of all the shots and things." Adam ran his hand through his hair sadly and looked away. "They signed up for adoption years ago, but it hasn't worked out yet either."

I dropped the piece of grass in my hand, flabbergasted. Thought of Becky bounding down the stairs at her little brick house, flashing her bright, naive smile. How she talked about children in the parking lot of Jerusalem Chapel. She'd even tried to convince me to have kids, for goodness' sake! And tomorrow she'd feed Cheerios to other people's kids while they enjoyed the couples' service.

I hung my head. "I'm so sorry. I had no idea."

"Don't tell her I told you. I think it's best if she tells you herself. But I wanted you to know."

I nodded, resentment washing over me. Everything in Staunton was wrong—death, dying, problems. Even Becky, the friendliest girl I'd met, lived her own sad nightmare, and I couldn't do a thing about it. I was stuck in the spiderweb with them.

"I hate this town," I finally whispered, kicking the lawn.

Adam looked up. "What? Why?"

"I've seen nothing but trouble in Staunton. Everybody's sick or dying or struggling with something. It's not normal! They must have done nuclear testing here in the '50s or something." Anger pumped through my veins, and I threw the handful of grass I'd picked out into the yard.

"What are you talking about? You've only been here a few days."

"Five. Enough to recognize a giant redneck pit when I see one. Before the day's over I'll probably sprout buckteeth and a gut, and tomorrow I'll be dead of high cholesterol from that hominy stuff!"

Dead. I actually said the word, sitting on Mom's front porch. I rolled my forehead in my hand.

Adam obviously missed my gaffe. He laughed out loud, which only made me madder. "Hominy doesn't have cholesterol, Shiloh. It's corn."

"Yeah, soaked in lye! Try soaking our pizza in lye and see what happens! Maybe that's why everybody's so weird and backward. Bible thumpers and racists!" I waved my arms. "I'm going crazy here surrounded by weirdos! Nobody has any brains!"

A too-long silence. "You think everybody around here is weird and backward?"

"Are you kidding? People don't even know how to conjugate proper verbs, Adam! They watch cars go in circles for hours! If anybody actually made sushi in Staunton, they'd use squirrels or—what did you call them. . .starlings?—shot out of their front yard. Everybody's nuts! Every single person."

I started to hurl another insult about dumb Southerners then abruptly shut up. My mouth had run away again, leaving me in a hazy stupor of anger and grief. But nothing really mattered anymore. Things couldn't possibly get any worse.

"Now that's not fair," said Adam, a hint of coldness in his voice.

"No? Well, that's what I see. And did the KKK run all the African-Americans out of town?"

"You haven't been here long enough to see anything!" Adam retorted, arms crossed in the darkness. "Yes, there are racist people in the South. But it's a sin, Shiloh, that God will judge. It's one hundred percent wrong, and those who know God know it. No one can love God and hate his brother. The Bible says so."

"The Bible." I rolled my eyes.

He didn't take my bait. "And a lot of those people who go around calling themselves Christians are liars. Fakers who use the Bible to accomplish their twisted agenda. Don't judge everybody by the sins of a few."

"As if that makes things any better!" I faced him, gripping the porch with white knuckles. "I can't find one redeeming quality around here. Greasy food, run-down shacks, and too many bugs!" I swatted violently at one buzzing near my head. "Ignorant people who want nothing better in life except working at dead-end jobs and mental institutions! No wonder my mom lived in Staunton. She was in her element!"

My cheeks flushed. I buried my face in shaking hands, hearing my heart pump angry blood past my ears. My breath shuddered.

Even in the moonlight, I could see Adam's gaze chill. "That's what you really think about everybody?"

"Yes, and a lot more."

"Well." He stood up and put his wallet in his pocket. "Good night then, Shiloh."

And with that, he picked up his tools leaning against the pillar and got in his truck and left.

I watched his truck pull out of the driveway like I'd watched my dad's retreating back. Mute, powerless to speak or call him back. I was frozen, a stone.

The taillights disappeared. I sat on the porch for a long time, devastated at what I'd done. I didn't mean it. I really didn't. *What on earth got into you? Honestly! You need help!*

I'd just insulted one of the only friends I had in the city, after he'd bought us all dinner and helped me move into Mom's house. He'd trimmed my hedges and mulched my plants. Told me how often to water my roses and promised to bring more plants.

And here I sat, under the condemning gaze of Mama Bird. Even she saw what a heel I'd been.

Shiloh P. Jacobs found her roots all right. A chip off the crabby old block.

I guess some things never change.

The dew suddenly felt cold, and I wrapped my arms around myself, shivering. I was lonely and tired beyond words. I longed to call someone, but there was no one to call.

I walked back into the empty house, locking the door behind me. Threw myself on the newly made bed in the spare bedroom, not even bothering to undress, and wrapped the thin blanket around me for comfort. Scrunched my eyes closed, wishing I could wake—by some miracle—to the sun-smoggy haze of Shiodome's brightness.

A rattling blast echoed outside my bedroom window. I threw off the blanket and fumbled for my cell phone, forgetting I could only reach Kyoko with it, or, heaven forbid, our editor Dave.

I imagined a crazed Appalachian farmer, like the *American Gothic* painting, at my front door waving his pitchfork.

Then the rumble of a car engine faded, complete with horn blasting the first notes of "Dixie." And another smaller backfire as it careened down the road. Drunken idiots!

I slowly released the cell phone, heart pounding, and plopped back on the bed.

You're not in Tokyo anymore, Toto! I scrunched angrily in a ball. You're in Churchville! The only gunshots I'd probably hear would be aimed at birds or badgers or something.

Stillness returned, and I tried to relax. Pressed my nose to the blankets to find any trace of Mom's scent. They smelled like her, as did the whole house: soft and floral, like fabric softener. She wore Avon perfume. On her good days, with her light brown hair pulled up and amethyst earrings dangling, I'd even thought she looked pretty.

Forget sleep. I balled up the blanket and marched down the hall to the living room. Flipped on the TV, blinking in the bright blue glow, and watched a silly British comedy on PBS. But I couldn't laugh. Couldn't even smile.

Everything, from the carpet to the wallpaper to the pictures on the wall, reminded me of Mom. The whole house breathed her; unfamiliar and strange, yet vaguely comforting.

I stared at the flickering screen and tried to blot out the emotions that materialized without warning, like clouds over the moon.

I slept on the sofa, blanket wrapped around me like a cocoon, and woke only when early morning thunder rattled the windows. I felt leaden, zombie-like. Didn't even put on fresh clothes. Just padded around in my house slippers, hair a mess.

The thought of seeing the rest of the house sickened me. It belonged to Mom, not me—no matter what the lawyer's papers said.

I was intruding on a stranger. Because that's what she was to me.

I considered calling Adam to apologize. If he couldn't forgive me, at least I could thank him and say good-bye civilly. I stared at my cell phone for twenty minutes rehearsing my speech with the international card in my hand.

Pressed the buttons, and. . .nothing. Not even a dial tone. I dialed Faye in a panic, but again, nothing.

They've disconnected my service. My last bill in Japan. . .I probably hadn't paid it.

I shut my cell phone and dialed Adam from the house phone. Stood there stupidly, cord dangling, waiting for him to pick up before I realized it, too, had no dial tone.

The Internet. They're probably connected to the same plan. Maybe. . .

I rushed into the library, trying not to look at the Mom-world of books or the icons splashed across her screen as I jiggled the mouse, computer groaning to life. The clunker of a computer obviously still worked, although her waterfall-Bible-verse wallpaper stopped me in my slippers. Wouldn't spaceships landing in Arizona be more appropriate?

There. The blue Internet icon. I reached for it, poised to click.

AP. The PM's wife. Forty-five minutes. "Did you get Schwartz to edit this? Because I'm not wasting any more time doing it myself!"

I dropped the mouse like a hot Japanese sweet potato.

Chapter 23

I switched off the computer and stormed out of the room, a lump forming in my throat. A little Internet icon had ruined my entire life.

No, you ruined your entire life, Shiloh P. Jacobs!

I didn't even need to click, thanks to the red bar across the bottom of the screen before I shut it down. *Internet disconnected*. Last night's brief phone call with Adam had been the last gasp.

At least the electricity and water still worked. Then again, who really cared anyway?

A chill settled over the house. I grabbed another blanket and put on socks. Poured a bowl of cereal and slumped at the table, watching tree branches shiver in the stormy breeze. Normally a good run, even in the rain, would have pumped some life and cheer into my heart. But not today. I left my gym clothes and tennis shoes in the suitcase.

If I'd ever felt hopeless in my life, it was now. I was cold, exhausted, and utterly drained. It could have been ten in the morning or ten at night. I had no idea. And I could care less.

Sunday rolled in blearier than Saturday, shrouded in cold

grayness. All the green that had enchanted me before seemed soggy, dark, and mute, as if it had fled with the sun.

Stifling memories suffocated me, and I abruptly picked up Mom's car keys and slogged out to the car.

Sat there in the driveway, looking out at the drizzly morning and inhaling the sweet berry smell of Mom's car air freshener. Not a single crumb littered her super-clean carpet. A Virginia School for the Deaf and Blind cup sat suspended in the cup holder, as if caught in time. A sweater and manila folder of student work on the passenger seat.

I reached out unconsciously to touch them, to hold what Mom had loved, but I couldn't. I drew back. Turned on the car and backed out of the driveway.

I reminded myself not to do anything stupid like I'd done at Jerusalem Chapel. After all, I couldn't call Adam now. But I needed to get away.

The streets shined rainy and empty, and warm, yellow-lighted windows gleamed back at me across the gloom. All the houses in Crawford Manor looked pretty much the same, save different paint and shingle colors: blocky, quaint, country-cute. Wooden shutters. Trimmed shrubs. Front porches. American flags.

Some houses had been dolled up nicely with expensive grass and dark brown mulch. Others, sporting dilapidated siding and old car parts, looked like they harbored criminals. One was painted. . .

Purple?! I braked, staring in disbelief as rain poured outside.

I thanked my lucky stars I wouldn't live in Crawford Manor long. Especially when I spotted an actual PINK FLAMINGO stuck in one yard—no, make that two—along with random tufts of faded plastic flowers in unnatural colors like turquoise blue and bright red and a couple of plastic chipmunks.

If I'd had my head about me, I would have snapped some pictures for Kyoko. But today it just made me more depressed.

I slushed my tires out of Crawford Manor and sat at the

intersection, not knowing which way to go. Turned right. And passed, after a parting of trees, a neat little country church crowded with cars.

Right. Today's Sunday. Faye had invited me to church.

Loneliness came so strongly I actually considered going just to see some fresh faces and smiles, but then looked down at my rumpled clothes and changed my mind. Drifted past the church and rainy hills. Gazed at the houses and long brick high school appearing on my left. Counted cows munching soggy grass.

The road forked. I glimpsed, through wiper blades, the redneck-est gas station on earth, and signs for other towns pointing down desolate roads toward the mountains.

Nothing else. I turned the car around in the gas station and headed back, marooned on a lifeless planet.

I found myself pulling into the church parking lot and just sat there on the gravel, not sure why I'd come. Just like the time I found myself in front of Mrs. Inoue's shop in my house slippers.

A lump tightened in my throat as I remembered Mrs. Inoue and her wrinkled hands. Her ginger candy. I never got to say good-bye. I squeezed the steering wheel as if to crush out the memories. Mom had found peace in church; perhaps in some small measure I could, too.

Under the pines the rain had mostly stopped, save a few random spatters and taps on the windshield and roof. A soft mist settled. I rolled down the window to breathe in fresh air then froze, hand on the button.

The sound of singing.

I listened, both awed and amused by the melody rising and falling from the quaint white-and-brick chapel. I'd stood on the sidewalk in Shibuya and heard voices and someone banging on a piano and felt contempt for white men bringing their religion to an Asian people who did very well, thank you, without it.

But try as I might, I could never shake the sense of reverence and even wonder that swelled when I heard voices lifted in worship. Buddhist priests chanted in cold, dark, ancient Japanese temples, but they did not sing. At least not like the Christians I'd heard. Those Jesus freaks seemed alive, if not slightly out of touch with reality. But still they sang.

A raindrop from a pinecone splattered on the windshield in a flurry of silver, as if to shatter my prejudices.

On Monday morning the clouds broke up, and I felt like Cro-Magnon woman stepping out of her cave. I opened the windows, pulled back the curtains, even opened the doors. A fresh breeze poured through the house and open screen doors, echoing blue sky and bright sun.

My reflection in the bathroom mirror frightened me: hair unwashed, face pallid and depressed. I'd eaten all the cereal over the weekend (it served double-duty for breakfast and lunch).

I pulled on gym clothes and jogged around the neighborhood in early morning white-gold sun, heat already beginning to swelter, letting my thoughts ease with the joyful pounding of my heart. By the time I got back, a small measure of sanity had crept back into my panting skull.

I sponged my sweaty face with a clean towel and drank some orange juice. Stepped into the shower and let the warm water lift my spirits with clouds of steam. Mom had some kind of grapefruit-ginger body wash in the shower, and it smelled heavenly.

I dried my hair with an ancient hair dryer. Put in a pretty barrette. Took my time putting on makeup and donning a fresh little sundress and sandals.

Poured the last of the orange juice, and then dug in the fridge to see what I could eat for breakfast. The milk was gone. I could make a turkey sandwich, I suppose, or. . .

I opened the cabinet and shook the box of grits.

I can't believe I've stooped to making grits. What if they've been soaked in lye, too? And just what is a "grit"?

Still. I was hungry. I read the directions on the side of the box, poured the water and salt, and added the grits. Pushed the button on the microwave, waited, and stirred. Suspiciously sniffed the scent of corn.

Added some butter and some more salt. Shook in a few drops of hot sauce. Tasted. Grated a handful of cheddar cheese. Stirred. Nuked. Tasted again.

Okay. I took another bite. This I can at least eat.

Feeling slightly proud of myself for conquering this new cooking feat, I sat at the table and stirred my steaming grits, looking up at the one black-and-white photo of our hands I'd left on the wall. I wondered if, in some small way, Mom would be proud of me, too.

Then to my surprise, I saw the outline of a blue pickup truck through the living room sheers. Turning into my driveway.

I stood at the screen door in disbelief, bowl still in hand. And saw Adam Carter walking up to my front porch.

Chapter 24

"What happened to your phone?" Adam asked a little gruffly. I searched his face for anger but found none. No smile either.

"I guess the phone company cut it off." I stepped out onto the porch. Surprised that Adam would still speak to me and at a second chance I didn't deserve.

"We were worried about you. Faye said she tried to call you like a hundred times."

We? Was Adam worried, too? Or just Faye? My heart picked up slightly in hopes that I could still repair the damage I'd done.

"Really?" I gulped, unable to meet his eyes.

"Of course. Nobody heard from you all weekend, and I know it's not easy to stay in. . ." He shifted his weight uneasily and put his hands in his pockets. "In your mom's house."

"No."

"But. . .I see you're moving up in the world." He gestured at my bowl. Still no smile. "Did you make them yourself?"

"The grits? Oh. Yeah. My first time."

"Congratulations. Those are number one of the redneck food groups."

"Oh?" I blushed, embarrassed now. "What are the. . .um. . .

others?" I stammered, not sure if he was joking.

"Biscuits, cornbread, possum, and pecan pie."

"And collards," I added soberly, afraid to laugh.

To my relief, he gave a slight smile. "And beer, of course, if you're a drinker. I'm not."

No surprise. Adam the teetotaler, in women and beer.

I took the moment to prepare my words. "Listen," I began, clutching my bowl and spoon and looking down at the porch. "I'm really sorry about what I said. I was horrible and completely out of line. I didn't mean any of it. I was. . .I don't know. Frustrated about my life. I'm so sorry."

"No, it's okay."

I looked up in disbelief, letting out the air I'd unconsciously squeezed in. "You mean. . .you forgive me?"

"Sure."

"I mean it. In Japan we eat some pretty weird stuff, too. Like *natto*, which is fermented soybeans with these long strings of fermented slime still clinging to them. And then there's jellyfish, and sea anemone like orange mush, and my friend ate horse sushi once, which means raw—"

Adam blanched and waved his hand. "No, really. You don't have to elaborate."

We stood there awkwardly a moment, and then Adam fingered his keys. "You busy today?"

"Me? Uh. . .no." Understatement of the century.

"Then hop in the truck."

"Why? Where are we going?"

He didn't answer. Just walked to the truck and got in. I wasn't about to lose him a second time, so I grabbed my purse and keys and locked the door. Jumped awkwardly up in the truck, still holding my bowl of grits.

I hesitated before slamming the door. "You're sure it's. . . okay?" I asked meekly, glancing over at him and then out at the neighboring houses. "I'm not making fun. I'm just. . ."

"We'll be in public, Shiloh," he said shortly, looking annoyed.

"Oh. Okay." I pulled the heavy door shut and clipped in my seat belt as he backed out of the driveway.

Neither of us spoke.

"Did you water your roses?" he finally asked, turning at the stop sign.

"No. It rained yesterday though."

"How much?"

I stared at him. "I don't know. Rain."

"You'd better do it when you get home then. They looked a little dry last time I checked. Roses need a lot of water."

Leave it to Adam to fill up our empty space with Mom's old dumb plants. But at least he was speaking—and not preaching—to me. Although I figured a sermon would come in due time, since I so obviously deserved one.

He'd probably stuck a Bible on the dash, right? Or a Billy Graham tract? No? *Hmph. He'll find a way.*

But Adam didn't say a word. Just turned down the same country road I'd followed on Sunday.

I ate without speaking then put my bowl on the floor. Drummed my fingers on the seat belt.

"Did I tell you I'm sorry?" I finally broke the silence. "Because I am. I felt terrible all weekend. You have no idea."

"You told me."

What else could I say? We passed the little country church on the right, and I didn't have the courage to tell him I'd actually pulled in and parked.

"Do you go there?" I gestured.

"Not now, but I did years ago. Now I go to a bigger one in town that's closer to home. My parents go to a different one—a really good one. But I prefer mine."

"Oh."

No questions about my churchgoing habits. No invitations or urgings to go. Just. . .nothing.

I didn't know what else to talk about. I felt like a child, chattering away, and stayed quiet like Adam. I sneaked a peek at him, still feeling guilty, and found his face far away, with no trace of emotion whatsoever.

The pastures were lined with rustic fences and white Queen Anne's lace, and we meandered out toward the mountains. Away from the city.

As the outskirts of Churchville faded behind me, my eyes practically ached from green, green, green forever—rich and brilliant—as if the rain had saturated the hillsides with vitamins. Lush pastoral landscapes, interspersed with occasional houses and blue mountains jutting through the trees, always morphing and changing shape. The hum of the truck soothed me.

I put my window down like Adam's and inhaled the clean and heady mixture of fresh-mown grass, damp leaves, and clean, pine-scented air swept in from the mountains.

We passed a field full of bright white grasses glowing in the morning sun like opal fire. Pines jutting into slate-blue hills. Red barns and silos. A turquoise sky shouting overhead.

Cows everywhere, in black-and-white patchwork. Swallows swooped in open sky, over waving fields of shining corn. Wooded bends with large, ancient trees, their arms loaded with swaying, glittering leaves. Fairy-tale-green moss carpeting creek banks. I lost myself in the dizzy color, forgetting where we were.

"Are we in Staunton anymore?" I asked cautiously.

"Not really."

"Don't you have to work today?"

"I should."

I rested my hand across my mouth and leaned against the door, feeling—with relief—like we were a hundred miles from Staunton, from anywhere. As we passed occasional cars on the road, people lifted one or two fingers lazily, buddy-like, and waved.

"Do you know them?"

"Nah." Adam lifted two fingers from the steering wheel in reply.

I stared out at an apple-green field and a weathered-looking man on a tractor. He tipped his hat as we went by, and I waved back.

The field widened, and there were fluffy, whitish cotton balls strewn across the grass. "What are those?" I gasped.

"Haven't you ever seen sheep before?"

"Not in. . .uh. . .person. They're in a bunch. A herd. Whatever you call them." I pressed my nose to the glass like a child, and Adam slowed. Idled the truck.

"A flock. Go on. Get out and take a look."

I hopped out of the truck and stepped over tall grass in my dress. Then stood by the fence while a gentle breeze ruffled my hair, watching the sheep wander and munch. They were soft and woolly, docile-looking, with black faces and perpendicular, black, floppy ears. Little fluff-ball babies frolicked nearby, fat and clumsy, watching me.

At my feet a brilliant puddle of golden dandelions spread out in all directions. I picked one, nuzzling my chin with it while a baby sheep—sheeplet?—bleated in my direction.

I climbed back in the truck and clumsily slammed the door. "Thanks."

"No problem."

I still held my dandelion. We continued down the road in silence. But peaceful silence. He kept his gaze, which had turned soft and pleasant, even wistful, on the road. Pushed PLAY on his CD player.

The music that began to flow—I say "flow" because it did, liquid-like and ethereal—rose up beautiful, emotional, unearthly. I'd never heard anything like it. The voices and gritty guitar chords were solid and real, but it had a sort of sunshiny feel that made it glow.

"What's this music?"

"This? Tomorrow." He didn't move his eyes from the road. Green and bright sun splotches from leaves reflected in them.

"What's Tomorrow? A band?"

He smiled briefly. "You've been away that long?"

"Guess so."

"They're a Christian band from Britain. They sing praise and worship music."

Now I get it. The otherworldliness of it all. I listened in awe as the guitar faded and the voices fell and then crescendoed, sounding like something from a choir, yet raw and U2-esque, skillful enough to play on any radio station. I thought Christian music was all stodgy stuff on pipe organs.

I heard snatches of words: *mercy, God, love, light, glory, forever, forever, forever*. . . Just like the blue and green sliding past the window, all colored by brilliant sun that dazzled my eyes. The most peaceful thing I'd ever heard.

Everlasting. . .never-ending. . .the cry of my heart. . .give You praise. . . The words kept pouring like water into my thirsty soul. I turned them over and over in my mind, trying to understand.

The chords haunted me, struck something deep I didn't know existed. A sensation like tears prickled in my throat, and I had no idea why.

The tune changed, and one song streamed into another. "I will not die but live, and will proclaim what the Lord has done. . . ."

I rubbed my ear to see if I'd heard right. "What did that just say?"

Adam replayed the song as something cold crept up my neck. It sounded almost word-for-word from that radio-preaching show, the one with. . .

"Like it? It's from the Bible."

I slumped back in my seat, tickling my chin with the dandelion. Surely not the same verse. Could it be?

"It's a new one. I like it, too."

I tipped my head back and let the music, like medicine, pour into the sore spots in my heart, my past. I didn't know why, or how, but I wanted it. Needed it. Felt like raising my hands to the sunlight and inviting Him—whoever He was—inside.

Singing wafting out of churches intrigued me, but these words—these throbbing chords—called me. By name.

"In my anguish I cried to the Lord, and He answered by setting me free. I will not die but live. . . ."

The painful ache expanded with each second, like a shimmering bubble, and I longed to lift my life up to Someone greater, Someone stronger, and let Him hold it in His hands as Faye had suggested. My job, Carlos, Japan, my family—all of it. Could He really take it? Make something good of my mess?

I couldn't look at Adam. He must think I was a pagan. Or worse, he'd think he converted me.

The Brit was speaking over the music, praising God, praying as if on behalf of all of us. I dared to let the prayer pull me along, the way a stream pulls fallen leaves. I mean, how could I pray? I didn't believe in Him. Not exactly.

I listened to that voice, that hush, those guitar chords in the background, afraid to make a sound and ruin the sacred moment. The truck transformed into a chapel. Nothing would ever be the same.

Relationship. Adam had called it a relationship. Tim called it a romance.

"You all right?" Adam looked over at me, tone softer than before.

I nodded curtly, afraid if I spoke I would cry. I am Shiloh P. Jacobs. I do not cry.

A thousand questions danced in my head, sparkling with blinding radiance like stream ripples as we rumbled over a bridge, wet rocks shining.

We pulled into a small country town announced by a couple of old trailers. Adam slowed the truck and turned down a dumpy-looking side road then parked in front of what looked like a shack.

"Come on. Let's have lunch."

"Lunch?" The music stopped when he turned off the truck.

"Sure. Aren't you hungry? It's noon already. After."

I glanced at my watch, surprised. I hadn't felt a thing.

Adam held the door for me as we entered—I kid you not—Bubba's Diner. The paint (if you could call it paint) peeled like a moldy onion, and it looked about a hundred years old. It had definitely survived air raids and probably a couple of fires.

"Now, this isn't anything fancy like you're probably used to, so don't get your hopes up," he said with a little jibe at the look on my face. "Just give it a try. Okay?"

The place was dingy, but something did smell good. Adam pulled up two bar stools in front of a long counter with an old guy working steadily behind it. Several men were already eating and talking loudly about NASCAR and taxes, slapping their knees, over the country music. I awkwardly scooted onto the bar stool in my dress.

"Whakinnadawgyawantdahlin?" the old man asked, leaning on the counter.

I stared at him and then at Adam. "Sorry? What?"

"He wants to know what kind of dog you want. You do like hot dogs, don't you? I guess you have those in Japan."

Was he mocking me? "Hot dogs? Of course. I love hot dogs. Um. . .what are the options?"

"Up there." Adam leaned back and pointed to a white plastic placard over the counter with movable black letters, many of which were missing. Chili Dog. Chili Cheese Dog. Chili 'n' Kraut Dog. And so on. If I could guess past the blanks.

"I don't see a Collard Dog," I said, scanning the menu.

Adam rolled his eyes. "Funny. He'd probably make it for you if you asked."

"No thanks. What do you recommend?"

"Chili dog with mustard. Todd's favorite."

"Todd?"

"My younger brother."

I still had all kinds of things to learn about people. "I didn't know you have a younger brother."

"He's eleven. A great kid."

"Well, I'll trust his taste in hot dogs then, if he thinks they're okay."

"Okay? These are fabulous."

"They're just hot dogs, aren't they?" From a joint called Bubba's Diner?

Adam smirked and turned to the man. "Two chili dogs with mustard."

As he made our "dawgs," I looked around the place for an inspection sticker or a sign that any reputable person, governmental or otherwise, had ever set foot in Bubba's Diner. I was still looking for it when the man appeared and slid two plates in front of us.

Adam bowed his head—the prayer thing again—and I tried to do the same. Whispered something along the lines of, "Please don't let me get food poisoning." Then took a bite.

Wow. I mean, WOW. The spicy homemade chili took me by surprise, and the soft, warm bun housed a tasty, fat little sausage inside. Grilled, not dunked in a pot of boiling water. The mustard had a nice kick, too—not the cheap stuff.

I ate my hot dog in four bites. Relived carnivals, fairs, and baseball games I'd never attended all rolled into one.

"Another one?" asked Adam, wiping his mouth with his napkin. I nodded, mouth stuffed full. The warm, squishy bread and tangy mustard were addicting.

We ate, and I took my time, imagining what the *New York Times'* food editor would write about Bubba's Diner. I'd seen articles about thousand-dollar balsamic vinegar and imported Italian prosciutto, but never an article about a hot dog.

I wonder if they'd pay me if I floated the idea. Hot dogs were, after all, one of Americans' top comfort foods, if they ever stopped to think about it—so long as you didn't buy them at the gas station or on a turning spit at the roller rink. I made a mental note to write up a proposal later. If it went to press, Bubba's Diner would have to rent out an empty lot just to contain all the Yankee foodies on pilgrimage.

"Why don't you have an accent?" I blurted.

Adam finished chewing and reached for a napkin. "Why should I? My family's not from Tennessee. That's where the good accents come from. Or Alabama."

"But everybody else around here has one. How did you miss out?"

He shrugged. "Actually a lot of people don't have accents. But in my case. . .beats me. I guess exposure to other people and places. Education and all that. Sort of neutralizes it a little."

So practical. I'd hoped for something a little more exciting. I wiped the last bit of chili from my plate while Adam paid. He thanked the man, and we pushed back our stools.

"Thatnsagudn," the man said, winking at me. Adam reddened and nodded politely.

"What did he say?" I asked impatiently as we headed for the door. "Why doesn't he speak English?"

"He was speaking English." He held the door for me.

"Well, not any kind of English I've ever heard. Can you translate?"

He hesitated and fumbled with his keys in embarrassment. "Nothing important."

"Yes he did, too! What did he say?"

"He said, 'That one's a good one.' Meaning you."

"Me?" I looked accusingly back over my shoulder. "He doesn't even know me!"

"I know."

"Then why did he say it?"

"I guess there are things every Southern man looks for in a woman he can respect."

I rolled my eyes. "I bet I can guess what they are."

"No."

"Then what?"

"Forget it." He strode across the gravel and opened the truck door for me.

"No," I insisted, annoyed. "Tell me!"

Adam ignored me, and I stopped in the middle of the parking lot. "Tell me! I'm waiting."

He turned to look at me. "You really want to know?"

"Yes."

"He saw you pray."

"Pray?"

"Yes, pray. It's important to find a good woman who loves God. That's more attractive than any pretty face."

I harrumphed. Like I believe that! "Anything else?"

"You're dressed like a lady. And not a streetwalker."

It was my turn to blush. "It's just a dress."

"Well, a man wants a woman who saves a little something for later, if you know what I mean. Some girls let it all hang out or come right up to the edge. It's not attractive. At least not around here."

"So all a woman has to do is wear a dress to catch a man in these parts?" I asked sarcastically, unfolding my arms and climbing up into the truck. "She can be dumb as a rock, but look pretty?"

"I didn't say that. Southern men aren't scared of a smart woman. In fact, she's a real catch. But they want her to be a woman."

"And wear a dress."

Adam looked annoyed. "I didn't say that either. You just asked what the man said, and I told you. It's a plus to dress decently. That's all."

I couldn't believe my Yankee ears. "Now don't try to sound all high and mighty, Adam Carter!" I snapped back. "If a woman walked into that diner in a miniskirt, every man in the place would bug his eyes out."

"You're probably right. But they'd never respect her."

"What's that supposed to mean?"

"They'd consider her a cheap item, like a Wal-Mart clearance special. 'A piece a work,' they'd say. But nobody wants a piece a work for the mother of his children and the woman he loves."

"I can't believe you!" Adam Carter, a landscaper, lecturing me on how to dress in the South and talking about women having children. I saw red. Of all the backwoods, ignorant, chauvinistic, sexist. . .

I grabbed for my seat belt, still steaming. "Is that all?"

He closed my door and got in on his side. Didn't answer.

"There's more and you're just not telling me. Go on! Spill it!"

Adam buckled his seat belt and leaned back in his seat, looking hard at me. "Why do you want to know if you hate it so much?"

"No reason." So I can know what kind of redneck creeps I have to deal with! "Just tell me."

"Fine." He started the truck. "You let me pay for your lunch and open the door for you."

"And that's supposed to mean something?" I crossed my arms.

"It means you're not a man-hating feminist." He glanced at my scowl. "Although I could be wrong."

I turned up my nose. "As if you would know."

"Southern men appreciate women who aren't too frilly," he said as if he hadn't heard me.

"I promise you, I'm frilly!" I snapped back. "Just because I'm not wearing heels today doesn't make me a Betty Sue or Daisy Mae or whatever her name is. I'm definitely frilly!"

"No you're not."

"Yes I am!"

"No you're not. You ate two hot dogs on a bar stool, without worrying about your lipstick, and you still have mustard on your chin." His mouth curved into a self-satisfied smirk. "You asked. Not me."

I cried out and pulled down the visor, finding the spot in the mirror and angrily wiping it off.

"And now you're going fishing."

"Fishing?" I retorted indignantly. "Who said I wanted to go fishing?"

Adam didn't answer. Kept on driving. Turned the music back on. Pulled into a gas station to get gas.

"Why don't you wear cowboy boots if you're such a Southern man?" I shot back as he took the keys out of the ignition.

"I'm not a cowboy," he said. And disappeared with a slam of the truck door.

And to my fury, it made perfect sense.

Adam came back out of the gas station with a paper bag, which he put on the seat between us.

I was still steaming. "Those better not be live worms. I'm not putting a worm on a hook, and that's final."

"They're not worms."

We didn't say anything more until he pulled up to the entrance of what looked like a national park. It stretched out green and tree-ful, with a few cars parked at the entrance. Adam dug two fishing poles out of the back of his truck, plus a tackle box, and I reluctantly carried the paper bag. Cold condensation on the sides told me there were drinks inside. Probably not beer, knowing the king of temperance.

We wended our way through a lush, meadowy area with picnic tables, and Adam set his stuff down on one of them. At least the picnic table was clean enough not to ruin my dress.

I couldn't say as much for the lake.

Squirrels chattered in the oak trees overhead, which groaned and swayed in the breeze. Everything smelled fresh, like it had just been washed, and the heat stuck my formerly cooperative bangs to my forehead.

Adam opened the bag and took out two frosty bottles. "A redneck meal isn't complete without processed soda laced with chemicals."

"Thanks for ruining my appetite." I pulled my hair to the side to cool my sweaty neck.

A cold Coke did sound good though, after those two spicy chili dogs. Sort of like pairing wine and cheese. Maybe we could have a redneck version? With Tang and grits? Or root beer and potted meat stuff in a can?

Adam opened the bag one last time and tossed two more things onto the picnic table. My vision blurred.

It's not. . .oh no. It's not possible. I paled, looking at the two round circles shining in clear plastic.

No, God, noooo. . . . Anything but that! Please!

"It's one of the redneck food groups," said Adam as he folded up the paper bag. But I barely heard him.

He put one of the silver disks in my hand, and I dropped it like a cup of scorching green tea—not believing what I saw. It can't be the same one. The same one! Even the same brand!

And then without warning, I, Shiloh P. Jacobs, burst into tears—right in front of Adam Carter, landscaper, and two fishing poles, in the middle of Nowhere, Virginia.

Chapter 25

When it rains, it pours like Japan during monsoon season.

I sobbed for three or four minutes without stopping, barely coming up for air when Adam, horrified, thrust me all the napkins in the bag, one by one. I used them up as fast as he gave them.

He paced anxiously, jaw hanging open, running his hand through his hair in absolute disbelief.

"Are you all right?" he asked over and over, until I tuned him out. "What's wrong?"

I didn't answer him. Just kept on crying, making little tear puddles on the wooden picnic table. The last time I'd cried I was seven, so I wasn't very good at it. I mopped my face with soggy napkins.

I saw Adam get out his cell phone and think of who to call then dialed Becky, but nobody answered. Left a muffled message for Faye that I couldn't hear.

I finally hiccupped and tried to talk through my sobs, but nothing intelligible came out.

Adam stood there stupidly then opened my can of Coke and slid it across the table. I took a few swigs. The cold, crisp fizz helped. I caught my breath and mopped my face some more.

"What happened?" he demanded, mutating back to broken-record form again. "Are you all right?"

"Mom," I finally managed, sponging my cheeks and wiping where my mascara had run. I couldn't even imagine what a fright I looked like now.

Adam stared at the pecan pie I clutched and then at me, obviously trying hard to understand. "Did she. . .uh. . .like these or something?"

I nodded and burst into tears again.

"I'm so sorry, Shiloh. I had no idea." He ran his hand through his hair again, looking terrified. "Really. I should have asked you first."

I shook my head no, still bawling.

"I shouldn't have brought you out here." Adam stood there, white-faced. "I just felt sad for you, with your world all turned upside down, and I wanted to give you a break from—"

"No. It's not that." I glanced at the pie again, tearing up. "It's just that Mom. . ."

Adam pressed the Coke into my free hand, and I swallowed. Then took a long breath. Another swallow. Felt my senses coming back to me.

He passed me another napkin, and I turned my head and delicately blew my nose. Crying is awful for a woman's appearance, Southern or otherwise. I drew in a shuddering breath.

He sat down on the bench and waited. "I thought you didn't. . . I mean you and your mom weren't. . ." Raised his hands in desperation.

"Close?" I sponged my nose.

He hesitated.

"It's okay. You can say it," I snapped, wiping my wet cheek. "We weren't."

I knew he'd look up at me in sheer confusion. I was confused, for goodness' sake.

So between sniffles I blurted out a little about the cults, the hungry school days, the nights not knowing when she'd come home. Dad and Tanzania. The boxes she'd sent me in Japan, and the pecan pie I'd pegged up on my corkboard.

"I can't ever forgive her," I said, dabbing at my nose. "Not that she matters to me anyway."

His tone softened. "Well, she obviously does."

"She shouldn't." I tossed down my balled-up napkin.

Adam sat intently, thinking, jaw cupped in his two hands.

"I'm sorry," he repeated.

"Stop apologizing," I snapped. "It's not your fault."

A look I couldn't place passed across his face. "No, I mean I'm sorry for you. I didn't know you'd been through so much."

"I know. And now my life is over."

He shook his head, looking up at me. "You keep saying that, Shiloh. But you're wrong. It's not."

"Of course it is." I rubbed my swollen eyes. "I've lost my job. Lost Mom. Lost everything."

He picked up the pecan pie. "The way I see it, you have a new start."

"What? Here?" I teared up again.

Adam pursed his lips. "Can I ask you something?"

"Sure."

"Did you ever taste the one your mom sent?"

I shook my head.

"I think if you open up to this new life, and all that God's doing in it, you might be surprised."

I sniffled. Adam opened the pie for me and took off the wrapper. Tipped it so it fell out of the little metal pan (which I had to admit was pretty ingenious—almost as clever as the Japanese onigiri rice triangle wrappers). Put it back in my hand.

I blinked wet lashes at him then at it. "Go on," he said. "It's your second chance. Take a bite."

"Isn't it full of. . .you know. . .formaldehyde and stuff?"

Adam sighed and rubbed his forehead in irritation. "You have the weirdest ideas."

"You never know. Have you ever read the ingredient list?" I took a reluctant sniff of the pie. It actually smelled good. Sugary, like vanilla or caramel.

"Have you?" He thrust the wrapper at me. "Last time I checked, flour and sugar weren't anything to report to the Bureau of Public Health."

I took a bite. Chewed. Tasted buttery crust, some kind of crunchy nut, and a wonderfully sweet goo. Took another bite. Funny, it was gourmet, in a trailer-trash sort of way: the salty crust balancing the sweet filling. I liked it even better than the hot dog.

No wonder Mom had sent it to me. It encompassed her life. Simple but sweet, made with ordinary, day-to-day stuff. Flour. Molasses. Pecans that thrive in the warm sun. Nothing fancy. But together it becomes a little poem of contrasts: crisp and soft, dark and light, making something entirely new. And she'd wanted to share it with me.

Adam was beaming. I tried to smile back through my tears, and he opened his Coke and pecan pie and ate with me. Two rednecks sitting on a picnic table strewn with fishing poles and a tackle box, eating snack food from a gas station. If only Kyoko could see me now.

If only Mom could see me now.

"How do you like it?"

He didn't need to ask. He could see it on my face, but I answered anyway.

"I love it." I sniffled, taking another crumbly bite. "I wish. . ."

"Wish what?"

I shuffled my feet and looked down at the wrapper. "I don't know. Maybe that I'd been able to. . .to tell her." Not just about her food but about her life. Her mistakes. Her victories. To call her now and then and hear about her job. To listen. To care. To try again.

Tears streamed down my cheeks again and dripped off my chin, and I dug in my purse for a tissue.

"You are telling her now."

"How?"

"By going forward. Trying new things. Looking at the world she loved and giving it a chance. Giving yourself a chance to make mistakes. And get up again. Like she did."

He lifted his eyes to the oak trees, all golden-shiny and bright in the summer heat, and so did I. Listened to them rush and swish in my ears. Looked through the leaves to the turquoise sparkles of sky, and further, wondering if I could open my heart to God.

I put the pie wrapper in the bag and patted a fishing pole. "We're really going fishing?"

"If you're up to it. You don't have to, you know."

"No, I'm up to it." I finished the last of my pie and picked up my Coke bottle. "Just no live worms."

Adam kept his word. He got out rubber lures, the color of greenish motor oil and sparkly. We sat on the grassy banks of the lake, our lines sinking into the mirror-blue depths with barely a stir. Other fishermen lolled in shady areas, laughing about bait and football and hunting. Far out on the shimmery plane I saw a canoe, floating like a leaf on a puddle.

I watched rings on the water spread wider and wider, disappearing, like the walls of my heart slowly expanding. Adam told me about his older brother, Rick, about the daily rituals of medicines and bandages and physical therapy. About Rick's anger and loss and faith that ebbed and flowed from a wounded heart.

Adam rested his chin in his hand and seemed to drift far away, and I let my mind lose itself among the clouds slipping slowly by, reflected in the upturned water.

We walked down a creaky wooden dock, water lapping at the posts, and I sat and dangled my feet in cool water. Forgot the rest of the world. Wiggled my toes and laughed as tiny, glistening minnows tickled them with curious mouths.

When Adam dropped me off in the late afternoon with a couple of pathetic-looking little fish, I didn't gripe like I'd planned to. I thanked him and took my cold grits bowl and spoon then chucked the fish in the freezer.

I sat in the rope swing and dangled my feet on the grass, not quite ready to bid the summer day good-bye. I watched the mountains turn blue-violet like a Japanese iris. Fireflies sparkled in the dusky twilight under spreading trees, enjoying the reprieve from the hot sun.

The sermon never came. All afternoon I'd braced myself for the big "God Talk" I was sure Adam would give me, and instead we went fishing. I had fun. My heart was full, and I felt clean. Healed.

And I was baffled, just like after eating hamburgers at Becky's.

What is it? What's the secret? What am I missing?

I was still thinking when the offending smell of tobacco smoke invaded my thoughts.

Chapter 26

I swiveled on the swing, half expecting to see Kyoko puffing her Mild Sevens. Instead, at the edge of Mom's property emerged a hefty woman in a housedress, mostly identifiable in the murky twilight by the glowing orange tip of her cigarette. Her white-vinyled house, exactly the same shape as Mom's, stood almost within throwing distance. Next to the largest satellite dish I'd ever seen.

"Hiya." She fumbled in her pockets with embarrassment. "Ya must be Ellen's girl."

It took me a minute to understand her thick accent, compounded by her puffing. I scooted off the swing.

"I'm Stella Farmer. Her next-door neighbor." She held out a ham-like hand and shook mine firmly.

"Shiloh Jacobs. From Japan."

I waved her smoke away as politely as possible, trying to place where I'd seen her before. The funeral. The big-haired woman crying into a handkerchief.

"Shiloh?" laughed Stella. "I fergot Ellen named ya after a battlefield." She shook with laughter and took another puff. "Don't she know the Yankees won that'n?"

Ice slipped into my gaze, and I nearly forgot all my nice manners with Adam.

"That battlefield was actually named after a city in Israel," I replied in clipped tones. "My mom referred to the city."

"I'm shore she did." Stella suddenly grabbed me in a tight hug and kissed my cheek, smelling like cigarettes and hairspray. And then she teared up, lips wobbling. "I'm so sorry about yer mama. She. . ."

I stood there listening to Stella cry then awkwardly put an arm around her shuddering shoulders. Walked her over to the porch steps and sat down.

"I'm so sorry, honey. She was jest such a nice woman. I miss her somethin' awful." She sobbed, rocking back and forth, and I ran inside for some tissues. Fed them into her hands one by one like Adam had done.

Stella mopped her face and blew her nose. "Thank you, sweetie. Yer a doll." She put an arm around me and hugged me tight, which I didn't particularly like with all the perfume and smoke and the stale odor of her housedress, but appreciated nonetheless.

"I know she thought the world a ya, that's for sure."

"Really."

I must have sounded skeptical because Stella raised her wet face. "Oh, lands, Shiloh, I know ev'rything about ya! Ya live in Japan, ya write for newspapers, ya eat sushi, ya got a good-lookin' boyfriend!"

I didn't tell Mom that stuff. She must have read it off my blog.

"Wait, ya'll got engaged, right?"

Stella didn't wait for me to correct her. "Ellen was always out here takin' care a her flowers an' tellin' me about ya. Proud as a June bug, buzzin' around. Showed me your pitchers she printed off the Internet."

The summer air and smells of Stella and evening roses were suddenly intense, and I stood, tears burning my eyes. The sensation was still new; until today, I had almost forgotten what tears were.

Stella fished in her housedress pocket for a lighter and lit up another one. "Sorry, doll baby. It's just real sad, ya know?"

"Yeah." I stared out into the blue depths.

"So you gonna go back to Japan or what?"

I cleared my throat. "I. . .uh. . .think I'll stick around here a little while longer. Mom left the house to me, so I've got to decide. . ."

I didn't need to finish. "If yer gonna sell it or not, an' whatnot. I figger'd. Well, whatcha gonna do 'round here until then? You gonna rent the place out? If ya do, take care who ya pick. Some of them renters ain't worth a lick. They'll tell ya they're havin' problems an' they'll pay ya next month, and the next month goes by, and they skip town. Happened to my cousin loads a times. Tore the place up, too—he had ta redo the whole house. Cost him more than what he'd a paid in rent himself!"

Stella lowered her voice. "Now see that house over there? The Jesters? They're renters." I followed her finger. "They seem like okay people an' all, but they throw parties sometimes. Had to call the po-lice out here on 'em. People like them bring down the property value."

I couldn't help noticing Stella's giant satellite dish over her shoulder and tried to force my attention away. "So is Crawford Manor safe?"

"Safe?" Stella cackled and took another puff. "Ain't nobody does nothin' except set off some firecrackers every now an' then."

"And shoot starlings." I meant it as a joke.

"Oh, well, shore." Stella craned her neck to look at me. "I mean of course, right? That goes without sayin'."

My leg slipped off the porch step in disbelief, and I yelped. Sat there rubbing it angrily and wondering how far I could flee in Mom's Honda before nightfall.

"The folks 'round here are the best." Stella puffed again. "Ya get some jokers, ya know. But most of 'em are good folks. Back behind our houses here we got Earl Sprouse, an' he's jest salt a the earth. Widowed some years back, an' a real nice fella. Call him if yer pipes freeze in the winter."

I'll be a thousand miles away when anything of mine freezes over, Stella Farmer!

"On the other side a yer place ya got Greg an' Lou Campbell. Real good folks. Their girl's in the army, an' they got their grandson livin' with 'em. Seems like a good kid." She tapped her cigarette. "They just got a new Datsun. I think Greg got a raise or somethin'. He works for State Farm."

"He's a farmer?"

Her shoulders shook. "No, city slicker. State Farm's a insurance place. If you need insurance, talk to Greg. He'll set ya up."

I had a hunch Stella could give me the beef on everybody in Crawford Manor. Not a bad thing. Then again, what was she saying about me?

Stella lowered her voice. "But down the street ya got Misty Wilcox. Now she's a piece a work." I whipped my head up. That phrase again! "Boys think she's mighty fine, but let me tell you! That girl oughtta get some sense before she turns out like her mama. Gettin' married to that dumb Wilkes fella! Shewwweee! Makes ya wonder why God made brains."

I smiled up at her in newfound admiration. Stella, in three minutes, had probably just filled up the rest of my "Southern Speak" notebook.

"Do you believe in God?" I asked out of the blue, surprising myself.

Stella puffed a few minutes, averting my eyes. "I reckon so. Elvis sang gospel, ya know? I think that's what makes a person good. Stickin' to their roots."

"Okay."

"I'm a good person and all. Don't get me wrong. Jest don't think I need to go to church. Me and God are close. Real close. That's all I'm sayin'."

Stella seemed edgy and even defensive, so I changed the

subject. "So what do you do?"

"I drive my school bus. Ain't ya seen it over there?" She shook her head, tapping ashes off her cigarette. "Sheeewwwee! Kids shore ain't what they used ta be, but it beats food stamps!"

Stella eyed me, trying to figure me out. "Yer a reporter, ain't ya?"

I toyed with a wooden post on the deck. "I. . .well. . .yes. I was." If I spilled to Stella about what happened, everyone in Crawford Manor would know by morning. Maybe before.

"Goin' back real soon then, ain't ya?"

"Maybe."

"Well, if ya ain't, Staunton's got a paper! Good'n, too. I get it ev'ry mornin'."

My heart picked up. "Really? Can I see a copy?"

"Shore, honey!" She eased herself up off the steps. "Come on over and take a look!"

I wandered over into the dimly lit house, which at first breath I realized wasn't fresh and airy like Mom's. Dusty. Dark. Full of carpet and aged fabrics in browns and greens—sofas, chairs, rugs. I felt suffocated.

Stella turned on an orange hanging light over a dining room table, which gave a creepy Halloween glow to the whole musty room.

But then a crisp newspaper folded next to her ashtray made me tingle. I snatched it up, smelling the clean scent of newsprint ecstatically, and opened it.

Newspapers. Words. Columns. Articles. Reports. Newsprint. They whispered to me like long-lost loves, sending secret messages in black and white. I looked down into the first familiar face I'd seen in days.

"Can I borrow this?" I asked, heart pounding. Staunton was small enough that *The News Leader* might not recognize me if I kept my mouth shut. I could earn a little money, pay off my debts, send myself back to school, and start over in New York.

"Barr-ee it? You ken have it. And here—take some a these."

Stella shoved a glass jar of gumdrops at me. "I certainly don't need any more on these big ol' hips!" She snorted in laughter.

"An' if ya need a job, just lemme know. My brother runs a restaurant up'n town. Real nice place, kinda upscale. I know they always need folks."

I swallowed my gasp. "Thanks, Stella. But don't worry about me. I'll call the paper tomorrow."

"You do that, darlin'. And if you wanna talk to my brother, just gimme a call."

Never in a million years! Instead, I thanked Stella, folded the newspaper under my arm, took my gumdrops, and headed home.

Chapter 27

We're not hiring now." The unsmiling receptionist at the *The News Leader* looked up at me with frosty eyes. She wrinkled her lip as she took my crisp stapled sheets, like I'd handed her a used flypaper.

"It's my résumé," I said tartly, in case she didn't recognize one.

"Um. . .okay." She shoved it under a stack of papers with the tips of her fingers. Then rudely waved me aside. "Sir? Can I help you?"

I put my hands on my hips in disbelief. This is the Staunton what? From where?

I've worked in better places than your fly speck on the map of mediocre, little-known, who-cares rags—a hundred times over! I fumed as the man stepped in front of me.

My heart pounded, ready to give Lee Ann whoever a piece of my mind. But it suddenly dawned on me—with cold realization—that I'd lost my right to fight. What could I say? I was a journalist fired for plagiarism, and now I depended on something new: grace.

I swallowed hard then walked out to the car, pride slipping away with each step. I pulled out of my hard-won parking space and thought murderous thoughts toward the *Leader* while I followed traffic under a train track. Past a giant metal flowerpot. A retro '50s diner. The old county jail, which had been broken up—so Becky told me, dead serious—into a spiffy little apartment subdivision.

Not a skyscraper or neon sign in sight on Greenville Avenue, the main drag—if you could call it that.

I was desperate for money. I needed a job.

The power company waived my late fee when they heard about Mom, and I paid the next installment so they couldn't cut me off. But the phone and Internet company didn't give a hoot about sob stories. They just put me on hold another hour.

Churchville offered no opportunities whatsoever, either for employment or cultural advancement. Long runs through the looped streets of Crawford Manor revealed endless rows of redneck cookie-cutter houses, most of them flanked by jacked-up trucks or discarded beer cans, and the narrow roads eventually disappeared into uninhabited pastureland.

I was, for all practical purposes, marooned.

Now I stared at my *omamori* good-luck charm dangling from my rearview mirror as I pulled up to a red light, fast-food joints blinking on either side.

Come on. . .work! Work! Just a phone call from the New York Times, *or even the Post. Just one measly little. . .*

All I got was the car behind me honking impatiently as the light turned green and a greasy, tattooed redneck leaning out of his mud-covered pickup to grin at me.

I found the mall and dismally parked then wandered aimlessly inside. Everything glowed strangely with natural light, all trimmed with polished tiles and plants. I felt unreal, like I'd dropped into Second Life by accident and suddenly gone virtual. I waved my hand in front of my face to make sure I was still breathing.

No sushi in the food court—if you could call a couple of

dinky, run-down food stalls a food court. No chips for my cell phone. Just tiny, kitschy stores that made me rethink driving to New York overnight. At least there I could panhandle.

But then I spotted a Barnes & Noble complete with Starbucks and counted out my precious change to buy the first espresso I'd had since touching down in Chicago. Surrounded by books, words, and coffee, I felt somewhat comforted.

As I stirred sugar into my espresso at a side table, a girl with a shiny Barnes & Noble tag and even shinier dark hair smiled at me briefly—but sincerely—before sitting nearby with her own cappuccino.

I looked up in surprise. In New York, no one smiled at strangers, and in Japan it was unthinkable. I'd just spent two years in a culture where people desperately avoided eye contact—always looking at the ceiling, the floor, or an advertisement for noodles with profound interest, eyelids blinking nervously.

Wait a second.

I choked on my coffee, wiped my lips with a napkin, and rushed, uninvited, over to her table. "I'm so sorry to interrupt, but are you reading. . .kanji?" I gasped and turned over her Asian-character-covered book.

Her dark eyes smiled back at me. "Not really. I studied Japanese my first semester in college, but I don't remember it anymore." She handed me the book. "Do you?"

"Sure!" I followed the characters with my finger. "'North Star Angels.' It's a new manga comics series. Kyoko loves it."

I flipped through the book, enthralled at seeing those familiar characters and cartoons—then realized I hadn't even introduced myself. "Sorry." I stuck out a hand. "I'm Shiloh Jacobs."

"Jamie Rivera." She gestured to an empty chair. "Want to join me? I've still got twenty more minutes before I go back to work."

It didn't take me long to learn Jamie was Puerto Rican-American and on summer break from college, getting ready to start her senior year. Paying for her college mostly herself, like me, and working to make ends meet.

"Too bad you're not looking for a job," said Jamie finally, stirring her coffee. "One of our guys just quit, and we're a bit short staffed these days."

I wiped the expression of derision off my face. Me? Work in a bookstore? I averted my eyes and flipped through the book some more.

Then thought, with tightening stomach, of the bills on my kitchen table. The way Lee Ann had tossed my résumé aside like bird-cage newspaper. The red needle on Mom's Honda pointing to empty.

Jamie had already changed the subject and was talking about something else.

"Did you say there's an opening?" I heard myself ask, hands nervously gripping my coffee cup.

So at least I hadn't stooped to waiting tables. I could sell books a few weeks—just until I got caught up.

Back home I checked for cell phone service again, but no such luck. My international card had run out, and I didn't have money for fancy electronics anyway. I flipped my old cell phone closed for good.

In Tokyo I'd have gone right out and bought the nicest model, with all the bells and whistles. But those days were gone.

I suppose I could pray, but I wasn't a praying woman. So I didn't exactly. But I thought it. A lot. And hoped maybe God would notice. After all, Jamie said God brought me—that Travis the boss had spent two sleepless weeks wringing his hands over a hole in the staff, and I was God's answer.

I didn't completely believe Jamie, but it made my lonely heart feel warm to imagine a God who had plans for me—a liar and a plagiarizer reduced to shelving books.

So imagine my astonishment when, around six, someone

knocked at my front door. I opened it, soap still dripping from the dish in my hand, and found Adam Carter standing there on my front porch. Holding out a cell phone.

"Becky said you don't have a cell phone that works here," he said, ignoring my bewildered expression. "So you can use mine as long as you need it."

"Me?" I stood there dumbly, so he reached for my one nonsoaped hand and plopped the cell phone in it.

"Go on. I've got another one I can use."

"I can't, Adam. You need it for your business." I tried to hand it back.

"Nah. I can do with my old one. I switched the chips, so I've got all the info I need. It's set up with my payment plan, which has a bunch of free minutes. You won't run out."

"But why? I can live without one, you know."

"You drive around a lot, and Becky and Faye and I just wanted to make sure you're safe. You do have a tendency to run out of gas in weird places, you know." He smirked.

I looked up into Adam's eyes, which I'd once written off as nondescript bluish. They didn't dance with black fire like Carlos's. But they were kind, in a way I'd rarely seen kindness, and I felt protected.

My cheeks burned, half from embarrassment and half from the unexpected feeling of someone—anyone—caring. I didn't deserve it, and I knew it.

I lost any desire to jibe him about not coming inside and instead closed the screen door chastely behind me. I felt the golden evening breeze on my face as I thanked him, and he shrugged it off.

"Barn swallows." Adam glanced up at Mama Bird, who sailed in gracefully.

"You mean target practice?" I turned the phone over in my hands.

He chuckled. "Not barn swallows. They're good birds. You

just have to clean your porch a lot."

"Tell me about it. The real estate agent I'm meeting this week is going to want them gone for sure. I hear he's a real stickler."

"So you're going to tear out the nests?"

"No." Mama Bird gave a yellow-beaked smile, preening politely under one wing. Three fat baby heads poked out. "I just have to figure out some way to hide them."

Adam looked pleased then glanced around the side of the house. "If your agent's a stickler, you'd better water your roses. They look kind of dry."

Out of the corner of my eye I glimpsed Stella in a hideous orange-flowered housedress, stepping out in the yard for a closer look. And trying to hide behind a shrub. She sized Adam up, still smoking.

Adam wasn't kidding about nosy neighbors forming opinions in a hurry.

His truck was still running. "Well, I've got to take care of Rick. Give us a call if you need anything. Congratulations on your job."

He waved politely to Stella, who scuttled behind her satellite dish like a hillbilly hermit crab.

I still had one more important task.

Which is why I found myself on the steps of Titanic Farm & Real Estate house/office decorated with potted plants and cheerful red geraniums.

You. Are. Kidding. Me.

Titanic? The boat that sank? I looked at the simple sign over the door and down at the printed Internet map. The five stars and 162 top-notch reviews, plus six real-estate awards. No mistake about it.

Our deals aren't big—they're titanic! read the slanted font over the name. *Sell your property and make history with Titanic*

Farm & Real Estate today!

Oh my word. I folded the paper. Didn't anybody in Virginia hire marketing professionals?

I rang the doorbell, not sure if I should bring business cards or a Bundt cake to such an establishment. It was weird how many house/businesses there were in Staunton, as if someone had just moved the sofa out of the way and shoved in a desk, secretary, and multiple phone lines. I shielded my eyes in the warm morning sun and waited.

"Well, welcome, Shiloh!" said Lowell Armstrong, pumping my arm like an old friend. "Come on in!"

"No icebergs?" I looped my purse over the chair back.

"Sorry?"

"Never mind."

I sat at the desk while a distracted secretary tap-tap-tapped away at the computer screen and answered phone calls. Lowell brought me a glass of water and tap-tap-tapped on his own computer, nodding and entering information as I talked about the house. A lot of tapping.

It felt odd to list Mom's assets out like so much wampum, wanting to know how many dollars I could squeeze out of it. But this was business. Titanic Farm & Real Estate's business, and unfortunately, mine, too.

"So." Lowell stared at the screen. "Here's your house. I can see it. Wanna take a look?"

He rotated the screen so I could see Mom's roof on Google Earth. And right next to it, Stella's bright yellow school bus.

"Look! I see it!" I pointed to a round, whitish smudge.

"Your mom's house? No, it's here."

"I meant Stella's satellite dish. You can see it from Google Earth." I laughed.

Lowell scrunched his eyebrows then chuckled blandly. "Oh. Well. I suppose so. Now, let's take a look at your mom's house and her land. If I'm not mistaken, the acreage for this particular plot is a little larger than the rest, encompassing. . ."

I slumped back in the chair, feeling like a traitor. Lowell set up an appointment for the following week to come by and see the house before my training shift at Barnes & Noble, and I thanked him and gathered up my purse to leave. I sensed, however vaguely, that I was stabbing Mom in the back.

She left the house to me. She would have wanted me to do what's best.

And I clopped my way uneasily down the wooden deck steps to the car, which was already heating up in the summer sun.

"Faye, you won't believe all the stuff that crazy Realtor wants me to do to the house!" I crabbed, still stewing. "I guessed he'd want the barn swallows out of the eaves, but that's nothing compared to the rest of his list!"

The fat packet he left me still lay on my kitchen table, papers ruffling in the window fan breeze. "Paint the kitchen? Pull up the bedroom carpet? He says a house is impersonal, like a can of tuna, and I have to make everything neutral and erase every trace of my existence! Poof!" I waved my arm like a wand.

"Tuna? Huh. That's odd." Faye pulled a whole chicken out of plastic, naked and pale, and I almost forgot what I was ranting about. She was here to teach me how to cook, since I knew squat about Southern food and most of what they sold in the grocery store, and I was here to complain.

She plopped the cold chicken, still oozing pinkish blood, onto a plate.

"Are you sure it's safe to eat?" I poked the rubbery flesh, momentarily forgetting Lowell. "Doesn't it have bones inside? And. . .contaminants?"

"Well, if ya eat it raw, yes," said Faye, lifting an eyebrow. "Better roll up yer sleeves though. You ain't never cooked nothin' before, sugar?"

"Not from here, no," I replied carefully. Leaned on my elbow, dreaming of the beautiful sushi rolls stuffed with egg and ginger I used to roll in my bamboo mat, slicing carefully in perfect disks. I couldn't even find rice vinegar in Staunton.

"Well, chicken 'n' dumplin's is easy. Yer gonna love it!"

Sweat already beaded under my crisp dress shirt. I washed my hands and opened another window. Wiped my brow. Mom's house sure did suck up the searing July heat, and no air-conditioning. During our Fourth of July cookout, the grass in my backyard was so dry Stella actually caught it on fire. Scorched it right to the ground in an ugly black patch. I forgave her, though, over watermelon, potato salad, and plates of her famous caramel-chocolate-chip cookies, sparklers raining brilliant drops into our sunburned faces.

I just hoped I could find a gigantic potted plant to cover the scorch mark when Lowell came to show the house.

"Now what?" I asked Faye as we salted and peppered the chicken and pulled it off the bones.

"Let's make the dumplin's while the chicken cooks." Faye reached for a rib of celery. "This goes in with the onion for flavor."

"What should I do?"

"Pour some flour in a bowl. About that much. Good." Faye guided my flour-stained hands and got some on her glasses. I sneezed when a puff clouded up, and we laughed together.

"How much should I measure?" I jotted things down in a now flour-spattered notebook, moving aside a bunch of fresh parsley from Faye's herb garden.

"I don't know, sugar. Start with a cup. We'll test its consistency. Now pour the milk on."

What I saw when I mixed up the flour, milk, and salt made me seriously question why I'd agreed to dumplings. They'd go in my "Southern Speak" notebook as pure slime.

I kept my mouth shut and minced parsley. Then pressed and patted little wads of the flour/milk mixture, once it had formed a disgustingly sticky mass, into dumplings. Dusted them with flour. Waited for the chicken to cook and then cool a bit and dumped them into the pot with the chicken. Added some broth from a can. And shoved the whole thing on the stove top in a covered pot to cook.

"Do you really think I have to stage Mom's house?" I complained while we cleaned up the mess and washed the dishes. "I can understand taking down the wallpaper, but I'm not redoing the whole place. People won't buy a house just because I put colored pasta in the cabinets and tie ribbons around the towels."

"Well, sweet pea, if ya wanna to sell it, ya'd prob'ly better do what Lowell recommended. After all, he don't get paid if you don't. He sees a lotta houses. Titanic Real Estate's the best around."

"But look, Faye! This is ridiculous!" I jabbed my finger at the list. "I'm not keeping wine glasses and a cheese wheel on the table. I'm not French, and neither was Mom. Besides, they're saying now wine and cheese don't actually go together so well after all. The wine overpowers it. It's just a quirky affectation from the '60s."

Faye stared at me over her glasses. "Well, sweetie, I don't know nothin' about wine. But I reckon we can do a couple of these things. Whaddaya think?" She looked over the list. "Here. 'Plant flowers in colors that sell.' You can talk to Adam."

I hadn't seen that one yet. "What does he want me to do, arrange them in the shape of McDonald's arches or something?"

"Dunno, sugar. Ask Adam. But this one you can do. 'Organize your cabinets. Turn cup handles facing the same direction.' "

"If you think I'm going to. . .," I grumbled, but Faye got up and opened my cabinet doors. Turned a few cup handles. Pulled the glasses forward. Wiped a spot on one with a dish cloth until it shone.

"See? It don't take much, honey. I'll he'p ya put it in order."

We were still working on the spice rack, which I grudgingly helped dust and organize with labels facing forward, when my nose picked up a delicious, savory aroma. "What's that smell?" I demanded.

"Chicken 'n' dumplin's, honey."

"Really?" I pulled the top off the pot. Took a whiff and staggered back in surprise. The fluffy dumplings reminded me vaguely of. . .*mochi*? pounded Japanese rice?. . .and the chicken sported a nice golden-brown color. Pepper flecks dotted the creamy gravy.

"Mmm-hmm," said Faye nonchalantly. "Lookin' good. Another five more minutes or so."

Excitement rushed in with my hunger. "Do I put it in bowls? Plates?"

"Whatever, doll baby. I usually use a plate."

"What do we have with it?"

"I dunno. Usually collards or some kinda vegetable. Corn on the cob if you got it."

I looked in the fridge. "Baby carrots?"

"Well, maybe if you cook 'em. 'Course, the dumplin's are almost done now. You could use the microwave."

I sliced the baby carrots and nuked them. Set out plates. Poured some lemonade I'd made from a packet. Snapped two pictures with my camera—one with Faye smiling and one with the food.

We sat down, and I waited for Faye. "You want to pray?"

She gave me a funny look. "Why don't you, sugar?"

"Me?" I stared back at her. *Why me?* "What am I supposed to say to God?"

"Whatever ya want."

I started to complain, but Faye had been kind to me. I sighed. "Okay, but it won't be anything spectacular."

"The best prayers ain't."

"Well." I closed my eyes and squirmed uncomfortably in my

chair. "God, I thank You for Faye. And for this food."

I didn't know what else to say. But Faye said to talk to God, so I laced my fingers together and tried hard. "By the way, God, I'm not entirely sure You're there. So please show me if You are. Because I'd kind of like to know. Amen."

Faye had probably never heard a more pagan prayer, but her expression did not change. She smiled at me and lifted her head. "Now, doll, which do ya want first—carrots or dumplin's?" And began to serve me.

Chapter 28

I felt Adam's cell phone buzzing in my pocket and surreptitiously put it up to my ear.

"Shiloh? Ya workin' now?"

"Just clocked in. Where are you?"

"At the mall. Ken I come by a second? I've got some news for ya!" Becky sounded jubilant.

"Sure! We're dead right now." I met eyes with Jamie, who was busy shelving books. She grimaced and nodded.

"Okay. I'm almost there. See ya in a jiffy!"

I put my phone away and walked through the racks and bins of CDs, organizing and shoving them back in their slots. I loved working in the music section. Just walk and straighten and occasionally change the CDs playing across store speakers—which meant I got to choose.

If I could find something other than country music.

In the few weeks I'd worked at Barnes & Noble, I'd started to get in the swing of things. Buy food at the grocery store and cook it. Or if Tim was around, grill it. Discipline myself to keep the house neat as a pin, even if it meant staying up late just to scrub the tub and dust the windowsills.

I even bought boxes of stupid pasta for the cabinets, and Adam told me yellow is the "buying" color, à la McDonald's arches (I'd guessed correctly), the Wal-Mart smiley face, and so on. I bought marigolds from the nursery where Faye worked, and Adam helped me plant them.

But Lowell would not budge on the wallpaper. He said if I didn't get it down and paint the walls off-white, he wouldn't sell my house. Ugly wallpaper would knock thousands off the sale, he griped.

Now I just had to figure out how to (1) strip wallpaper and paint like a pro and (2) do all of it with my busy work schedule. Maybe I could just stop sleeping. Or eating. And send Faye home with all the food herself.

I adjusted my scarf—a pink silk Louis Vuitton—and caught a glimpse of myself in the glass. Crisp button-up shirt, knee-length skirt, knee boots. The normal summer outfit of preppy Japanese girls. If I blinked, I could be back in Tokyo, standing in line for cream puffs at Beard Papa's or shopping for expensive stationery.

But my eyes were too sad for that. Just rows and rows of books and a browsing teenager with a tattooed head.

Just then Becky peeked around a CD display, flushed and happy. "Shah-loh!" She bounced over and hugged me. "I heard ya got phone service again!"

"And Internet. You can thank Barnes & Noble." I hugged her back. "Skype's free, you know." Which meant, thanks to a few days of surviving on crackers and baby carrots to make my first Internet hook-up payment, I could now talk to Kyoko all I wanted.

Becky rolled her eyes. "You and yer fancy computer lingo. Well, anyways, I'm happy for ya. How's yer cookin' with Faye comin'? She's so excited about it, ya know. Tole me y'all made a apple pie last week!" She seemed ready to burst, suppressing a grin with great difficulty.

"And sausage milk gravy." The gravy was actually really tasty—peppery, hearty, flavorful—so long as you didn't look at it, spread there across the golden biscuits like pallid vomit.

"Lands, ya made gravy?"

I dropped my voice. "Did you know Faye keeps bacon grease in a cup on the back of her stove?"

Becky blinked. "Don't everybody?"

My hand slipped on the CD I was straightening. "Uh. . .so what's the big news?"

She whispered something in my ear.

"What? Tim's wearing a hairnet?" That couldn't be true, or good news, but that's what I heard.

"No, silly!" Becky hit me jokingly. "I'm pregnant!"

"What?" I shouted.

Even Jamie dropped the scanning gun and covered a scream. "Oh my goodness! Congratulations!" And she threw her arms around Becky like an old friend.

When I came to my senses, we all jumped up and down and shouted together. People buying books frowned, but I didn't care.

"She's pregnant!" I called out to anyone who would listen, making Becky blush like fire and try to shush me.

"I cain't believe it," she repeated, shining tears pooling in her eyes. "God's so good ta me, Shah-loh! I jest knew He'd make it happen! I knew He'd give me my miracle!"

It certainly seemed like it. The hand holding Becky's purse shook so much I steered her to a table, which a polite high-school boy vacated immediately.

Jamie trailed along, beaming something I couldn't figure out, and suddenly I got it. "You're a Christian, too, aren't you?"

"Sure I am. Since middle school."

"I thought so." I pushed her down next to Becky. "Talk, then, since you can understand each other."

I thought Jamie would be uncomfortable, but instead she clasped Becky's trembling fingers in her own and closed her eyes. "Dear Father," she whispered, "we thank You for this miracle. How You've given life and brought a new child into the world. Most of all, we thank You for Your Son, Jesus, who died to make life with You possible—on earth and in heaven forever."

Becky's happy tears made little circles on the table as she whispered a prayer in reply, and I just stood there dumbfounded—an outsider interloping on something unspeakably sacred.

An instant warmth flowed between them that I couldn't match, no matter how I tried. As if they shared a past, present, and future—and a family, too—even though they'd just met.

Miracle. Life. New. Those words again, fresh and heady like the green glens I'd passed with Adam, listening to Tomorrow fill the summer air. I wanted to swallow those words and make them mine.

I sensed something inside me like Becky must feel—pushing, growing, begging for breath—breaking open the hard walls of the seed and lifting a curling green tendril to the sun.

What is it? I fidgeted with a random book from Jamie's cart, trying to stop the swell of emotion that both frightened and intrigued me at the same time. *Is it You, God, I'm feeling? Is it even possible that You would love me or that I would need You? How can I know? Did You even hear my prayer?*

As if on cue, I looked down at the book in my hands—emblazoned with a silhouette of a man on a cross.

I jerked my fingers off like I'd grabbed a searing Japanese hot pot, and the book dropped with a clatter. Then I hesitantly knelt to pick it up, heart in my throat. And oddly on my knees as if in prayer.

I scrambled to my feet and smoothed my skirt, tossing the

book on the cart like an old banana peel. Where did that come from? My omamori good-luck charm? But my curiosity tickled, relentless, and I turned the book over with the tips of my fingers.

"I was pushed back and about to fall, but the Lord helped me," the glossy jacket quoted from the Bible in clear white script. "I will not die but live, and will proclaim what the Lord has done!"

I pushed the cart away from me with a start.

"Amen!" Jamie beamed, raising her head and releasing Becky's hands.

So let it be done.

I shoved another book on top of the cart and covered it with the scanning gun for good measure. Becky threw her arms around Jamie and then practically knocked me down with her hug. I felt strangely honored to enter her life, her struggles and joys.

We'd only known each other a month or so. *Why is she so kind to me? Why does she care about me, honoring me with her news, grilling hamburgers for me?* I mulled this over as she hovered like a happy moth, wiping her tears while I straightened CDs. And tried to forget the book on the cart as Jamie wheeled it away.

"When's the baby due?"

"Wale, it's July now, so 'round April, I reckon."

"Do you want a boy or a girl?"

"Both! I don't care! Twins! Triplets! Bring it on!"

"Do you have names picked out?"

"Not yet. Ken ya he'p me find a baby-names book? I wanna get started thinkin' right away!"

At last—something I could do for Becky! We pored through book after book, sliding them off the shelves with our heads hunched together.

"What's yer middle name?" Becky hovered in the *P*'s. "Don't it start with a *P*?"

"Pearl," I lied.

"Aw, that's sweet!"

I didn't meet her eyes. "Maybe a hundred years ago."

"Yeah. I reckon so. I had an Aunt Pearl though, an' I loved her."

"How about. . ."—I thumbed through some pages—"Brooklyn?" Wow, a New York name! "Or Bronx?"

"Bronx? That ain't in there!"

I smirked. "No. But Brooklyn is."

Becky wrinkled her nose. "Too city slicker. No offense. But look here." She slid her finger down the list. "Macy. Don't it sound nice?"

"Like the department store?"

"Macy Alyssa." Becky turned a page, not hearing me. "Alyssa with a *y*. I think it's real cute."

"And what if it's a boy?"

"I dunno yet, but he ain't gonna be no Arthur or Fred or nothin'. This baby's gonna have style!"

Given that Becky sported too-big denim overalls, a green plaid shirt, and her hair in a messy ponytail with a frizzy hot-pink elastic band that had (maybe) seen better days, the comment was rather funny.

I closed the book. "Speaking of style, I need to get my hair cut. Want to come with me?"

"I usually go ta Hair Corral. It's fifteen bucks. How 'bout it?"

Any hair salon with the word *corral* in it gave me shivers, like I'd come out of a hay-filled stall with a perm and feathered bangs. "Umm. . .I was thinking of a place in the mall Jamie recommended. Since it's so close to work."

Becky looked up. "Crystal? That place costs fifty bucks or more!"

It probably did, but I wouldn't walk out with a mullet. "I'll pay for you."

"Shucks, Shah-loh! You don't have ta do that!"

"Consider it my prebaby gift." *I'll work overtime. Please, Becky, say yes.*

She beamed. "Okay. It's a deal. When?"

"Friday morning, ten o'clock. Before my shift."

"Got it."

Becky smacked my leg suddenly. "Hey, I heard ya went fishin' with Adam!"

"Me?" My voice came out loud and squeaky. "Why, did he say something about it? Because it wasn't my idea. He just came over and invited me."

"Yeah. He said ya was havin' a rough time adjustin' and all."

He said that? I stiffened. "Yeah? Well, I'm fine. I'm making it."

She studied me a minute, finger holding her place in the book. "Ya know, I'm always prayin' that Adam'll find a real good Christian gal. He wouldn't settle for less than that in a woman. He's a keeper, ya know. He don't take things lightly, 'specially when it comes to faith and God."

"Well, there's always Jamie." Oops. She's taken. Long-time boyfriend.

Becky peeked over the shelves. "Nah. Jamie's real sweet, but I don't think she's his style."

"You don't even know her!"

"I jest have a feelin'."

I looked around for an exit. Got out my cell phone to check the time. "Adam's. . .well, really serious, Becky."

"Yep, I reckon a little too much sometimes. I always tell him to lighten up. But that's jest Adam. He'll figger out a good balance one day." She closed her book. "But he's one in a million. That's fer sure."

Uh-oh. I needed to end this conversation fast, before—

"Is that his cell phone?" she yelped, snatching it out of my hand.

"He's just helping me out!" I put my hands up, panicking at her smug smile. No way I'd hook up with somebody from Staunton, no matter how nice he was.

I shoved the phone back in my pocket and flipped through Becky's name book. "How about Clive?" I suggested. "Or here... Chanticleer?"

And got out of the way before Becky whacked me with it.

I was still thinking about Becky when I pulled open my metal mailbox door. We didn't have cute little mailboxes in Japan—just professional red mail drops. In the South mailboxes were art. Decorated with eagles, flags, paintings, all laced with blooming clematis and lilies. Stella said if her mail-carrier cousin got a dime for every bee sting around those dumb flowers, she'd be a rich woman.

I stopped thinking about Becky, though, when I pulled out a thick plastic package of forwarded mail covered with labels. Probably for Mom. I still got her mail, which weirded me out.

But this bundle boasted a Japanese postage stamp. I tore open the plastic, curious.

Envelopes. Fat envelopes. From. . .American Express. Daimaru.

Uh-oh.

I sifted through them, still frozen to the side of the road. Comme des Garçons. And on. For infinity. Bills and more bills. They kept coming—remorseless white rectangles, staring angrily back at me.

I knew they'd come one day, but I didn't think they'd come so fast. And so many. Did I really spend that much money in Japan?

"You did!" screamed Louis Vuitton. Visa. Taiyo Internet and phone company. Motorola. Costco.

I'm in big trouble. My shaking fingers found two last

envelopes in the mailbox, one with an official-looking font. An apology letter from Dave and a plea to come back? Or a severance check?

Chicago Tribune. I ripped it open.

"Thank you for sending your résumé. We regret to inform you. . ."

I didn't bother to finish. Balled it in a wad. Another silly paper not hiring—or not hiring me.

The last envelope simply contained the water bill. Changed to my name and due in a week.

A car whizzed by, blowing my hair, and I realized I was still standing there, hand on the mailbox lid. Mouth like a round ramen-noodle bowl.

All I could think of was Adam's cell phone in my pocket and two people I needed to call, right now: Tim, and as much as I never, ever wanted to admit it, Stella Farmer.

"Hello, Stella?" I tried to keep my voice from quivering.

"That you, Shiloh?"

"Yes." I slumped at the kitchen table in utter despair, envelopes everywhere. "I. . .uh. . .never thought I'd ask you this, but what restaurant does your brother own?" I choked the words out.

"The Green Tree, downtown. Why? Ya need a job?"

I covered my face with my hands. I hated, hated to answer yes. How on earth could I, Shiloh P. Jacobs, need a job from Stella Farmer's brother?!

"Maybe."

"I thought ya done found somethin'! What about the paper? Didn't ya tell 'em yer a big-shot reporter in Japan?"

I wiped my eyes, which suddenly started to fill. Crying came so much easier since that day with Adam, as if making up for seventeen years without tears.

"They're not hiring now, but they'll. . .um. . .keep my résumé for the future." I stretched the truth. "I sent my résumé to some other papers, too, but. . ." I didn't bother to recount the rejection e-mails—and three rejection letters, four including the *Chicago Tribune*—I'd received since.

"Aw, sugar. I'm sorry. But don't worry! Ya ever done rest'rant work before?"

I stoically wiped my nose with a tissue. "No." Even in my toughest bill-pay days I'd managed to get cushy, air-conditioned office jobs. At my one stint serving coffee and taking jackets at Neiman Marcus, I got a four-hundred-dollar tip from a wealthy (and lecherous) senator.

"Well, that's all right, Shiloh. Jer'll hook ya up. He's a doll. I'll give him a call."

I sniffled. "It's not on. . .you know. . .Greenville Avenue, is it?" I saw myself on roller skates carrying fried-apple pies.

"Naw. In the historic downtown. Kinda near the Wharf."

"Staunton has a river?"

"No, by the clock tower. The part a town near the train station where. . ." Stella belly laughed. "Never mind. They got some nice places there." Her comments should have added points, I suppose, but I was too depressed to reply.

"Ya ever drive a bus before?"

"You mean like a school bus?" I wiped my eyes in shock.

"Sure! You should try it! Ya take some classes and go to lots of boring safety meetings, and jest make sure them blasted kids don't throw lunch boxes, or nowadays laptops. Great day in the mornin', Shiloh! When one a them whops ya—"

"I think I'll stick with something a little more. . .temporary." I felt dizzy, and my pulse picked up a panicky rhythm.

"Well, The Green Tree's great! You'll see. Lemme talk ta Jer." And then, "Hey, ya waterin' them roses? Yer mom sure loved 'em. I been waterin' 'em ev'ry now and then, but we've had some sorta heat wave lately, an'. . ."

Roses? How on earth could I think about roses when collection agents would probably come pounding at my door any minute?

I hung up and plodded out to the deck, staring down at the rose bushes. They did look a little dry, I guess.

I half-heartedly dumped a few buckets of water over the roses, feeling like them. Withering and dwindling, soft blossoms raining petal tears across the hot mulch.

Chapter 29

Good thing Crystal opened early because I needed a good haircut. A haircut that would dazzle my soon-to-be redneck restaurant boss and his hillbilly patrons into big tips. Then as soon as I sold Mom's house and paid my bills, I'd be out of Staunton so fast they wouldn't be able to read my blue-and-white Virginia license plates.

Becky met me outside the empty mall, the parking lot shrouded in early morning quiet. We pushed open the glass doors, footsteps echoing.

"Joo have breakfast?" She narrowed her eyes at me as my nose picked up a whiff of vanilla waffle cones from Big Dipper Ice Cream.

"Does green tea count?" I shrugged. "I had two cups after my run."

She smacked me again. For all the demure manners Southern ladies were supposed to have, they sure made a lot of painful physical contact.

"That ain't breakfast! Don't ya know it's the most important meal a the day? Here." She rummaged in her big (denim) purse and found a granola bar. "Eat. Now."

Never say no to a Southern woman. You'd get smacked again, or argued with, and sooner or later she'd get her way. So I opened it and munched.

"So whatcha gonna do ta yer hair?" Becky asked. The mall smelled of fountain mist.

"A trim, so it's still swingy." I showed her between bites. "Bangs to the side. How about you?"

She shrugged. "The usual."

"Do you have straight-across bangs?" I stopped short and eyed her fluffy bangs for the first time.

"Sure. Since sixth grade. Why?"

I almost choked on my granola bar. "Oh no, Becky! You can't!"

"Cain't? Why ever not?"

"I mean, haven't you ever wanted to try something different?"

She shrugged again. Then again, she did have on that horrible Bean Festival T-shirt and ragged corduroy pants that bagged around her thighs.

"Nah. I cain't never find nothing I like. I figure same ol' me's good enough."

Despite being stunned by the number of negatives Becky just used, I steered her to a curvy, black wire bench under a skylit tree. "Sit," I ordered.

"Why? What'd I do?"

I felt a sudden rush of emotion for the girl who'd taken me in. She practically oozed sweetness. And I wanted to do something back. Besides, it would probably be my last gift for a long, long time. Maybe forever.

"Trust me, Becky. I've got an idea."

She scrunched an eyebrow skeptically. "A perm? I done tried that in middle school. Wasn't nice."

"No, Becky! Forget middle school. You're a grown-up now—twenty-five, right?—and you need to have hair to match."

The eyebrows. "I ain't shavin' it off neither, like them girls do. Shoot, Tim'd kill me if I come home lookin' like I joined the marines! No sirree! I'm havin' hair." She lifted a blond chunk to demonstrate.

"I think if you parted your hair on the side—like this—with some long bangs, and made it nice and swishy, you'll be a knockout." I squinted at her. "You know, you could add some highlights, too. What do you think?"

"I dunno, Shah-loh. My pocket's only so deep."

"So's mine, but we can do this! Tim will love it! I'm sure of it."

At the mention of Tim, her eyes brightened. "Think so? I ain't so shore. He likes me the way I am, and he says he don't want no flashy woman."

"No piece a work. I know. Well, you won't be. Do you trust me?" My excitement swelled.

She squinted at me a long time. "I reckon. But if I come outta there with a Mohawk, I know where you live."

"Deal." I grinned. "Let's see what they can do."

Everything in Crystal gleamed black and silver, stiff and angular and cold. Perfect. A woman with sawed-off auburn hair directed me to a hard, glossy black chair.

"Bet you got you a cute fella back in Japan," said Trixie to my reflection in the mirror as she tilted my head. "With them gorgeous eyes—all green and gold. You must have a mob comin' after ya!"

"Me?" I laughed ruefully, staring back at those eyes and wondering if Carlos missed them. Apparently not enough. "Nah. I got dumped for a blond."

Trixie's head spun around toward Becky. "No kidding!"

"No! Not her. Becky's great. But Mia's eyelashes were just too irresistible, so. . ." I broke off, surprised at the lump forming in my throat.

"Aw, honey, I got some stories that'll stand this hair up

straight," said Trixie, snipping expertly with the scissors.

By the time we'd exchanged sob stories involving lousy men, Trixie's black eyeliner began to run. We looked ridiculous—a bunch of bawling women in front of a mirror.

"Look," I said in low tones, "if you want to do something nice, give Becky a good haircut."

We both looked over at her where she sat, oblivious, reading *Good Housekeeping* and swinging one knee over the other.

"She's scared to try something different. I thought she might look good in something like. . ."—I paged quickly through a magazine—". . .this. See? Feminine and loose, but not sloppy. Natural, but with a bit more edge. What do you think?"

Trixie nodded at Becky. "Some highlights, too. I'll take a look."

"Okay, but make it good, and I mean good. If not, she'll hate me forever. Not too short."

"Mmm-hmm. I got it. Let me finish you up."

She swished my hair over her fingers and snip-snip-snipped. Worked in some fruity-sweet shine serum. Fluffed the ends. Handed me a mirror.

I smiled, impressed. "That's exactly it, Trixie. Exactly. You're amazing. Do you have a business card?"

Trixie's face had brightened, and now it began to shine. I received her card with two hands, Japanese-style, and bowed slightly. Let her untie my silver apron lightly strewn with hair.

"I've got an appointment, but I'll be back in an hour. Will Becky take that long?"

"With highlights, prob'ly."

"Great. And do me a favor—don't let her run away!"

And with that, I bolted out of Crystal before Becky could fry anything with the curling iron.

I got lost up and down the one-way roads in downtown Staunton, went the wrong way, got honked at, banged my steering wheel, and finally parallel parked, mad, beside a fire hydrant.

I checked the address again on a street lined with old brickwork then halted in front of a window clouded with white-clothed tables. Saw my reflection in the glass, complete with sassy haircut, and wavered there, immobile. THE GREEN TREE read the swirly font.

You are in Staunton, Virginia, about to go in a hick restaurant and ask to wait tables.

I was still riveted there when the glass door swung open.

"You Shiloh Jacobs?" asked a redneck-looking man in jeans, tennis shoes, and a neat haircut and mustache. He looked vaguely like Stella minus a lot of pounds and a housedress.

I tried to answer, but words stuck in my dry mouth.

"Well, are ya?"

"Yes, sir," I stammered, feeling like an idiot. *You were a star, Shiloh P. Jacobs! An award-winning writer! You worked for Associated Press, for crying out loud, in a posh apartment building in Tokyo! And here you stand, calling a redneck restaurant owner "sir"?*

He grinned broadly, looking even more like Stella with his jowly cheeks—but somehow higher class. "Well, come on in! We've been waitin' for ya!"

I gulped, squeezed my eyes shut, and followed him through the doorway as if I were taking my last steps. I wished Becky knew where I'd gone in case I turned up missing.

Jerry, who reminded me of a cross between a beardless Bob Seger and Captain Kangaroo, gestured to an empty table, and I sat meekly while he hollered for somebody named Flash back in the kitchen to get me a Coke. (Do I want to know why he's called that? I don't think so!) Then Jerry plopped down on the opposite side of the table and folded his hands.

"So, Shiloh. That your real name?" He grinned, but to my relief he didn't leer. Shook my hand, all friendly like. "I'm Jerry Farmer. Pleased to meet ya."

As the lanky guy missing some teeth brought me a glass goblet of Coke, Jerry gestured to a shy girl at the register. "Say hi to Dawn." She waved.

"Well, Stel says you're a top-notch gal, Shiloh. Let's see what you've got." He skimmed my résumé, massaging his chin with his hand. "Huh." Nodded and stuck out his lip. Turned the page. "Wow. AP? Pretty doggone good! Cornell? Mercy. And. . .uh. . . why do you want to work here again?"

He lowered my résumé, one eyebrow raised.

I cleared my throat. "Well, you see, normally I would work as a reporter, but"—think fast!—"since my mom died, I. . ."

My statement generated the hoped-for sympathy. "Oh yeah, that's right. Stel told me. I'm real sorry to hear it, Shiloh. Losin' a parent can be mighty tough. I lost my dad a few years back, but ol' Mom is still hangin' in there. She's a trouper."

"Well. Good for her." I flexed white fingers.

"You ever done restaurant work before?"

"I served coffee at Neiman Marcus, if that counts." I pointed nervously to the résumé.

Jerry chuckled. "Uh, yeah. I see it. Not exactly the same thing, but okay." He flipped to the second page. "So who else do ya know around here besides Stel?"

What a weird line of questioning! "Not many people, actually," I squirmed. "Faye Clatterbaugh and Becky Donaldson and. . .well, Adam Carter. . ."

His eyes lifted. "You know Adam Carter?"

"Um. . .yes. Sort of. The one who's a landscaper?"

"Yep. I don't know Adam much, but his brother Rick got himself all torn up in the military. Cryin' shame. There's a good family if God ever made one."

"I guess so."

"Ain't no guessin' about it! They's gold. Adam gave up a college scholarship to stay and help his folks take care a Rick."

I sucked in my breath. "He did? Nobody ever told me that."

"Don't get much better'n that. We don't have much landscapin' that needs done around here, but if we did, you better believe I'd call Adam."

Jerry closed my résumé and tapped it on the table pensively. "So what are you doin' in Staunton, Shiloh? I know you've got bigger fish to fry than here."

"Well, I need to sell the house and put it on the market. Pay off some bills. That sort of thing." I licked my lip-glossed lips nervously, still mystified at how Adam seemed to follow me. Did everybody in Augusta County know him? Or did everybody just know everybody?

"Gotcha. Good head on your shoulders, Shiloh." Jerry grinned. "Well, we ain't Neiman Marcus, but I think ya can handle it. You'll just need to come in and train, and you'll be up and runnin' in no time. What's your schedule at the bookstore like?"

"Pitiful. Part-time."

"Write it down." He shoved a piece of paper and pen at me.

Does this mean he's hired me or. . . ?

Jerry disappeared to take a call. I scratched out my measly hours and put down the pen. Waited for Jerry then glanced around, taking in the white Christmas lights glinting off mirrors. Gleaming silverware. A chandelier. Dazzlingly clean and un-country, upscale, with glass and crystal accents. An ugly Hellenistic white statue, the only Greek throwback in the room.

Nice. Not Chez Panisse, but definitely not a dump either.

I picked up a menu and looked over the fare: pumpkin ravioli, sweet potato fries, turkey sandwiches with sliced green apples and Brie. . . . I blinked to see if I was reading correctly. Brie? In Staunton?

Not a single collard green or pig's foot on the whole menu. Why, if I blinked, I wouldn't even be in the South!

"You're gonna love workin' here." Dawn hovered shyly by my shoulder. "It's a great place, and people are just packin' in here these days. Jerry's the best. I've been here about a year now."

"Is the food good?"

"Fresh, modern, and emphasis on vegetarian. That's our slogan. Jerry made it."

I had no idea Staunton sported any tree-hugger types, much less vegetarians. I turned the menu page.

"Ain't all vegetarian," said Dawn, bursting my bubble. "We got meat, too. But you should try the roasted red pepper soup. Outta this world. The guys grill the peppers, skin 'em, then cook 'em with shallots and cream."

"What's a shallot?"

Dawn gave me a funny look, as if amazed a Staunton-ite rather than a Cornell graduate would be able to identify a prissy French vegetable. "Kinda like an onion, but with a lighter flavor."

"Are you a waitress?"

"Not yet. But I guess you and I'll train together."

Train. Waitress. HELP! Before I could throw the menu and flee screaming, Jerry came swinging through the kitchen doors.

"Sorry about that, Shiloh." He slid into the booth and scratched his head. "Business call. So. . .where were we? Training?" He picked up my paper. "Can you come in tomorrow morning?"

"Saturday? Sure." Duty calls, Adam told me once, loading up his truck for Saturday work.

"Good. You'll need a uniform, too. A white shirt like Dawn's. Collared. Make sure the sleeves fit to your wrists, all the way down, and absolutely no spots. We're a clean place, as you can see." He gestured around. "Ever use starch before?"

"Like. . .cornstarch?" I rubbed the side of my fragrant post-Trixie head, trying to understand.

A grin flickered across Jerry's face. "No. As in spray starch. For shirts. Buy a can and spray that shirt good while you iron it. Make sure it's wrinkle free because we don't do wrinkles here either."

My eyes popped. An awful lot of requests for a little hillbilly restaurant, classy as it may look. Jerry must have seen because he leaned back and crossed his hands behind his head. Winked at me. "Relax, Shiloh. It's easy. You'll pick it up in no time."

"I hope so." I clenched and unclenched my shaking fingers. "What else?"

"Black pants and black shoes. Closed-toed in case of spills. Make sure they've got good tread and ain't slippery on the bottoms."

His eyes turned serious. "Our rules. First off, always be here on time. We don't hire waitstaff to keep customers sittin' around suckin' their thumbs and checkin' watches. Got that?"

I gulped. "Yes."

"Rule number two: you're always happy when you arrive at The Green Tree. No matter what might have happened during your day, you leave it at the door. The Green Tree is a fun place. A happy place. We reflect it to our customers. No complaining, grumping, or frowns."

I was seriously having second thoughts. And third and fourth ones.

"Rule number three: the one people like most. You try everything and learn how to describe it to customers. None of this, 'How's the steak?' And, 'I dunno. They say it's perty good.' No. Not here. When people ask, you describe. You paint a picture that makes their mouth water. You say, 'The prime rib is a tender cut, piping hot, well-grilled with black pepper. We serve it with herb butter melting on top. It's delicious.' Now, don't that make you wanna order up?"

As much as I loved food, all of these rules were a little too deep for me. I'd hoped to. . .well, plop food on the table, disappear, and collect big tips.

"You ever been a food writer at any of them papers?"

"No, but it's one of my aspirations." Writing plus food—an ideal combination.

"Well, have at it! I expect great things from you, Shiloh P.

Jacobs! Stel's right about ya. Yer an angel. What's the *P* stand for anyway?"

"Phyllis," I lied. Why did everybody have to ask me?

"Hmm. I had an Aunt Phyllis." Jerry stroked his chin again. "What do you say, then, Shiloh Phyllis Jacobs? Any questions?"

"Pay?"

"Oh, sorry. The most important part! We pay half of minimum wage."

I choked on my Coke. Ice lodged in my throat. I coughed, set down my glass, and Jerry rushed over to pat my back. Dawn stopped punching the register and leaned over the table.

"You okay, Shiloh?"

"I'm fine. Thanks." I tried to smile. Wiped the front of my shirt and the table. "Sorry about that."

"You sure?" Jerry hesitantly sat down, handing me another cloth napkin.

"You get to keep your tips, too," said Dawn, obviously not dotting the lines between my choking fit and Jerry's "half of minimum wage" bit. "No tip sharing. It's a really good deal, you know. Not all restaurants let you do that."

"Just make sure you record 'em for taxes." Jerry eyed me. "You really all right, Shiloh? Ya look a little pale."

I put my glass down, willing myself not to be rude. "How much could I make in one night, Jerry?" Two-fifty? Five bucks? I bet that's not even taxable.

"Aw, shucks, I can't say for sure, but most of the waitstaff make around eighty a night. Maybe a hundred. Who knows."

"Dollars? You're talking dollars?" I leaned forward.

"Well, we ain't payin' ya in pesos. Or yen, or whatever you made in Japan."

At least Jerry knew his international currency. I considered.

"Blake got three hundred bucks for one birthday party," added Dawn the Helpful. "You get the best tips on Friday and Saturday nights."

"Okay, Jerry." I saw dollar signs. "Count me in. But I've got to make money. If I don't, then I'll have to move on. I'm sorry, but I really need it."

"Don't we all," he replied with a friendly smile. "You do your part, Shiloh Phyllis Jacobs, an' don't stand around whining to the kitchen boys, and I'll make sure you get some full nights. Deal?"

We shook hands over the table. And I hurried back to the mall to see if Trixie had turned Becky into one of Kyoko's close-shaved punk chicks.

Chapter 30

When I found Becky sitting nervously in the chair, I almost didn't recognize her. Becky's frizzyish mane had somehow tamed itself into a sleek, shiny blond waterfall, woven with artful highlights as if she'd been out playing on the beach. Trixie cut side-swept bangs and a longish, choppy style that fanned out slightly as it fell over her shoulders. Becky looked polished, pretty, like she'd just stepped out of a magazine.

"Where'd ya go?" Becky accused hotly. "Ya just up an' blazed outta here like Sherman on the way to Atlanta!" She looked mad.

But I was too busy gawking to reply. Clapped my hands over my mouth. "Becky, look at you!" I cried, throwing my arms around Trixie.

"Huh? Do ya really like it?" Tears pooled in Becky's eyes.

I froze. "You're crying? You don't like it?"

"I reckon I do." She laughed and reached for a tissue in her purse, still sniffling. "My hormones are jest a little crazy, ya know, and. . ." She blew her nose. "Wow, I ain't never. . .Tim's gonna like it, don'tcha think? Is it too blond? It is, ain't it?"

"Too blond? No way! He'll love it!" I gasped, drying her eyes with a tissue. "As a matter of fact, wait just a second. . ."

I flipped open my purse and pulled out a smoky gray eyeliner pencil. Dabbed a little at the corners of her eyes and smudged it. Brushed on some blush.

My berry-rose lipstick was too stark for her, so I mixed a little with some lip gloss and daubed it on with a Q-tip.

"Well, look at that," grinned Trixie. "If she don't look like Faith Hill and Shania Twain all rolled into one!"

I had no clue who they were talking about, but it must be good. Becky laughed and cried again, and I frantically dabbed at her eyes to keep her makeup from smearing. "Don't cry!" I ordered. "Think of tomatoes, fire hydrants, anything—but don't cry!"

"Okay." She sucked in her breath. "Far hydrants. Here I go!"

I paid Trixie, trying not to flinch as she riffled through my dollar bills, taking almost all of them, and handing me the change. I handed it back to her as a tip. It hurt, but the gorgeous new Becky was worth every penny.

"Come on," I said, marching Becky out the door. "We've got one more place to go."

She wiped her cheeks. "Where?"

"Here." I steered her into a cheap clothing store. "We're buying you at least one new outfit so you can knock Tim out when he comes home."

We haggled and pinched pennies, managing to buy Becky a cute pink top that added color to her face and a pair of dark, fitted, boot-cut jeans just right for her. The jeans took the most convincing, as she kept worrying about being "too city slicker" and "too modern" and "tryin' ta show off." I finally started paging through my checkbook until she quit complaining and got out her purse.

"Whaddo I wear with 'em?" Her green eyes shined and filled at the same time as we hauled our goods out to the car in the swelling heat. Blue sky from horizon to horizon, not a cloud in sight.

"Do you have any heels?"

"High heels? Shucks, no. I got some flip-flops though."

I thought. "What do they look like? Are they platforms?"

"I don't reckon. They're brown and pretty old. I ken show 'em to ya."

"Uh. . .no. What else?"

"Tennis shoes?" She hopefully showed me the sole of her worn green Nikes.

"No way."

She glared at me. "What are you, the Fashion Nazi?"

"Becky, these are classy jeans," I pleaded. "Understand? You have to dress them up."

She thought hard. "I got some purple jelly flats somewhere. . . ."

"Jellies?" I ran an anxious hand through my hair. "No heels?"

"'Course not! Do I look like some kinda yuppie, heel-wearin', black-dress kinda gal?" She thought hard. "Wait—maybe I do. I wore some silver ones to my cousin's weddin' a long time ago."

"Silver?" I repeated with a sigh. "Silver's. . .no."

"No?"

We were running out of options. "Okay, fine. We'll use them. But you've got to have heels. Classy. Remember?" I dug the shirt out of the bag. "That's solved. Now let's get you ready."

"But ya gotta work, don't ya?"

"At one."

"I ken gitcha back here by then."

Becky was already sweating, about to ruin her beautiful hair. I rushed her into the car, air conditioner turned full blast—me momentarily forgetting about The Green Tree, except for the cheap black pants I'd bought that I wouldn't mind getting covered with mustard and fry oil.

At her house Becky dug through some hideous bridesmaid's dresses and taffeta who-knows-what until, at long last, she unearthed the silver heels. And they were. . .perfect. I turned them in the light, afraid the vision would vanish. "Let's just try them and see."

"Now?"

"Of course now! Tim's coming home early this evening, isn't he?"

"At five."

"Well, you'd better be ready! If these shoes don't work, we'll have to go get some of mine."

My threat did the trick. Becky pulled on the shirt and, reluctantly, the jeans. Gordon watched lazily from behind his chew bone, tail tapping.

"And the shoes," I bossed, and she stepped into them. I fastened the sparkly buckles around her ankles.

We surveyed her in the full-length mirror, and even if the shoes were a bit shiny, they didn't hurt. You could hardly see them under those nice, long denim flares. I unclasped my silver bracelet and put it on her wrist.

And wow, I do declare—our little Becky was a stunner!

"Sheewwweee!" I mimicked Stella. "You look hot! Tim's going to go wild!" I flipped her hair over her shoulders. "What do you think?"

I saw the tears starting and shoved a tissue in her hand. "Fire hydrants!" I shouted. "No crying!"

She laughed and reached into my purse to get the little pack of tissues I'd offered, but to my horror, picked up my notes from The Green Tree by mistake. Jerry's business card fell out.

"The Green Tree?" she read, putting it back in my purse. "Ya went there fer lunch while I was at Crystal?"

I blanched. "No."

I hastily occupied myself zipping my purse, hoping she'd drop the subject.

"I never been to The Green Tree. Hear it's a real nice place. Got some awards 'n' such. Tim 'n' I'd like to go there sometime."

"Ah. No. It's not all that." I waved it away with my hand, imagining—to my horror—Tim and Becky sashaying in while I stood there covered in ketchup. "I'm sure there are better places in town."

I turned her around and straightened her hair in front of the mirror, stepping over snoring Gordon. "Why'd you go there in such an all-fired hurry anyway?" Her eyes looked curiously back at me from her reflection. Then at the bag with my black pants.

Doggone it, Becky, if you'd just. . .

"You got a job, didn't ya?"

I tried to laugh derisively. "Me, waiting tables? Don't be silly!"

"Yes, you, Shiloh Pearl Jacobs! A job! That's why you bought them black pants!"

I couldn't answer. Becky spun around and put her hands on her hips. "And you didn't tell me?" She looked mad again, all blotchy. Those hormones must be working overtime.

My notes were there on the bed, and we could both see them. "Hold the glass by the stem, never by the top."

I ducked my head and lowered my voice to a mumble. "Yes. I got a job, okay? At The Green Tree."

"As what, a table dancer?" she snapped, eyes flashing fire. Gordon's tags jingled, and he jerked his head up.

My eyes popped. "Excuse me?"

"If you're so doggone ashamed to tell me you got a job at a restaurant, that's all I can imagine!"

I whirled around. "Now hold on just a second, Becky! You don't know what it's like to have to scrape for jobs, do you?"

"No? Well then maybe you'd like to know I worked sellin' car batteries at AutoZone when I was in high school, and at Hardee's, too! A lot lower on the daggum totem pole than The cotton-pickin' Green Tree. So are ya embarrassed to be seen with me now?"

My heart froze. Not Becky, the last person on earth I wanted to be fighting with. "Of course not! Don't be ridiculous." I sat down on her bed and knotted my arms. "I'm just not used to. . . that. . .kind of work."

"Well, git used to it! Ain't nothin' wrong with honest work, woman! You ain't gotta put on airs for nobody!" She let out her breath huffily. "You done lived too long in that world a yours tryin' to impress people, haven't ya?"

She didn't wait for an answer. Plopped down on the bed next to me and looked in the mirror. "And that's just what I done today, ain't it?"

"No, Becky," I managed, fixing a strand of her hair. "You made yourself beautiful for the man you love most in the world. I can't think of anything more honorable than that."

She sat there a long while, and then the waterworks started again. She reached for my purse then drew back and wiped her eyes with her fingers. I snatched up my purse and threw it in her lap.

"Get it yourself!" I snapped, trying to make her smile. "You might find my off-duty numbers in there."

She grinned then wobbled into a sob. I wrapped her in a hug, and she cried into my shoulder.

"I'm so sorry, Shah-loh! I shouldn't have said nothing. I don't know what got into me. Will ya please forgive me? I can be so stupid sometimes! An' this ol' mouth a mine. . .forgive me, too, Lord! If You don't fix me, I'm always gonna be sayin' stuff I shouldn't!"

And she bawled some more. I just sat there, chin in my hand.

"You're right about one thing, Becky." I picked at my purse strap. "I've lived in a world where the main goal is to eat or be eaten. Like a river full of piranhas. You always have to be the best, the brightest, the top. It's an obsession. It's in your blood. You just. . .do."

I stared down at my hands, ringless and empty. "I guess that's why I. . .you know. . .racked up so much debt. It's hard to start over."

"I know." Becky sniffled and balled up her tissue. "I pray for you ev'ry day 'cause I know it ain't easy. You done better than most of 'em would, an' I'm real proud of ya."

"Proud of me? For what?" Of all the times in my life to

receive praise, now certainly didn't rank near the top.

"I know waitin' tables ain't your thing, and Staunton ain't your kinda place neither. But ya stayed." Becky's voice started to choke up again. "I didn't know if you would, with so much hard stuff in your life, but ya did. You got guts, Yankee! And I'm proud to know ya."

I looked up, embarrassed. "Did you say you pray for me every day?"

"Sure I do. Look." She pulled a notebook off her shelf and flipped through it. "Back here, last week. I prayed for you to smile. An' ya look happier lately."

"What day?" I demanded, laughing. "I don't believe it."

"Thursdee."

"See? Nothing happened on Thursday. Just. . ." I chuckled. "Oh yeah. That's the day Kyoko got her *omiyage*."

"Her what?"

"A present. Souvenir. I sent her pork rinds."

"Pork rinds?" Becky scrunched up her face. "What for? At least send somethin' she ain't never seen before!"

This time I laughed so much my sides hurt. If Becky could have heard Kyoko's words over the phone, she'd be praying for her, too.

"What is this?" It was my turn to snoop. I reached for the notebook, but Becky had squirrel-like reflexes.

"And here." She flipped another page and pulled it away when I grabbed again. "I prayed for ya to make friends, and the same day you called an' tole me about Jamie and your new job." She followed something with her finger. "I prayed for yer meetin' with the Realtor to go good. Yesterday I prayed for somebody to do somethin' nice for ya. Don't know if it happened or not."

Instantly I remembered the basket of garden vegetables Earl, my plumber neighbor, left on my front porch after he mowed my grass. I didn't know what to do with a bunch of zucchinis and string beans, me being the supreme non-Southern cook, but the thought warmed me.

"Does a gift on my front porch count?" I asked, feeling hair stand up on my neck, like when I found that book in my hands at Barnes & Noble. The one with the cross. Right after I prayed.

No way. I rubbed my forehead, glancing uncomfortably at the notebook. Don't be silly!

"'Course it counts! Then that'n's answered!" Becky was beaming now, all tears gone.

"Are you serious?"

"Shore! Whaddaya think I do, make these things up?"

"No, but. . .isn't that luck? Omens?" I remembered the omamori charm hanging from my rearview mirror. I had to admit it had been pretty useless the day some idiot dinged my parked fender, but it still mattered, right?

"Luck? Ain't no such thing as luck, woman!"

"Of course there is." I folded my arms, feeling chilly. "How else does all this stuff happen? And don't say—"

"God." Becky's eyes met mine soberly. I gazed back at her sudden intensity, startled, then abruptly started folding up the shopping bags.

"I don't believe He answers prayers like that."

"Well, ya oughtta. 'Cause He does."

"Did you pray for me to get a job today or something?"

She flipped the notebook page and read. "Nope."

"Well, what did you pray then? Let me see." I held out my hand for the notebook. She didn't give it.

"For you to know He's with ya."

Which is sort of what I prayed with Faye.

"Well. I'm. . .well." I sat there tongue-tied. I hoped it wasn't like voodoo. What if Becky prayed for me to get fat or marry a hillbilly or start growing a mullet?

"Does He answer everything you pray?" I got up and shoved a hanger in the closet.

"At least you recognize He answers prayer." Becky flicked

an eyebrow. "And no, He don't give me ev'rything I want. Don't ya think I'd have a houseful a kids by now? And a bigger house? Mercy, an' all kinds a stuff!"

"Then I don't get it." I untangled some more hangers, feeling grumpy. "Either God answers prayers or He doesn't. Which is it?"

"'Course He does! But His plans and His timin' ain't always ours."

I turned to face her. "You're telling me God has plans for me? For my life? Here in the middle of nowhere, working at restaurants and shelving books?" My cheeks reddened with anger.

"I'm sayin' exactly that, Shiloh Pearl Jacobs! But sometimes you gotta wait to see His answers."

Her words hung there, over the littered hangers and discarded tennis shoes. I twisted the metal neck of a hanger back and forth, thinking.

"How about Mom? Faye said she believed in God, but He let her die of an aneurysm in her own backyard. How's that for an answer?"

The room fell silent as a Japanese subway car, nobody speaking above a whisper. I heard Gordon snore and roll over, crinkling a fallen bag.

"You don't have any idea what God might a been doin' in her life," said Becky, face turning blotchy as tears swelled in her eyes. "We ain't the judge."

"Well, I wouldn't have answered her that way."

"You ain't God! An' how are you to know what she prayed for?"

"Not this," I retorted, gesturing out the window at country pines.

"All's I know is that God loves ya, my friend." Becky spoke strong and clear over her tears. "An' He loved your mama, too, more than life itself. I'm leavin' it in His hands. I trust Him."

"Yeah. I said that about Carlos, too." I turned back to the closet, but Becky snatched my hanger.

"God ain't Carlos." Her eyes flashed. "He loves ya, Shah-loh!

Don't ya get it? What Carlos did ain't love."

I didn't reply. Just rummaged in the closet, my eyes starting to water.

"Shucks, I done prayed for ya to come to church a bunch a times so you'll hear how much He loves ya." She whapped me facetiously with the notebook. "But He ain't answered that'n yet."

"Hmmph." I shut the closet door. "Keep praying. But I make no guarantees."

"Believe me, I will. And there are some other things I might show ya one day when they come true."

"Like what?"

"Hmmph yerself! Reckon you'll jest hafta wait."

"Well, maybe I'll just pray some things about you. What do you think about that?"

Becky stuck her chin out. "Go right ahead! I ain't scared."

"I'll start by praying for you to name your little boy Arthur." I tickled her belly.

"How do you know it's a boy? And he definitely ain't gonna be no Arthur, although you can pray all ya want! Lord knows He'd like to hear ya talk to Him ev'ry now and then!"

Chapter 31

"You memorize the orders for each person, never 'auctioning' food," Jerry was saying. I'd stumbled through two weeks of training, and my exhausted brain could barely cram in more information, much less scribble more notes. My writing sagged as I yawned, bleary-eyed.

"None a this, 'Who ordered the tuna salit?' and looking around for somebody to grab it. This ain't a warehouse!" Jerry shook his finger. "This is The Green Tree! You remember what people order because it's important. You're friendly but not chatty. You serve, smile, and disappear. You refill glasses before they ask. You watch but do not loom."

Dawn rubbed her eyes, and I reached down to massage my aching feet with my free hand. I wondered if I'd ever snubbed a waitress. Or a bookseller. They sure worked a lot harder than I realized. Reporters, on the other hand, got to spend much of their time in comfortable office chairs.

My head crowded with plates. Salad dressings. The grills where the cooks sweated, yelling orders. Flash's grin, missing a tooth. The dishwashing area clouded with hot steam and smelling of sanitizer. The frosty freezer room opening with a big metal door.

When Jerry finally spit us out with a friendly good night, I could barely keep my car on the long, winding country roads and stumble into Mom's house. I threw myself on the living room carpet in sheer exhaustion, peeling off my shoes and sliding my sore feet into comfortable Japanese house slippers.

I tried to rid my head of whirling images of plates, wine-glasses, and shiny metal kitchen counters. The odor of frozen cheesecake and pungent black olives. The soda machine's hissing roar. Clinking of glasses and ice.

My humiliation as I practiced taking orders then delivered the wrong glass of soda. The shiny blond customer with too-cute Dolce & Gabanna sunglasses, probably younger than me, turned up her nose and shot me a hateful look. I wanted to ring her scrawny, California-wannabe neck.

And all of this back-to-back with Barnes & Noble shifts, changing clothes just to go to work again. I fell asleep this morning at the break-room table.

I flipped wearily through the CDs in Mom's tower, neatly stacked in the corner, to see if I recognized any of her tunes. Nope, nope, and nope. Christian artists, probably, judging from their names. I twisted my head to read more. The Beatles, toward the bottom, and the Statler Brothers.

And there near the top: Tomorrow. Really? I snatched it up in surprise, turning the artsy cover over in my hands.

I slipped it into the CD player and rested my exhausted head on the floor, listening as edgy guitar chords and voices swelled and filled the room, drifting through my cluttered mind. Pulling me back to that peaceful afternoon in Adam's truck where all that mattered was God and eternity, life and light and faith.

It seemed so long ago now in the clatter of real estate agents and bills and jobs. It was August already. Back in Japan, August sizzled with festivals: fireworks, *taiko* drums, steaming food stalls selling shaved ice and hot *yakisoba* noodles. I'd put on a pretty cotton *yukata* robe, sash around the middle, hair pulled up.

Instead I modeled wrinkled, soda-stained pants.

"God, what on earth am I doing here?" I whispered, running a hand through my sticky hair. I couldn't even pour the first glass without spilling, and Jerry laughed at me. "I'm so lost. Where are You?"

Even Mama Bird, swooping into the eaves in the deepening dusk, had a home. So did her fat babies, who bulged out of the tiny nest. Ready to fly away to bigger and better places.

And I could not.

No answer. Just silver chords of the guitar and a voice lifted over the lush notes: "We are hard pressed on every side, but not crushed; perplexed, but not in despair. . ."

Wait. Crushed? Perplexed?

Didn't Christians live on a cloud with their pie-in-the-sky-by-and-by nonsense?

". . .persecuted, but not abandoned; struck down, but not destroyed."

The words wrapped me like a blanket. I thought of Mom and her heartache, our dark memories, and yet the music kept singing, weaving, unafraid—as if one did not cancel the other out.

No toy in every Happy Meal, like Becky said. Her unanswered prayers. But still her smile, her faith. Her miracle child.

Pain and beauty, strangely coexisting.

As if God, in His infinite power, could handle both without crumbling. The thought had never occurred to me.

I rubbed my forehead with a grimy hand, mystified by the smiles I'd seen gleaming from Mom's pictures before I stowed them in boxes. Laughter. Hugs. Hands holding crooked arms. Peace softening the lines in her face.

What was your secret, Mom? I slid a photo album from the shelf and reluctantly squeaked it open. *All this time I've been playing hide-and-seek with what it was. And, perhaps, even with you.*

I traced the lines of her cheek with my finger as she laughed with a group of friends in this living room, a bouquet of snow-white roses on the table. Bad Polaroids of a boy with twisted hands grinning up at her. An African-American girl in a wheelchair, unseeing, Mom's arm around her shoulder. Hiking. Gardening in gloves and trying to shoo away whoever was taking the blurry photo. Snapshots of her roses, looking neon-red in the sunlight, and dewy shots of pink and white buds.

A card fell out, tucked in the back of the album. *Thank you for the beautiful roses for our wedding,* read the handwriting. *You blessed us with such beauty, and we'll always remember your gift. God bless you.*

A snapshot inside the card showed a radiant bride clutching a ribboned bouquet of white, arm around my smiling mother.

I sat back, chin in hand. I'd imagined Mom sometimes over our years of frozen hurt and anger, but these happy faces didn't match. Giving hugs. Giving flowers. A completely different woman than I knew before. . .and I started to wonder if I'd ever really known her at all.

The house was quiet like after a snowfall, hushed, wrapped in cotton. I closed the photo album and walked down the hall to her room, which I always avoided. Switched on the light and just stood there, taking in all the details Lowell and I tried so hard to sponge away: framed paintings of roses, Bible verses, an antique trunk covered with a colorful gypsy-patterned cloth.

I ran my fingers over her brush and hair clips on the dresser, left just as if she'd put them down a moment ago. Touched my little elementary-school picture she'd tucked in the corner of her mirror. Her tube of lipstick. My favorite amethyst drop earrings in a dish.

I took the top off her golden-yellow globe of Avon perfume and smelled summer evenings in New York, elegant purse tucked under her elbow as she led me off the subway to a modern art gallery or weird museum. . .those amethyst earrings glinting. I could recall a few pleasant days.

A Bible verse on a card: "For we are God's workmanship,

created in Christ Jesus to do good works, which God prepared in advance for us to do."

I covered it with my palm, wondering over the words, which pricked me with surprising emotion.

And there, a little framed photo of Mom as a high-school graduate. Even in black and white, I could see her hazel eyes, multicolored like mine—the only thing about her that looked like me. And held just as much promise and sorrow.

I could scarcely breathe, so thick were the images and scents of the past as I slid open her dresser drawer, staring down at the neat boxes of hair pins and earrings. Her slim gold watch still gleamed in its box, tick-tick-ticking as if waiting for Mom to slip it on.

"For we are God's workmanship. . ."

For an instant I felt like an intruder, a stranger, invading Mom's private spaces after years of absence. But I had to. Pain welled up, but it was good pain, like the sting of removing a splinter. She would have wanted me here, sifting through her colorful tangle of necklaces like all our memories, intertwined forever.

A covered velvet box hid in the corner. I pulled the top off, curious, and couldn't believe what I saw: Mom's gold wedding band and engagement ring.

I hadn't seen them since New York as a little girl, after Dad left. Sure, she'd worn them a year or two longer, in vain hope, but they eventually disappeared. I assumed she'd pawned them or thrown them away, but no, they hibernated here, outliving even her. They still gleamed so bright I could see my reflection—and at the same time looked unspeakably lonely, cordoned off and lifeless all these years.

I took them out and held them, cold, in the palm of my hand until they drew warmth from my skin. Closed my fingers over them and then opened them again, watching the gold and diamonds gleam and sparkle as they were made to do for a lover.

It ached to see them, and I couldn't explain why.

And then suddenly, as my eyes hovered over my empty left ring finger, I understood. Dad. Carlos. Good-byes. Mom felt that ripping in her chest, just as I had.

She knew how it felt to reach out for love, to feel her heart leap up at the sound of a name, the warmth of a hand in hers. To ride the subway through the city and know that out there, somewhere, across those millions of hearts, one beat only for her.

And then, in one horrible moment, to have it snatched away forever, like a blanket on a bitterly cold night. Promises broken, words severing in an instant what had taken years to build. Separation. Divorce. Arguments. Eviction. Alone.

No wonder she seemed to die not in Virginia but years ago, succumbing to the illness and depression that tormented her. Black and lonely nights. Reaching out for anyone and everyone who offered hope, no matter how shoddy or half-baked.

"For we are God's workmanship. . ."

I squeezed the rings in my hands as tight as my eyes, remembering how I'd thrown Carlos's ring in the mail within a week. Mom had kept hers for nearly twenty years, throughout all her moves and houses, and stored them close to her heart.

Perhaps Dad meant more to her than I ever realized.

I slipped the rings on my finger for safekeeping and sat down on her bed. Smoothed her blankets and bedspread. Wondered, for the first time, if she'd missed Dad like I missed Carlos. If she'd missed me, too, as she slept there, knowing she'd lost me just as surely as she'd lost Dad.

The weight was too heavy. I placed the rings back in their box and silenced their memories with a pop of the velvet lid.

I was just sliding the drawer closed when my fingers touched something hard and beaded, tucked loosely under a silk handkerchief. I thought there could be no secret more overwhelming than Mom's rings, but when I brushed aside the silk to find a beautiful little book, I couldn't resist.

The cover sparkled with tiny Indian mirrors, beads, and embroidery. Colorful and exotic—just Mom's style. In fact, I'd seen lots of these books years ago in New York. . .in Mom's eccentric collection of "mind help" stash, along with the Raelian pamphlets and self-hypnosis mumbo jumbo.

It dawned on me slowly at first then like a grim wave. A book of wisdom from some Indian guru, or Hindu life forces, or whatever. Another church. Another wisdom. Another sham.

Next time Faye says something about her "new life" with God I'll. . .

I opened the cover and, to my astonishment, found no elephant goddess or guide to karma. It wasn't a book at all. It was a journal—blank-paged, marked with a pale-blue silk ribbon—like the ones we sold at Barnes & Noble. Filled, from beginning to nearly the end, with Mom's familiar blue ink handwriting.

Oh, Mom's journals. I remembered those.

I flopped down on the bed, recalling her notebooks stuffed under chairs, shoved in wads, scratched on napkins—usually when Mom went off her medication. She'd rant about her problems with Dad, wanting to die, and waiting for her "celestial family" to take her from our cold and evil earth. I threw them in the trash and tried to sponge those words from my mind.

I recognized Mom's script all right—swirly, loopy letters as if running away from her. Fields of blue words planted in row after row, as far as my thumb turned the pages.

The cover sparkled like the rings, and I wavered. Maybe it was better to let sleeping dogs lie and just leave the past in the past. And as I closed the journal, several dried and pressed roses, nearly transparent in their fragile beauty, sifted into my lap.

I cupped them in my hand. Roses? In Mom's journal? I would have expected astral fortune cards, not roses.

My brow furrowed as I flipped through the pages, finding several more paper-thin specimens, all cream and pink with age but still lovely.

And then—the word *Shiloh* caught my eye.

I just sent Shiloh another package. She might not receive it, but at least I've done what I could. I know I messed up. I'll never be the mom—or wife, for that matter—I always dreamed of. But all I can change is today. Live differently now. Smile now. Pray now. Working in my garden and in my classroom strengthens me, invigorates me—and promises me something better. A better life. Yes, that's it! A better life with God. I see His glorious creation, without explanation and reason (no scientist can create a zucchini or a child!), and I'm invited into it. I water and trim and fertilize, and fat blooms smile back. Red tomatoes fall round into my hands. A blind girl learns Braille. Adyn writes his name.

But it's my roses that speak to me at home when I'm alone with my thoughts. Why? Because they carry thorns. Reminders of this fallen world, our sin—my sin—and how it hurts. How thorns pierced Jesus' forehead and nails pierced His flesh for me. When I was still His enemy. And yet when the blooms come, they carry scents of heaven.

A perfect picture of our sin and God's mercy. Beauty and pain, all woven together—just like my life. Oh, what an amazing work God has done in this cold little heart of mine!

My jaw fell open. Mom? Mom wrote THIS? It's not possible! She wasn't lucid enough! Wasn't. . .I don't know, but it couldn't be her!

That's why the Bible says, "We have this treasure in jars of clay to show that this all-surpassing power is from God and not from us. We are hard pressed on every side, but not crushed; perplexed, but not in despair; persecuted, but not abandoned; struck down, but not destroyed." That is me, and I will never be the same!

Beauty and pain side by side, just as I had considered in the living room. Right in front of me, in Mom's frilly letters.

"I was pushed back and about to fall, but the LORD helped me." I pressed my eyes closed, remembering the book in Barnes & Noble with startling accuracy. "I will not die but live, and will proclaim what the LORD has done."

"For we are God's workmanship. . ."

Astounded, I paged through the journal, staring at the lines of blue and hardly believing my eyes. I knew this writing. Those loopy l's and a's. But had Mom—my unstable, ranting, suicidal mother—actually penned these lines?

Her words called like a clear stream, whispering, enchanting. I couldn't stop reading.

> *I see the work of God again as I prune and trim my roses, getting ready for the big frost that will put them all to sleep for the winter. And yet today, on an Indian summer morning reprieve from the cold, I found they had burst into bloom again! Without warning, just a chorus of fresh, bursting pink and white flowers as if a wedding party paraded through my garden.*
>
> *One last flourish, ill-timed but unspeakably beautiful in its quiet fanfare. In fact, more beautiful than all the summers put together because around it, life has bled. Dwindled. Slipped into the silence of autumn and fallen leaves. It is here, where life seems most drab, that these shining pink voices call the loudest.*
>
> *My life again, in flora. When I should double over in despair from my past, never to rise again, suddenly I shout! Dazzle! And come to life!*
>
> *This is my moment. One last flourish. Not for me anymore, thank the Lord. But for Him. I see it now! Even the coldest fall can no longer silence my voice. Come, fall!*

Come, winter! I am not afraid. I will keep on singing until my last petal falls.

The pages blurred. If I was a betting woman, I would have given all my money (if I had any) to prove these words imposters. Just like Mom.

Impossible! She couldn't have written this! I pressed my palm to my forehead, turning pages in disbelief.

Mom studied religious philosophies and cults from all over the world, giving all her money and her mind to follow the weirdest beliefs ever invented. But nothing, nothing had ever caused her to speak such beauty—from her heart, a heart so glorious and confident it moved me.

I ran my finger over her words again: "One last flourish." Did Mom know she was going to die?

I no longer cared about The Green Tree or Lowell or Barnes & Noble. I had to know. Now.

With shaking fingers I switched off the bedroom light and plopped down in the warm lamplight of the living room, journal in hand.

★ ★ ★

When I awoke, Mom's journal had fallen in my lap. My face pressed against the side of the armchair, leaving deep marks across my cheek. Yet none of it mattered. I had crossed over into another world, right there in the living room.

Mom. I couldn't shake the beauty and poetry echoing from her words into my very marrow. She whispered, she cried, she missed, she reached out. She had spoken to God in tender joy, like a relationship. . .a romance even. . .and He to her.

For a moment I felt like an outsider again, standing by the table while Jamie and Becky prayed, watching something unspeakably precious unfold.

Instead of the old complaints, I found faith and thanksgiving.

Instead of anger, I found peace. And instead of bitterness and hate, I found—to my utter astonishment—forgiveness.

Not perfect forgiveness, but real. Aching. And still stepping forward, one foot at a time.

If I dared to make such a statement, it was as if Mom had come to life.

She prayed for strength. Prayed for courage. Prayed for me. For Shiloh P. Jacobs, who wouldn't even take her phone calls.

My hands trembled on the pages as I saw my name written in her distinctive lettering, spotted with wrinkled tear marks. I followed them with my finger, line after line, and then abruptly stopped: "And that's why I planted my white Kobe roses, named after a city in Japan that rebuilt itself after the earthquake."

I knew the Kobe earthquake, for crying out loud! I had written about it! The Great Hanshin earthquake in 1995 that destroyed one of the biggest cities in Japan—in the world, even. How on earth did Mom know? Had she read my articles?

Like me. I lost everything, too. But it was that loss, perhaps, which made me rebuild stronger this time. I will never be the same. Like Kobe, my foundations have been dug deeper now. My buildings strengthened from within. I am a new city built on the ruins of the old. Always remembering, but looking to the future.

"For we are God's workmanship, created in Christ Jesus to do good works. . . ." Works prepared for me from the foundation of the world.

And every time I see those clouds of white in my rose garden, I'm reminded of who I am. And Whose I am. And Whose I'll be until the day I die. . .and then for eternity. "God's door" indeed! "I am the door," says Christ. "If anyone enters by Me, he will be saved." My destruction is what brought me to the Door that leads to life, true life, with Him. Only He is a foundation worth building on.

I wanted to scream! Mom knew the kanji characters for "Kobe" meant "God's door"?

Mom had written about Japan—my Japan—in such tender color and poetry it put me to shame. All my award-winning articles suddenly seemed like they'd been written by one of those wind-up monkey toys banging cymbals.

"I will not die," she wrote, "but live, and proclaim what the Lord has done!"

I couldn't read another word. Felt sick, stifling. I closed the book and pressed it to my heart. Slipped to my knees and let my tears soak the flowered upholstery of Mom's armchair.

When the sky turned the pale blue color of the silk ribbon in Mom's journal, I found my feet on the smooth kitchen linoleum then on the cool, rough wood of the deck.

I had to see Mom's roses. Touch them.

And I tripped down the last two steps in horror.

Chapter 32

They hung ruined, scorched. Dried, brown, lifeless, the leaves withered and tattered. Carmine petals scattered the flower bed. Only a few green leaves survived the mayhem, looking out of place in the faded canes. The white ones, if I remembered correctly (I couldn't tell for sure because the petals had all dropped) looked like they'd been struck by lightning.

"What have I done?" I cried, rushing inside and fumbling for a watering can. I doused the roses in a sparkling shower then raced back for another. And another. When I'd finished, I stood there dumbly and surveyed the mess.

It was my fault. Adam told me to water her roses. So did Lowell, for crying out loud. I hid my face in my hands.

Dawn suspended a pearly, diaphanous mist over the morning. Calm, without a car stirring. The sun still sat below the horizon, and dewy grass sparkled in gray tufts. A night chill hung in the air.

"Noooo!" I moaned, getting on my hands and knees and studying the dried rosebushes, wishing I could do something—anything—to help. Like. . .mouth-to-mouth resuscitation? I felt more foolish by the minute.

Finally, squatting on my heels in despair, I remembered. I rushed into the house, stumbling over my tennis shoes, and grabbed my cell phone. Called Adam, not realizing it was six in the morning.

"Hello?"

"I think I killed them," I said, tears streaming down my face and choking my throat. "They're all dead—every last one of them!"

A long pause. "Shiloh?"

"Yeah. Sorry." I drew my sleeve across my eyes. "Mom's roses. They're all dried up."

I heard some muffled noise in the background. Another pause. "Did you. . .um. . .water them?"

"Some." I tramped through the mulch and knelt by a formerly pale yellow bush that now stood limp and shriveled. "It rained the other day, too, so I thought. . ."

"A drizzle, or a good, hard rain?"

"I don't know. Maybe. . .in between. I don't know." My voice choked up again.

More noise on the line. "Can you wait thirty minutes?"

"Thirty minutes?" I repeated, uncomprehending.

"Just give me time to get there, okay? I'll take a look."

"Really?" I sniffled, not believing what I heard. "You'll come here? Now?"

"I'm on my way out the door."

Not again. Not after the gas can, after. . . I smacked my forehead in frustration. "Adam, I'm so sorry. I'm an idiot. I just. . ."

"Don't say stuff like that, Shiloh." He sounded annoyed. "You should know better."

I gulped, not sure which astonished me more: his scolding or his offer to come.

"Sorry. I take it back. But I woke you up, didn't I?" For some reason that made tears come again. Everything I did was wrong.

"No, you didn't. I get up early."

I scrubbed my toes miserably in the mulch. "Should I water them some more?"

"How much did you already give them?"

"A couple of buckets."

"That's enough. Don't do anything else. Too much water and you'll shock their root systems or drown them."

"Should I put. . .fertilizer or anything?"

"No, just wait. I already put fertilizer plugs last time I came. Just wait until I see the extent of the damage, and then we'll see if anything can be done."

I hung up and wiped my face. The words "extent of the damage" rang in my head like one of those awful songs you can't get rid of.

Damage, broken, ruin. I've just killed Mom's roses.

I looked down and saw pajamas, so I rushed inside and threw on the first thing I found. Pulled my straggly hair into a ponytail and washed my tear-stained face. I was still crouching by the flower bed when a crunch of gravel made me look up.

"Had breakfast yet?" Adam slammed the truck door shut. Dropped a packet in my hands, paper-wrapped and steamy warm.

"Breakfast?" My eyes glazed over, uncomprehending.

"Breakfast. Food." He looked ready for work in a baseball cap and work boots. "Remember what that is?"

He was speaking another language. All I could think of was Mom's poor, crumpled roses in the dry flower bed and those beautiful lines in her journal. We stood there as he surveyed the damage. Then he knelt and checked the leaves. Touched the soil at the base of the canes. Gave a low whistle.

My eyes spilled over, and I left him there, letting the screen door slam behind me. No way I'd stand there in front of a man and cry. And for Adam, this would make the second time.

Adam looked up at me when I came down the steps, still squatting by my ruined roses.

"It's pretty bad," he said finally, gently twisting some leaves in his fingers. They fell like powder, disintegrating.

"Then that's it." I tried to suck back my tears. "I've done it. I've destroyed her rose garden."

"Not necessarily."

"What do you mean not necessarily?" I snapped. "They're gone! They're dead! There's nothing we can do, right?"

"I can't make promises," said Adam, scratching his head. "Not in this condition. But there's a good chance the roots are still alive."

"Like that's going to make any difference." I kicked a piece of mulch.

"Of course it does! It makes all the difference in the world."

I raised my head.

"The roots are like the heart, Shiloh. If they're alive, there's still hope for the plant. It can grow again. It can produce leaves. It can live. It can bloom."

I couldn't look at him. The perfumed morning hung between us, and I scarcely dared to breathe. "Even if there are no leaves left?"

"Even if there are no leaves left."

The force of his words echoed in my soul. He was no longer talking just about Mom's plants but about me. My life. My heart.

"You mean. . .there's hope?" My pulse quickened. "They can come back?"

"Maybe. Like I said, I can't promise anything."

I bit my lip, trying to keep my pulse from surging. "But what if they're really, really dead?"

Adam rested his hand on his knee. "Well, Shiloh, there's where God comes in. He's the only One who can raise the dead. That's beyond watering. That's in the realm of miracles."

"God can. . .raise the dead?" Strange, but it seemed exactly what He had done to Mom. Brought her dead and broken spirit into extraordinary life and beauty. Caused her to burst into bloom. There wasn't much I wouldn't believe anymore.

"Sure He can. Nothing is impossible with God. He's already

raised His own Son back to life for us, and I can't think of anything more impossible to fix than death. Can you?"

I touched a broken rose twig, shriveled like an autumn leaf. "No."

"Then pray. No promises, but let's do what we can and ask God to spare these poor, dried-up roots. Some of them, at least, look. . .well, somewhat salvageable. It's pretty bad, Shiloh, but believe it or not, I've seen worse."

"Worse than this?"

"Look." He touched the red rosebush, which still clung to a few normal-looking leaves. "See this green? It's getting water from somewhere. It's not healthy, but it's trying. Somewhere down there it has a lifeline. The heart is still pumping." He lifted blue eyes to mine, and something in my heart stirred as if waking from sleep.

It's trying. The heart is still pumping. If it's still alive, then there's hope. It can live again. It can bloom again. Fragile jars of clay, but still holding treasure. Struck down, but not destroyed.

Choose life, that you may live!

I buried my face in my hands. "What about these white ones? They're all brown. And they're the most important ones of all. I can't. . .explain why right now, but they are."

Adam patted the soil below the thorny canes tenderly, as if tucking them in for the night. "Then we have to take care of its heart. Coax it not to give up. Give it what it needs, and see if miracles happen. Does your mom have a hose?"

We split up, and I found it against the back side of the house, wound in a neat coil. Adam dragged it around to the flower bed. Went to the back of the truck and got out something silver.

"What's that?"

"A sprinkler. To keep the waterings even throughout the day." He hooked it up to the hose, and out sifted a soft little shifting spray that turned, turned, turned with sibilant sounds. I watched the fine mist gently bead the dried leaves and brown branches like healing tears of repentance.

"So what do I need to do?" I crouched next to him as he adjusted the sprinkler.

"Well. For starters, you need to remember to water your roses," he said sternly, tugging on his cap in irritation. "Maybe we can save them this time, Shiloh, but I can't promise next time. Miracles happen, but I don't run my business asking for them every time I forget to do my job. You need to water them every day, just like I told you. Morning and evening, without fail, even if it rains."

"So the sprinkler doesn't do it for me?"

"No way. The sprinkler serves as a backup, not the real watering. I can't tell you how many desperate phone calls I get from people and companies telling me their roses dried out. Roses need water, lots of water. It's that simple. You can't count on someone else to do the job for you. That's what I tell all my clients."

Adam, still miffed, sat down on the deck steps as the sun began to rise, leaving a place for me to sit.

"People who won't invest the time shouldn't buy roses or dahlias or varieties that require a lot of care. They need crown vetch or a cactus or something you can just throw in the garden and forget about. But they won't have bouquets of roses in the spring. You can't have it all. You have to choose what you want in life and go after it."

I hugged my knees on the deck steps, thinking of Becky's prayer journal. So much like Mom's, lined day after day.

"What do you want in life?" I heard myself say.

"Me?" Those bluish eyes met mine then lost me somewhere over the trees. "God. To know Him better and honor Him with my life. To. . ." He stopped. "Basically that."

I wanted to ask him what he almost said but didn't, but thankfully kept my mouth shut. Instead I breathed in fresh dawn as orange clouds turned gold. Up in the dome of blue sky a group of birds flew together, almost too small to see.

Adam turned to me there on the deck, thick sandy hair poking out from under his baseball cap. "And you, Shiloh? I think that's a fair question. What do you want in life?"

My eyes watered as I remembered Mom's journal and all my spiraling thoughts since I'd come to Staunton. My proddings and searchings. My emptiness, and my old dreams of glory.

"I don't really know," I replied, looking down at my hands. "I wish I did. At one time I would have said to write more or win more awards or. . .something like that. But I really don't know now." I rested my chin on my knees pensively. "But when I figure it out, I'm going after it with all my heart. That much I know."

Adam nodded. "I believe you." He nudged me with his elbow, hands tucked in his pockets. "You can start by eating breakfast."

I remembered the thing in my hand. I opened it and found a sausage biscuit with cheese. Adam got his biscuit, which had grown cold on the car seat, a thermos of coffee, and an extra mug from the truck as the sprinkler whish, whished beside us.

We sat there on the porch steps and munched, listening as a blue jay shook the leaves and shouted his familiar cry: "Thief! Thief!" from Stella's silver maple tree. Sunlight climbed across the land in a brilliant burst. The grass sparked blue and red fire.

"People don't shoot blue jays, do they?" I bit into my biscuit.

"Huh? No." Adam's paper crinkled.

"Good."

"I mean, not usually."

The spicy sausage and cheese opened a well in my stomach and I ate hungrily, feeling light and strange and almost delirious. Lack of sleep and deep thinking had turned me inside out. I folded the biscuit paper into neat, tiny little triangles like the Japanese did.

"Did you need all that stuff to fix the roses?" I blurted in midsip of steaming coffee, seeing the back of Adam's truck for the first time. The bed spilled over with big bags of mulch and soil, potted trees, and all kinds of garden tools, everything tied down with rope.

"No. It's for work today."

"You still work on Saturdays?"

"Sure. I'm doing part of a new subdivision in Fishersville."

"Where's Fishersville?"

"A few miles outside of Staunton. And I'd better go before I'm late." He drained his coffee. "They want me there by eight thirty."

"Oh." I felt silly for calling him all the way over here. No amount of apologizing could remedy the situation, so I just thanked him instead. Felt like a heel.

He stood up and took my little biscuit-paper triangle and tossed it in his bag. "You fold all your trash into geometric shapes?"

"A Japanese thing." I stuffed my hands in my pockets. "I'll fold a bird for you next time."

I tried hastily to finish the too-hot coffee, but Adam waved it back. "Keep the mug. Give it to me next time I see you." He stood up and got out his keys. "Hope your roses make it, Shiloh. Just remember what I told you."

"Lots of water. I know. I'll do it. I mean it this time."

"Good because you might not get a next time." His face was serious. "If you keep letting them dry out, you'll damage their root systems for good, and there's no fixing it. God's creation can only take so much trauma without long-term effects."

"Believe me, I know," I said, thinking back over my life. Tears stung my eyes again. "I just didn't. . ."

"Didn't what?"

"I didn't know Mom's roses meant so much to her." I pawed the gravel with my sandal.

Adam's face softened. "Does that matter to you?"

"It does now."

"Good." He seemed pleased. "I'm proud of you, Shiloh."

Proud of me? Was he praising me or patronizing me?

"And as for the trauma and long-term effects, well, remember how we talked about miracles. God can raise the dead. Don't be afraid." His eyes met mine one last time, blue across blue morning.

Chapter 33

Water spilled across my dirty fingers in the Barnes & Noble bathroom sink, bright and sparkling. Sprinkler-like. My thoughts leafing like my roses, bright and thick with green. I couldn't stop pondering this strange and powerful Jesus. Speaking in parables, in riddles. Tongue-lashing hypocrisy. Turning over tables. Touching the leper.

His startling words leaped from the Bible pages as I read through them, chapter after chapter. I blinked back yawns in too-late lamplight, unable to put the Bible down.

I was still thinking of how Mom and Jesus both cared for the blind, when, in the mirror, I saw Jamie emerge from a stall, eyes red from crying.

"Jamie?" I turned in shock, hands still dripping.

"Hi. Sorry." She wiped her eyes and tried to laugh.

Normally Jamie's angelic smile glowed a permanent fixture, but today she looked like a fallen angel, crumpled and sad.

"Are you okay?" What a dumb question! Of course she wasn't okay. I modified. "What's wrong?"

"Nothing really. Nothing that won't solve itself in a year or two."

I waited for her to elaborate. "Money problems," she finally said, turning on the faucet and dabbing her eyes with a tissue. "I know it's silly, but I just didn't expect to wait out my last year of college again."

I raised my eyebrows. Twenty-two definitely wasn't late for finishing college.

"Why do you need to wait another year?" I asked delicately. "And why do you think it's late?"

"Well, I started college early—at seventeen. I expected to finish early. But now I'm stuck again. My parents don't have a lot of money, and right after I graduated from high school Daddy got laid off from his job. So we couldn't afford college for two years."

"No scholarships?"

"Some, but not a free ride. I did some volunteer work and went to a cheaper community college then transferred credits little by little."

I'd known drunk football players at Cornell who'd gotten "free rides" and partied their time away. And hard-working Jamie Rivera went to community colleges because her family couldn't afford tuition.

It smacked of unfairness. I scrunched my paper towel harshly.

"But I'm fine with waiting. I saved enough to complete my senior year last year and planned to start again this fall. But they canceled my biggest scholarship."

"Why?"

"No idea. Lack of funding or something. I talked to the dean and he said cancellations happen, and I should try to apply for more financial aid. I've already done that, and I've taken out the maximum student loans I can. So." She shrugged and wiped her face. "There's nothing else I can do. If God wants me to start next year, I'll start next year."

I turned away and folded my paper towel into a tiny rectangle, Japanese-style. "That's a bit fatalistic, don't you think?"

"What do you mean?"

"You know—things just turn out the way they're going to because of God. That there's no such thing as our actions or coincidence or just plain injustice."

Jamie's hands paused on the faucet. "Yes and no. We do face consequences for our actions. But coincidence? No. Things happen because God ordains them."

Somehow Jamie's word *ordain* sounded holier than mine, although we meant the same thing.

"The Bible says not even a sparrow falls to the ground apart from God's will. So whatever He plans, happens. I can trust Him with my life. If I don't go back to college this fall, He must have a reason and a purpose."

There it was again—God, not good-luck charms, or even pure fate—behind the events of our lives.

I stared at Jamie in amazement. This was what set Christians apart from non-Christians: their unfaltering trust and optimism, like the people singing in the rain at that little country church. If something turned out badly, God had still ordained it—and for their good. In all my years I'd never entertained notions like Jamie's. Life, as I told Kyoko, sometimes just stank. Period. And I rose above it with my own skills and know-how.

What was I saying? I was in a Staunton mall bathroom. I'd bombed, not succeeded. My mental-illness mom had actually found more peace in her life than I had.

"So no fatalism." Jamie tossed her tissue and washed her hands. "I trust God no matter what. He's never let me down."

"But isn't this letting you down? You were crying."

She looked surprised. "Would you give your little child anything she asked for?"

"Jamie, sorry, but you're not a little child. You're a twenty-two-year-old woman. The analogy doesn't fit. It's always bugged me about. . .you know. . .Christianity."

"We're all children in some respects," she replied without changing her expression. "We don't always know what's good for us. If I'd gotten everything I'd asked for, I'd have a mansion and nasty Bobby Stimpson from sixth grade as a husband."

My thoughts flashed briefly to Becky and her dream of a house full of kids. "What's the problem with getting what we want? Why is it so wrong?"

"It's not wrong. Sometimes God does give us what we want. But. . ." She pursed her lips in thought. "Sometimes we need to grow, Shiloh. We need to be stretched, and it's not pleasant. It's painful. We change through suffering."

"Sure we do. We become bitter and twisted old hags who hate life."

She briefly beamed a smile. "Maybe. Or maybe we become more compassionate or gentler toward others. We learn from our mistakes and become better people. And maybe, just maybe, we reach out for God."

"So it's back to Him again." I unfolded my paper-towel-rectangle and wiped my hands some more, even though they didn't need it. "I don't need suffering to change me, Jamie. I just need a couple thousand bucks, and all my problems will be over." Okay, more than a couple thousand. A couple ten thousands.

Jamie's dark eyes glinted back at me in the mirror. "You really think money will solve everything?"

"Sure I do."

"Well, it certainly hasn't solved anything in Hollywood. Do you read the tabloids, Shiloh? Cheating? Adultery? Embezzling money? Shoplifting? Because when you're missing God, nothing fills the hole." She gestured around us. "God made everything—every molecule, every breath. We're made to give Him glory, not stuff ourselves full of things of no importance."

" 'For we are God's workmanship, created in His image. . . .' " My lips formed the words in a whisper.

"Exactly," Jamie's soft voice echoed against the cold tiles. "The word *workmanship* also translates as *poem* in the Greek. We are God's poem."

Words stuck in my throat. I dried my hands some more, not meeting her eyes.

"He gives us a choice of blessing and cursing," added Jamie, "and urges us to choose life. To choose Him. Because only He brings real satisfaction."

The hairs stood up on the back of my neck. "What did you say?"

"What? About Hollywood?"

"No, the part about choosing life. Choosing God. How He wants us. . ."

"To live for Him, even with all our problems and hurts. And we're not satisfied until we do."

Persecuted, but not abandoned. Struck down, but not destroyed. For we are His workmanship. . .

Those verses were following me, stalking me, even into the Barnes & Noble bathroom. Pursuing me. I looked behind me for a split second, half-expecting to see someone standing there.

"You really think He doesn't solve everything for us on purpose?" I finally asked, beautiful words from Mom's journal swelling up painfully. "That He knows we're suffering and allows this horrible stuff for our good?"

"I really do." Jamie looked at me just a little bit stubbornly. "And I wish you did, too."

Everybody in this town, it seemed, wanted to evangelize me. Except Lowell. He just wanted to evangelize buyers with my perfectly staged house.

"Well, I still don't like the child imagery. We're the child, He's the father. The immature and the mature. The unwise and the wise. I think it's insulting." I threw my paper towel in the trash and checked my watch. "Besides, I have to go to work again."

"Shiloh, don't you long for a father? The way a father is supposed to be?"

Her question hung in the air like a breath of summer breeze penetrating the stale Barnes & Noble bathroom walls.

"Me?" I stalled for time to come up with a better answer than the one that rose, like an ache, to the surface.

"A father who loves you infinitely, who adores you no matter what you do, who would rather die than live without you?"

Suddenly I couldn't see. The mirror and Jamie smeared together like weird stained glass.

"There's no father like that," I whispered hoarsely. "If he existed, I'd do anything to be with him."

"Well, He does. And He's waiting for you to see it."

Our voices had fallen to near whispers. If anyone pushed open the door now, they'd break the sacred calm settling over us, just like in Adam's truck. I prayed they wouldn't. That they'd leave me alone with this moment, this hope that Jamie just wouldn't let fizzle out.

"My dad isn't like that."

"God isn't your dad."

"God gave me my dad, who doesn't care if I live or die."

"God wants to show you how different He is from your dad. And He's arranged everything in your life to bring you to where you are now—so you can find Him. Every bit of love, mercy, or anything good you have in your life is from Him. His gift. Because He loves you."

I thought suddenly, wildly, of Becky and Tim and their smiles, their faith. . .of steadfast Faye. . .of Mom's prayers for me in her journal. Those blue-penned words speaking hope, life, and victory. Rebuilding on the ruins. Her smiling photos with a face so peaceful it almost didn't look like her.

"Come, fall! Come, winter! I am not afraid. I will keep on singing until my last petal falls."

"What if I don't believe it?"

"Tell Him you want to."

"God can raise the dead," Adam said as he stood over Mom's roses.

And then without a word, I turned on my heel and fled.

Chapter 34

I could hardly hear my own thoughts over the din of the kitchen. Banging pots, short-order cooks calling orders, the hiss of fry oil. Jerry shouting left and right, and waitresses frantically dodging each other with loaded trays. The crash of silverware and roar of the sink as two cleaners struggled to wash and sanitize the growing mound of dishes. Busboys kept scurrying, dumping more loads.

My mouth hung open. Not one inch of my overloaded brain could have prepared itself for the chaos I found upon entering The Green Tree for my first work night.

"The Harlem Globetrotters!" Jerry shouted. Wearing a suit and tie. "Brace yourself, Shiloh, because tonight's gonna be big!"

"What?" I shouted back over the noise, terrified. "The Harlem Globetrotters are in Staunton?"

"Made a reservation for thirty-seven people just this morning!"

I felt like I did in my recurring dream of being chased by a herd of black-eyed peas. "Please tell me you're joking!"

I pressed my hand to my forehead, trying to block out the noise. Jamie's words. My stomach heaved. "Why does everything have to happen at the same time? I need to go home, Jerry."

"Nonsense!" He flashed a gleeful smile and tossed my apron at me. "Live a little, Shiloh! This is what it's all about! Keepin' up with what life throws at ya!" He tapped me affectionately with his notebook. "It's insane!"

Insane indeed! Jerry was insane.

I felt like one of those Black Cat firecrackers the neighborhood kids popped after dark (probably bought in South Carolina, where Stella told me they sold every kind of explosive known to man).

"I'll introduce you to the staff better another time, but for tonight, you're on! And thank goodness for that—you couldn't have come at a better night!"

I gaped at him, open-mouthed. "You're serious."

"Didn't you say you wanted to make money?"

"This isn't what I had in mind!"

"Aw, quit whinin' and get to work! It'll be a blast! The Harlem Globetrotters—in my restaurant!"

I slowly dumped the apron over my head. "Where are you going to put them all?"

"They'd be sittin' on each other's laps if I tried ta stuff 'em down here! I opened the overflow space on the second floor and spent the day puttin' tables up there. Got some extra cooks and dishwashers and a couple of busboys, but still short on waitstaff. But. . .this is as good as I can do, Shiloh! We're sizzlin'! Ain't it fun?"

"Fun?" I tied my apron and glared.

"A little bit a mayhem ain't gonna kill ya, Shiloh! It'll make ya stronger!"

Jerry was starting to sound like a mustached Jamie. I scowled.

"The Harlem Globetrotters, Shiloh! You're gonna be servin' some of the most famous people in the world!" Jerry hit me again with the notepad as if to knock some sense into me, still grinning. "You can git their autographs! Just do your job and you'll have the best night of your life."

"I seriously doubt that."

My fingers shook as I hung up my purse. I'd held interviews with Japanese heads of state without a nervous butterfly, and suddenly a bunch of hungry Staunton-ites and traveling basketball players scared me out of my wits?

"Start with these tables out here." Jerry rushed me to the kitchen door and handed me my tray. Pushed me into the main room. "Good luck, kiddo!"

A couple scanning a menu looked up expectantly. Quiet music tinkled overhead, and an older couple gestured to their water glasses. I took a halting step forward then ducked back into the kitchen.

"Git on out there!" scolded Jerry over his shoulder. "Tonight ain't no night to get nervous and freeze up. Now go on! Git!"

"I'm not freezing up, Jerry!" I argued back. "I need a water pitcher. And I just had an idea."

"What idea? Make it fast."

"You need more waitstaff. Can I call a friend who might want to fill in?"

"You can call the Pope! And if he showed up, I'd put him to work."

"You're serious? Even without proper training?"

"As a heart attack! Anybody can pour a glass of water! Now make your call and git back out there in sixty seconds or. . ."

"Or what? You're going to fire me?"

"Not tonight," said Jerry facetiously. "But don't tempt me."

I fumbled for my cell phone in my purse, tray under my arm, and hastily dialed.

Chapter 35

Silence. Pure, beautiful silence.

I opened my eyes weakly, and I tried to remember why I felt like watery grits, exhausted and poured out. Why my hair reeked of fry oil and my arm was sticky with. . .ketchup? I sniffed. Dried and caked like blood.

Ugh. Not a nice premonition.

As if the shi in my name didn't sound enough like death. Danger. Mishaps.

My eyes focused on the delicate Japanese fan ruffling across one pale blue wall I now called mine. Sunshine. And a pile of reeking restaurant clothes scattered across the carpet.

No Barnes & Noble. No Green Tree. Just beautiful, blessed quiet.

I rolled over with a yawn. Didn't even lift my head to look at the time.

Last night I stumbled into bed around three in the morning, waving good-bye to a bleary-eyed and soiled Jamie Rivera—both of us with aching feet and covered with coffee and roasted red pepper soup. We'd served hundreds (or so it seemed)—and they just kept coming, no matter how fast we scurried. We even rang people up with the credit card machine and booked reservations for the following week.

Reading specials and memorizing orders and running for heavy, steaming plates, over and over, all endless night long. Dawn the Helpful burst in, called in on emergency, and eased our load by commandeering a busboy and ordering him to stay with us. Our trio kept the entire restaurant in order—seating people, taking orders, serving plates, refilling glasses.

Only after nine o'clock we realized we were alone—the hostess didn't show, Jerry never reappeared, and all the other waitstaff stayed upstairs serving the Harlem Globetrotters, who'd slipped up the back way.

At ten Jerry closed the restaurant and ushered us upstairs to gawk at the famous-of-all-famous basketball players. They looked ten feet tall—giants in the little room—surrounded by agents and coaches and personal members of their own press.

Press? I ached to see their press releases—proofread them and correct the misspellings and dangling participles. To whip out a notebook, ask friendly questions, and then bang out a story on my laptop before you could say "Kareem Abdul-Jabbar." And then listen to my boss pour on the praise.

Instead I meekly extended my hand and let them shake it heartily in their huge ones. I meant nothing to them. A waitress. A hick. A nobody. Not a soul in the room would guess, in my frazzled ponytail and stained apron, that I once worked for the Associated Press in Shiodome, Tokyo. That I accepted one of the highest journalism awards this side of the Pulitzer, auditorium hushed as I rose to my feet.

"Well done," Jerry had said as we filed out, clapping me affectionately on the shoulder. "Shiloh, you're an angel. You'll share tips with everyone else, ya hear? We're splittin' it up fair and square tonight. You guys were gold." He always said that. "And Jamie?"

"Yes, sir?" Under the exhaustion she looked nervous, like showing up at the wedding of someone she didn't know.

"Sir nothing. You were fantastic. You want a job?"

And that's how Jamie joined The Green Tree staff. I guess so, after Jerry took us into the hallway and counted out a staggering five hundred dollars—in real dollars—right into our hands. EACH of us. Told us the Globetrotters were generous men.

Jamie and I staggered, dream-like, into the black and empty Staunton streets. I stayed awake on the long drive home by listening to right-wing talk radio host Michael Dewberry, a new guy, who advocated a return to militias and spent an inordinate amount of time talking about guns and deer hunting.

And here I lay, comatose. With. . .the phone ringing?

I groaned. No way on earth I'd swing my legs over the bed and plod out to the kitchen just to answer the phone. Please. All I needed was more sleep. I pressed the pillow to my ears and buried my face.

Pause. More ringing.

Please, please, go away! I threw something at the door, trying to close it.

And then—the buzz of my cell phone vibrating from my Green Tree pants pocket. I grunted angrily then reached over and clumsily dug it out.

I flipped open my phone with a scowl. "Becky?"

"Rise and shine, sleepyhead!" she chirped, forcing my closed eyes open. "Yer goin' outta town today!"

"Out of town?" I repeated incredulously, fumbling for my alarm clock. "What time is it anyway?"

"Seven thirty. Time for ya to be up, Yankee!"

"Seven thirty? Are you crazy?" I hollered, scrunching the pillow around my head. "The Harlem Globetrotters ate at our restaurant, and I just got home!"

"Shore, an' I'm Bob Hope!"

"No, Becky! I'm serious!"

I heard her giggling and covering the phone. "Shah-loh thinks I'm gonna believe the Harlem Globetrotters was at The

Green Tree last night," she guffawed to Tim.

I glared, grumpy enough to give a lecture on the verb "to be." I was, they were. Is it really that hard?

"So, can we come pick ya up now? Are ya decent?"

"Decent? What are you talking about? Where are we going?"

"To reenact the Civil War."

This conversation made no sense. "The war ended over two hundred years ago, and we're not bringing it back."

"A little over a hunnert 'n' thirty," Tim corrected me in the background. "Check yer hist'ry books! If they ain't made in Jersey, that is!"

"You've got me on speakerphone?"

"Okay, we'll pick ya up in 'bout half an hour. See ya."

I don't know if I was more astonished at Becky's "invitation," which I still hadn't accepted, or how we managed to have parallel conversations among three different people. Maybe I was still asleep. I closed my eyes and opened them. Nope. No such luck.

I groaned and rolled out of bed. Stared at my haggard reflection in the mirror. Crawled in the shower and scrubbed Coke and marinara sauce off myself then dried my hair and put on fresh clothes, feeling slightly better in clean jeans and a green print top. Clear kelly green made everything better.

Then, per my promise to Adam, I lugged the water bucket down into the flower bed.

I ate some cereal, puffy eyed, then heard Becky knock cheerily on my front door. Jerked it open and promptly spilled orange juice all over myself.

"What ON EARTH?!" I shrieked.

Instead of Becky, there stood a bearded Confederate soldier—as authentic as I'd ever seen—pointing his very sharp and very real bayonet right at me. His unsmiling eyes bulged large and angry, matching his gray battle uniform, and every single button and badge shone. His boots—real period boots—gleamed, and I jumped back as another Confederate peered up at me through the bushes, clutching his saber. I didn't know whether to freeze or flee.

The sound of laughter shook me. I looked up and saw, through my haze, Becky doubled over with laughter. She finally straightened up and slugged the soldier with the bayonet in the arm.

"Tim?" I managed.

He dropped the pose and guffawed, putting the sheath back on the bayonet and leaning it up against the porch pillar. "Shucks, Shah-loh! I didn't think ya'd fall fer it!"

"What on earth are you doing?" I burst out angrily, wiping orange juice off the front of my shirt. "It's not Halloween!"

My breathing gradually slowed down as I saw Tim's face underneath his Rebel-flag hat. He'd grown his beard out and everything.

Tim and Becky only laughed harder. The soldier in the bushes with a CSA belt buckle (Confederate States of America?) stood up and slapped his knee. "Good one, Donaldson! That's the ticket!"

"Who are you?" I demanded, not quite believing the charade was really fake. They looked so authentic. The Rebel in the bushes even had bright yellow chevron stripes on his shoulders and a real leather saber case.

"Randy Loomis." He had penetrating green eyes and a goofy sort of smile. Rusty-colored hair hung over his collar. "Tim's cousin." He doffed his cap and bowed then held out his hand for mine.

"Hmph." I offered it reluctantly then snatched it away when he tried to kiss it. "Hope you didn't ruin my marigolds. They have to sell this house, you know."

I let them into the living room and went to change (ironically) into a New York Mets T-shirt then stomped moodily back out with a baseball cap in my hand. "This better be good."

"It will be." Becky put her arm around Tim the Confederate. "Tim's a reenactor."

"I'll give him something to reenact," I muttered.

"Aw, now, Shah-loh, don't be crabby. You'll love it." Becky patted my arm. "Tim an' his dad have been doin' reenactments for years. His dad's a brigadier general. You'll see him there."

"Where's there?"

"Winchester."

"Where's Winchester?"

"A short piece up 81," said Randy. "We just gotta pick up that Carter fella first."

I turned to Becky for translation—hilarious as that sounds—who fortunately had kept her sweet blond hair nicely styled. She wore lip gloss, too. The closest thing she'd come to lipstick. My "Chapstick-doesn't-count-but-is-better-than-nothing" speech must have gotten her attention.

"About two hours'r so north on the interstate. Perty drive and ev'rythang, an' you ken see some new places." She peered at me worriedly. "You really okay? Ya look kinda like tha livin' dead."

Death. *Shi.* Four of us in the car.

"Firing real cannons doesn't sound safe, Becky."

Randy's green eyes lit on me, glowing like overeager embers. "I'll take care of ya." He inched closer, breath prickling my hair. "If yer scared, 'cause there's a lotta smoke an' all, I'll. . ."

"Forget it. I'll be fine," I said shortly. And reluctantly grabbed my purse.

We stopped by someplace to pick up Adam (the only non-Confederatized male), and then Adam, Randy, and I packed into the backseat of Becky's sedan like Japanese smoked squid in vacuum-sealed bags, suckers smooshed against plastic.

Good thing her car was roomy because I had no intention of being pressed against Randy's prickly bronze stars for the duration of the trip. Although from his grinning stares, he certainly wouldn't mind.

A hot cup of coffee from Hardee's, although not the snazzy stuff I liked, helped wake me up enough to absorb the conversation about the Civil War and Tim's reenactment history as we sped toward Winchester. All the sabers, emblems, uniforms, and hats, all identical to those used in the 1860s—even down to the stitching. Homemade hardtack, from real nineteenth-century recipes.

The soldiers, all having honest-to-goodness ranks, actually drilled and practiced and shot blanks from cranky old muskets and cannons.

Tim and Randy talked excitedly about war tactics and battles lost and won. What the Confederacy could have done to improve their strategy and win the ones they lost.

Personally, I thought they were all Looney Tunes. But I was outnumbered four to one, so I kept my snarky comments to myself. And tried to ignore Randy's too-friendly manner when he grinned at me, like a creepy old photo come to life.

"If we lose the Shenandoah Valley, we lose Virginia!" Tim waved an impassioned hand. "That's what Stonewall Jackson said. And he got it right!"

"Stonewall who?" I lowered my sunglasses.

Utter silence descended, so quiet I heard a gnat hit the windshield. Tim pushed a button and squirted it off, still not closing his mouth.

"A Confederate general, Shiloh," Adam intervened quickly. "One of the best either side ever saw."

"She's jokin', ain't she?" chuckled Randy, waiting for some sort of punch line. "Ain't she?"

"Oh. There were a lot of them, so. . .they all sort of run together in my mind." Frankly, I just didn't care. And I had a sinking feeling I was wasting one of my few free Saturdays doing something that would make Kyoko have me committed.

"Look over there," said Randy, putting his arm around my shoulders and scooting closer. "Them's the Blue Ridge. Can you see that mountain over there?"

I slid closer to the door and shoved his arm off. "I can see just fine. Thanks."

"I can show ya all the battlefields 'round these parts an' teach ya all the hist'ry." His smile showed big teeth. "Just me 'n' you."

I sipped my coffee and paid great attention to the hillsides, a few trees slightly yellow along the tips. September whispered just around the corner.

"Really." Randy winked at me and tried to slip his arm back. "Jest name the day. You're a fine little woman, ya know? Yer just on the wrong side. I'll teach ya right."

"Cut it out, will you?" I snapped, putting his arm back in place.

"Hey, Randy," Adam interrupted, gaze dark as I met his eyes. "Can you tell me why the Confederate tactics failed at the Battle of Antietam?"

And that kept Randy's full attention for the next hour.

Cars clogged the grass at the enormous parking lot. People everywhere—some clad in period garb and others dressed in jeans like me. Confederate uniforms sprouted like gray mushrooms, polishing rifles and sabers, pulling on boots, straightening caps.

I stood there, caught between two eras. The Confederate gunner yakked on his cell phone, while on the other side of me, a gray-clad hospital steward with a Bluetooth in his ear snapped his car doors locked with a chirp, chirp.

"Where's the blue side?" I shielded my eyes.

Tim, unloading his gear out of the trunk, gestured without looking up. "Over yonder."

Sure enough, another field of cars glittered in the hazy sun, with spots of blue covering the green grass.

"Why are they separated?"

Tim shrugged. "They ain't all. If you look around, you can

see some minglin'. But ya know." He shot a big grin. "Can't get too friendly with the enemy before the big battle."

I couldn't tell if he was joking.

Without a doubt, this took the proverbial cake—or hardtack, I should say—as one of the weirdest things I'd ever experienced. Even weirder than pouring Coke for the Harlem Globetrotters.

The battle would start at eleven o'clock sharp, so Tim and Randy gathered up their gear and strode through the parking lot to find Tim's dad.

"Hey, son," Tim Senior beamed, dropping the act long enough to slap his son's back. Other officers smiled and shook hands, uniforms studded with bars and medals. "Ya made it! How's the little squirt?"

At first I thought (in horror) he referred to Becky, but then Tim patted his wife's belly lovingly. "'Bout the size of a goldfish. Reckon it'll be able to shoot in the next battle?" And they guffawed together.

Becky blushed and pretended to be scandalized, but Tim Senior hugged her like a long-lost daughter. Even kissed the top of her head.

"Let's hope it takes after yer side," he joked. "A cotton-pickin' shame to have him look like this Tim fella. And who's this lovely lady?" He touched his hat, and I saw Randy glance furtively at me.

"Yankee, sir, unfortunately. . .but a keeper." Randy gave me another too-warm smile, trying to twine his fingers through mine. I pulled them away. "A definite keeper. Hope we can win 'er over to our side."

I took a step back, glaring, but nobody seemed to notice. Tim Senior shook my hand warmly, pressing my hand with the top of his. Despite his fierce countenance and imposing uniform with all his stars, stripes, and bars, he seemed gentle and humble.

"She's a keeper all right," he said kindly. "Welcome, Shiloh. Great name. Great battlefield." I opened my mouth. "And even greater city in the land of God's people. And a reference to the Messiah Himself."

"You knew!"

"It's in the Good Book." He winked at me. "Don't get no better'n that."

We made our way over to a hillside, where Becky spread a blanket out in a somewhat shady spot. Even the sunny patches were filling up with people, lawn chairs, umbrellas, and picnic blankets.

"Wish me luck," said Randy, face close to mine. He lowered his voice. "I'll look for ya up in the stands."

He tried to kiss my hand again and then my cheek, but I made a beeline over to Tim, who had just finished loading up his gear. Pretended great interest in the rucksack he was strapping closed. Becky smiled up dreamily at her 1860s husband, oblivious to my plight.

We waved as Randy and Tim finally headed down to the huddled masses of troops gathered in the field below, weapons and buttons gleaming.

"Whew!" I fanned my face violently as the morning sun warmed up the hillside. "Glad they're gone."

"Ain't it excitin'?" said Becky with a swoony sigh. "I just love Tim in that uniform."

"I'd like to deck him," grumbled Adam, looking moody. "I mean, not Tim, of course. That obnoxious Randy fellow."

"Me, too." I crossed my arms. "Does he have to ride home with us?"

"Huh?" Becky finally turned to me.

Hopeless. I rolled my forehead in my hand. "Which battle is it?" I asked, watching rows of troops assembling in the distance.

"The Battle a Winchester," said Becky, not trying to be funny. "The Third Battle a Winchester, ta be specific. They call it the Battle a Opequon, too, after a river 'round these parts."

"Look! Horses!" There in the crowds of blue and gray

soldiers, gradually assembling en masse across the giant field like brewing storm clouds, strode rows of officers mounted on horseback. Tails swishing, tall and gallant, sniffing the air in an excited frenzy. One jumped a little too nervously, and his Union officer reined him in.

An eerie spectacle stretched out below us.

The props were so real I could imagine, if I tuned out the noisy crowds and teenagers with white iPod buds stuck in their ears, more than a hundred years turning back like pages of a book.

A low ripple passed through the crowds. People sat down on their lawn chairs and grabbed their binoculars. Women dressed in period hoop skirts ushered children to their places. Laughter evaporated.

A tense silence hung over the field, and just as the crowd started to whisper again, a blue speck of an officer on horseback—barely visible—rode toward the middle. And a gray dot mounted on a chestnut galloped out to meet him.

We watched them: an entire war boiled down to two people, not so different from each other, there on horses with swishing tails. They talked, drew back, tried again, and then galloped off in opposite directions.

There would be no peace on that green field. There would be war, and soon.

Suddenly there came the thump of battle drums, shouts of soldiers, and the masses of blue and gray surged forward. Rifle shots. Puffs of smoke. The front lines running toward each other and mingling in a tangle of weapons and soldiers.

I watched in silence, seeing men in blue and gray fall and roll in the grass then lie motionless as troops poured over them. Battle standards waved in the breeze as rank after rank charged forward, meeting for a melee on the rolling grasses. Smoke from muskets and rifles made a haze over the fighting. Bugles blared.

It was impossible to find Tim or Randy—just face after smoke-obscured face.

"Tim lost two great-great-grandfathers in the war," said Becky in low tones. "Both officers. And three great-great-uncles. A father and two sons. An' loads a cousins. One of 'em infiltrated enemy lines, got captured and sent to an internment camp, then escaped and helped the Rebs win the Battle of Harpers Ferry in West Virginia, all while he was sixteen years old. Fighters, my husband's fam'ly! An' mine, too. I lost three great-great-uncles. One from a bad amputation."

"Stonewall Jackson led that battle in Harpers Ferry, didn't he?" asked Adam, eyes drifting out over the smoke-filled valley. "And the First and Second Battles of Winchester, if I remember right."

"Shore did. Greatest general to walk the earth 'cept Robert E. Lee. And he won both o' them battles here. Yessir, great man." She shielded her eyes and winced at an artillery blast. "Most of Tim's fightin' family and most of the Rebs all together weren't much. A bunch a farmer's boys. They couldn't read 'r write. They were kids, mostly. Outnumbered, outsupplied, and outmatched in ev'ry area militarily. But they fought ta tha last drop a blood."

" 'Lost Cause' propaganda. I've heard this stuff before," I muttered to Adam.

"Maybe so." He shrugged. "But there's some truth in it, too, I think."

A picket line of bearded, rugged Confederates charged a Union cavalry, and I watched several of the men in gray crumple and fall. One struggled and charged again then fell clutching his side, staggering. I saw him draw himself up and take a final shot at a mounted soldier, causing him to tumble off his horse.

"Fighters," said Becky again, looking as if she would cry. "They were all fighters. Everybody down there in gray."

I remembered a children's movie about the Civil War with the Confederates portrayed as buffoons—hairy and unshaven, burping and falling over their own cannons. But seeing Tim's stately father and the mock Confederate General Jubal Early down below, strong and steadfast, made me have second thoughts.

Second thoughts about everything. Even the way I'd always snapped, "The war ended—get over it." It did end. But that war, that division, and their wounds affected people more deeply than I'd ever realized.

These were battles fought in people's backyards. Fathers and husbands and brothers lost forever, leaving behind only letters, pictures, and legends. Memories based on which side of the border people stood or how they pronounced a vowel.

Even the South Carolina capitol building still shows its scars—cannonball blasts in the mortar—until this day. Virginia was irreconcilably divided into two states.

Time does not, in entirety, heal all wounds.

I had to remind myself the bugles and the picket lines and the bayonets weren't real and that the men strewn across the ground in various expressions of agony would eventually get up and walk again. It was strange, too, omnisciently knowing the outcome—the South would surrender, Lincoln would play "Dixie," and the two halves of the US would reunite.

"Who won this one?" I asked Adam.

"You really want to know?"

"Yes."

"The North."

I turned back to the battle, somehow disappointed. I knew the North won the war eventually, and I was glad, but it seemed sad somehow to watch these boys in gray fall over Virginia soil.

"The South gave a good fight though. Only twelve thousand troops to the North's forty thousand. And heavy casualties for the North. They were fighters, just like Becky said."

The sheer force of the numbers stunned me. I strained my eyes to see the gray coats, shouting and thrusting swords and bayonets with all their might. Going up to meet wave after wave of blue without faltering.

"Oh! Aunt Wilda!" said Becky abruptly, interrupting my

thoughts. "There she is! Hold my place, y'all!" And she scampered off through the crowds.

Adam and I watched in silence, and then I turned to him. "Do you really wish the South had won the war? And seceded?"

"I never said that."

I was taken aback. "No? But you're. . .here!"

"So are you. And you're not waving stars and bars."

"Yeah, but that's different. I was abducted."

"Well, the Battle of Opequon's history, Shiloh. Think what you want, but the Civil War really happened. My brother Todd found a Confederate button in our backyard."

I gazed down at the field through my sunglasses. "I thought every Southerner believed 'The South Will Rise Again' and all that."

Adam laughed. "Well, a lot of them do. But I'm not everybody else."

"Right. If you disagreed, you'd get strung up the nearest tree."

"Probably."

"Well, that just proves it then."

"Proves what?"

"That Southerners are bigoted and intolerant. Just like everybody says."

Adam took off his baseball cap and scratched his head. "Well, I don't really agree, Shiloh. That's an awfully harsh judgment. If you went back to Brooklyn and told everybody the South should've won, you might get a similar reaction."

I choked back a laugh. Come to think of it, yeah. Definitely. They'd brand me a racist, tell me to go back to my trailer in Alabama and shoot a squirrel, and make snarky comments about deep-frying and inbreeding.

"But they fought the war over slavery, Adam. Anybody who wanted to keep slavery is wrong, and I'll never change my opinion."

"Well, you shouldn't. Slavery's always been wrong from the

beginning. But a lot of people who fought for the South disagreed with slavery completely. Like Tim's family. They fought for their homeland. Their wives and daughters whose farms were invaded and burned. Whose sons were killed by Northern gunmen.

"Most of the battles took place right here in Virginia and elsewhere in the South, and they were the ones who stayed out of the war until their houses burned down around their ears. You'd better believe they grabbed their muskets and joined the Rebels. Regardless of what the Confederacy advocated or didn't."

He shrugged, hand on his chin. "I could be wrong, but it's a different perspective. At least for consideration. There are usually two sides to everything."

I watched the sea of soldiers across the meadow. They seemed so real now, so human—all of them, both colors. Things weren't always as clear-cut as I'd imagined.

"Don't misunderstand me, Shiloh. Slavery was and always will be a terrible evil. The KKK and thugs who harassed abolitionists? The worst. Despicable. People try to defend slavery by showing how well some families treated their slaves, but it misses the point. It's wrong. Period. And if Southern commerce couldn't continue without slavery, it deserved to collapse."

"Well said."

"It's not me who comes up with all this. It's God."

I pushed my sunglasses up on my head. "Slavery's in the Bible, Adam! Even I know that much!"

"A lot of things are in the Bible that God didn't necessarily approve of. But Southern slaves didn't go free every seven years like Israelite slaves did in the Old Testament, so it's not really a good comparison."

Seven years? What on earth was he talking about? I ran my fingers through the grass, feeling like that night on my front porch with Adam.

"If you look at Paul's letters in the New Testament, he asked the owner of a runaway slave to welcome him back as a brother, not a master. Which speaks more of God's heart than anything else."

"But a lot of people claim to be Christians and racists, too, like those KKK nuts."

"They haven't read First John."

"Who?"

"In the Bible. It says if we claim to love God and hate our brother, we're deceived. You can't be a racist and love God. Ever."

"You believe that?"

"Absolutely. The Bible doesn't address all of our modern social issues directly, Shiloh. God's left that task up to us. He's given us His heart and His ways to change the world. But if you wonder about slave traders, First Timothy lumps them with adulterers and perverts."

I harrumphed. "Well, good." Finally something in the Bible I agreed with.

Actually I agreed with a lot of things. More than I cared to admit. I played with a dandelion stem, trying to press down the emotions surging within me.

Adam crossed his legs and leaned back. "Be careful judging the gospel by a few loudmouths who call themselves Christians. Jesus warned us a lot of people who think they're saved, but He'll say, 'I never knew you.' "

A chill crept up my arms even in the heat. "Saved?"

"From sin and from hell." He met my eyes. "It's real, Shiloh. The wages of sin is death. The Bible says so. And you have to choose."

Just like the battle on the green field, two sides warring against each other with all their strength. Only one side would win.

"I have set before you life and death, blessings and curses. Now choose life!"

I jerked my head up. The words whispered through my mind like wind tickling my cheeks, pulling strands of hair from under my baseball cap. I took it off and let the breeze blow through it, wild and free.

"Would you have fought for the South, Adam?" I switched subjects, Kyoko-like, as something like tears welled in my throat.

"I don't know."

"You don't?" I swiveled to look at him. "Are you really a Southerner?"

"Of course I am! I love the South. But I can't tell you if I'd have fought for the South or not. Even Jesus warned the Pharisees about bragging over what we'd have done in past generations and thinking we're somehow 'better' than our fathers—because we weren't there.

"It's a dangerous thing to put ourselves and our modern values back into pasts we know nothing about, especially when we puff ourselves up with pride and say, 'I would have done differently.' No. I choose to live now and make my decisions now. This is who I am."

And at that moment, a great respect for Adam Carter welled up inside me. Adam might be stuffy and odd and serious, but he was real. Just like any of the men down on that field, gray and blue, believing to their dying breath.

We looked down over the valley as a bugler on a horse led another blue cavalry into the fray. A wall of Southern gunners disappeared into a puff of smoke. Horses reared up, and troops scattered over the clatter of artillery fire.

"What a messed-up world," I whispered, blinking fast to hide my tears. I hurt for Tim's brave warriors, cut down in their prime. For the ranks in blue, wanting to preserve the Union. For slaves torn away against their will, never again to breathe the air they once called home.

For everyone who'd ever suffered and bled and forced himself to stand again against great odds, like the outnumbered Confederates in the field below.

Like Mom.

And also like me.

"So much bloodshed. So much fighting."

"You're right, Shiloh," said Adam gently. "We live in a fallen world. The only way to free yourself from those evils comes through Christ. He cleaned people up back then, and He still does it now."

Those words seemed to carry across the centuries like an urgent whisper. I need Him. It caught in my throat like a sob, the way I'd felt when Jamie begged me to tell God I wanted to believe. That I wanted Him for a Father.

I leaned back in the grass, and my fingers barely touched Adam's. They were warm among the green. He didn't pull away.

I sat up quickly, face flushing, but a strange quiver coursed through my veins. Hugged my knees and looked out over the smoky valley, strewn with men who had given their last.

I didn't need a new battle. I was sick of battle. I needed the whole war to end. To surrender and accept His terms. To discover that instead of death, I'd find a whole new life. A whole new Father. A whole new love. The way I'd always longed for deep inside.

My prayer rose up like a puff of musket smoke, dissolving into clear sky overhead. Invisible, yet spreading out into eternity.

I want to believe, God. I don't know why, or how, but I want to. I need to. Help me believe in You.

I turned to find Adam's blue eyes looking at me with an expression I couldn't describe. Without a word, he gently brushed a strand of my hair out of my eyes and tucked it behind my ear.

"Say yes," he whispered. "To God."

My cheek burned where his fingers had touched my skin, ever so slightly, as if unwilling to forget.

The sun dipped low and golden when we rejoined Randy and Tim's family, taking pictures and talking with other reenactors.

The next reenactment was the Battle of Stanardsville in Greene County, and everybody couldn't wait to trounce General Custer and ride alongside the famous JEB Stuart. A Confederate victory!

I'd actually felt disappointed when Union General Philip Sheridan surprised the troops with two fresh divisions of cavalry, forcing the strong Confederate lines to sway and eventually break. Cocky Sheridan, waving his hat and proclaiming victory even before the battle ended, made me despise him.

Sheridan, people told me, burned and laid waste to the beautiful Shenandoah Valley. Oaks whispered golden leaves against a distant ridge, joining in his condemnation.

Victory was victory, but as I helped Becky roll up the blankets and pack Tim's gear in the trunk, I couldn't forget those fallen gray coats—exhausted after struggling valiantly with an enemy more than triple their size.

I knew exactly how they felt.

We were still loading up when I noticed my purse didn't jingle like it normally did.

"Has anybody seen my keys?" I dug through my purse frantically, finding nothing, then dumped it upside down on the seat. Pawed through cell phone, sunglasses, and cap.

"Didja lose 'em?" Becky looked worried, peering around Tim Senior's now dust-stained uniform. "We got your spares at home."

"Yeah, but Mom's keychain." I could get another one probably, but I wanted hers. The one she held. Tucked in her purse.

I pressed my hand to my lips in thought then groaned. "I know where they are. I took them out at lunch when I was talking to that woman."

"The one who knew yer mama?"

"Yep. I'll be right back." I tossed my purse on the seat.

"Wait! I'll go with you!" Randy trotted forward excitedly, giving me an eager grin.

I shot up a hand. "I'm fine! It'll just take a minute!" And I sprinted off.

Ugh. I certainly didn't need some creepy cousin coming off into the nearly deserted hillsides with me for so-called protection. Give me a break! We're in Winchester, Virginia, not New York!

Besides, the hillsides dazzled with honey-colored sun, and I could see perfectly.

I skirted the area, hill after hill, coming around the lightly wooded glen where the food area peeked between trees. It stood deserted now, and cicadas creaked in the woods, swelling up with a dizzying sound.

Fallen twigs crunched as I ran down the path, veering off at the edge of the woods where we'd eaten lunch. One more bend and the tree should. . .

Wait a minute. It didn't look right. My oak stretched into the sky, towering, and I didn't remember any pines nearby.

I paused in the middle of the pathway, pulling my sweaty hair off my neck. Crunched a few more steps through the leaves. Checked at the base of another tree and found nothing. Stood there with my hands on my hips, wishing I'd brought my cell phone. The food area was a lot farther from the parking lot than I remembered.

I closed my eyes and retraced my steps. Then hurried down a smaller side path, wrapped in forest, a few bends just out of sight. A giant oak. I recognized its spreading branches.

I pushed fallen green leaves aside, digging around the roots. And, to my relief, snatched up my precious VSDB keychain. Held it up in the fading light and jingled it just to hear the sound.

Winchester was cooler than Staunton, farther north, and a chilly snap descended as the sun lowered, turning the glen pale blue. I sat back on my heels to rest, wishing I'd brought a jacket.

Something flickered through the trees. A sound, a movement. A ripple of wind in the leaves. I stood, one arm against the oak.

Then again, a flash of lighter color. Sure enough, several figures lurked in the shadows near the empty food buildings, all closed and boarded up. Probably cleaning people or something.

I tied my shoe and started quickly back toward the main trail. And scuffed to a stop on the leaf-covered earth.

Two guys blocked the path, looking in my direction.

I backed up a few steps then headed around the food area the long way, into the woods, hoping to throw them off. But as soon as I ventured beyond the buildings I heard laughter, low voices, and footsteps. And a whistle. Calling something in low tones.

The sun slipped another notch, turning everything an eerie dusky color, just like a scary movie. Summer crickets began their night calls.

I walked faster, pushing overzealous branches and leaves out of my way. But when I came around the next bend, there stood the guys again, still blocking the path. Closer this time, so I could see the leering grin of the tall one, shining dimly in the dusky twilight.

And I was farther away from the parking lot than ever.

Someone bird-called through the trees, rustling branches, and I stepped back, swiveling my head at a twig snap in the other direction. *Probably just some dumb Boy Scouts clowning around, Shiloh! Chill.* I wiped sweaty fingers on my jeans and surveyed my options, determined to walk out calmly, head up.

But on the trail behind me emerged another silhouette, too big for a Boy Scout. Or a boy anything. Barring my access back to the main path. The two guys in front of me whispered and sidled closer.

Instinctively I shrank behind a clump of pines, ready to scream.

No! Don't do it! You'll give away your location, and besides, nobody up in the parking lot can hear you anyway.

My heart thudded, and I slipped through the pines and off the trail. Dark woods closed in around me, drowning the foliage in darkish blue-gray. The color of battle uniforms under smoke. The color of dread.

Angular shadows slithered closer. Footsteps crackling twigs, muted whispering. That silly bird call and the shiver of leaves as a tree branch wobbled.

I was hemmed in, just like the Confederates at the Battle of Opequon. And even more outnumbered.

Great. I pressed cold fingers to my cheeks, crouching under a leafy maple branch. *Think, Shiloh! How on earth did you get yourself in this mess?*

I ducked through a thick shrub and into shadows, breath coming fast. Sweaty hair sticking to my forehead. If I could just make it to the food buildings, their dusky outlines still visible through a gap in the trees, I could hide there—and slip up the trail when the guys left.

My footsteps vanished across a carpet of moss and fallen leaves, and I flitted between two buildings like a nervous butterfly. I crouched near a patch of overgrown weeds, breathless, and forced myself to ignore the cobwebs tickling my neck and bare arms.

I leaned my cheek against the cool wood, waiting for footsteps to fall on the soft trail with muffled crunches. Closer and closer. Low voices, a whisper.

Shuffling past me.

And growing fainter.

I let out a shuddering breath, hearing nothing but birds twittering. The low groan of a towering elm, swaying gently in the evening breeze. A single acorn that fell with a plunk on a shingled roof.

Legs shaking, I eased onto my toes and then stood up. Peered around the side of the building and into the murky dusk, breath going out of me in relief. *You're free and clear, Shiloh! Make a run for it!*

The empty trail gleamed pale in the fading sun.

Jennifer Rogers Spinola

I maneuvered a tentative toe over the underbrush, and then an arm grabbed me roughly from behind. A hand clamped over my mouth, swallowing the scream that tried to escape.

Chapter 36

I tried frantically to pull away, but he held me like a vise. I kicked his shins and rammed my elbow in his stomach, drawing some curses, but even after my most solid kick he grabbed me in a sort of headlock. He shoved his hand over my mouth, and I bit his fingers hard, which made him yell in pain. I squeezed out a partial scream.

But he smacked me in the head, making my ear ring, and this time he covered my mouth with the crook of his beefy elbow.

I tried to slide to the ground and out of his grasp, pounding him with all my strength, but he twisted my arm behind me until I cried out.

Then he dragged me, still kicking his ankles and punching with my free arm, away from the buildings.

I swiped for his shoelaces, making him stumble, but he cursed, righted himself, and caught my punch just as the other three guys sprinted through the trees, out of breath.

"What a little fighter!" he laughed, passing my flailing arm to one of the guys while they dragged me into the woods.

I dug my nails into the new guy's wrist, making him yelp, and then punched him in the jaw while he momentarily loosened his grasp. It didn't hit him as hard as I would have liked since he stood at an angle, but he still rubbed his chin and swore. I squirmed away from the third guy and tried to twist free when he grabbed my tennis shoe. Tore it away and kicked him square in the chest.

God! God! Save me! I'd never been a praying woman, but after my prayer on the hill, now seemed like a pretty good time to start in earnest.

"Careful! Hold her!" One of the guys grabbed my arm as I ripped it free, uppercutting into somebody's nose and nearly squirming loose. "She's a slippery one!"

My heart hammered in my chest, pinpricked with adrenaline as they pulled me through the trees, farther and farther away from the food buildings and any place I'd ever seen. I'd been mugged three times in New York and had my purse and wallet snatched four times. Once Mom and I had been carjacked. But never had anything gone this far.

It's a nightmare! I told myself as I twisted furiously, limbs hobbled. *Just a nightmare! It can't be real!*

Any second now I'd wake up and find myself in Staunton and thank my lucky stars to be in one piece. Forget lucky stars. I'd even thank God.

One painful wrench of my arm when I sank my teeth into somebody's bony wrist reminded me I was very much awake.

"C'mon! Hurry up!" one guy urged under his alcohol-laced breath, jerking my hands away as I grabbed at tree branches. "There's the trail!"

This is bad, God! Oh. . .this is bad!

I didn't recognize anything. Shoot, I couldn't even recognize Winchester on a map. I screamed at myself for not letting Randy come with me.

The woods opened to a deepening blue path, dead-ending near a neatly gated and locked Dumpster. Wild, patchy shrubs fizzled into dark, scrubby forest on all sides beyond a thin fence.

I panicked when I saw we'd come to an end, ramming

whoever was behind me hard with my head and giving a jagged blow with my elbow.

The guys dumped me on the ground, knocking my breath out, and I managed one scream before somebody wrenched my head to the side and stuffed a bandana in my mouth. He sat on me when I scrambled partially to my knees and grabbed his musty-smelling shirt around his throat, twisting so hard it tore.

I groaned under his weight, barely able to gulp air. Then as he wrestled for my arms, I managed to yank fistfuls of his long, greasy hair. Hard enough to rip some out. He bellowed. Two other guys seized my wrists while he wrapped duct tape around them, once, twice. All the while fending off my kicks.

"Sheeewwweee!" crowed the oaf as he finally got off me, brushing himself off. Still laughing as I tugged at my wrists, rolling my head in the leaf-covered dirt and trying to spit out the bandana. Somebody pinned my shoulders to hold me still. "Never thought it'd take four a us to hold one gal. Reckon she's one a them women wras'lers!"

The thought popped incredulously into my racing brain as I tried to memorize their shadowy features for police reports: Rednecks? I've been kidnapped by rednecks?!

Then again, there was duct tape. I'd seen a car bumper held on with it.

"Well, looky what we got here," said one guy with a patchy beard and leering grin. "Looks like we caught us a perty little jackrabbit."

They'd all moved a safe distance from my tennis shoes, but one of them got too close, and I kicked again, this time knocking off his baseball cap. Underneath it gleamed a completely bald head, covered with creepy tattoos—a swastika, a Rebel flag, and a snake.

I stiffened against the cold earth, muscles paralyzed.

Uh-oh. Big-time.

Somebody shined a flashlight in my face, blinding me, and

the angry scowl of the skinhead bulged inches from my nose. Breathing those noxious alcohol fumes. He whacked me in the face with the cap before plopping it back on his head.

"Look at them fine-lookin' eyes," said one of the dumber-sounding guys as their illuminated heads filled up the deep-blue sky overhead, harsh light making me blink back tears. "How many colors ya reckon she's got there?"

Something made them jump, and they turned back to me nervously. "Hurry up, y'all!" They seemed amateur, clumsy, and even skittish. "See how much she's got on 'er! I bet she's loaded!"

"Shoot, she ain't got no purse," muttered somebody in a plaid jacket, jerking my jeans pockets inside out. "And nothin' in there, neither, but some keys. Ya got a car here?" His eyes lit up. "She's gotta car!"

"What's yer plate number?" one asked excitedly, whispering to split up and go find it.

Someone jerked the bandana out. "Gimme yer plate number!"

I screamed, tugging on my duct-taped wrists, and Patchy Redneck Beard clapped his hands over my mouth. Stuffed the bandana back, spilling cigarettes from his shirt pocket. "Doggone it, ya idjits! Fergit the keys! She ain't got no car." He threw my keychain on the ground and hunted for his cigarettes.

I reached over and defiantly shoved my keychain back in my pocket with my fingertips, wrists still stuck together.

"Shoot. No cell phone neither." I had no more pockets. Then they pulled off my tennis shoes to check for money, as if I'd really be so afraid in Winchester, Virginia, that I'd hide rolls of bills in my shoes. Ridiculous! I guessed correctly—they were amateurs. Amateurs who'd watched too many cop movies.

Still, the one with the plaid jacket held my head down while he stripped off my watch—a green plastic one from Japan—and pulled out my earrings.

Morons! They cost $8.99 at JCPenney!

"Wait a minute. Whadda we have here?" demanded the skinhead, focusing the flashlight beam on my T-shirt. Ice-blue eyes crinkled into a scowl. "New York? A stinkin' New York Yankee?"

In other circumstances his comment would be funny. *No, Mets! Can't you read?*

But they outnumbered me, and besides, I couldn't talk with the awful dusty bandana in my mouth, foul and sour. I tried to spit it out and had almost succeeded when I saw a glint of metal. I froze.

"That's right, little Northern trash Yankee. If you wanna come invadin' our land, you'd better be ready to take us on! The South will rise again, and we'll wipe all you cheatin', commie Yankees off the face a God's earth—right down the toilet with Israel!"

I had no idea what he was ranting about, but he pressed something sharp to my throat. Amateur or not, he was dangerous. The others followed his lead, murmuring angrily about Yankee invaders and making racist cracks.

One of them missing a tooth gawked at me, looking like Flash turned evil. "New York?" he wheezed. "Lot a blacks up'n New York, ain't there?"

My pulse pumped with anger even through my fear. What is it with these racist people? I wanted to knock another tooth right out of his jaw.

"Well, yer a perty little thang. Betcha had a black boyfriend up there, didn'tcha?" Missing Tooth winked at me, but his smile was ice cold.

"Answer!" shouted the skinhead, poking his blade painfully deeper into my neck.

Let's see. . .one. . .two. . .no, two and a half because Ryan was mixed. . . Oh, and that guy with all the nationalities—didn't he have a black. . .grandmother? Uncle? Brother-in-law. . . ? I guess my total came to something like two and three-fourths. Would these creeps even understand if I used fractions? Or should I just round to the nearest whole number?

"She didn't say nothin'," croaked Plaid Jacket. "Ya know she had a couple!"

"'Course she didn't say nothin'! She got yer bandaner in 'er mouth!"

"Looks like she needs a lesson in hist'ry," Missing Tooth said in a raspy voice. "'Bout people who got strung up tryin' to befriend Uncle Tom."

The skinhead glowered then slowly removed his knife. Blinded me with his flashlight again. "It's not the Civil War," he growled, lowering his face so I could see his crazy, ice-blue eyes. They terrified me. "It's the War of Northern Aggression!" He tapped out each staccato word. "Did you know that? Did you?"

He put his boot on my chin, and I nodded yes.

"And the world won't miss one less Yankee, will they?"

"Should we get her ta call her folks?" the other guys were whispering, already forgetting about the "his'try lesson" and going straight to money. "See how much rich Yankee money they'll send?"

Good luck with that, buddy! And then my pulse chilled at his words: "We can take her out ta yer place, Jimmy! Ain't nobody gonna find 'er there. But how're we gonna get her back to the car without—"

"Shut up, man!" Plaid Jacket hissed and smacked him. "Don't say my name!"

"I wasn't sayin' nothin'! I jest—"

"Shh! I heard somethin'!"

The skinhead ignored them. He cursed me some more then yanked the bandana out of my mouth so abruptly I didn't even have time to think. "Where're you from?"

I started to tremble, from fear and from cold. If those clowns put me in a car, I might as well write my own obituary.

"Virginia," I blurted. "Staunton."

"Liar!" he shouted, spitting at me and kicking me in the ribs. The blow glanced off, but it hurt. I rolled onto my side, groaning.

I was sorry I cried over Sheridan. Sorry I'd ever come to this Southern stink hole, and if I ever saw another gray uniform or stupid Southerner I'd. . .

The skinhead flicked open his shiny knife. "You ain't got no accent from Staunton, you dirty Yankee liar! I'll show you what we do to Yankee scum who defile our land!"

The next thing I knew, my ears roared with the crash of underbrush, a hundred voices shouting—and a Confederate soldier clocked the skinhead hard with the butt of a Civil War musket. The snake tattoos spun, and the musket cracked him again, opening up a gash on his forehead and putting him out cold.

I crawled partially out of the fray as arms swung overhead, people everywhere.

Missing Tooth and Plaid Jacket cried out and tried to flee over the fence, but two other gray-clad Confederates and someone who looked like Adam tackled the two of them to the ground. Another soldier in gray with yellow chevrons bolted over the fence and went in hasty pursuit after Patchy Beard.

Shouts roared, and someone dragged me away from the fighting. He pulled my wrists free and thrust me to a Confederate soldier who looked fifteen. I screamed, seeing another Confederate after all the "Yankee" abuse, and tried frantically to jerk free.

"Get her out of here!" Adam yelled, shoving us away. "Shiloh, go with him! Now!"

He punched the squirming guy he was holding in the face—once—twice—and then passed him to another soldier who whacked him with his musket until he fell, limp.

"Come on! Quick!" The kid wrapped an arm around me, and I stumbled over tree roots with him, still gawking over my shoulder.

Without a doubt, this constituted the most bizarre thing I'd ever seen in my life: a pile of Confederate soldiers brawling with a couple of rednecks and a skinhead.

Nobody would believe me! Nobody! Where on earth was my cell phone camera when I needed it?

"You mangy coward dog!" yelled one of the soldiers, wrestling the remaining redneck into the dirt. "Beatin' up on a girl! I don't give a care whar she's from!"

"Hey, you one a us, man!" Missing Tooth squealed in protest, punching wildly. "Ya s'posed to be fightin' the Blues!"

And then a long, deep groan as the soldier punched him hard in the stomach. He wilted like a rotten magnolia. "I ain't one a you, ya stupid bonehead! I fight coward idiots! Don't matter what color they're wearin'!"

Adam caught up as High School Confederate whisked me down the path and up out of the woods. My breath came in ragged gasps, and I groped for support.

"It's all right now." Adam put his arm around my shoulders and got the high schooler to support my other arm. Someone put my tennis shoes back on my feet. "Are you okay? Are you hurt?"

My side throbbed, pain spreading across my abdomen. "What happened?" I bawled as shock turned to tears, arms and legs wobbling. "Who are all these soldiers?"

"We came after you." Adam's chest rose, out of breath. "It was taking too long, so Randy and I decided to separate and see if we could find you."

"He'd just come down the hillside lookin' for ya when we told him we'd seen somethin' weird," said the kid, identifying himself as Trevor. "Couple a guys lurkin' around down here, up to no good, and we thought we heard a girl screamin'. So we came up kinda quiet-like to see what was goin' on." He shook his head. "Bunch a idiots! My dad's done called the cops."

Of course. Cell phones. And people smart enough not to leave them on the backseat of the car.

I shivered. Trevor gave me his handkerchief like a gentleman and called me "ma'am." It was probably a period handkerchief, too, and not a Wal-Mart knockoff. But I thanked him and sponged my face.

When we came up out of the trees, a scattered cheer rose across the dark hillside.

"Hoo-rah!" shouted a crowd of soldiers and bystanders with thick accents, high-fiving Adam and Trevor and pushing us up the hill. And then: "Let's git 'em, boys!" Our reinforcements poured into the woods at top speed. That pro-militia Michael Dewberry talk-show host would've been proud.

They hustled me up the hill, never stopping. Darkness had settled, purple, and a dim orange horizon still flickered over the empty battlefield. I thought of the men who'd crumpled there in the heat of the day and how I'd prayed to God, feeling for the first time a bit of kinship with the ache of battle.

Stupid Southerners! My stomach heaved, gray coats swirling in my head. Side pulsing angry and sore.

Southerners had attacked me, but they'd also risked their own blood for my safety. I doubled over in pain, not sure what to think anymore.

"Over here!" yelled Adam, and we ran smack into Tim and Randy.

"For Pete's sake!" shouted Tim, practically popping an artery. I'd never seen his face so furiously red. "Egg-suckin' scumbags! I can't believe it! Shiloh, are you all right?"

Randy threw his yellow-chevronned coat over my shoulders, which I gratefully accepted in the cold fall chill. I didn't even care when he kissed me and called me "honey." I just wanted out of there as fast as my legs—or someone else's—could carry me.

Tim Senior hollered on his cell phone, giving directions to the officers and directing patrols to the opposite side of the woods to catch the one that got away. He crushed me in his hug, cheeks wet, then boosted me up onto his shoulder.

Everybody was yelling, even as we ran, stumbling to the top

of the hill where a small crowd had gathered. And then, beautiful flashing police lights.

"Did you find it?" Adam asked, out of breath, as the officer approached me, pulsing in blue and white.

"Find what?"

"Your mom's keychain."

At that moment, if he'd asked me to marry him, I would have said yes.

I arrived home at two in the morning again, after an X-ray at the emergency room and chat with the police. My ribs weren't broken—just badly bruised. The doctor gave me a medical excuse from work for the next five days and an ice pack.

I thought I wasn't hungry, but when I left the emergency room, I could have eaten the leaves off a tree.

So we stopped at Cracker Barrel around nine o'clock, where I tasted corn muffins, pinto beans, mashed sweet potatoes, and sugar-cured ham for the first time. And learned that on Southern menus, macaroni and cheese counted as a vegetable.

After bawling out the police, the two Tims paid for dinner, as well as my X-ray, and Becky cried most of the way home.

They dropped off Randy first, but not without him offering—no, begging—me to stay at his place. Even started getting my stuff out of the trunk. Adam and I both argued with him, but he grinned anyway. "I'll call ya first thing in the mornin'," he said, covering my face with kisses until I pushed him away. Hard.

When I hobbled out of the car, all my strained muscles and ligaments starting to stiffen up, Stella ambled over from her yard, caught in their headlights in her nightdress. Out for a late-night smoke.

"What on earth happened to ya?" she crowed, puffing smoke across the gravel. "You drunk?" She sniffed me.

Nosy Stella, wanting details. I groaned and sat down. The

thought of all Crawford Manor knowing I'd been attacked by hicks didn't set well with me.

"No." I eased across the driveway with worried Becky's help and sat down on the top step. "Long story, Stella. I'll tell you later. And Becky—stop worrying. It's just sore. The doc said I'm fine, remember?"

"He said nothin's broken," Becky corrected sharply. "Don't ya wanna come with us? We'll put ya up, Shah-loh. I mean it! I ken. . .I dunno, make ya chicken soup or somethin'." She wiped her eyes.

"I'm not sick."

"But ya hafta go ta trial! Back up'n Winchester in a few months!"

"Trial? What'd she do?" Stella repeated, her wild thoughts swirling and circling like the moths around my porch light.

Becky teared up again. "Git in the car. Come stay with us."

To tell the truth, bunking at someone else's house just made me feel even more out of control. Just like I'd felt in the woods. I couldn't explain it. I wasn't sure I even understood.

Shiloh P. Jacobs may carry an ice pack, but she's no coward.

"I just want to sleep in my own bed, Becky. Please? Trust me?"

Becky hesitated, sniffling. "Ya shore ya ain't mad? 'Cause I don't blame ya. It's my fault."

"The only thing that'll make me mad is you calling me at seven thirty in the morning again." I shook my finger at her. "I'm sleeping in tomorrow, and that's final!"

She laughed through her tears. "Well, ken we come getcha t'morrow after church? An' have lunch tagether or somethin'?"

"I'd almost go with you," I heard myself whisper, remembering the open pages of Mom's journal. The dried roses tumbling out, fragile as butterfly wings. My prayer as the battle roared around me.

"Huh?" Becky hollered. "What did ya jest say?"

I know! I'm out of my mind! Medication or stress overload. Something.

"Nothing. Just. . .maybe next Sunday. . ." I didn't finish. I wasn't committing to anything—just learning more. Any good reporter would do the same.

"Church? You wanna come ta church?" Becky sniffled.

I ducked my head in embarrassment and scowled. "If you don't tell the whole neighborhood, maybe! Now let me go to bed."

Becky sniffled and stepped down the driveway. "Gracious, Shah-loh, take it easy, and call me if you need anything. Ya hear?"

I watched their car disappear then pulled Mom's precious keychain out of my pocket. I'd paid dearly for it; I should have it enshrined. Then eased myself up and unlocked the door.

"Where you goin'? You didn't tell me nothin'!" yelped Stella.

"Just wait."

I wrapped a fresh bag of peas in a clean towel, replacing my soggy ice pack. Filled the watering can halfway and plodded stiffly down the deck.

I should have been depressed, angry. And I was, on some level. But something unexpected bubbled up: a giddy delight in Mom's creaky old house and broken-down roses, which I thought I'd never see again. Stella's infuriating cigarette smoke.

And my ridiculous life, so absurd I nearly laughed out loud. Broke! Fired! Mugged! And surrounded by crazy Southerners who drove me NUTS. All of them! If the deep fryer didn't kill me, Southerners would.

I laughed and cried at the same time, hugging my aching side as the screen door banged behind me. I was coming unglued; my mind spun.

And yet I'd been rescued. Bought by someone's blood. Given a second chance.

A second chance at life.

The dark woods. The green hillside. Another hillside where crosses jutted into the sky, like the cover of the book in Barnes & Noble.

"I meant what I told You today, God," I whispered, joy leaping up at the sound of my heartbeat. My breath. My pink skin, alive, where the duct tape had stuck. *I want to believe in You like Tim and Becky and Adam do. Like Mom did.*

I don't yet, but I want to.

I tried to lift the heavy watering can, but it hurt. Stella barked at me to "let that fool thing alone" and watered for me. I wrapped my arms around my middle, watching dark sparkles trickle down over the rose canes in the porch light.

And then I clapped my hand over my mouth. Screamed.

"What's a matter?" shrieked Stella, dropping the watering can like a hot biscuit. "Snake?"

"No." I dropped to my knees. "Mom's Kobe rose bush. It's alive."

Chapter 37

I couldn't sleep after verifying with a flashlight, again and again, that Mom's white Kobe rose plant was indeed coming back. It had bushed out all over, green and leafy, new and tender shoots in midsprout. The first sign of something stirring beneath the soil.

Just like me.

I plodded up to the shower, still in awe, and scrubbed off Winchester dirt. Washed my hair and put on pajamas. Padded toward my room, checking and rechecking my door and window locks.

And just as I passed the library, I heard Skype ring on my computer.

Kyoko. Nine missed calls. I groaned out loud, face in my hands. I'd promised to chat with her since Wednesday. I glanced at my watch, my bandaged side, and then reluctantly slid my sore body into the chair. Clicked past all my open windows of job postings, AP wire service, and newspaper sites and answered.

"Kyoko?" I rubbed my narcoleptic face in an attempt at coherency. Warm water plus painkiller definitely took their toll. I was turning to rubber.

"Shiloh P. Jacobs!" Kyoko roared into the speaker, jolting me awake. "Where on earth have you been? I've spent three days searching for your face in the Missing Persons file!"

"You won't believe—"

"Try me!" she growled. "And it better be good!"

"Well, in the space of twenty-four hours I've met the Harlem Globetrotters, witnessed part of the Civil War, been attacked by rednecks and a skinhead and rescued by Confederate soldiers, and a rose bush I killed came back to life. And I'm kind of thinking of becoming a Christian."

Total and utter silence on the other end of the line.

"Kyoko?" I rubbed my eyes and jiggled the mic. "You're not watching movies with the sound off again, are you?"

No reply.

"Kyoko? Are you there?"

"Oh no." Her voice dropped to a near whisper. "You've gone mental on me. I worried all the stress might do it to you, Ro. But it's so much worse than I thought."

Kyoko didn't believe me. I could tell by her voice. She said she did and gave all the appropriate comments and "uh-huhs" when I offered more details, but she seriously thought I'd lost it. Asked the same questions in different ways to catch me off guard and see if I'd change my answer. An old reporter's trick.

I didn't know what else to say. So I bid her good night and dreamed of skinheads and knives until I woke up and turned all the house lights on.

When I finally dozed off at dawn, the first thing that jarred me awake was the endless ringing of the phone.

"Shiloh. I'm comin' by yer house. Whatcha need?"

"Who is this?"

"Your true love."

I groaned and leaned against the wall, blinking bleary eyes at the answering machine, which showed eleven messages. "Randy."

I rubbed my face, wondering why nobody in this town ever let me SLEEP.

"So can I come?"

"No, Randy, just. . .thanks but no thanks. I'm going back to bed."

After his fourth phone call "just to check" and a pounding at the front door that I didn't answer, sleep was impossible. I made a pot of hot green tea. I carefully maneuvered myself and my teacup in as pain-free a position as possible in front of the computer, hoping to explain things to Kyoko in an e-mail. I was always better with words.

But. . .I just sat there. Cursor blinking. Tea steaming. Writing about guys lurking in the woods didn't sit well in an empty house, especially as rain began to drizzle on the windows.

I'd try photos instead.

Kyoko had already received my most recent batch of uploads, which included a hat with an enormous bass attached to the top, three versions of the mullet, cowboy boots with flames up the sides, a license place reading "DUMHIK," some homemade deer jerky at a gas station, and—I kid you not—a guy on his riding lawn mower with a "farm vehicle" license plate on the back.

I hadn't even uploaded the reenactment pictures yet. To tell the truth, I might not. Ever.

I clicked on a photo of Stella in her housedress, smoking like a furnace, and slowly withdrew my mouse. Not after she'd spent all night making a huge cheese, egg, and bacon casserole for me. Left it on the side porch with a *Git well soon!* note when I'd gone out to water my roses. Found them already watered and the sprinkler turned on.

Same with the photo of Tim's truck with big old Gordon in the bed, baying his head off. Kyoko would certainly have some colorful adjectives for the people I called friends. Especially since she thought I was losing it.

I sheepishly squeezed my bag of frozen peas, trying to shake off the chill. Maybe Kyoko was right. Had I forgotten my purpose here? That Virginia served as a temporary stopover, and (earth to Randy!) I'd come to Staunton solely to sell the house and move on?

Girl! I could hear Kyoko say. *What are you gonna do, sell pork rinds in Podunkville to pay off your bills?*

I limped stiffly to the bathroom, muscles screaming. Scrapes and scratches covered my arms and legs, unnoticed in all the fuss, and my side bloomed bright blue-purple and angry. I could kiss my morning run good-bye for a while.

I turned on the weepy faucet and filled the tub. My tired body needed to soak. And I needed to think of how to finish what I'd come to Staunton to do. The perfect opportunity: five days of medical leave.

I finished my bath and slid on comfortable sweats. I checked for any trace of Randy Loomis hiding out in my bushes then grabbed an umbrella, marched over to Earl's house, and scheduled him to fix my faucet Friday evening when Faye arrived, for propriety's sake. And he sent me back with homemade cornbread and beef stew.

Because that's the way people did business in Virginia.

I poured some hot cocoa mix in Adam's mug and nuked it in the microwave then dug hungrily into the stew. It slid over my tongue delicious and meaty, piping hot—just the thing for a cold day. Then I turned my attention to the bedrooms. My first job: move the furniture out of my bedroom and start pulling up the carpet. Presumably before (1) Randy called again and I had to take the phone off the hook, or (2) he came by and offered to help.

I hauled, pushed, and grunted for about an hour, sliding the heavy chest of drawers out into the hallway. I found a tool kit and started to take apart my bed, sitting cross-legged with heavy iron beams across my lap and the floor strewn with screwdrivers. Awkwardly shoved the weighty mattress up against the wall.

Then I got out some heavy-duty pliers and started ripping the old carpet up from the corners. I rolled it across the room into a bundle, displaying the dusty, honey-colored wood flooring, and then hauled part of the carpet out to the laundry room. I could barely wedge my way between the furniture in the hallway. I dumped the carpet and then found some needle-nosed pliers to pull up the sharp little carpet staples, all the while answering two more of Randy's calls with diminishing increments of politeness.

Whew! Talk about a job and a half! My side throbbed. I held my trusty bag of frozen peas against my rib cage until cold numbed the pain then took more pain medication. Ripped up some more carpet. Picked up the scraps, dumped the rest. Got a broom and some cleaner and went to work on the floor.

I'd just dipped the rag in the can of wax again, half the floor shining, when my body seized up.

Either I'd overdone it or Earl poisoned the beef stew. A jagged shot of white-hot pain through my ribs quickly convinced me it wasn't the stew.

My hands shook, dropping the wax-covered cloth. I clumsily shut the can and took an aspirin then stumbled onto the softest place I could think of: Mom's bed. Rolled over on my side and groaned, wheezing as the pain radiated throughout my rib cage.

I'd been stupid to think I could get the house cleaned up in my state—and so soon after a traumatic attack.

Perhaps I had an ulterior motive all along—to forget my humiliation as if it had never happened? To prove, once again, I could do it all?

Tears stung as I recalled the curses, the blow to my head, the taunts and laughter. My utter powerlessness, despite my best efforts. Struggling with duct-tape-bound wrists is for wimps, not strong girls like me. Not Shiloh P. Jacobs, who had always controlled her own fate and pulled herself up with her own two hands.

We are all powerless. We are jars of clay.

Rain pattered softly on the glass, and I hugged my bag of peas, feeling the pain ease slightly as the aspirin took effect. Let my stiff legs relax. The phone, for one blessed minute, finally sat quiet.

I pulled open Mom's bedside table drawer and lifted out her Bible. The one I'd been reading night after night, left splayed on the sofa or half-open on the kitchen table. Her yellow highlights and notes scrawled in the margin lighting up like signposts.

First John. I have to find 1 John. I flipped to the table of contents then paged to the back of the Bible.

"That which was from the beginning, which we have heard, which we have seen with our eyes, which we have looked at and our hands have touched—this we proclaim concerning the Word of life. The life appeared; we have seen it and testify to it, and we proclaim to you the eternal life, which was with the Father and has appeared to us."

I squinted at the black words, running across the page in blocks and columns like signposts. The language sounded funny, but something deep was coming—I sensed it.

"This is the message we have heard from him and declare to you: God is light; in him there is no darkness at all. If we claim to have fellowship with him yet walk in the darkness, we lie and do not live by the truth."

It sounded like Adam's verse—the one about true Christians not harboring racism. Why? Because they reflect God. "For we are God's workmanship, created in the image of Christ Jesus. . ."

I followed the words with my finger: "But if we walk in the light, as he is in the light, we have fellowship with one another, and the blood of Jesus, his Son, purifies us from all sin."

The words pounded into my brain like the crashing waves boiling up on the Rio de Janeiro beach that Carnaval so long ago. Smashing down into the sand. The blood of Jesus purifies us from all sin.

So that's what the whole Jesus business meant! No wonder Mom seemed different. She was different! She hadn't just practiced "positive thinking" or mind games. Jesus had cleansed her. Set her free.

He'd given her life.

The thought was so bizarre—so strange and yet magnificent—I just lay there on the bed, staring up at the ceiling until a loud knock at the door jolted me to attention.

"Randy, go away!" I hollered, pulse pounding. "How many times do I have to. . ."

Huh? A hound? Gordon? I pulled back the curtain to find Tim and Becky standing on my front porch.

"Good night, Shah-loh," drawled Tim, hauling in a bunch of steaming plastic bags as I opened the door. "You look like you done seen a ghost!" He'd shaved off his reenactment beard, but his mullet and mustache were still very much alive.

"Ya all right?" Becky worriedly took my hand. "Y'oughtta sit down a bit. How ya feelin'?"

She'd make a great mom the way she was always fussing over me. "I'm fine, y'all," I joked. "Just working around the house and avoiding your crazy cousin." I scowled at Tim.

"Which cousin? What are you talkin' about? I got sixteen first cousins."

"That figures," I muttered. I tried to explain about Randy, but Tim's train of thought had already jumped the track. He set the bags down on the kitchen table, yakking about somebody from church who killed a rattlesnake with a slingshot.

"Hope it's okay we brought Gordon," said Becky, still looking over me worriedly. "He was alone all day yesterdee and don't do too well by himself, so I figger'd we'd just bring him along."

"I love Gordon." I knelt and petted as he wagged his tail and licked my cheek with a nasty, stinky, loveable tongue. "If you take your eyes off him for one second, he's mine." Lowell had said no pets for me, but he didn't say no friends' pets. So there.

"Hope ya love good ol' Southern fried chicken, too!" grinned Tim, opening up the heavenly smelling boxes. "Ya got'ny tea, Yankee?"

"Green tea? I drink it every day." I waved my teacup.

"Green what? Naw. I'm talkin' sweet tea."

"Oh. I don't know how to make that."

Becky and Tim both stopped in their tracks and stared at me. "You don't know how ta make tea?" asked Becky, not understanding. Even Gordon jerked his head up, tags jingling.

Hopeless. That's what Becky-who-can't-conjugate-the-verb-to-be thought of my prissy Yankee self. Shaking her head in pity.

"You got some tea bags?"

I rummaged through the cabinets and found a metal tin. "Darjeeling?"

"No, that ain't for iced tea." Becky made a face. "Interviewed the daggum president a Japan and don't know how ta make sweet tea!"

"Prime minister."

"Whatever." She rummaged and pulled out an unopened box of Luzianne. "Now we're talkin'! Ya just bull some warter and dump some a these tea bags in a pitcher with a cup of sugar."

"A cup?"

"Some folks put two."

"Lands," I said in jest. "One's fine!" Japan's less-is-best sweet mentality had warped me forever.

Becky scooped sugar. "Now when the warter bulls, just pour it over and let it sit 'bout two hours'r so. Then take the tea bags out, top it off with some cold warter, and put it in the fridge. Ain't nothin' better in the world!"

"Amen!" said Tim. "In the meantime, let's eat up!"

He'd just pulled the top off the gravy container when he noticed the chest of drawers standing in the hallway, parts of the metal bed frame leaning against it. Gawked like it was Shenandoah-Valley-burning General Sherman come back to life.

"What'n tha tarnation. . . ?"

"What's a tarnation?" I peeked around him. "Oh, that. I was just taking up the carpet." The big toolbox still sprawled in the doorway, tools and cleaning supplies strewn about.

"You?" He jabbed a spoon at me, still dripping with gravy.

"Yes."

"Today?"

"Guess I overdid it, huh?" I crinkled the frozen peas. "I got the carpet up though, and it just needs a good wax job before I work on Mom's room. I figure I can probably get it done by—"

"See-it!" he ordered, scowling at me and crossing his arms. "Right now!" Nodded to the chair with his head.

"What?" I raised my eyebrows and sat. Becky put her hands on her hips to join in my condemnation. "What did I do?"

"Yer under doctor's orders, Shah-loh Jacobs! Yer s'posed to be restin'! If ya needed that carpet outta the room so doggone fast, why didn'tcha say somethin'? One a us'd helped ya!"

"For goodness' sake! Y'oughtta know better!" scolded Becky.

"No fair!" I yelped. "Tag-team setup! And our biscuits are getting cold." I snatched one from the bucket.

"You ain't seen tag team yet!" Tim rolled his knuckles playfully on my head. "But I wawnt ya ta promise not ta touch nothin' until. . ."

"Until when?" I lifted my chin.

"Until you're better and git some help." His eyes were serious. "Sometimes ya gotta have the sense to know when enough's enough!"

"Or ta ask fer help." Becky flounced down in the chair. "Miss Independent."

I took a bite of my biscuit, enjoying the buttery golden crustiness on the outside. "Well, since you're leveling with me, I'll level with you. I'm behind. I spend all my time working to pay my bills, and I'm not getting the house ready for sale. I'm worried."

"'Bout what?"

"My house is just sitting here. It's not even on the market yet, so I've got no buyers and no prospects." I picked at biscuit crumbs on the table and ate them. "And you know I didn't come to Staunton to sit around and do nothing."

"Ha." Tim sat down and pulled up a plate. "If there's one gal who don't sit around and do nothin', it's you, Shah-loh! Down here we tend ta. . .I don't know. Take our time. Right, sugar?" He kissed Becky on the cheek.

She opened the chicken box. "I reckon you was countin' on those five days off a work, weren't ya?"

Tim mused awhile as he fixed his plate. "We'll he'p ya. And believe me, I understand what it's like ta need moolah. Shucks—we all do."

"Exactly. I. . .well. . .look." I reached over and grabbed a stack of envelopes. Plopped them at his plate. "There. Go ahead. I trust you."

He glanced at me then opened some envelopes. Read the numbers. Kept a straight face. "What's yer income, Shah-loh? Ken I ask?"

I told him. He rubbed his chin with his fist. "I gotta crunch some numbers, but the first thing we gotta do is get ya on a budget. Start the snowball effect."

"The what?" I imagined the Yeti peeking in my window.

"Where you pay off the smallest debts first and then use tha money yer not spendin' on interest to pay off tha next biggest ones. An' keep goin' up the chain. Gives ya confidence and gits things paid off as fast as possible."

"Can you teach me? My independent self welcomes any help." I sniffed playfully at Becky, and she threw a napkin at me.

I sobered, looking into their earnest faces. "I really need to get back into my area of work. I can't wait tables and work at Barnes & Noble forever. You know that as well as I do."

A bittersweet glow radiated from the gray windows outside, and the yellow light overhead reminded me of where I'd come from and where I still needed to go.

We all avoided each other's eyes, and for the first time I felt a twinge of sadness at the thought of leaving. But that was life, and I needed to find mine. Far away from here.

"Wale," said Tim, extending his hands to us. "There's one thing we do at these times. We pray."

We bowed our heads over the table, three sojourners, as Tim prayed for me and my finances, for Mom's house, and for Becky and the baby. Then we raised our heads and dug in like old times, passing biscuits and gravy. Laughing as if we'd share meals like this forever and none of us would ever leave.

After lunch Tim flipped through all my envelopes one by one and totaled them without flinching or fudging. I was ashamed at the debt I'd managed to rack up, as if snooping in a stranger's bills. How could that have been me, spending six hundred dollars on a Gucci bag?

It felt an eternity ago. Now I checked prices in the grocery store. Bought generic and store brands. Cut coupons. Turned off the car air conditioner to save gas. Checked my weekly hours at work to see if I'd have enough to pay my bills.

Becky sat there quietly, never making a snarky comment. Patted me on the shoulder. "Don't worry. Tim'll getcha outta yer fix as fast as he can. I know you're tryin'."

I looked for judgment in their faces as he opened the Louis Vuitton envelope, but found none. With the $390 I'd spent on a silk scarf, I could have gotten Adam's brother some new medical equipment. Bought Becky some smashing maternity clothes. Invested in tickets to come see my mom, even if out of principle.

But I had been so intent on playing the part—a woman above my means—and snagging a man like Carlos, who in the end didn't even want me at all.

Tim watched me redden and squirm as he wrote down the amount and finally smacked me with the corner of the envelope. "Gotta face 'em, Shiloh! Face 'em head-on. That's tha way ta do it."

"I know. I just can't believe I was so stupid with money back in Japan. I'd have a nest egg saved up by now."

"How much'd ya make?"

I gulped. Covered my eyes. Told him. In the past I would have lied, but his "face-'em-head-on" speech emboldened me. I'd pretended too much of my life away already.

"Yep. But that's how ya learn. No sense cryin' over it now."

We did some more budgeting, and then Tim told me to call every single one of the companies, on Skype if I had to, and ask them to waive the late fees. To tell them the truth and see if they'd cut me any slack.

In the past my pride would have refused, but now I obediently jotted it down in my planner.

Tim wrote me out a weekly budget for necessities and added another small category: house repairs. To get me in Lowell's good graces again. Said he'd help me if I promised not to do anything myself.

Then suddenly: "What time is it? Shoot, we're late! It's on!"

"What's on?" We all jumped up, including Gordon, who bayed and wagged his tail.

"The race!" And he dashed to the living room and turned on Mom's TV. "It's in Daytona ta boot! Shewwweee!"

"NASCAR, silly!" giggled Becky at my blank face. "Siddown right here and watch!" She smacked the sofa.

"NASCAR?" I repeated stupidly, not moving. "We're really watching NASCAR?"

"Watch and learn!" Tim gave a silly grin, stretching out his gangly, cowboy-booted legs and hugging a couch pillow. "And let's see if our sweet tea's ready while we're at it!"

I'd never seen cars go around a track so many times. I got dizzy after a while, but between Tim and Becky's excited cheers and explanations about drivers and crews and sponsors, and who cheated and who didn't, the whole thing began to make. . .well, a bit more sense. Maybe.

I memorized a few car numbers and who was "pole position" and absorbed (not necessarily intentionally) all kinds of weird information about the greats. Tim liked a new upstart named Vic Priestly, number 54, who drove for John Deere. He'd come in the top five in the last four races and won the Brickyard 400, beating all the favorites.

When I decided to cheer for Juan Montoya, it made things instantly easier. I now had enemies.

And every time one of us said "Jeff Gordon," Gordon bayed and waggled his backside. I hauled him onto my lap, where he snoozed comfortably.

"Doggone it, Vic!" yelled Tim, throwing the couch pillow. "Now don't go runnin' inta the wall! Git 'em! Show 'em how it's done!"

I grabbed the pillow and dusted it off. "Quit throwing my house-staging props!" I scolded. "They're supposed to make rich people buy my house!"

"Oh, and this, too?" He picked up my basket of half-folded, wrinkled laundry. "Yer smelly ol' socks oughtta bring 'em in by the truckloads!"

"Go! Go! Go!" screamed Becky to Tony Stewart, sitting on the edge of her seat. "You ken pass him! Pass that ol' Jimmie Johnson and leave him in the dust!"

Then she let out a soft groan and doubled over.

"What's wrong?" I put down my iced-tea glass. "You okay?"

"I'm fine." She waved me away. "That chicken must a woke up! Don't worry 'bout me."

Then Jeff Gordon crashed with Vic Priestly, and we all turned back to the TV screen. Tim stood up, arguing with the commentators and waving his arms. Plopped back down in frustration, slapping his knee.

And then Becky, "Ow!" Sharper this time.

Tim and I both turned. "Sugar? What's wrong?"

She sat up again, brow wrinkled. "I don't know. Prob'ly nothin'. I just. . .felt some pain outta nowhere. Just some cramps, I reckon."

We turned back to the TV, but something niggled in my brain. I watched her profile out of the corner of my eye as she sipped her tea and followed the race. Cheered when Tony Stewart sailed past Vic Priestly into first place. But she massaged her belly as if something still hurt.

Kyle Busch cut off Juan Montoya with a buzz of tires, grabbing third—and then Becky's face furrowed in pain, so strong she gasped.

She frowned and stood up. "I'll just use the bathroom real quick."

The race shifted to a commercial break, and Tim and I followed her, exchanging silent glances. Cold uneasiness crept over me, like when I'd seen shadows on the trail in Winchester.

"Go on! Y'all don't have to listen!" Becky called through the closed door.

"What?" Tim hollered back. "Cain't hear ya! We was just listenin' ta Becky use the bathroom!"

I chuckled and emptied another ice-cube tray into the pitcher. Sweet tea sure made us go through ice awfully fast.

The race came back on, but neither Tim nor I made a move for the living room. Becky hadn't come out yet, and I busied myself with washing the table, trying not work myself up and upset Tim. But I worried. Especially when I heard her groan in pain again. And give a sharp cry.

"Baby?" He rapped at the door anxiously. "You okay?"

No answer. Then a weak, "Yeah, I think so. I just don't know why I. . .oh no. Oh no. That ain't good. Oh God! Tim?" She opened the door a crack and peeked out with scared eyes. "I'm bleedin'!"

"Bleedin'? You mean. . .sweetie? You think. . .?"

Becky doubled over again, looking pale. "I think we'd better. . ."

I felt cold all over so quickly goose bumps prickled on my arms.

"Let's go! Right now!" He helped her put her shoes on, coaching her to take it easy. Put her arms through her jacket and zipped it up in such a gentle way it nearly made me cry. "Shiloh, I'm sorry ta bail on ya, but—"

"I'm going!" I shouted. "Just get in the car! I'll drive you!"

"But yer all banged up, an' Gordon's here. . . ."

"Get in the car!" I ordered. "Gordon'll be fine. You take care of Becky. Just tell me how to get there."

And we bolted into the rainy evening.

I drove as fast as I could, Tim and Becky sitting in the back, praying in low tones. Fingers laced together. Becky's groans punctuating the swish of wet tires.

I stopped at a red light, windshield wipers swashing back and forth, and prayed myself. Wished I could send out a red alert for everybody to pray at top speed. Maybe numbers made a difference—like in finances.

The hospital hid in the middle of nowhere, clear on the other side of the county—or state. I wasn't sure which. I pushed the Civic as fast as possible on the rainy roads, gripping the steering wheel until my nails dug into my palms.

The baby's fine! You'll see! I calmed myself into a numb oblivion, pressing the accelerator and signaling and watching for signs. Squealed into the hospital parking lot and unloaded Becky and Tim at the front door.

"I'll find you." I squeezed her hand tight. "Don't worry! Just get in there! Everything's going to be all right."

I parked the car, shaking all over, and then rushed inside the spacey-looking complex of white, metal, and glass. Sat down on the hard hospital seat and clasped my hands tightly together and waited. And waited. And waited.

I tried not to look at the people around me, all in various stages of worry or stress. This made my second visit—in one weekend—to the emergency room. My stomach heaved at the smell of antiseptic.

I called Faye. Called Adam. Sat riveted to the seat, waiting for any movement from the emergency-room door. Waited for Tim to come out with a grin, telling me Becky had swallowed a fly or some silly joke. All would be fine. We could go home, recap the race, feed Gordon, and get up tomorrow smiling.

Please, God. . .please, God. . . I prayed, hands wrapped around my still-throbbing abdomen and half-thawed peas, which did little to relieve the pain. Two children played with blocks in a corner, the girl's blond hair in pigtails.

Please, please, God. . .

Time dragged on, and I ached. Shivered in air-conditioned blast. Wrapped my jacket tighter and wished I'd brought some aspirin or a fresh bag of peas.

Faye called, on her way, and Adam promised he'd leave as soon as his dad arrived to stay with Rick.

Adam and I texted back and forth:

ANYTHING?

NOTHING.

ANY WORD YET?

NO. I'LL LET YOU KNOW.

The white ceiling and beams screamed futility. People walked into hospitals one way and out another—either saved, like I'd been in Winchester, or changed forever in an instant.

And all out of our control.

At nine p.m. the emergency-room door opened, and I saw a flash of Tim. I jumped up and ran to him, heart in my throat.

Chapter 38

I knew immediately the news wasn't good. Red rimmed his eyes, and his face gleamed wet. He reached up in a daze and wiped it with his hand.

"Tim?" My eyes filled. I took a step back, shaking my head.

"She. . .uh. . ." He struggled to keep his voice steady.

"Did she. . .lose. . .?" I couldn't say it. I felt small, like a speck on one of those immaculate white walls. I was helpless; I could do nothing. Just like at Winchester. Duct tape on my wrists.

Tim closed his eyes, drew in a sharp breath, and nodded. "Yeah. The baby's gone."

I crumpled, gasping, covering my face with my hands.

"It's okay, Shiloh," said Tim in a hoarse whisper, tears streaming. He knelt beside me. "God is good. He gives an' He takes away."

I inhaled a sob then reached up and clasped his hand tight. He squeezed it in both of his, shoulders shaking.

"You're sure? I mean, maybe they're wrong, and. . . ?" I bawled, tears dripping on the floor in glossy little dots.

"No mistake. I shore wish it was." Tim wiped his face and helped me stand up. "I'd. . .uh. . .better get back with Becky. I done called my parents, and. . ."

"How's Becky?" My throat swelled so tight I could hardly squeeze out her name. I saw her there in Barnes & Noble buying a baby-name book, glowing, and in the parking lot at Jerusalem Chapel Church. Becky's miracle. And now it was gone.

"She's okay. Sad, but. . .she'll get through."

"Give her my love, Tim. I'm so sorry."

I couldn't find anything else to say. He clapped me on the shoulder and disappeared, cowboy boots clacking mournfully on the shiny floor.

I struggled to steady my ragged gasps and made my way back to my seat. People averted their eyes, hiding behind magazines. I pulled out my cell phone and sent a message to Adam: BAD NEWS.

My nerves frayed an inch away from snapping. The cell phone shook in my hand and then clattered to the floor. I didn't pick it up or even see if Adam wrote back. Tears dripped down my chin.

I barely noticed when the door opened and a figure came in, clad in a rain-spattered dark jacket, and sat down next to me. Touched my shoulder.

I turned and saw Adam, eyes red. He picked up my phone and put it in my purse. Reached out a hand and wiped my wet cheek.

Without a word, I buried my face in his shirt collar and wept. And he wrapped his arms around my head and wept with me.

Without a doubt, I had just experienced the worst weekend in my adult life.

I slumped in the hard waiting-room seat, exhausted and emotionally shot, side pulsating so much I doubled over. Adam brought me a cup of tepid water and found some aspirin in his truck, but on top of my already-strong pain medication and my mood, I threw it all up in the bathroom anyway. I just sat there stiffly, arms locked around my waist.

When Faye arrived, wet from rain, I didn't even look up. I left my keys with Tim so they could use the car, and followed Faye for the ride home, wincing and clutching my drippy pea bag.

Gordon was still sprawled in my living room, and the thought of wrapping my arms around something soft and squeezable made me tremble. I needed him. His silly grin. His heavy head across my foot, stinky dog breath and all.

Adam and Faye spent a long time in the lobby, speaking in low tones, and I heard my name repeated quietly—and the words "alone." Adam worried about leaving me by myself.

It made me angry, but he was right. I had no one. Tim and Becky, after all, had loving family and friends to surround them. They would grieve and cry and heal, circled in protective arms. Cared for. Cooked for. Loved.

And although I bitterly resented the implication, I didn't. I could call Kyoko, but she already considered me mentally unstable. Kyoko, mind you, who had skulls on her purse and dated men who won green peppers.

Dad and Ashley? Hmph. They might as well live on the moon for all we kept in touch.

So Adam told me I was staying with Faye. He put his hands on his hips in a way that suggested he'd argue if he had to, but I didn't even care to pick a fight.

As we trudged through the rainy, copper-lit parking lot to Faye's car, I hated Staunton. Hated everything. Hated that I'd ever come here and gotten all tangled up with Tim and Becky. It hurt too much. I should've just let Ashley and Wade sell Mom's house and keep the money. At least I wouldn't be stuck here in Hickville, Virginia, trying to keep down aspirin and crying over another tragedy.

I remembered the first night I left Best Western with Faye, my job loss fresh and aching and the streets unfamiliar. Now I felt the same way again, watching telephone poles flash past and wondering why on earth I'd come.

"Now, you just relax, sugar." Faye patted my knee. "Everything's gonna be all right."

"That's what I told Becky," I snapped, wiping my swollen eyes. "And it isn't!"

"Oh, but it will be. It'll hurt for a while, but it's never the end of the world. They'll come through."

I stared at Faye, an inch from spouting something rude, but then remembered what she said about Mack. About children. "Did you ever. . .you know. . .?"

Faye didn't make me finish. "Yes. Twice." She turned a sad smile in my direction. "It was real hard. Mack gave me a lotta support, though I do remember feelin' he could never understand my pain. But it was okay. The Lord did. And He got me through it."

In my mind I saw Mom's Kobe rose bush, leaves beaded with rain. I forcefully pushed it away.

"I don't understand, Faye. How can you say, 'The Lord did'? From my perspective He didn't do anything! He got your hopes up for nothing, just like Becky and Tim. And then took it all away. I thought maybe I believed in Him, but. . ."

We stopped at a red light, and I listened to the signal click, click, click. Such an empty sound.

"We chose it, sugar."

"Chose what? To lose babies and suffer?" My words came out harsh and angry, stomach roiling with fresh nausea.

"Honey, God didn't create this mess. We did. If we'd a listened to Him, we wouldn't be in our fix. Life would be perfect."

"No, I didn't eat the forbidden fruit. Adam and Eve did."

Faye chuckled. "Doll baby, there's a little bit a Adam and Eve in all of us."

We drove through town in silence, and I stared out at the bright gas station signs and dark houses. Steel-gray ribbons of shiny streets. Each window hiding its own pain and memories.

"The Bible says His mercies are new ev'ry morning," said Faye softly. "We'll cry some, Tim and Becky'll cry some, but we'll get up t'morrow lookin' for His mercies. 'Cause they're there, just waitin' on us."

I turned my head so Faye wouldn't see my tears.

Chapter 39

Unexpected scarlet stole through Faye's woods in a late August cold snap—the earliest in more than fifteen years. My rose blooms fell like Becky's hope, still lush with color. When Adam brought my car over Wednesday evening, sporting paint-flecked hands and dirty jeans, he suggested we prune the rose canes that bloomed on old wood.

The other roses, he said, would need pruning in early winter or late spring, if whoever bought Mom's house knew anything about plants.

I reminded him at my house-staging rate, nobody this decade would be buying squat.

"Looks like summer's over." Faye stood beside me in her tennis shoes, face lit with glowing gray sky. She said it matter-of-factly, without any hint of sorrow.

But as I remembered Becky and Tim, I felt that summer had indeed slipped away. I couldn't imagine Becky without her smile, and yet it seemed gone for good, never to return.

"Yeah. I guess so." I shoved my hands in my pockets and trudged next to her, down over the sloping cow pasture bordering her backyard.

"Thank ya for yer help, Shah-loh," Becky'd said over the

phone, her voice blue and lifeless. "You did great ta git us out to the hospital so fast. And the flowers you an' Faye sent were jest beautiful."

"Ah." I brushed it away. As if flowers could help anything. "Don't mention it. I just want to see you happy again."

"I will be. Don't ya worry none."

Words stuck in my mouth like dry rice. "Becky, it was supposed to be your miracle," I finally whispered. "I don't understand."

"It was still a miracle. Just 'cause it didn't turn out tha way I wanted, don't make it any less of a miracle."

Words imploded.

"We's jest the vessel, Shah-loh. We ain't in charge. God forms the clay, an' I done give Him my life. He knows what's best. "

Vessel. Jar. Of fragile clay. God's workmanship.

My fingers fluttered to my forehead. "Well, if there's anything I can do, just tell me. Please, Becky. I'd do anything for you."

"I know you would. You're such a good friend to me." Her voice crumbled. "Just keep prayin' to the Lord. He'll bring us through. Ain't nothin' ever too big for Him to handle."

Such strange hopes, these Christians. That God would hear and understand and somehow make something beautiful from the mess.

"There's a purpose in ev'rything," I could still hear Tim drawl, relieving a tearful Becky of the phone. "We jest don't always git it. But He sees the whole pitcher, start ta finish."

Just speaking about their loss made me feel worse, not better, reminding me it was startlingly real. Being believers in God hadn't protected Becky and Tim. And yet, neither had it broken them.

Strange. I racked my brain, trying to come up with some logical explanation. Grief and denial. Something like that.

My flowers fade, and the petals shiver and drop, Mom had written, as I paged through her journal in Faye's pretty spare bedroom, quilt around my shoulders.

Winter comes barren across the land. But you know what I've discovered? Barrenness sets the stage for miracles. So many holy women of the Bible were barren. And yet God reserved His greatest miracles for them—to bring forth nations! Rulers! Prophets! Forerunners of Christ! Can a woman ask for more?

And winter, in fact, is not an image of loss but of fullness. Of culmination. Of brilliant fire and gleeful cold, hands rubbed together against our breath. Breathtaking mornings and stars over ice. A picture of the gospel: "though your sins are like scarlet, they shall be white as snow." Snow that covers. Snow that blots out. Snow that promises shouts of victory just beneath the surface, all the roots and shoots and stirrings waiting, joyfully, to erupt at just the proper time.

Do not be so smug, Death. Sin. Pain. Your victory is short-lived. Mine is forever!

"You gonna keep walkin'?" asked Faye, bringing me back to reality. "You been lookin' out at that field an awful long time."

"Huh?" I looked up and saw a cow staring at me, cold wind rippling the tawny grasses. "Oh. Sorry. Just thinking."

"'Bout?"

"I don't know." I scuffed the grass with my foot. "Why didn't God give you children, Faye? What you wanted most?"

"It ain't what I wanted most. Or Becky either. We want a life spent lovin' Him."

These Jesus people had a way of catching me off guard every single time. I had to be on my toes with them, too, just like with Kyoko. Although for slightly different reasons.

"But I know you wanted children. Why didn't God give them?"

Faye reached a sweatered arm around my shoulder. "I dunno, sugar. Mebbe it's for you. You ever think a that?"

"Me? What do you mean?"

"Lord knew you'd need somebody in your life right now, doll. An' here I am."

The breath went out of me, and my cheeks burned angrily. "But that's not fair to you, Faye!"

"It is fair! We don't deserve none a this." She gestured around at the fields and silver-gray sky.

"That doesn't make everything all right!"

Faye turned her face to me almost severely. "You wanna talk about fair, Shiloh? While the Lord Jesus was up on that cross bleedin', it wasn't because a Him—but because of me. Because of you. And our sins."

I started to protest, but this time Faye stood her ground. "We rejected Him and went our own way, just like them cows over there, always tryin' to bust through the fence an' wander out in the road. No, Shiloh. I done tried that. I'm His now, for better or for worse."

Like wedding vows. Didn't Tim call it a romance?

A smile flickered on Faye's wrinkled lips, rosy with lipstick. "But with God it's always better. He works out every single thing in our life for our good. Bible says so."

"You believe that, Faye? That this pain means something? And that God uses it to make us better people?" Pain oozed from my side in fresh waves. I stumbled, arms around my middle.

Persecuted but not abandoned. Struck down but not destroyed.

Faye was either a lunatic, stark raving mad, or she was right. She couldn't be both. I opened my eyes.

"With all my heart, doll. That's what faith is."

"And you'd still say yes to God's plans for you? Even if it was only for me?" My voice broke.

"It'd be my privilege." She smiled and circled me with her arm. "His plans for me are always better than anything I could dream up for myself. Just wait an' see."

Right then and there on that slant of waving grass, I made

up my mind not to let Faye go. I would not be Carlos. I would not replace her. I would not forget to write and call like I'd done with Mom, even when I moved away.

For the first time in my life, I would be Hachiko the dog. Waiting, waiting at Shibuya Station. Or more precisely, somewhere in redneck Staunton, Virginia.

Friday marked the coolest day yet, even with the sun, and Faye and I headed to Mom's house early to make hot chocolate for Earl when he arrived at six.

"My roses are dying." I leaned sadly over the railing in my jacket, purse, and reporter's notebook under my arm. The flower bed was scattered with carmine petals. Faded green leaves, pocked with yellow, shivered in the wind.

I imagined the thorny canes poking through white, like Mom had written. Snow that covers. Snow that blots out. Snow that promises shouts of victory just beneath the surface. Roots reaching down into frozen soil, waiting for spring.

"It's about that time," said Faye, tenderly touching the leaves. "They'll look real good next year though. Your mama always had the prettiest flowers around."

Even the Kobe bush, full and leafy, boasted thick green spades all over. I hated that its season would end so soon, after such hard work.

But still—it lived. It had survived. Next year I'd see blooms. . . or whoever bought the house would.

We spun around as country music blared from a rusty pickup, careening into a driveway down the street. A dilapidated Dukes-of-Hazzard-like car squealed in behind it. Hooting. Yelling. Somebody threw a wheelbarrow.

Back in Tokyo I'd lived between a six-figure endocrinologist and a famous news anchor. Neither of whom owned a wheelbarrow.

"Oh brother," I muttered, fumbling with my key. "Here they go again. The Jester brothers."

"They drunk?" Faye whispered.

"Who knows." I pushed open the door, and a sharp, strong chemical odor slapped me. I backed into Faye. "Phew! What's that smell?"

"Smells like varnish! Ya workin' on something for the house?"

"No. Just moving furniture."

The smell increased as I stepped inside. "Faye, do I have a gas leak? I might have to call the fire department!"

I rushed into the kitchen, forgetting my stove was electric. Not gas. Then halted there, breath sucked out. My keys dropped with a clank.

"What's a matter, sugar?" asked Faye sharply, her mother-hen instincts coming out. "Did ya—"

She saw it, too, and gaped, purse strap falling limp over her arm. "Well, I'll be."

I clapped my hand over my mouth, fresh tears beginning to flow. I tried to speak and couldn't.

"Who do ya suppose. . .?"

From top to bottom, all the ugly brown-and-white wallpaper had been stripped from the kitchen and dining room and the walls covered with a silky coat of eggshell-white. It glowed apricot in the last rays of evening. The rooms now looked large, airy, and modern.

The chest of drawers was gone. I rushed down the hall, and sure enough, my bedroom floor gleamed honey-colored wood. A thorough cleaning and fresh coat of wax. Mom's, too. Carpet staples taken up. All the furniture put back where it belonged, reflections shining on those warm wooden beams.

In an instant, Mom's house was transformed. All insults about Southerners—Jesters or otherwise—stopped in my throat. My "Southern Speak" notebook splayed on the floor.

"Ya didn't contract anybody?" Faye asked in bewilderment.

"Who do ya think did the work?"

My hand rested on my forehead as I searched my brain. "Adam's the only one who had my keys. And. . .remember? He had paint on him when he brought my car Wednesday!"

"But he couldn't have done ev'rything by Wednesdee." Faye ran a hand over the wall. "This here's a lotta work!"

"Hold on." I marched over to a kitchen chair and snatched up a baseball cap with a fleck of paint on the back. "Aha!" I waved it as evidence. "Tim was here, too."

"How do ya know? Ain't that Adam's?"

"Nope. Vic Priestly, number 54, John Deere. Tim's favorite driver."

And I bawled into his cap.

The phone trilled. I was still sponging my face and thinking of the sacrifice Adam—and especially Tim—had made for me. I loved them fiercely, like family. Family in a way I'd never known.

"Hello?" I tried to steady my voice.

"Lowell Armstrong from Titanic Farm & Real Estate. How's the house coming, Shiloh?" I detected a note of sarcasm.

My hand quivered on the receiver. One of those astonishing, rare moments when everything in the universe lines up exactly right. If I tried, I couldn't make this happen.

And now, for my moment in the spotlight. "Lowell, the house is ready."

A surprised pause. "What do you mean ready? Wallpaper down, walls painted?"

"Yes, sir."

"Carpet taken up, hardwood floors polished?"

"Yes."

I heard him banging and shuffling through papers, obviously not expecting to get so far with me. He was hunting for the list. "Really? How about the. . .uh. . .leaky bathroom faucet?"

"The plumber's coming in fifteen minutes."

Silence.

"Well," Lowell finally said. "Wonderful! So are you ready to put it on the market?"

"Absolutely." I grinned at Faye. "You can start listing it anytime."

"Good, because I have some folks who might be interested in a little place just like yours. Are you ready to show?"

"Just name the day."

Lowell's voice sparked with excitement. "Great, Shiloh! I'll come over tonight and put our Titanic Farm & Real Estate sign in your front yard."

I hung up the phone then screamed and hugged Faye. And we jumped up and down in that beautiful kitchen like two giddy high schoolers.

Chapter 40

"So what happened next?" asked Jamie, gripping her tray in excitement. We dodged busboys in the busy Green Tree kitchen, waiting for two orders of roasted red pepper soup. Trinity Jackson, a tall African-American waitress, crowded next to us, listening in.

"Remember when Earl fixed my faucet and had hot cocoa with Faye and me? Well, the next Sunday evening he came by again to check the faucet. When she was there for our weekly cook-fest." I lowered my voice conspiratorially.

"Did he know she was coming?"

"I mentioned it." I scooted plates around on my tray to make room for the soup. "I thought it was a coincidence, but last Saturday he stopped by again."

"When Faye was there?"

"Yep. I think he saw her car."

Trinity bent close, trying to hear over the dishes and pans banging and the hiss of steaming pots. "You think he's. . .you know, sweet on her?"

"I don't know, but I think so."

"Talkin' about me again?" asked Blake loudly, smacking Trinity with his notepad. "The answer is yes."

"No!" She smacked him back. "Not now, not ever!" But her dimples curved into a grin.

"Aw, Trinity," he sighed, grabbing a handful of silverware and grinning, his pale blond face gleaming like a chubby moon behind glasses. "I love older women. You know that."

"I don't know a thing except you're my nephew's age," she retorted, raising an eyebrow. "Why don't you go find a freshman?"

"Never, Trinity," he quipped, pretending to look rapturous and offering her a silverware bouquet. Or maybe he wasn't pretending. I didn't know. "You know I'll always love you."

"Get out of here!" I snapped. "We're trying to talk!"

"Men." Trinity laughed and rolled her eyes. She'd done some modeling, and at twenty-six was a knockout. Slim and dark-lashed with impeccable makeup. "Isn't Blake like nineteen?" she whispered.

"I think so," Jamie whispered back. "But you have to give him points for effort, right?"

Trinity rolled her eyes. "I guess. He's a nice kid."

"Faye's older than Earl by a couple years," I said smugly. "Doesn't seem to deter him any."

I grabbed the bowl of soup from Flash and gave him a thumbs-up. Gratefully accepted a couple of hot sweet-potato fries.

"Ha. Blake is Blake. I don't care how old he is." Trinity shoved off the counter and went to grab a pitcher of ice water. "So tell me about your lovebird friends."

"Well, they're not lovebirds yet. But every time I visit Earl, he's always listening to Bible Today. That radio program with the sermons."

"You're kidding!" Jamie arranged salad plates carefully on her tray. "Faye loves that one, doesn't she?"

"Exactly." I wagged my eyebrows.

Trinity's amber eyes sparkled. "So are you gonna set them up? I love mushy stuff. Come on, Shiloh! Let's plan."

I cupped the second bowl of soup from Flash and carefully set it on Jamie's tray. "Give me some ideas then. Becky thinks we should move fast because there's an older guy at church who's been asking about her."

Trinity's face clouded. "How is Becky? She hasn't been here in a while."

"Not a hundred percent, but better." I'd spent all the time I could with Becky, taking her out for ice cream and shopping. I convinced her to buy a smashing pink dress that matched her pale skin. And, of course, to get her highlights and hair done again at Crystal.

After seeing the new Becky, Tim already didn't mind shelling out a few bucks—and I helped with the clothes. She was smiling again. I know she still hurt, but as she told me, life went on.

After I told Jerry about the newly painted kitchen, he'd given Tim and Becky dessert on the house. Even he seemed a little protective of me after what happened in Winchester. He didn't take flak from his employees, or excuses, but he also played Papa Bear—making sure people treated us right. I liked being in his good graces.

I was still thinking about Becky when the last customer paid, and I slumped, bleary-eyed, into an empty booth to pick up stray napkins the busboy had missed.

"So you sold your house?" Trinity looked up from the booth where she was rolling silverware in cloth napkins.

Waitresses never really stop conversations. We just spread them out over several long, interrupted, noisy hours. Or occasionally, days.

But this time her words made no sense. "Huh?"

"You said there was a couple scheduled to look at your house. After your. . .uh. . .fiasco." She gestured to my side with a fork, and I cringed. I still popped an Advil every now and then, but the swelling had gone down, and most of the time I barely felt it.

"Oh, them." I sighed, wiping a sticky hand through my

normally obedient bangs, which straggled down into my face. "They didn't make an offer."

"No?" Her hand paused on the silverware. "Bad news then, huh?"

I picked at my nails, which used to shine like satin, always polished. Now I clipped them short from repeated washings and harsh chemicals. "Another hope deferred."

Trinity wrinkled her nose. "You reading the Bible? You sound like Jamie. Or my grandma." She rolled her eyes.

"Actually, yeah, I am. But it hasn't sold my house yet."

I shouldn't have said that. It made the Bible sound like another omamori good-luck charm, when in reality it turned me on my head. Stunned me. Defied me. Half the time I wanted to chuck the whole thing out the window and read cereal boxes instead, but something glorious and wonderful stopped me.

Jesus and His crazy disciples made me alternately doubt my sanity and cry for joy. Sort of like Southerners—but without mullets and gun racks.

"You'll sell your house." Trinity reached out a warm hand, rings sparkling. "Hang in there. The right person will be ready soon."

Yeah, and *Chicago Tribune* will recant its rejection, Carlos will apologize, and people will actually leave tips instead of change.

And possums will fly.

I squeezed Trinity's hand and stacked the tray with dirty dishes. Yep. That's what I got these days. People's leftovers. Cold and crusted to the sides of sticky bowls.

I clanked everything together when Dawn tapped my shoulder, startling me.

"There's a guy here for you."

"What?" I lowered my tray. "For me? It's almost nine! We're getting ready to close."

Trinity half rose in her seat. "Maybe it's that cop who comes by sometimes? He's hot, Shiloh!"

"Nope. Not Shane." Dawn shook her head.

"Well, come on—is he cute?" Trinity whispered impatiently, and Dawn blushed. Glanced around the corner and shrugged.

"I don't know. Normal."

Trinity peeked. "Hmm. Kinda," she said, showing her dimples. "But not my type."

"It's not Tim? Or Tim Senior?"

After the Winchester incident, Tim Senior and Jeanette became my new best friends. Or patrons, I should say. Jeanette dropped off tons of homemade pound cake and banana pudding, and Tim Senior installed brand-new locks on my door. He checked my car and put in new brakes, all without taking a cent.

"Nope, neither of the Tims. I've never seen him before."

"All right. Hold on." I tossed my damp cloth onto the tray. "What is your type, anyway, Trinity? Short blonds who love older women?"

"Get outta here." She sized me up. "Latinos. It's what I tell Blake, anyway."

"Ha. I've got one for you back in Japan. He's probably free now, too."

I hurried between the tables with my dirty tray, practically running smack into Adam Carter, sans baseball cap.

"Adam?" I was a mess—hair straggly, clothes smelling like coffee and fry oil. A two-year-old had sprayed mustard on my once-white apron.

"Hey, Shiloh. Sorry to bother you," he said, looking anxious. "If this isn't a good time, I. . ."

"No, it's fine. We're closed, but Jerry'll keep it open for you."

"No, I'm not here to eat, although the place looks nice. I need an emergency favor."

"Sure." I wiped my hands on my apron. "Anything." After what he and Tim did for me, I'd scrub their tennis shoes if they asked.

"My dad sort of. . .uh. . .fell off the roof, and Mom's out of town. I need somebody to stay with Rick while I take Dad to the emergency room."

Forget possums flying. "What?" I squealed.

"I know, it's crazy." Adam chuckled. "Dad wanted to fix something up there, even though we told him to call a repairman. But he's stubborn and, well, looks like he broke his arm. We didn't think so at first, but it's starting to swell up, and he's in a lot of pain."

"Is he all right?"

"I think so, but Rick's been having a lot of bad reactions to his new medications, and I don't know just how long it'll take with my dad. I tried to reach Faye and Tim and Becky, but they're all out. Nobody answers. I'm so sorry. I'm desperate."

"It's no problem," I said quickly. "I can go."

"Todd's there, too, so he can help you out."

"How old is he again?"

"Eleven. A great kid. But I don't necessarily trust Todd to manage Rick's medications, if you know what I mean."

"Sure." I thought fast. "I clock out in thirty minutes. Can you wait that long?"

"You can go now." We turned to see Jerry standing there, reaching out to clap Adam's shoulder. "Anything we can do to help, my man. She's all yours."

I flushed red at his choice of words, but Adam—thankfully—didn't seem to notice.

As the two of them chatted, I ran to the back to change clothes, flinging off my dirty apron. Short of a full shower, a splash of water on my neck and hands worked in a pinch. I sprayed something fruity to cover the food stench. Threw on jeans and brown heels. Then my delicate knit summer-weight shirt, short-sleeved, and brown velvet jacket—all of which Faye'd altered, since clothes practically fell off me now that I spent so much time on my feet. I brushed my hair and pulled it back in my little mother-of-pearl clip then tucked it up and off my sweaty neck.

The weather had been crazy lately—cold for two weeks and now hot again. I was living in the Bermuda Triangle.

"Ready!" I said breathlessly, hauling my soiled waitressing clothes in a tote bag.

"And out you go, Shiloh Phyllis Jacobs!" Jerry gave us a push. "You were gold tonight. Did I tell you that?"

Another crisis. My life was just one big crisis after another. Handing out pills seemed minor, comparatively, and besides, it had been a few weeks. I suppose I was due another one.

"Come in." Adam ushered me through the simple foyer. He waved at his dad, who stretched out on the sofa, face pale and gray. "Dad? How ya doing?"

Cliff, as Adam introduced him, groaned and gave a wry smile. "Been better," he managed. "Been worse. Maybe."

"Don't worry, Dad. Just let me show Shiloh where to find everything, and we'll leave."

I clutched my purse nervously as Adam led me quickly through the house, pointing out things in rapid-fire fashion: the bathroom, the kitchen, Todd (who looked up from doing his homework with a friendly smile), and two dogs, both chocolate labs. Then Rick's room.

He knocked and opened the door a crack. "Rick? Shiloh's here. She'll help you with your medication and anything else you need, all right? I've got to take Dad." He stuck his head in the kitchen. "Todd, homework. Okay? And help Shiloh."

"Okay." Todd smiled at me again from the table, tapping his pencil and swinging his feet. He looked as interested in his homework as in a cross-stitching of a sheep.

"Shiloh. Here you go." Adam thrust a piece of paper, typed, into my surprised hands. "All of Rick's medications in order, with times. The labels are easy to read, no guesswork. Everything else is on the paper—how many, what he needs to take them with, and so on. Here's where we keep his medicines." He waved at the boxes lined up on the kitchen counter. "Sorry this is so fast. I really am. I just. . ."

"Go!" I shoved him toward the living room. "Your dad's waiting! Don't worry about me."

"Are you sure?" Adam hesitated a split second then bolted for the living room, keys jingling.

I don't know why I said it. I was in someone else's house with two brothers I'd barely met—and dispensing enough pharmaceuticals to kill a horse.

The front door latched, and silence fell. Todd looked up at me with expectant blue eyes. Tapped his pencil on the book again. Then pushed back his chair and came over to where I stood, still holding the paper.

Oh, God. . .don't let me mess anything up!

"Rick has to take all of those," said Todd, leaning against the counter. "He hates those two right there." He pointed to the paper with the list of medications.

"Why? Do they taste bad?"

"Naw. I guess not. They're capsules. But they make him feel bad sometimes. Doc says he needs 'em though. I dunno why." He shrugged. "I take vitamins. Mom says they're not the same as medicine. Do you take vitamins?"

"Sometimes." I started to say more, but the two gentle chocolate labs nosed my legs, tails wagging excitedly. They reminded me of Gordon, but a lot more aesthetically pleasing. And they smelled better, too.

"Wanna say hi to Denny and Dale? The big one's Dale."

We scratched behind their ears, eliciting happy whines. Denny pushed his cold nose into my hand and sat expectantly, tail thumping.

"I named 'em after Dennis Hamlin and Dale Earnhardt."

"Who?"

"NASCAR," said Todd in surprise, as if everyone knew. "Number 11 and number 3. But Dale Earnhardt died, so he doesn't race anymore."

"No, I guess. . .uh. . .not." I raised an eyebrow. "Let me ask you something, Todd. Does everybody around here name their dogs after NASCAR drivers?"

"Hmm. . .naw, not ev'rybody, I reckon. Some people name 'em Bud and stuff. We've got a cat, too. Wanna see him?" And without waiting he rushed off.

"Here he is." Todd lugged a giant (and unwilling) black tomcat, who pushed and swished his fluffy tail in a vain effort to flee.

"Did you name him after a NASCAR driver, too?"

"Naw. My mom calls him Speck."

"That's an awfully big speck."

"Yeah, but he was little a long time ago."

The cat meowed in displeasure. "All right, Todd. I'd better see Rick, don't you think?"

Todd's shoulders sagged. "I guess so. But then can I show you my army men? And Rick's Purple Heart? They're in my room."

"How about after your homework?"

"Okay." He reluctantly hauled Speck back to the laundry room and plopped down at the kitchen table. And I took off my too-hot jacket and gauzy scarf. Dumped my purse. Gathered my courage and knocked quietly on the door to Rick's room.

"Rick? Can I come in? It's Shiloh."

"Well, hey, Shiloh. I've been waiting to meet ya! Come on in."

I pushed open the door and took a step back, astonished. The room was a maze of weight benches, tables, and medical equipment, and a closed wheelchair stood next to the bed. Two prosthetic legs reclined on a table, one long and one short. Boxes of bandages, gauze, and topical medications piled in a mountain against one wall.

And there sat Rick, leaning against pillows. The curves under the sheets where his legs should have stretched were truncated, making a spiteful optical illusion. Just like the prosthetic legs—one long and one short.

I wanted to cry, flee, or say something, but I couldn't. I tried to cover my shock, but it wasn't fast enough.

Rick chuckled. "Adam didn't prepare you for all this, did he?"

"No, it's nothing."

"C'mon, Shiloh," said Rick with a grin. "I've seen that look a million times. It's no biggie. Have a seat. You'll get used to my little scientific lab soon enough." He patted a chair next to his bed. "Make yourself at home."

I entered like a robot and planted myself on the seat. Wondered what on earth I should say to someone who had lost two limbs.

"Rick Carter." He extended a hand and groaned slightly with the effort.

"Shiloh Jacobs." I shook his hand. "I'm so sorry." I'd just breached all disability etiquette, but it came out anyway.

"About what? This?" He rubbed his five o'clock shadow. "I know. I try to shave it, and it just keeps coming back."

It took me a minute to realize he was teasing me.

"Oh, you mean my legs! Yeah, well, just between you and me, I did it for the VA benefits. They're pretty good these days, you know—early retirement, monthly paycheck. . ."

I laughed and felt my body untense slightly. "So you're. . . fine? Basically?" I let my breath out. I don't know what I had expected, but this wasn't it.

"Well, when a pretty girl says I'm fine, I take it as a compliment." Rick winked at me, his casual demeanor taking me off guard. "Well, leg-wise, I suppose I'm not in the greatest shape, but I'm alive."

"That's great." I tried to sound cheerful.

"I keep telling myself that."

I glanced at my fingers, fidgeting in my lap. "Actually I'd. . . uh. . .imagined you'd be in pretty bad spirits. You seem, well, wonderful."

I couldn't imagine not being able to run again, to stand and feel the wind against my face. To climb Mount Fuji at daybreak, coarse earth crunching under my tennis shoes as my lungs filled to shouting with crisp, thin air.

"Well, you're lucky you're here today. This morning I heard I can rejoin the army in the future, although I doubt I'll be a gunner again. But I can do lots of other good jobs. It's not the end."

His pillow was sliding, and before I could reach out to adjust it, he'd fixed it himself. I jerked my hands nervously back to my lap.

"Relax, Shiloh," said Rick. "I ain't made of glass." He put his palm over his chest. "My heart's still beating. The most important part's still here."

"If the heart's alive, then there's still hope. It can grow again. It can live. It can bloom. Even if there are no leaves left."

I closed my eyes, feeling the rush of memories. Adam's blue eyes at dawn, bending over the roses. Mom's white Kobe bush, leafing out green in the bright glare of a flashlight.

"You're right." I twirled a ring on one finger. "You have everything that matters. It takes most people their whole lives to figure that out."

"Well said."

I swallowed hard. "Your brother told me something similar. I. . .I've been thinking about it for a while."

"Todd? Yeah, he's pretty deep for his age." He was teasing me again. "Oh, you mean Adam. He's a thinker, that's for sure. He. . . uh. . .told me some about your mom. I'm sorry to hear it."

Two thoughts hit me at once: First, Adam had spoken of me. And second, Rick Carter, who had lost two limbs and had bandages on his arms and under his shirt, was comforting me.

I felt ashamed of everything I'd complained about—my messed-up family and Staunton life. Even my injuries from Winchester didn't compare with what Rick had suffered.

"Thanks. I'm learning a lot. More than I ever thought I would in a place like Staunton."

"Tell me about it." He rolled his eyes.

"So. . .what happened? Do you mind if I ask?"

"'Course not. It's simple. I was patrolling in Afghanistan and stepped on a land mine. Boom! End of story. I didn't feel a thing at the time, but when I regained consciousness, I was on a medic's table. They tried to save both of my legs, but the injuries were pretty bad, and they could only save one leg. I lost the other foot just below the ankle."

He looked like Adam as he spoke, brown hair falling over his forehead. But thicker eyebrows that raised like punctuation. A wry laugh etched in little lines around his mouth.

"I'm so sorry." I blew out the breath I'd been unconsciously holding.

"Well, that's the way it goes sometimes."

"I know, but it's still hard."

"Well." Rick rearranged his pillow again with some difficulty, grunting. "Everybody's amputated in some way or another, Shiloh," he said pensively. "We lose loved ones, cut off memories forever, end relationships. Go down paths we can't return from. We can't always have it back."

I held my breath. The room was so silent I heard the oscillating fan across the room, quietly droning as it rotated on its stand, softly ruffling Rick's dark hair.

"I know, it might seem far out there, but I think there's some truth in it," Rick continued. "We all experience loss. And that's what amputation is all about: irretrievable loss. A part of you that's no longer there."

I thought of Mom, the Mom I wish I had known. Of Dad and his silence across the years. Of Tim and Becky rushing to the emergency room. Faye and her empty double bed.

"And sometimes what we amputate needs to go. Like my feet. If you keep them, they'll squeeze the life out of you."

Carlos. After all these weeks, his name felt strange on my tongue. I missed him, and maybe still loved him, but memories of his old affection now chilled. Whatever he had for me, it was never love.

"But"—Rick raised a finger—"you have to choose life, regardless of how much it hurts."

Life. That word again, whispering itself to me over and over. *"I will live and not die. . . ."*

I vaguely remembered Pilgrim's Progress in literature class, and how the man Pilgrim ran from his old loves. Plugging his ears and shouting, "Life! Life! Eternal life!" My heart beat faster.

Rick smiled. "And when we make the choice to live without, that's when we learn to walk again."

I glanced at the wheelchair.

"Yeah. Walk again." He winced as if in pain but didn't want to stop the conversation. "I can't yet, but I will. That's what all those weight benches are for—to strengthen my muscles so they can support my weight again. Unused muscles atrophy. They've got to become stronger than ever and get used to the discomfort of the prosthesis.

"Although it's painful, I tell ya. You have no idea. Sometimes I break out in a sweat just thinking about it."

"So there's a purpose in all your suffering." I laced and unlaced cold fingers.

"Sure there is!" His dark eyes sparkled. "Did you know I can run again with all the new-fangled technology? Swim again? Maybe even ski?"

"I can't even ski on the two legs I've got, Rick!"

He laughed. "I could before. Who knows? Maybe I'll improve."

"I believe you. You'll probably have better success than me."

He studied me for a minute, fan blowing my hair. I brushed a strand behind my ear, remembering—inexplicably—Adam next to me on a sunny green Winchester hillside.

"And one day I'm going to walk again on my own two legs. In heaven, Shiloh. Do you believe it?"

His question took me off guard. "I want to," I said, suddenly blinking back tears. "I think maybe I'm starting to."

My heart beat faster, as if giving me a surge of adrenaline. To do something. Say something. Step forward.

"The blood of Jesus purifies us from all sin." I trembled.

"Well, it's real," Rick went on. "You can't possibly hope to find everything you're created for in this little fallen place called earth. I've learned that now. We're all broken up. We're sinful."

"Jars of clay." I heard it come from my mouth.

"That's right, Shiloh! Jars of clay. But one day we're gonna walk with the King—in new bodies that don't wear out and hearts that only do good."

He looked up at the ceiling, seeming to forget I was there. "I never used to care about heaven much, to tell you the truth. I had my own plans and things for my life. But now I realize we're dust. Our kingdoms are dust. We're made to reflect the glory of the Creator."

"For we are God's workmanship, created in Christ Jesus to do good works. . . ."

"And we aren't satisfied until we do." I remembered Jamie, standing there in the Barnes & Noble bathroom.

"Exactly. We are His. And what's real is eternity."

The room hushed. I pressed my lips together, willing myself to keep back my words. "Rick." I hesitated. "Can I ask you something?"

"Go ahead."

"Don't you hate those people who did this to you?" I longed to go forward, toward this strange and amazing Jesus, but something dark held me back. "Who took your legs away from you?"

"They didn't take my legs away from me." Rick gazed at me steadily. "God's still in charge, Shiloh. It was His decision."

I inhaled sharply, remembering Becky's tears. The boot kick to my side. The power we thought we had dissolving like mist in God's strong and tender hands.

"But don't you hate those people anyway?"

"Hate them?" Rick furrowed his brow and brushed his hair back from his forehead. "Sometimes." He grinned sheepishly. "I know it's wrong. But mostly no. There's no way I could ever really hate them."

"Why not? I could! I'll hate them for you right this minute!"

He chuckled. "Thanks, Shiloh, but you don't want to do that."

"Sure I do!" I glanced at the shape of his footless legs beneath the blankets.

"No. I promise you don't. Hate just kills you slowly from the inside, like a disease. Besides, we've all done sinful things."

I raised an eyebrow. "Sorry, but I've never blown anyone up, Rick. There's a big difference."

"Not so much of one as you might think."

My eyes bugged out. "What are you saying? Killing and maiming people is wrong. And I'm not a murderer, last I checked."

"Jesus says you are if you've ever hated somebody."

"What?" I sputtered, halfway standing up in my chair. "Me?"

"All of us. Look at it this way. Have you ever told a lie? Or. . .I don't know. . .stolen something?" Rick looked so unafraid of our delicate topic, as if he were out fishing on a lazy Sunday afternoon. He put an arm behind his head.

Both his question and manner took me aback. My cheeks flared as memories of AP surfaced with frightful clarity. We called it plagiarism, but it was stealing. Stealing someone else's words and lying about them being mine.

I cleared my throat nervously, not liking where our

conversation was going. "Yes. Okay, yes. I have. But lying doesn't make me a murderer."

"No, but God says it's wrong."

"It didn't hurt anybody!" My own conscience suddenly shook off the dust and leaped into action. *How can you say that? You hurt Kyoko and Dave, and even the prime minister's wife. Did you ever think of that? Did you?*

No, I hadn't. Ever. I sat there frozen. *And you hurt yourself, too—God's creation, made to give Him glory. His poem, Shiloh, created to do good things!*

"Even if it didn't hurt anybody, it still hurt God. He says so in His Word."

I opened my mouth and closed it. "But. . .why?"

"Because God is good, Shiloh. And we aren't. End of story." Rick shrugged. "So in the end, we all do things that hurt someone. We fall short, and God forgives us. And that's why I forgive others."

"Forgive." I stared off into the distance, drifting from Rick to Mom. My thoughts brewed like storm clouds, hovering on the edge of something electrifying. "How, Rick? People always talk about forgiving, but frankly, I can't."

He looked up at me curiously. "Well, that's a good question. It's not easy. I'm hardly the expert on forgiveness. Just ask my family." He rolled his eyes.

"I'm not going to sugarcoat wrongs, Rick," I interrupted, crossing my arms. "People don't deserve excuses. Sometimes Christian forgiveness seems so silly, like it all doesn't matter."

Rick winced and pointed to the blankets, voice suddenly hoarse. "Of course it matters, Shiloh. What's happened sometimes can't be undone."

I sat back in the chair, silent. Palms cold with emotion.

"But I know one thing: if God forgave me for what I've done in my life, and He made me His child, how can I say no? Once He comes into your life, He gives you power to do things you could never do on your own."

"Like raising the dead."

"Yeah," said Rick. "Kind of like that."

Suddenly everything snapped into focus, as if I'd been seeing in blurred vision all these years. I couldn't forgive Mom because I hadn't asked God to forgive me!

It had never occurred to me that I'd actually done wrong. That I'd sinned against God—not just with AP, but in thousands of other ways, big and small. That I had done things my own way, without His help and without His power.

It's no wonder I couldn't forgive. I was a car with no gas, vainly trying to rev it in the parking lot at Jerusalem Chapel Church.

I needed more than trying harder. I needed a gas can.

God had brought me here to Staunton, shouting His message of love for me through more people than I could count. *Come home!* He was saying. *Come home to Me!*

It was almost too much to bear. Tears dripped down my cheeks, right there in front of Rick Carter as I clutched my seat, knuckles showing.

"I'll just. . .um. . .be right back."

Before I could make it to the bathroom, Rick's face turned pale, and he gritted his teeth.

"Are you okay?" I turned back and snatched up the paper. Wiped my face. "What do you need?"

"Sorry, Shiloh. I just need the. . ." He grimaced. "Sorry. The first one." He jabbed in the direction of the paper.

"Okay!" I replied, trying not to panic. "I'll get it! Just hold on." I checked my watch. Thirty minutes late. I ran out of the room and fumbled for the box. Emptied two pills into my shaking hands and quickly read the instructions. "Take with food."

"Food," I said out loud. "It must be a strong one. Todd?"

"Yes, ma'am?" He dropped his pencil and jumped up to help

me. His response was so endearing I wanted to hug him, but first I needed to get Rick stabilized.

"I need to find Rick something to eat with his medication. Do you know what he likes?"

"Oh, that one? He usually takes it with dinner. Soup or something."

"He's had dinner already, right?"

"Yeah, but he don't mind eating." Todd pulled open the refrigerator. "How about green beans and Jell-O?"

I made a face. "Maybe just the Jell-O."

"Yeah. It's strawberry banana. Rick loves it."

We scooped some quivering red stuff into a bowl. "Looks like what happens when we skin a deer," Todd said casually.

"Ugh, Todd!" I groaned. "Please!"

"Well, it does! Ya ever eat venison?"

"No!" I wrinkled my nose. "Thank goodness."

He dug in the refrigerator for some Cool Whip. "Wait. It's Rick's favorite combination. He'll love it." He glopped some on top and took it to him.

I poured Rick a glass of water and handed him the two pills. He swallowed them and then rested, eyes closed. Ate some Jell-O with a spoon, hand shaking. I grabbed a paper towel and shoved it under the bowl in case it spilled, trying not to think about Todd's venison comments.

"Here's where you have to watch him," whispered Todd. "Sometimes he feels bad after he takes 'em. But if he don't take 'em, he has pain all night."

Beads of sweat broke out on Rick's forehead as he rested there. He massaged his one whole leg and let out a groan then sank against the pillow. A slow sense of relief spread over his face.

"Better?"

He nodded without answering. Let out a deep breath.

I looked over the paper. Thirty minutes after those started to work, he needed a small white one. I scanned the rest of the paper and made a mental checklist.

"Still hungry?" I asked when Rick finished his Jell-O.

He nodded, still gritting his teeth against the pain.

"What do you like?" I jumped up. But he was pursing his lips and squeezing his eyes closed, so I didn't force him to answer. I dug in the kitchen cabinets and found some Ritz crackers. Another Southern staple, apparently. Everyone had them—and blocks of orange Colby cheese.

I sliced some cheese and turkey and ham then sandwiched them between crackers. Southerners also tended to have vinegary pickled things like olives or—I opened the fridge door—baby dill pickles. Exactly. See? I'm learning. I arranged them in a little dish on the side of his plate.

Todd watched hungrily, still bouncing his pencil and swinging his feet, so I made him a plate, too, and slid it across the table.

I chomped a pickle as I dug in the freezer for some frozen blueberries and ice cubes. Threw them in the blender with a container of strawberry yogurt and a splash of orange juice. Two minutes later, voilà! A berry smoothie. I poured it in a tall glass and gave the leftovers to Todd.

I carried the plate and glass to Rick with a fresh napkin and watched as he opened his eyes in surprise. "You made all that for me?" He grunted, forcing a smile. "Thanks, Shiloh. You're a lifesaver."

When I went to clean up the kitchen, I found Todd pouring half his smoothie into another glass and dividing his crackers on either side of his plate.

"Ain't you gonna eat, too?" he asked, pulling out a chair. "See? I saved ya some. We can eat 'em together."

For a split second I understood why Becky wanted so much to have children. A little guy like Todd could light up your world. "Sure." I sat down next to him with a smile. "I'd love to."

When Adam found me, I was sound asleep at the kitchen table. I'd helped Todd finish his homework after our snack, taken the army-men-and-Purple-Heart tour, folded and flicked paper footballs, sent him to bed, and doled out the rest of Rick's medications.

Rick asked me to bring his Bible when the pain hit especially hard, and I read for him from Psalm 139: " 'O Lord, you have searched me and you know me. You know when I sit and when I rise; you perceive my thoughts from afar. . . . If I rise on the wings of the dawn, if I settle on the far side of the sea, even there your hand will guide me, your right hand will hold me fast.' "

"Read to me," he said, "how we are made."

" 'For you created my inmost being; you knit me together in my mother's womb. I praise you because I am fearfully and wonderfully made. . . . All the days ordained for me were written in your book before one of them came to be.' "

It was medicine, it was music. A song swelling inside me I could barely contain.

I read with voice choked, blinking back tears. If Rick noticed, he never let on. When I left him around midnight, he slept peacefully, chest rising and falling in the gentle rhythms of slumber.

"Shiloh," whispered Adam, brushing my hair back from my cheek.

I opened my eyes and saw Todd's math book inches from my nose. I jerked my head up and rubbed my eyes.

"We're back. I'm so sorry."

"It's okay." The kitchen was dark, but the microwave glowed a bright green 1:39.

"How's your dad?"

"He broke his arm in two places. Took awhile to set the bone, but he'll be fine. Guess he won't climb up on the roof anytime soon."

I fumbled for my purse. My eyes felt stuck together.

"I'll take you home. Just jump in the truck."

"No, I need my car tomorrow. I work."

"No problem. I'll bring your car by in the morning."

"You don't have to do that."

"That was a statement. Not an offer. The truck's unlocked." He squeezed my shoulder affectionately and disappeared into Rick's room with me staring after him. If his dad was stubborn, Adam was a chip off the old block.

I yawned, forgetting what I was supposed to argue about. And let Adam drive me home. I saw nothing except warm summer stars, balmy night breeze, and locking the front door behind me.

Home. Quiet. And my own comfortable bed, so warm and welcoming.

But I had one more thing to do.

I switched on my bedroom light, seeing the soft shine on the golden floor, and grabbed Mom's Bible.

Mom's journal lay there, sparkling blue in the lamplight, but for once I needed someone else's words. God's.

I paged back to 1 John with trembling fingers. And spotted it in verse 9, waiting for me exactly where I'd left off: "If we confess our sins, he is faithful and just and will forgive us our sins and purify us from all unrighteousness."

That was it. That was what I hadn't done. I believed—I saw—I knew—and now I wanted to come home. Forever. Like Mom had done. To hang up my coat of anger and hurt and let this Jesus, whoever He was, bathe my feet with His tender mercy.

I wanted not just to sprout but to bloom and grow and multiply. To explode with life. To trade my selfish, near-sighted ways for His eternal vision.

God can raise the dead.

Like Indian summer, I'd been given another chance.

I slipped awkwardly onto my knees in my jeans and heels, pressing my face into the blankets. I knew I didn't need to; if God was as powerful as He said, I could pray standing on my head. But I wanted to remember this moment. To remind myself that I was dependent—not only on grace, but on Grace-in-the-Flesh called Jesus Christ. That my own self-sufficiency was no better than the smelly Green Tree clothes moldering in my tote bag.

"God," I whispered, voice echoing against the remnants of Mom's life that colored the room, "I don't really know You. You know me though. You created me. I read it tonight in the Psalms. But. . .I want to change. I want not just to know You, but to come home to You."

I scrunched my eyes closed, aware I'd missed a Billy Graham prayer by a long shot. But something inside urged me to go on. To speak. "I don't really know how to do this, but I'm sorry I sinned against You. That I've built my own kingdom like Rick said—which is nothing more than dust."

Sin after sin came to my mind—the lies, lots of lies, the puffed-up pride and unforgiveness, the self-righteousness and words I'd spoken in anger. My fracas with AP. My arrogant judgment of those around me, including Adam and Faye and others. Dark and painful images stabbed me with regret.

"I've sinned against You, and I've hurt others, too. It's too late for me to tell Mom I'm sorry, but I have a feeling it's not too late with You." I took a deep breath. "I want to be different, God. I want what Mom had. I want Jesus. I want Him to raise me from the dead and forgive my sins. I want to live and not die and give You glory, all the days of my life."

Chapter 41

The phone was ringing.

I rubbed my face, blinked, and then stumbled out to the kitchen, squinting at the bright sunlight. Put the phone up to my ear and plopped down in a chair. Yawned. Realized I hadn't said anything.

"Hello?" Randy better not call me again. I'd talked to him several times, making it clear he'd receive nothing more than my friendship, but he still kept offering to take me to battlefields. And e-mailing goofy pictures of us Photoshopped together, along with lengthy love poems.

No one spoke on the line, and for a split second I thought maybe Carlos had called. I reached to hang up.

"Shiloh?"

Odd. "Stella?" I sat down again.

"You okay, honey?"

"Me? I'm fine. Why?" I rubbed my eyes again, still feeling groggy. The kitchen sweltered, and I stretched the cord to the window to let in the fresh morning breeze.

"Oh, I just didn't hear nothin' on the other end. Wondered if you was there."

"I'm here. Just half asleep. What's up?"

"Yeah, I saw ya come back real late last night with that fella in the blue truck."

I yawned. "Adam? I was helping his brother."

"He's a nice one, Shiloh."

"His brother? You've met Rick?"

"Naw, Adam. The blue-truck fella. Such a gentleman. Sheeewwwweee!"

"Yeah, he's a good guy." I rubbed my eyes, which had fallen shut again.

"You ken say that again! Come by and give me yer keys this mornin' 'cause you was sleepin'. Real nice and polite. Didn't know God still made men like him!"

"He dropped my keys off?" I glanced out the window, seeing the back curve of the Honda.

Stella kept right on going. "He always waits for ya outside when you're alone, like he's got some kinda class or somethin'. I noticed he was differnt right off."

"Yeah, he's got this thing about always waiting out. . .what? You noticed?" I wrinkled my nose.

"Well, it's a small world, hon, and these eyes don't miss much." She tittered. "Ev'rybody round here's talkin' about ya, tryin' ta figger out what kinda gal you are. They think you're a peach by now! A good head on yer shoulders, yessiree! I told 'em myself! Not like Misty Wilcox, always foolin' around with whatever Tom, Dick, or Harold shows up in her livin' room. Why, jest last week she an' that Shifflet fella. . ."

This was a really weird conversation, albeit enlightening. I didn't know people actually paid attention to anything I did, good or bad. However, we're talking about Stella here.

"Um. . .so maybe I should come over and get my keys?"

"Keys? Oh sure, honey. But that ain't why I called. I done fergot." She giggled. "It's about yer roses."

"My roses? What's wrong with them?" I was already scrambling for my sandals.

"No, hon. They look fine. It's just that white bush."

"The white one? That's the most important one, Stella. Did something happen to it?"

"No! That's why I'm callin'! I don't know what kinda fertilizer you been usin', but it's workin'!"

"What do you mean?"

"You jest gotta see it! I went out this mornin' for a smoke, and there it sat, all. . ."

The phone clattered to the floor. I ran, still in my pajamas, and threw open the door. Jumped the deck steps two at a time. And stopped short at the snowfall of lush white blooms covering Mom's Kobe rosebush, petals sifting lightly to the ground in the gentle breeze.

I stepped through the warm mulch and knelt there, gawking at the spectacle of sparkling white rimmed with faint pink like a sunrise. Thick blooms loaded on the leafy stems, mounded like scoops of ice cream and perfuming the breeze.

Mom's Kobe rosebush bloomed.

The one as good as dead. The one without leaves. The one that hung brown and bare.

I felt déjà-vu-like there on my knees, remembering last night's prayer by my bed. Everything became new. The dead rose to life. The heart beat clear and strong. I can live again! I can bloom again!

"Jesus," I whispered. "You did it. You really did it!"

A whiff of smoke tickled my nostrils, and Stella's flip-flops came skooshing through the grass.

"Toldja it was bloomin'," she crowed, letting out a hazy breath. "Ain't it something? What'd ya put on it?"

"I didn't do anything." I couldn't tear my eyes from the piles of white, shimmering in the morning sunlight and bending down the branches with their weight. "It's just. . .God."

I sounded like Becky, but with proper grammar. It felt weird. I wiped my eyes.

"Hmm. Yeah. I reckon so." Stella puffed in silence. "Them's real pretty. Seems like I remember yer mom takin' special care of this'n. Always real careful prunin' it and stuff. Her favorite, I reckon."

I pinched off a perfect cup-like blossom and placed it in Stella's chubby hand. "Here. Mom would have wanted you to have it, too."

She turned the white bloom over then shyly pressed it to her nose. Snuffed out her cigarette and plopped down on my porch in her housedress, eyes pooling with tears.

I sat down next to her, not saying a word, and we watched the morning together. The blue jays and finches in Stella's tree. Squirrels scampering across my yard. Mist rising over the pastures, pearly pink.

And then I bade Stella farewell. There was still one more thing I had to do.

The narrow road up to Green Hill Cemetery twisted through emerald woods, long and lonely. The iron gate swung in the breeze, unlocked. I idled my car at the entrance and pushed it open then drove inside and parked. Listened to absolute stillness descending as I slammed the door.

Robins twittered overhead in the latticework of green and hints of yellow as I strolled quietly among the headstones. Some crumbled with age, dating all the way back to the early 1800s. I paused by a child's grave decorated with a lamb, imagining the black-clad crowd that gathered here so long ago. An eleven-year-old boy. No explanation, just a name and dates. Infection? An epidemic? An accident? I winced, thinking of Todd.

"Safe in the arms of Jesus," read the lichen-covered script. My breath caught in my throat.

From now on that would be me, safe in the arms of Jesus. No matter what happened, He would stay with me. In me. Living through me.

I walked through the years, watching them pass by me, ghostlike and silent. I touched stones so old the carvings blackened and faded with lichens, and a sudden rash of markers dated 1863. My spine quivered. The war? I wondered if any Donaldsons numbered among them.

Mom's grave lay toward the back, up where the grass met a thick stand of woods. I hadn't come here since the funeral, so I felt lost, weaving through the markers in search of hers.

I spotted it easily though—the gray granite shiny and polished. The rectangle still patched with brown earth where the grass had begun to grow over.

I stood there, feeling the warm fall breeze ruffle my hair and jacket and then stooped down to touch the newly carved letters: *Ellen Amelia Jacobs.* I ran my fingers over the dates of her death and birth.

Ellen Amelia Jacobs, sojourner in Virginia who decided to stay for good.

Ellen Amelia Jacobs, mother of a daughter who'd finally come home.

Ellen Amelia Jacobs, teacher and friend and lover of God, who'd gone through God's door and found life out of destruction. Who bloomed one last fantastic flourish. Who said to fall and winter: *I am not afraid!* And whose tender faith, like the white Kobe roses in my arms, carried scents of heaven.

I laid the thick bouquet on the grass, shocking white against dull green, an offering of my heart. Like Mom, it was late—but better late than never.

"I'm sorry, Mom," I whispered awkwardly, putting my hand on the sun-warmed stone, still cool on one side. Kneeling in the grass. "I'm sorry I didn't know you. That I didn't want to know you. That I missed the you I could have loved."

My tears were healing; they seemed to wash away all my malice and hardened anger. I could forgive now, just like God forgave me.

The gas was flowing into my tank. My heart had doubled in size, flooding out a love for Mom like I'd never known.

I couldn't erase our past or pretend it didn't happen, but I could cover it, like the snowfall of roses over her grave. "Though your sins are like scarlet, they shall be as white as snow."

No more lies. No more hiding. I could start fresh—from now—and let God reveal the new creation He'd started in me, just as He'd done in Mom.

His workmanship. His poem. His jar of clay, fragile, but holding treasure. Encircled by His powerful hands.

I passed my hand over the hard, carved letters of her name. "You're not the same person I remember, Mom, and I want you to know I'm not either. I've changed, too." I wiped my face. "And I think you'd be prouder of me now than when I won all my greatest awards. Thank you, Mom. Thank you for what you gave me—life and Life. The very best things of all."

The riot of birds cried out my joy in the green glory of the morning. Nothing else mattered. Not AP, not my debts, not the house. Not even romance or someone to love.

We could do anything, God and I. Together.

There in the middle of a hundred gravestones, I had never felt more alive.

About the Author

Jennifer Rogers Spinola, Virginia/South Carolina native and graduate of Gardner-Webb University in North Carolina, now lives in the capital city of Brasilia, Brazil, with her husband, Athos, and their son, Ethan. Jennifer and Athos met while she was serving as a missionary in Sapporo, Japan. When she's not writing, Jennifer teaches English to ESL students in Brasilia. Find out more about Jenny at www.jenniferrogersspinola.com.

Discussion Questions

1. Carlos' dashing appearance and handsome good looks earn him a lot of positive attention. How does he treat Shiloh and Kyoko? What characteristics does he exhibit through his behavior? Do his good looks have any bearing on his attitudes and/or actions?

2. At one point, Kyoko asks Shiloh if Carlos truly loves her, and Shiloh replies in annoyance, "Of course he does!" Do you agree with her? Why or why not? In your opinion, what is real love like? How is it shown?

3. Pressed for time at the Associated Press office, Shiloh makes a quick, one-time decision to plagiarize a story, thinking no one will find out. What were the consequences for her breach of integrity? Have you ever done something against your better judgment "just one time"? What happened? In Shiloh's case, if no one had discovered her error, do you think her secret would have still had an effect on her character? Her career?

4. Shiloh continually asserts that her mother means nothing to her, but Shiloh's shock, turmoil, and anger indicate otherwise. Why do you think this is the case? Have you ever struggled with a difficult family member or painful memories? What helped to bring you peace?

5. At Tim and Becky's cookout, Shiloh is surprised that something as simple as "a couple of hamburgers and a radio" could bring such clean, free joy. What do you think Shiloh senses in her friends that she's been missing? How do they receive her and her many problems? What does this tell us about the impact believers can have on near strangers for Christ? Has anyone inspired you in a similar way?

6. Adam makes a reputation for himself as an oddball by refusing to go in Shiloh's house alone. What reason does he give for his actions? Can you think of any other reasons Adam's caution might have

been a good thing? Have you ever "gone out on a limb" to make an unpopular choice based on your convictions? What happened?

7. Becky says once that Jesus isn't a "Happy Meal," and there isn't a toy inside every box. What does she mean by this?

8. When Adam takes Shiloh fishing, she expects him to give her a spiritual lecture or sermon. Why do you think he refrains? In what ways does Adam still share his faith with Shiloh, and what is its impact?

9. Have you ever had to wait tables, work in a store, or do a similar type of work? What was it like? If not, can you imagine the drastic life changes someone like Shiloh would face? Can you see any positive changes in Shiloh's character as a result of her hardships?

10. During a conversation about suffering and sin, Shiloh tells Faye that Adam and Eve, not she, ate the forbidden fruit. Faye replies that "there's a little bit of Adam and Eve in all of us." What did Faye mean by this? How is this reflected in Shiloh's life? In your life?

11. Toward the end of the book, Adam's brother Rick says "we're all amputated in some way." Are there any areas of your life or personal relationships you've cut off or left behind, either voluntarily or against your will? How has God brought healing to your life as a result?

12. After conceiving against all odds, Becky loses her miracle baby. Have you ever suffered a great loss of something? Why do you think God allows our sometimes best-laid plans or greatest hopes to be dashed? What reasons do Tim and Becky give for continuing to follow God in faith even during tragedy?

13. After reading her mom's journal, Shiloh comments that it seemed like her mom "came to life." What did Shiloh mean by this? How did Ellen's life change? And how did Shiloh's behavior exhibit the same transformation?